NECRONOMICON
The Manuscript of the Dead

Necronomicon

THE MANUSCRIPT OF THE DEAD

ANTONIS ANTONIADES

Translated from the Greek by
Maria Mountokalaki and Elizabeth Georgiades

Hippocampus Press

New York

Published by Hippocampus Press
P.O. Box 641, New York, NY 10156.
http://www.hippocampuspress.com

Cover art and cover by Fotis Papadopoulos
Hippocampus Press logo designed by Anastasia Damianakos.

First Edition
1 3 5 7 9 8 6 4 2
ISBN 978-1-61498-139-8

Contents

NECRONOMICON
The Manuscript of the Dead

1. Darkness over the Empire

Even though it was the beginning of November, there were signs that winter was approaching rapidly. A cold, fierce wind ravaged the bare plain of eastern Thrace and, undeterred by the massive unassailable walls surrounding the Empire's capital, continued to advance, whistling gruesome victorious tunes.

The guards of the notorious walls of Constantinople, dressed in extra woollen greatcoats, were hiding inside the stone towers, trying to keep warm beside portable iron braziers and looking forward to the change of shift. Numb with freezing cold, they seemed not to care about their duties, and with good reason: there was no information concerning threatening activity by barbarian intruders and, because of the bad weather, the country lanes were empty of pedlars and commercial caravans.

Behind the protective walls, the million-strong city seemed deserted, even though the church bells had sounded the end of the morning mass just an hour before. Not a soul was to be seen along the paved avenues, the marble squares with the deciduous trees, the cobbled streets leading to the wealthy districts, or even the muddy lanes of the slums. Not even the smoke of the forever burning hearths was visible, emphasising the city's abandonment. The gale cleared the smoke the moment it came out of the chimneys and then moved on its frenzied way, going past churches, monasteries, palaces, wealthy mansions, and miserable hovels, in order to reach the Bosporus, intending to cross through Europe to the opposite coast of Asia, like a ferocious warrior.

As far as the senior archimandrite of the Constantinople patriarchate Evangelos Danasses was concerned, both the chilling cold and the sweeping wind were of no significance; it was a common, seasonal phenomenon, a problem for farmers, fishermen, and all the rich men who couldn't visit any of the city's pothouses, in order to enjoy themselves with cheap, watered-down wine, all the while caressing the plump skin of sinful women who sold themselves for a song. Dressed in a luxurious cotton tunic, he was sitting at his desk and glowering at the seal on the document that the patriarchate guard had delivered to him. It was a reference letter from the emperor's adviser, Duke Vasilios Voreates, who was pleading with the patriarch to grant a hearing for the bearer of the letter.

Danasses glanced at the somewhat alarmed guard, scratched his forehead, and reread the document. Since he was very fastidious as well as naturally curious, he tried to read between the lines.

He was surprised that the duke was begging the patriarch, since in this case it was unnecessary. According to the letter, the bearer was a monk called Demetrius Meligrates, among the few survivors of the disaster that had struck the island of Patmos approximately a month before. This particular piece of information was enough for Danasses to receive him with no further delay. He was also suspicious of the duke's mild-mannered approach in making his request, since Danasses was aware of their disputes over both politics and religion.

These obvious incompatibilities made the perceptive and observant Danasses think hard before he decided to be the first to meet the monk. His thoughts, of course, were the result of suspicion. In Constantinople, malicious rumours were circulating that the emperor was planning on deposing Patriarch Theophylactus, especially after the complete failure of the latter's innovative idea to put up plays of biblical content in churches. To the zealots and the self-appointed protectors of proper faith, this novel suggestion proved that the prelate was an organ of Satan and an accomplice to the dark forces that lately had been working incessantly to destroy the world.

The reports from the Empire's bishoprics as well as the events that often shook the capital both made it clear that the situation was getting worse every day. Ever since some scholars announced that in less than two generations' time it would be a thousand years since Jesus' birth, the predictions about the imminent doomsday had reached epidemic proportions. Every day, passionate hermits came to the cities to preach God's Word and show sinners the righteous path, while at the same time every earthquake, plague, or thunderstorm was received as a sign that judgment day was approaching rapidly and nothing could stop it.

This is what prompted Patriarch Theophylactus to propose these ecclesiastical plays. He had thought that since the people didn't study books, the most suitable means of learning the true concepts of the Bible was theatre. As an experiment, he had successfully organised two performances in churches of Constantinople's rich areas. But during the third play, the last one, held at the temple of the manual workers' district, violent riots broke out when the comely duchess Helen Kastriotu, who portrayed Bathsheba during her bath, and whom King David had fallen in love with, got undressed not only in front of the actor, but also before the eyes of the uneducated crowd watching, thus challenging their morals and causing turmoil with her lasciviousness.

To the prejudiced and pharisaic crowd, the undressing of the beautiful lady was but a demonstration of the whore of Babylon, one more sign that the end of the world was near and that on judgment day, apart from all their other transgressions, they would have to account for one more sin. The plays came to an end forever, the duchess was banished from Constantinople to Syracuse, Sicily, and all the townsfolk, even the ones who hadn't attended the performance, hurried in confessing their lustful desires.

Fear and suspicion dominated the minds of the people in the Empire. To every one of them, an interlocutor, a neighbour, or even a relative could be an enemy, a conspirator, a heretic, or even a sorcerer. Nothing was excluded, everything was possible, and this silent acceptance led to misconduct and violent behaviour.

In the minds of the pious, not even the patriarch himself was innocent of the suspicion that he took part in the plan of the sinful to conquer and enslave the world. So any action or suggestion of his was examined in the light of possible treason by strict and vigilant critics who were self-proclaimed protectors of Christianity.

Danasses was well aware of all this. He also knew that conspiracy was secretly spreading its tentacles over the patriarchal throne. Power is sweet, no matter its kind or size. Knowing all this, he ordered the guard to present the monk to him.

Sitting at his oak desk, he rearranged his dark tunic and raised his bearded chin, having an air that befitted a man of his title. He would never allow any crude monk, because of ignorance or illiteracy, to reproach the patriarch. However, while he was mentally preparing to confront this supposedly malicious rumour, something inside him was stirring ominously. He felt that there was something he had overlooked.

He tried to think what he was missing, but to no avail. Only when he saw the guard opening the door again did he remember. He had noticed the look of repugnance on his face and forgot to analyse it. But the moment monk Meligrates appeared at the threshold, he understood why the guard was alarmed.

Danasses got frightened when he saw him and, as a reflex, pushed hard back on his chair. He had seen quite a few monks and hermits in his time and knew that their appearance mostly caused your flesh to crawl. Most of them wandered through the Empire dressed in shabby and completely filthy cassocks, unattended and smelling like skunks, with unruly hair and looks so hideous they

could make you sick, their cheeks gaunt with fasting, which com-
bined with their bristly beards made their face look like a scary
mask. All those men, at least externally, did not look at all like the
refined clergymen who lived in Constantinople or in other great cities of the Empire. On the contrary, they seemed like followers of an
uncivilised religion.

As soon as hermits and monks renounced worldly matters and
chose to lead a secluded life, the first victim to their twisted view-
point was personal hygiene. That is why they walked about dirty,
lousy, and sick, spreading disease in addition to horror. As a result,
the senior archimandrite expected to meet someone like that, filthy
and disgusting; but the man he saw gave him quite a scare and
caused a sense of threat inside him. It was so powerful that his heart
jumped with fear, his face turned pale, and he held tightly to the
arms of his chair.

Before the heavy desk, Meligrates stood straight and stared at
Danasses with a pair of big black eyes, the only discernible feature
on his face, as the rest of it was hidden behind soiled bandages,
from his forehead to his chin. The yellowed old cloth strips, with
purple spots caused by the oozing sores beneath them, were tied
around his head, leaving only his eyes uncovered. It was a countenance that usually belonged to lepers or other people suffering from
similar diseases, that caused the flesh to rot.

"Do not fear me, my lord, I carry no disease," Meligrates said,
rushing to calm the concern that had surged inside Danasses.

The nervous reaction and the heart palpitations that shook the
senior archimandrite subsided the moment he remembered that the
man came from Patmos, which had almost burned to the ground.
Hence, assuming that the poor monk had suffered nasty burns, he
felt somewhat at ease, breathed a sigh of relief, and was now calm
enough to notice the rest of his features, even though the dirty

bandages caught his eye, filling him with mixed feelings of repugnance and pity.

The man's black sackcloth was tied in the middle by a rope belt, and the sleeves and ends were all torn and muddy. That familiar element eased Danasses even more. Ashamed of his original reaction, he greeted and welcomed him in a milder tone than the one he often used for others. Even so, he kept contemplating every detail. He also made a mental note that before presenting him to the patriarch and the bishops in the city, he had to warn them about the man's ghastly appearance.

Meligrates introduced himself with humility and modesty, qualities that didn't usually suit the undisciplined and opinionated hermits who visited Constantinople. He then confirmed that he came from Patmos, which he had left several days after its destruction, and finally asked to meet with Patriarch Theophylactus Lecapenus, in order to raise the matter of a great danger that was threatening the entire world. While he was speaking, he was touching the wooden crucifix that hung on his neck with his gloved right hand, and at the same time he clenched the sack he was carrying in his left one.

Danasses listened to him silently, and the hair rose on the back of his neck. He wasn't scared but felt uneasy. This feeling grew stronger as a result of the monk's foreign accent and hoarse voice, which had a guttural sound, worse than that of the Syrians in the Empire. It was a sound that, in combination with his terrifying countenance, brought to mind sickly thoughts and fear of danger.

In spite of all this, when he heard the reason why the man wished to speak to him, and because he was tired of hearing daily about the imminent doom and was anesthetised by the apathy caused by the repetition of the same notion, he frowned and placed his hands on his desk, ready to turn down his request. He did not wish to bother the patriarch and the bishops over yet another speculative and imaginary danger, since the high priests had others, greater matters to attend to.

Guessing the senior archimandrite's intention, Meligrates rushed to say: "I have seen the monsters that destroyed Patmos with my own eyes, and I am sure that the Patriarch wishes to hear the message that Theodorus Philetas is sending him."

At the word "monsters," but more so at the name "Theodorus Philetas," Danasses jumped to his feet. He knew that what the deformed monk was going to tell him wasn't just another story or a prejudiced narrative. Moreover, he was certain that the patriarch would wish to hear any news sent to him by the man who had disappeared for six years now—his teacher.

The seats in the patriarchate boardroom were arranged in U-style, perhaps in memory or in imitation of the look the room of the Empire's senate used to have. In the centre of the horizontal seat row was the throne where the emperor sat when he took part in the conferences with the high priests. On the right of the artfully carved throne, which was covered in dark blue silk, was a similar one for the patriarch. Their only difference was the emblem they had on the top of their backs: the emperor's had a carving of the two-headed eagle, the symbol of the Empire, whereas the patriarch's had the monogram of Christ on it, the Greek letter *chi* overlaid by the letter *rho*.

The colours that dominated the room were crimson, gold, and blue, both on the chair covers and in the pieces of art. On the walls hung wooden icons of the apostles, the saints, and other biblical figures. Three grand chandeliers cast light all over the room, while at the corners stood silver candlesticks that could hold up to twelve candles. The centre of the marble floor was covered by a thick carpet along which a crimson-coloured runner reached the emperor's throne.

Monk Meligrates glanced at the priests and curtseyed. His movements, though calm, revealed a person who didn't know how to behave in the presence of high clergymen.

In the seats in front of the weary monk, apart from the patriarch himself, there also sat four more bishops from nearby cities, who had come to Constantinople for the celebration in honour of the archangels Michael and Gabriel. All five bearded men were wearing their archbishop vestments of gold and white and were politely looking at him, having already been informed of his gruesome appearance by Danasses.

They had heard about the disaster in Patmos, but they knew nothing of what exactly had happened, or how many victims there had been. The circulating rumours presented a disheartening situation, reporting that all the citizens had died in the fire, and the island had turned to ashes.

Naturally, because of the times in which they lived but even more so due to the incident in Patmos, the disaster was associated with the imminent day of reckoning. They were all aware that in one of Patmos' caverns, John the Apostle, the youngest and most favoured of Jesus' disciples, had written the Book of Revelation. When news spread about the unquenchable fire that had burnt Patmos to the ground, the believers shuddered with fear and considered the event as the most unshakeable proof that the end of the world was near. The only encouraging piece of news, which was considered an omen, was that the sacred cavern had not suffered in the least. That was why the priests did not mind the monk's clumsiness but kept silent, anticipating the details about all that had happened. The only one who looked at him anxiously was the patriarch.

Theophylactus Lecapenus, despite the importance of his title, seemed barely over thirty years old, whereas the other bishops were older than he. He had black hair, a rich beard, and a discernible countenance. Danasses had informed him that the monk was bearing an important message; at that moment, Theophylactus had spontaneously and rather thoughtlessly replied that the hearing would be held in the presence of the other bishops. But now, seeing him with all those bandages, somewhere inside him an alarm had sounded.

His uneasiness was quickened, not by the unfortunate man's appearance, but by the thought that certain words might be said, words that would reopen old, healed wounds. He was worried about what sort of message Theodorus Philetas was sending him, and about the possibility of stirring up forgotten matters, which would evidently put him in a difficult position in front of the other bishops. Nevertheless, he demonstrated calmness and repressed his growing fear and nodded icily, thus permitting Meligrates to speak.

The monk from Patmos moved closer to the archbishops and stopped two feet away from the gilded braziers that burned in front of their seats. In his left hand he was clenching his battered leather sack, while with his right he reverently touched the wooden crucifix on his chest.

"Dear brothers in Christ," said Meligrates and looked at the bearded men across from him focusing on the patriarch's face. With all the skill his poor vocabulary could offer, he struggled to speak formally and elegantly. Such an effort didn't go unnoticed by his listeners, since his speech did not flow; on the contrary, he paused and stammered a great deal.

"Forgive my confusion and the inappropriateness of my manners. Please let my misfortune be the excuse for my behaviour; do not judge my ugly appearance and unrefined conduct harshly, but pay due attention to what I am about to reveal to you. Above all, my brothers, listen to me unaffected by the import of my words but only focus on the essence of things, on the fact that at this very moment the whole world is at great risk, which we have to confront in a drastic and effective manner.

"Do not think that I asked for this hearing only to reveal a vision or a prophecy. I am not a daydreamer. On the contrary, I present myself before you as someone who has witnessed devilish works and knows about the satanic plans for the enslavement of the world.

"I saw the demons that attacked the holy island of Patmos with my own eyes. I myself read about their plans, in the book written by that damned Hagarene and translated by Theodorus Philetas."

The bishops and the patriarch kept studying the unfortunate monk in silence. What he said neither surprised them nor aroused their curiosity. They heard such stories and theories concerning the world's end on a daily basis; so many, in fact, that they remained almost indifferent to any new narration.

It was just the other day, at the time they gathered outside of Hagia Sophia, the world's largest temple, that some hermit named Vissarion incited the masses of believers, claiming that Satan himself had settled in Constantinople. His words made the flesh of the gathered people crawl, but all of them, having in mind the service that was about to take place, kept coming to church and remained seemingly calm.

The earthquake that at that moment shook Constantinople would at other times not have caused any fear, as it was such a common phenomenon, especially for the capital of the Empire; but it brought much terror to the faithful that were present, causing the death of fifteen people. Panicked by what had happened, they charged into the church thinking that inside they would find shelter and be safe. As a result, some people fell down and were brutally trampled underfoot.

Fortunately, the panic soon subsided, but the terror remained. Vissarion, pleased that the facts supported his words, was untroubled by the suffering and the casualties. Paying no attention to the dead and the wailings of their relatives, he climbed onto a marble fountain and offered the solutions to the imminent danger: "Watch, brothers! Watch, because judgment day is upon us! Send your women away, send them off to monasteries! Your daughters as well! Donate your riches to the church, repent and keep only one tunic, like our Lord and Saviour."

Incidents like that often took place in every city of the Empire. Fear directed the thoughts and the emotions of the people. It even dictated behaviour, rendering calm, innocent citizens suspicious and restless.

Hence, the patriarch and the bishops were unmoved by Meligrates' introduction and continued to observe him in silence. They wanted to hear about the events in Patmos, but the mention that demons had caused the disaster raised necessary suspicions and doubts. They could not accept what he was about to tell them without prejudice, in spite of his being a monk. They knew that most of the time, the prejudice of uneducated and God-fearing monks made them exaggerate insignificant matters and misunderstand simple ones. It was only natural now for the chief priests to remain quiet and expressionless in the face of the monk's words. They were not going to be carried away by the fantasies of just anybody, regardless of his title or position.

Meligrates immediately felt the disbelief his message had caused. He could see it in their grimaces of disdain and in their contemptuous looks. He had no time to lose and was fully aware that he had to convince them about the gravity of the matter. Fearing they might send him away, he recited in a strong and clear voice, barely pausing to draw breath:

"All the mystics know that the true sorcerers, the gatekeepers of the invisible world's keys are only those born dead. Only they, who were born dead but managed to live, possess the power to communicate with the creatures living beyond. In essence, it is from birth that they have the gift to see beyond this material world, as it is understood through the mathematical knowledge of the Greeks, and thus, provided they cultivate it, they can contact immaterial and, in a sense, otherworldly entities.

"I am such a person, who was first born dead but then came back to life and survived, the author of this book—"

"What profanities do you dare utter, you blasphemer!" the bishop of Thessalonica interrupted him.

"Who is writing all this? You?" asked the angered bishop of Adrianople.

Meligrates raised his gloved hands in an effort to calm them down. His eyes shone with satisfaction, as he had managed to catch the bishops' attention. He was aware that he didn't have much time, so he had to use every possible means in order to convince them quickly.

"Calm yourselves, brothers! These words come from the Hagarene's book, specifically from the introduction. I wasn't the one who wrote them. I've recited them as I remember them, without using the poetic metre they were written in. And I'm only reporting them so that you can grasp the importance of the threat and the risk that surround us—"

Patriarch Theophylactus raised his hand, silencing Meligrates. He glanced sharply at the bishop of Thessalonica and asked: "Does this blasphemous book contain instructions for the Antichristians?"

"Yes. According to the cursed Hagarene who wrote it, it is a collection of records of forgotten events, unknown myths, howling of demons, and descriptions of rituals bestowed upon our time by ancient sorcerers since the dawn of mankind."

The bishops looked at each other. Their expressions showed nervousness, bewilderment, and curiosity. They whispered a few words and remained pensive for a while.

Sensing their hesitant reaction, Meligrates decided not to allow them time to raise any objections. Pressed by the knowledge he was carrying, by the experiences that had left marks on his body, he didn't want to let them waste time with aimless musings and unfounded theological theories. So he recalled another passage from the introduction of the book and recited it with emphasis: "Apart from the sorcerers who were born dead, the others who also gain the gift of sensing the world of the dead are the ones who during their lifetime died and were later reanimated.

"There is truth in the text that states that the sorcerers who lived in ancient Babylon, or even earlier than that, in the badly constructed brick towns of Ur, but during the time when there were no cities, are one and the same with the sorcerers of today and those of tomorrow.

"Death is nothing more than another event, during which man pushes the limits of his natural senses, the natural laws, and enters the invisible world, gaining new, enhanced senses. The result of this limited contact between man and the beyond is the preservation of these new senses.

"This man is no longer ordinary like the rest, but a breaker of the laws of nature, a medium, or even a traveller between two worlds.

"Death is both the gate to other worlds as well as our birth inside them."

"Stop talking, blasphemer! You are a heretic!" the bishop of Philadelphia yelled angrily, getting up from his chair waving his fist to Meligrates.

"This is all I am stating, I, who was once known as the poet named Abdul Alhazred. I, the sorcerer, who was born dead, saw the world beyond our own, spoke with its odd creatures and heard the hum of their ill-sounding voices, will name my book *al-Azif*," Meligrates continued undeterred, seeing that he had caught the bishops' attention.

"What did you say the name of the book was?" asked the bishop of Nice in extreme curiosity.

"In Arabic, its title is *al-Azif*, but Theodorus Philetas translated it into Greek as *Necronomicon*."

Patriarch Theophylactus rubbed his chin with his left hand and looked at Meligrates pensively. On his left and right, the bishops were murmuring among themselves, upset by what the monk had said—things that were indeed diabolical and extremely heretical. Also, he did not doubt that his former teacher had translated such a book, a fact that further concerned him about what might be revealed later.

Gripped by ominous thoughts, he gestured at two guards to remove Meligrates from the room. He first wished to know his colleagues' opinion on the issue and give them some information about Philetas; and then, if they all agreed, they would listen to the monk.

Not knowing the patriarch's intentions, Meligrates tried to resist the guards. He thought he had missed the chance to speak, possibly because they thought of him as a heretic, and cried in complaint: "Brothers, I'm not a heretic! Everything I've disclosed to you was said by the Hagarene. You must hear me out, I beg of you! For the love of God, listen to me!"

"Don't be upset," Theophylactus interrupted him. "We intend to listen. I merely wish to discuss with my holy brothers about what you have revealed. You see, we haven't been prepared for this issue and we need some time to consider it—"

"There is no need, Theophylactus," snapped the bishop of Adrianople, Ignatius, who was the eldest and also the spiritual father of the patriarch. "Let him speak and we can discuss this later, after we know all the facts," he added and, turning to Meligrates, asked: "Tell us, brother, where did you find that book and what is its connection to the destruction of Patmos?"

Meligrates heaved a deep sigh of relief, freed himself from the guards' grip, and took a step forward. His gaze was fixed on the venerable, white-haired bishop. He had feared that they would turn him away, so now, reassured, he gathered his thoughts.

"I wasn't the one who found the book, it was Leon Peleuses in Damascus—"

"Who is that?" the bishop of Philadelphia interrupted the monk.

The patriarch bit his lip under his beard when he heard the name Peleuses. He was now certain that his fears would come true. He maintained his composure and kept staring at the monk.

"My dear brothers," said the bishop of Nice and stood up, turning all gazes toward him. He had recovered from the original surprise that Meligrates' words had brought him. The monk's attitude told him that he was anxious to relate everything that had happened, and he wanted to give him permission to speak freely, with no interruption. "I am of the opinion that we had better let him tell us his story, from the beginning, without us asking him questions and interrupting him," he stated and looked at his peers one by one. "Let us learn the general facts and then we can concentrate on the details," he added and, after receiving their consent, he gestured at the guards to bring a seat for Meligrates.

The weary monk breathed a sigh of relief and sat on the stool he was offered. Gingerly, he placed his sack in front of his shabby clogs and fixed his gaze on the bishops. He was one step from achieving his goal, that is to tell his story to the Empire's high clergymen, and yet he found it difficult to begin. He didn't know what event he should start his narration with. The image of Leon Peleuses came to his mind, when he first saw him.

"Almost six years ago, two consecutive conspiracies disturbed the Empire."

The patriarch gulped nervously. What he had wished to avoid was now before him. He had to interrupt the monk and prevent him from confessing the secrets of the things he knew.

"Dear Meligrates, you do not need to get into much detail," he said with a false smile. "We all know that my brothers, Stephen and Constantine Lecapenus, first banished our father, the co-Emperor Romanus Lecapenus, and then tried to steal the throne from our brother-in-law, Constantine Porphyrogenitus, God bless him."

All the bishops hid a smile beneath their beards, without turning their gazes to him. They knew of his brothers' conspiracies, just as they knew he had been anointed as patriarch thanks to his father and not because he had been more worthy than scores of the Empire's other bishops.

"This incident, the unsuccessful plot against Emperor Porphyrogenitus, was the reason why Theodorus Philetas, Leon Peleuses, and Doctor Bashar ibn Fathi were at the Hagarenes' kingdom," Meligrates pointed out. "The worthy professor of the University of Magnaura, Theodorus Philetas, along with Doctor Nicephorus Peleuses' grandson, Leon, had taken part in the plot and were on your brothers' side. Consequently, after they failed to dethrone our dear King Porphyrogenitus, in order to escape capture and punishment, they decided to take refuge with the Arabs."

The patriarch and the bishops and even the four guards that were present all recalled the events that had divided the Empire six years before. For a long time, ever since the heir to the throne, Constantine Porphyrogenitus, was still a child, Romanus Lecapenus possessed the title of co-emperor and ruled the Empire. When Porphyrogenitus became a teenager, Romanus gave him his daughter as his wife and kept ruling over the kingdom, since he was now father-in-law to the actual emperor. He also gave titles to his sons. He assigned the youngest, Theophylactus, as the Patriarch of Constantinople, whereas to Stephen and Constantine offered positions in administration and military forces. For himself, however, he kept ultimate and total governing power.

Stephen and Constantine were deeply overshadowed by their father. Being now two grown men, they wished to take over the reign themselves. Thus, with Porphyrogenitus in obscurity in the arms of their sister, they decided first to dethrone their father, since he seemed more dangerous to their plans. They captured him, forced the monastic life on him, and banished him to a monastery.

Everything was going well, but luck wasn't on their side. When Constantine Porphyrogenitus realized that his brothers-in-law were coveting the throne, he proved to be a worthy descendant of his glorious ancestors. Being sharp-witted and educated, he successfully dealt with the plot against him. He caught the two challengers, forced the frock upon them, and banished both to the same monastery where they had sent their father.

But apart from their relation, Lecapenus' sons and Porphyrogenitus had one more thing in common: the same teacher, Theodorus Philetas.

"Philetas," Meligrates went on, "knew that Porphyrogenitus was not going to show him the same generosity he had shown his two brothers-in-law. The reason he had been so magnanimous when he punished Stephen and Constantine was because you, my lord, are their brother, and your sister is his wife.

"You can see now that the enormity of the king's anger was to fall upon his teacher—the man who had chosen to support the usurpers over him. He had every right to do so in this case, for his teacher's betrayal weighed in his heart more than that of his brothers-in-law. The reason for their treachery was ambition, but what he blamed his teacher for was disloyalty and hypocrisy.

"We all know what happens to traitors: they have their nose, ears, and lips cut off, and then they are blinded with hot pokers. So Philetas, along with Leon Peleuses and Bashar ibn Fathi, in order to save themselves from such punishment and torture, dressed in monks' cassocks and crossed the eastern provinces of the Empire to find rescue in the Hagarenes' kingdom. For they knew that there they would receive a warm welcome."

Seeing that he had his prominent listeners' undivided attention, with no further interruptions or questions, Meligrates went on narrating his story. All he cared about now, apart from recalling what he had read and heard, was convincing them that the danger that was upon them was not a mere fancy of his morbid mind, but completely real—so real, in fact, that he bore its marks upon his body.

2. The Monk of Damascus

Every noon, because of the unbearable heat, Damascus is dominated by languor and inertia. The sun scorches the city under a dazzling, bright yellow light so intense that it can immobilize and subdue a person. If it weren't for all the flies and cicadas that ruined the impression of complete immobility, the city would seem abandoned, totally deserted. This doesn't only happen during the summer months but almost throughout the entire year, so it seems there are only two seasons of summer; torrid and mild.

There is barely a cool breeze to refresh the senses. Only the waters of the River Barada offer a dose of freshness, mostly for the children who, untroubled by grown-up problems, get the chance to play at any time of day. The wealthy Damascenes deal with the heat inside their mansions, at the foot of Mount Jabal Qasiyun. Built among the trees of the small wood—a sad remnant of the once thick forest, now destroyed by successive wars—the residences maintain a bearable temperature. The rest of the citizens, hidden behind dense shadows, drowsy from the high temperature, and soaking with sweat, lie down or sleep and wait for the intense heat wave to pass so they can go back out and get on with their work and interests. Only then, in the afternoon, with the muezzins' loud voices, does the city come alive again.

But on the day of the earthquake most Damascenes were upset and their heart-breaking cries had disturbed the usual midday peace. Moved by despair, they sat beneath the shadows of the trees, weeping and grieving, outside the collapsed or derelict buildings, holding on to whatever they had been able to save. They weren't bothered by the persistent sweltering heat. They cared about nothing but the dead, the injured, and their destroyed properties—everything they had been striving for years to make and protect, but had lost in the blink of an eye beneath the ruins.

Anguish and dread dominated the suffocating atmosphere. Everyone feared that there would be a repetition of the morning earthquake tremors and had no intention of returning home. Thus they endured the terrible, sizzling weather as an additional trial to their kismet, their fate.

The prevailing fear was palpable. No one would risk their own lives or the lives of their families. Even the emir was said to have left the palace and set up camp in the garden of the citadel, near the Dome of Roses. Besides, the news that approximately two hundred and sixty houses had been destroyed, crushing their owners and their families, had left no man unmoved. Especially the women, who wailed and beat their chests because of the disaster that had struck them and begged the mighty Allah to show mercy.

Wails, mourning, and heart-shattering whispers hovered over each neighbourhood, increasing the pessimistic feelings of the bereaved citizens who, as time went by, they learned more about the disaster that had struck them. Among the names of friends, acquaintances, and relatives were soon added the names of prominent Damascenes who had been either severely injured or buried in the ruins. As the stench of death spread, so did the pain that pierced through their hearts. Along with the tragic news there were references to supernatural elements that further exacerbated their anxiety.

Other rumours circulating were that the two flag posts that carried the black flags of the Abbasid caliphs had fallen off the walls. This was considered a bad omen for the emir's fate. It was also rumoured that the emirate's cadi, the prelate judge, had suffered a head injury from a ceiling beam and was now fighting for his life at

Bashar ibn Fathi's clinic. The most superstitious of the citizens associated this particular event with the future of the city and said that if the revered old man died, there would be another earthquake, which would raze everything to the ground.

Such and even stranger things were being whispered among the Damascenes, who were unable to gain a reprieve from the announcements about the disasters all over the Ghouta farms surrounding Damascus. Five villages had been completely crushed, while two market towns on the northern side were abandoned by their inhabitants, because they had fallen prey to the fire that broke out after the earthquake.

"Not at all strange," Theodorus Philetas said with certainty to his terrified students, who were discussing matters under the shadow of a tree in the court of the university and had attributed the event to supernatural causes. "The material that builders use to secure the bricks is tar. This fact proves that the fire was nothing odd, since tar is flammable."

The young students looked at him in confusion, and Philetas frowned, slightly irritated. In addition to the Greek language, he had also taught them about Aristotle and therefore expected from them to consider matters logically and not get lost in the superstition that always shrouded events. Nevertheless, knowing that people in general associate natural events with invisible demonic forces, he decided not to be too harsh on them.

"Tar," he said with an encouraging smile, then continued to explain his thought process. "Someone lit their oven, the earthquake occurred, the coals were all scattered, the tar caught fire, and the flames spread to every house. It's as simple as that!"

His students gave a resigned nod. Reason ruined the black, threatening image of the unseen evil forces that sought to destroy the world and, at the same time, neutralised the feeling of anxiety that comes from thinking about a supernatural situation. They accepted his explanation with measured satisfaction, because as much as they respected him, they couldn't be certain that his reasoning was right. Moreover, he was but a man, which meant that despite his education he didn't know Allah's plans.

"Don't jump to conclusions before considering the different sides and, above all, don't let yourself fall for the fantasies spread by the superstitious," said Philetas dogmatically and then lay on the grass and closed his eyes.

In the five years he had been living in Damascus, this had been just the second earthquake, whereas in Constantinople not even a month went by that an earthquake didn't shake the city. He wasn't frightened by this and of course knew that it had nothing to do with punishment or divine curse, contrary to what God-fearing people all around the world thought.

Of course, the destructiveness of this morning's earthquake was heinous. The subsequent terror stirred the public's imagination into mass hysteria. It was a common human tendency that he knew very well, and he wasn't going to let his students be affected by it. He did the same when he taught in his homeland, all the while realizing that eventually, if they didn't accuse him as a conspirator, they would definitely incriminate him as a heretic.

He smiled at that thought as he lay there, with the sunbeams peeking through the leaves and warming his face. Despite his greying hair, he had turned sixty a couple of years before, and the wrinkles on his forehead and around his eyes were now permanent features, and his muscles had lost the strength they once had. He wasn't going to change his views now. On the contrary, the older he grew, the stronger and firmer his views became. Not because his selfishness and bigotry had developed, but because he could now better comprehend the fallacies that dominated the human mind.

He had once hoped to see the world changed, free from superstition, free from the fear that comes with ignorance. This was his vision; he wasn't about to wait for someone else to make this change, but he himself would fight for his beliefs with all his might. He had offered himself to this ancient war, and exactly for that reason he was now away from his homeland, accused of treason.

Nevertheless, even though he lost and was later persecuted, he didn't feel defeated. The war was still going, and though he wouldn't live to see it to the end, he knew that he was a winner; one of the countless victorious warriors who fought for their ideas but, unluckily, did not taste the fruits of their efforts.

He had indeed won battles over the narrow-minded and prejudiced; he had instilled his views into his students, who, in turn, would instil them into others—until on that blessed day there would come a time when man would pull himself out of the pit of ignorance, cease being afraid of devils and fiends, and fear no punishment and torment in hell.

"Earthquakes are sent by God so he can teach us a lesson and advise us. It's punishment for our sins!" Philetas remembered the bishop of Smyrna claiming, when the latter had verbally attacked him during one of his lectures at the University of Magnaura. The passionate bishop was infuriated when he heard the various explanatory theories of the ancient Greeks and, boiling with anger, he yelled at him: "Your name shouldn't be Theodorus, but Antitheus!" Not God's gift, but God's enemy.

He wasn't hurt by the insult. He even understood why he might be considered an enemy. His beliefs were opposed to the superstition that many clergymen promised. He worked feverishly to undermine and defeat their distorted sense of the world. He was going to fight until the end, until he drew his last breath.

He realized, of course, that the day when the people would be free from darkness was still very far. He had made his peace with it, even though he didn't openly admit it. He saw that the way to the final goal was long and difficult. If you wish to save men from superstition, you must educate them, shed light over the darkness that surrounds them, explain the inconceivable notions and simplify the complex ones. In order to do that, though, you need schools. Schools, however, both inside the Empire and the caliphate, are scarce considering the population. Books are also needed, but those books that broaden the horizons of thought and judgment are considered redundant, useless reading materials, or are even banned.

He could still remember what his Arab colleagues at the university had told him when he was offered the chair of the translation branch with his five students. They asked him to translate only useful books, meaning all those that dealt with mathematics, astronomy, mechanics, medicine, and pharmacy. To his religious colleagues in the caliphate, all comedy, history, and the philosophical texts of the ancient Greeks, especially Plato's, were viewed as worthless, so they weren't to be translated.

In the past, when Damascus was the capital of the caliphate, this branch had ten times as many students, and books were incessantly translated from Greek to Arabic. Early on, however, the ulama, that is, the professors of law, had decreed that only the scientific texts were to be translated and not the rest; specifically, the ones that were considered to bear blasphemous thoughts and ideas of the infidels. They had realized that if the believers read all those books, they would question the Prophet's law, so they forbade people from translating or reading them, just as the Christian theologians had done before.

Later, when the capital of the caliphate moved to Baghdad, the copying of books increased in Damascus, but translations had declined. The teachers who knew the Greek language had moved to the University of Baghdad. In doing so, the former capital was thus preoccupied with copying already translated works.

Naturally, one of the reasons that made the Damascenes stop translating was that the diehard local muezzins and preachers passionately preached against the infidels. When you are near the enemy, intolerance increases as a result of fear, but when you are away, it decreases and almost disappears. And Damascus is a little more than a week's travel from the Christian kingdom of the *Nasraya*, that is, the followers of Jesus the Nazarene.

From the University of Baghdad, the professors kept writing to the emperor in Constantinople, imploring him to send them teachers of Greek as well as books. On the other hand, the Damascenes, in spite of the city's great Christian population, were indifferent. But ever since the day Theodorus Philetas took over the department, the work began anew. Under his supervision, his five students corrected the mistakes previous translators had made and translated new texts that they found in the university library or were brought to them, for a price, from neighbouring cities.

The rebirth of the department was such that all his students and colleagues, admiring the rate at which the works progressed, named the room where the copying took place "the monk's realm." It was a realm of knowledge and spiritual excitement, the fount of many ideas and theories for the development and improvement of the world.

But of course, even under his control, they only translated scientific texts, which were first scrutinized by the ulama, in case they contained anything opposed to their beliefs. If they discovered a writer's comment or idea that they found blasphemous, they demanded it be erased. They also made him teach only Aristotle, not Plato, because they found the Athenian philosopher's ideas corrupting and dangerous, especially when it came to religious matters. People with power, no matter where they are, never want to awaken the hypnotized flock they rule.

Philetas knew this. He had discovered it when he taught in the Empire, and his suspicions were confirmed after he had fled to the caliphate.

Fortunately, there were those few visionaries who believed in the power of education, and with their help Philetas could keep fighting against the multi-tentacled sovereign enemy. One of these men was the great *al-mu'allim al-thani*, the second teacher, as the Arabs call the philosopher Abu Nasr al-Farabi. The Arabs regard Aristotle as the first teacher and the very knowledgeable al-Farabi from Baghdad as the second.

During the first month he was at the caliphate, Philetas sent a letter to the wise Arab and, as a gift, he sent him Plato's *Republic*, the only book he had managed to take with him when he left home. He knew from his friend Bashar ibn Fathi that al-Farabi adored the Athenian philosopher, which is why he didn't hesitate to write him.

During their time in Constantinople, Bashar had told him about al-Farabi, who, influenced by Plato's philosophy, taught his Arab students the notion of *al-Imam al-'adel*, the Just Imam, who would govern the believers according to the rules of *Sharia*, the Prophet's law. Therefore, it was only natural, after the group had settled in the caliphate, that Philetas would seek the friendship of such a like-minded man.

Besides, the reason he conspired against the emperor by aiding Stephen Lecapenus rise to the throne, which then led to his banishment, was rooted in Plato. In order to make his vision real, he first had to alter the current political situation; thus he struggled to create a philosopher-king who would wisely rule over his subjects, according to the laws of the wise.

Theodorus opened his eyes and looked above him, at the wide leaves that seemed transparent in the bright sunlight that sizzled Damascus. Fearing that the heat would lull him to sleep, he sat up. He was the only professor present at the university, and he had to keep an eye on things. The rest of his colleagues had gone home and left him in charge, along with any students that were boarders there. Apart from that, he didn't want to sleep at noontime, because such hot weather usually gave him bad dreams. So he pulled the clay basin toward him and splashed fresh water on his hands and face.

He took a look at his linen cassock, which was now all soiled with dust and sweat. When he returned home that evening, he would wash and change clothes. He might walk around in cassocks and everyone might call him a monk, but he hadn't embraced the monks' hygiene standards as well. In fact, he did have standards, whereas the real ones didn't even have hygiene.

Most Damascenes thought he was a genuine monk and, even though they respected him, they still looked at him askance. He was amused by their behaviour, especially the first years. He could see their bewilderment, how they floundered every time they met him. They saw a foreigner, a nonbeliever mingling with his Arab students in the local *souqs,* the open marketplaces, or teaching at the city's coppices in fluent Arabic. They were pensive, all clearly wondering about one thing: how can an infidel hold a teacher's position and be respected by the ulama, the cadi, and the emir?

They were also put out by how much their students loved him. Nobody had forgotten the beating incident at the central *souq* of Damascus when a lout from Mosul tried to humiliate and offend him. The students who accompanied him that day caught the browbeater who had spoken ill of their teacher and gave him a piece of their minds. From that moment on, no one, either local or stranger, ever insulted the "monk" again. Nonetheless, they remained suspicious of him, despite his citizenship all these years.

Of course, the Damascenes had partially accepted him because of the reason he had taken refuge in the caliphate. They didn't know all the details, but they had been informed that the "monk" had helped an aspiring usurper of the throne take over power and had failed. He had betrayed the king, and this fact in their simple minds almost made him their ally. They also assumed that in the event of a war, he would definitely help them against the Romans, *ar-Rum,* as they called the citizens of the Empire. Hence, the more the years went by, the more they got used to him and respected him.

Philetas, however, was not a traitor to his homeland. He had made this clear to the emir of Damascus at the onset. He had asked for the Arabs' hospitality in exchange for his friendship and knowledge of sciences.

"That is all," he had told the emir. "If you ask me to embrace Allah or lead your army against my country, you can have my head right now, for I will never accept, no matter how much you torture me," he insisted. The emir, because he appreciated his morals—but also because he liked to boast that he was a man of letters, since he knew that the king of *ar-Rum* had turned down the caliph's request to send teachers of Greek to the University of Baghdad—accepted the offer smugly and swore never to bother him for religious or military reasons.

Philetas himself did not think of his participation in the conspiracy as treason, but as an opportunity for change and improvement. He was concerned with achieving a fairer and more harmonious society, without the issues of the throne caused by the lack of the council of the wise and by the lack of distribution of people according to their abilities. That was his goal; to transform the political situation of the Empire and see his fellow citizens happy. He didn't believe in the doctrine of the divine emperor. He was aware of the bad outcome this idea could have, so he tried to educate and shape a philosopher-king, constitute a council of first-rate men, and offer people a society of principles and values.

He wasn't fooling himself, though; he knew he had missed the chance to establish a political system inspired by Plato's *Republic*. But neither would he accept the thought that he might not see his dear Constantinople ever again. Everyone who knew him well could easily see the devastating sorrow that shattered him.

"Home is where you lay your head" is what they say of great

men, but this was not true for Theodorus. On the surface, anyone could assume that since Theodorus had been living in the Arabic kingdom for five years, he would have accepted his fate by now, enthusiastically working at the university, being a part of the exotic (for him) Damascene lifestyle.

However, that wasn't the case. If someone looked into his eyes, they would see the deep grief that was eating him up. One more thing that revealed his innermost thoughts was his clothing. He never took off the cassocks. He had worn them when he went into exile so he could hide from his pursuers, and had never removed them. Not because he liked to infuriate the fanatical muezzins, as he used to joke, but because he wanted to remember his failure and the hope that one day he too, just like Odysseus, would return home.

A teenager in a blue medicine student cap came running to the university yard. His black eyes scanned the students that lay beneath the shadows and paused on Philetas' face.

"Dear teacher," he said, bowing before Theodorus. "My teacher, ibn Fathi, sent me here to ask for your help."

Philetas handed him the wooden ladle and pushed the basin toward him. The young man took off his cap, filled the ladle with water, and poured some on his head, an ancient habit they had in the East to avoid sunstroke.

"Did he say it was urgent?" Philetas asked and urged him to pour more water on his pitch-black hair.

"No, sir," the boy answered and with the back of his hand wiped the water that dripped on his hairless chin.

"Then sit down and rest and we can leave after sundown."

Husni ibn Jaber opened his eyes and saw the ceiling coming down at great speed. He screamed in terror and lifted his hands over his face for protection, but then noticed that he was not moving but merely swaying along with the movement of his eyes and realized that it was all due to his dizziness. He breathed in a panicked sigh of relief and tried to calm down.

He felt his head heavy and swollen. He could not remember whether he had been hurt or was high on hashish. He raised his head and looked at the figures that rapidly swirled around him. He couldn't make out their features, because his eyes were throbbing and he couldn't focus on them. On top of everything, he felt his stomach turn.

His instinct was to rest his head upon the straw mat he was lying on and close his eyes. He tried to gather his scattered thoughts so he could remember where he was. He reopened his eyes and turned his head toward the sound of crying and weeping. Something inside him stirred at the heart-breaking sounds that jarred on his ears. Suddenly, he saw Jelal in front of him, rocking to and fro and hanging upside down.

"Jelal!" he screamed and tried to grasp his friend's body, but his hands only found air. Jelal was nowhere around.

Husni raised his hands to his temples and pressed hard, trying to stop the vertigo. He took a few deep breaths to calm the tension that overwhelmed him and focused his gaze on the ceiling beams. He knew then that he wasn't inside the tent at the cameleers' reservation and that the wailing didn't come from his companions.

Images flashed through his mind, reminding him of some of the latest events. He saw himself, in the morning sunlight, gazing longingly at the square walls of Damascus, the southern city gate. He remembered arriving on a camel and that when he saw the guard, he ran and dropped to his knees asking for help. The rest of his memories were all confused. A uniformed man was yelling in his face; two men were firmly holding him; he was on his knees, and his hands were tied behind his back; another man, in a blue turban that doctors wear, forced him to swallow a liquid concoction.

Husni turned away and violently vomited on the floor. He

coughed hard and felt his heart stifling in his chest. He propped himself up on his elbows and knees and tried to sit up.

From inside his open thobe, his family medallion could be seen on his chest. It was a burgundy stone, almost black in places, and chiselled in a way that it resembled a monster-like creature.

He didn't care if anyone would see it at that moment. He was dizzy and couldn't even hold a thought. The medicine they had given him when they transferred him to the clinic made him sick and disoriented.

The image of Jelal was again before him, clearer this time and in gruesome detail. His friend was swinging upside down, his ankles tied to the central pole that supported the tent. His stomach was torn open, ripped to shreds, and his intestines hung out, dripping fluids and blood down his suntanned face.

Husni's eyes darted to the other bodies that lay inside the tent. Everywhere around him there was blood, severed limbs, and hideously gutted bodies. By his left foot, staring at him, was the detached eye of a butchered cameleer.

"The demons!" he screamed, beating hard on his chest. "The demons killed them all!"

Bashar ibn Fathi's clinic, located next to his mansion, was a long, single-storey building that consisted of three rooms: the patient wards, the auditorium, and the pharmaceutical laboratory. Built of stone instead of bricks, like most of the city's buildings, it was a sturdy structure that hadn't been in the least damaged by the earthquake. It had been built on the northwestern side of Damascus, according to Philetas' architectural plans.

Bashar chose a building site near the city gate that led to Antioch. He might have done it subconsciously, as if he wished to be closer to his homeland. It was an odd habit of all the emigrants who felt terribly homesick.

At first, when they left the Empire and headed for the caliphate, they stayed in Bashar's homeland. The humidity, however, was really harmful to the health of Theodorus, who, after the hardship of their exile, felt the pain in his bones becoming more and more intense.

They had stayed in Antioch for two months before Theodorus mustered the courage to confess that he couldn't bear the wet weather any longer. The city was justly called "the Wetter" by the Arabs, because of the constant rainfalls.

He was sorry to have to leave his city yet again, but he eventually agreed to move. They ended up in Damascus, the former capital of the caliphate, with the dry climate and the intolerable heat. Nevertheless, they were both thinking of returning to their respective homelands: Bashar to Antioch and Theodorus to Constantinople. The third party, Leon Peleuses, the "boy" as they playfully called him, was the only one who wasn't interested in going back. But he, too, intended to leave the insufferable furnace that was Ghouta.

If someone had told them five years ago that they would all leave Constantinople to come and live in the caliphate, they would have laughed at the prediction, considering it feeble and stupid. Yet life has its paths, and what seems impossible eventually becomes possible, while what seems absurd turns into the only logical option.

Bashar ibn Fathi was better aware of that than his two friends, and that is why he didn't care about the future and its twists any more. Many years ago, when he was still a young doctor, he followed the emir of Antioch on a looting campaign against *ar-Rum*, which led to his capture and his transfer to Constantinople.

He knew of the histrionics of the fanatics and the seemingly God-fearing folk. He had the honour to have been taught the Quran by worthy ulama, who instructed him to keep an open mind to the cunning of all sorts of exploiters. These men tend to distort the Prophet's words in order to have their own needs met. So when he saw the passionate cadi of Antioch with a shaved head as a sign of mourning, complaining and shouting that the *Nasraya*, the infidels whose sins feed the demons, had to be banished, he realized that the campaign didn't have to do with faith, but with greed and profits from plundering.

Nonetheless, since he was the emir's personal physician, he couldn't help going with him, even though he knew that the war against Christians was irrelevant to the jihad, the sacred war, just as the *Mujahedin*, the warriors of faith, were merely a party of destitute and impoverished religious people who wished to get some land and achieve a better future.

Thus, using the excuse that "Allah dictates," the emir, who longed for more riches and beautiful maidens, gathered his troops and launched a sudden attack, aiming to catch the Empire's army off guard, but he failed. Unfortunately for him and for the exact same reasons, the enemy side, the general of the Seleucia province, also had his troops ready to invade Syria. As a result, the two adversaries confronted each other at the border.

The Arabs, who weren't expecting to face an assembled army, as soon as they saw the hundreds of waving flags and heard the horns signalling an attack, lost their nerve and took to their heels. During that hasty retreat, Bashar was captured and imprisoned, as were the lord of Antioch and other well-known sheriffs—nobility to the Arabs—who were later all released, after their relatives had paid their ransom. Bashar remained in *ar-Rum*'s captivity.

For a long time he wondered why his family and relatives hadn't paid the ransom for his release. His grief over this abandonment ate at him, until one day a merchant told him what had happened after his capture. A few months after the inglorious battle, his cousin Rashid al-Dur had married Bashar's wife, Afrah. That was when every torturing question he had was finally answered, and every suspicion was confirmed once he returned to Antioch.

Rashid, madly in love with Bashar's wife, embezzled the ransom money and spread the rumour that the doctor had succumbed to hardship and died inside a damp, dark cell where he was tortured by the ruthless Christians day and night. Finally, after the mourning period had passed, he married Afrah. That was why Bashar had remained a captive, but thanks to his profession and his knowledge about the Greeks, he ended up in Constantinople, where he met Theodorus Philetas.

During the years he had been living with the *Rum* he neither believed nor hoped that he would someday return to his homeland. But after the failed attempt against Porphyrogenitus, he followed his friend and succeeded. He returned to his native land, now a grey-haired man, and was informed that his beloved Afrah had died while giving birth to her second child, whereas Rashid had moved to Gaza after her death.

Despite the shadows that blemished his homecoming, he was quite content with it and very pleased to be able to return the favour to Philetas for the kind hospitality he had shown him during the years of his captivity. In fact, that is how he actually felt in Constantinople: more like a guest than a captive. He never knew the hardships and the troubles the captives went through. If they didn't get baptised as Christians, they died, either inside prison cells or in the fields and mines, working hard like slaves. He, on the other hand, without changing his faith, stayed in Theodorus' mansion, worked at the university, and felt more like an ambassador than a defeated enemy.

The friendship he had formed with Theodorus and Leon during his captivity was the reason why he had left his dear Antioch. Theodorus' health had deteriorated as a result of all the hardship during their two-month journey from Constantinople to the caliphate border. Throughout the journey, they slept outdoors, steering clear of villages and cities, fearing that guards might recognise them. They also ate frugally, and at times not at all, so all three of them fell ill, but especially Philetas, due to his advanced age.

They consequently left "the Wetter" in search of a drier place. They ended up in the beautiful and mysterious Damascus, which took them in its welcoming embrace and helped them get back on their feet. However, their seductive city was badly hurt by the morning earthquake, causing the clinic wards as well as the yard and the road outside to be packed with hundreds of casualties.

Since that morning, he and Leon along with their students had been helping the wounded, but found it hard to cope with the unprecedented circumstances. They had very few supplies to prepare the medicines and were saddened by the fact that the victims would double in number because of this shortage.

Bashar was drenched in hot sweat and was irritated by his students' clumsiness, but more so by the never-ending heart-breaking cries of the families, which wouldn't let him concentrate. He rushed wherever he was called to examine, suture, and dress wounds. Only at noon did he manage to rest a while, have something to eat, and drink some fresh water. The chaos surrounding him didn't leave him in peace, and judging by the number of casualties, he could sense that the following days would go by in the same way.

His short break, though, ended with the news Leon brought him. The emirate's cadi had finally succumbed to his injuries. This turn of events worried him because he had heard of his religious fellow citizens' predictions and knew that if news of the prelate judge's death spread, panic would shake the already terrified city. He decided not to announce it right away, but put it off until the following day instead.

He called two of his students and threatened to punish them if they didn't keep their mouths shut, and with their help he transferred the lifeless body to one of the mansion's guest rooms. He hoped that by the next morning the fear that reigned over the Damascenes' minds about the supernatural intervention would subside, and they would take the news with prudence, without mixing it with fantasies of disaster.

"The demons! The demons killed them all!" Bashar could hear on the way from the mansion to the clinic, across the covered corridor that connected the two structures. Puzzled by those words, he turned around to see who had uttered them and saw a sunburnt man crawling on a vomit-covered straw mat.

At first he couldn't tell who it was. Since this morning he had examined at least three hundred people and had seen as many of their relatives, who begged him in tears and kept pulling him by his thobe. So it was hard to recognise the man and his problem.

But as the man kept howling about demons and monsters, Bashar suddenly remembered: the guards had brought him in half an hour prior to the earthquake, explaining that he was mad and perhaps even possessed. He had tried to examine him, without any luck. The poor man was delirious, hallucinating, and prone to escape, so Bashar decided to administer a sedative. What with the earthquake and all the following events, it was almost natural to have forgotten all about him.

Husni, deep into his illusions, saw the demon approaching and screamed in utter terror. He looked around to find cover, but stood up in disappointment. If he was meant to die, he would die fighting, he thought, and it took all his strength to steady himself.

Desperate, he watched the deformed creature stretching its bony limbs to grab him and he retreated, until his back touched the wall. That was when he realized he had no other choice but to attack. He did so, letting out an encouraging, wild cry. He charged at it aggressively, averted its grip, grabbed it firmly by the neck, and tried to choke it.

Bashar, startled by the attack, didn't have time to protect himself. He felt the man's fingers around his throat squeezing hard, but not so much as to suffocate him; the madman wasn't strong enough to strangle him. His reaction was violent and completely justified.

He landed a heavy blow on Husni's face, freed himself from his grip, and, snatching him by the thobe, thrust him hard on the wall.

Shaken by the sudden attack, Bashar stood for a few moments opposite the unmoving body of the madman, whose name he couldn't remember. He waited a little to see any possible reaction and then, realising that his opponent had fainted, leaned over him. He also called his student, Khalil, who was at the medicine laboratory.

"Yes, sir—"

"Don't 'sir' me, and get me a rope so we can tie this one up; he's very dangerous," he barked at him, thinking that on top of everything he had to deal with, he had also been attacked by this crazy person.

Khalil came running and gave his teacher the rope. At the same time, he observed the man on the floor.

"Hold him by the shoulders," Bashar ordered and started tying Husni's hands. "He attacked me, damn it," he whined as he tightened the knot. "He would have killed me if he had been stronger."

Khalil, puzzled, looked at his teacher, who was so furious that he swore in Greek. He missed what had happened, so he couldn't believe that the man had attacked the doctor in order to kill him.

"Hold him tight, so I can tie up his feet, too," Bashar muttered with irritation. The more he thought about the incident, the angrier he got. He had made it safe through the battle against the *Rum;* he, unlike so many others, had survived captivity; he hadn't fallen ill to any of the transmitting diseases he had treated. And yet, a lunatic had almost choked him to death.

"A lunatic!" he said to himself and when he tightened the rope, he pushed Husni onto the floor.

The body of the man slipped away from Khalil's hands and fell sideways. From inside his saggy shirt, his medallion came loose and fell on the stone floor.

Bashar glanced at the strange figurine and turned to leave, but stopped as a question formed in his mind. He turned around quickly and peered at the burgundy stone that hung on the neck of the man who had almost killed him.

What had caught his attention wasn't the shape of the stone, but the stone itself. He then bent down, picked it up, and inspected it with great curiosity.

"Mnizurin!" he yelled and jumped to his feet, startling Khalil, who had been observing him.

Alarmed, Bashar took a step back and simultaneously wiped his hands on his thobe, as if he had touched something disgusting and slimy. He looked at his speechless student, who was astounded, and then he returned his gaze to the stone.

He had seen a similar stone at an alchemist's laboratory in Constantinople and remembered everything Theodorus had told him about it. It was considered rare and wasn't a mineral, but a living organism.

"Khalil," he said, his voice breaking. "Hurry to the university and ask Professor Philetas to come to the clinic."

Soaking with sweat and exhausted from performing countless operations, Leon Peleuses sat at a corner of the sanatorium and asked a servant to bring him some cool sherbet. He couldn't take it anymore. He felt light-headed from all the wailing, the blood, and the heat, which was still going strong even though the sun had started its descent in the horizon. He wiped his blood-stained hands on a linen hand towel and leaned his head backwards, a reflex position he used in order to calm the pain in his upper back.

A student came to tell him something about Bashar, but Leon waved him away. He was so exhausted that all he cared about was a short break. If he kept working, he would collapse.

Up to this day, he had never dealt with such a large number of injured people, and he was already hoping never to witness a situation like this again. He shivered when he tried to comprehend the enormity of the loss. He wasn't some young doctor who came face to face with death for the first time; but the numerous casualties, the dead children in the hands of their desperate parents, the wailing and the smell of blood that was filling his nostrils, disheartened him. He felt death hovering over him.

The only time he could remember something similar during his thirty-year-long life was when one of the "palaces of the poor," in Constantinople, collapsed. The so-called "palaces" were multi-storey buildings in which dozens of poverty-stricken paupers lived. Most of the buildings were made of brick and rotting wood and were divided in small rooms that were packed with large families. The buildings were filthy and shabby, but most of all, they were derelict and flammable. Every now and then, one of those blocks would collapse, due to bad craftsmanship or decayed building materials. Also, many times they burnt down, when a brazier would tip over by mistake or a few sparks escaped the badly constructed fireplaces. Both these cases resulted in dozens of deaths. However, the injured people he had had to deal with on that specific case were no more than thirty-five, not like the hundreds he was facing now.

The image of Constantinople, the largest city in the world, came alive before his eyes. He hadn't missed it, nor did he long for its adventurous lifestyle. All he craved for was its sea and its cool breeze. Ah, the sea . . .

His mind was flooded with images of turquoise waters, seagulls squawking, and crashing waves. He hadn't seen his beloved sea in five years, yet he knew it was only a few days to the west. He had forbidden himself to travel to a city near the sea, because he knew that when he saw it, he would board the first ship and leave. But he knew he couldn't travel further beyond Crete.

He had thought of escaping the caliphate countless times. Not that he wished to return to the Empire: he didn't even care about that. All he wanted was to leave this furnace and go live on an island. But he couldn't—not because the Arabs didn't let him, but because he didn't want to leave Theodorus on his own. Theodorus wouldn't prevent him from going, but Leon knew that his friend would wither away, because he regarded him as his last and only hope of ever returning home. Hence, all he was left with was dreaming of the sea. He would have to summon his senses and memory to feel its fresh breeze. This was the small price he had to pay to the man who saved his life.

Theodorus was the first to know that Porphyrogenitus had found out about the conspiracy against him. Without wasting precious time, he informed Leon about the treason. In fact, he and Bashar went to his house in a carriage and forced him to follow them to the caliphate. The teacher knew that the then twenty-five-year-old man would give in to what his age dictated, that is, stay and face the charges.

If Leon hadn't left with him, he would now be a blind and mutilated monk in a monastery, unable to do anything but pray for the salvation of his soul. Contrary to the Christian practices in the rest of the European kingdoms, they don't kill traitors in the Empire; they mutilate them, blind them, and put them in monasteries. Most of them, however, as a result of the hardships of a monk's life, don't survive long.

So if it wasn't for Theodorus, he would have neither hoped nor dreamt to build a home on an island someday. Above all, he would never have discovered the secret dens of Damascus, where you can get high on aromatic hashish and savour women from all over the Mediterranean.

Leon opened his eyes and looked at the sky to spot the position of the sun. When night came, he thought, he would go to al-

Mamun's opium den, which was two blocks east from the "gem of Damascus," the magnificent mosque with the three minarets that the Umayyad caliph had built to praise Allah in the capital of his kingdom.

He yearned to travel inside the dreamscapes that hallucinogenic drugs can offer, to surrender to the sweet intoxication of artificial happiness. He was in need of love and affection, just like any other man who has been alone for many years, without passion. He satisfied that desire for intimacy with short-term substitutes, the appealing Turkish women al-Mamun offered him in exchange for some money.

"My lord!" A woman's voice caught his attention. "May the mighty Allah keep you well and protect you," an old woman said gratefully and kneeled before him, took his hands and reverently kissed them.

Leon abruptly wrenched himself away and looked around to see if there was anyone watching them. He might be a doctor and a citizen of Damascus, but because he was of a different faith, there was always the fear that the fanatics might accuse them both of promiscuity. As kind as Arabs were, they forbade the infidels to have sexual affairs with the Arab women, unless they decided to convert to Islam.

As soon as he was certain that everyone was absorbed in their own problems and paid no heed to everything going on around them, he breathed a sigh of relief. He smiled to the old lady, who was thanking him profusely, and helped her to her feet.

"Only Musa! Of my whole family, only Musa survived thanks to you, doctor. My grandson, Musa. Only him—" The white-haired woman in the torn and soiled dress burst into tears and leaned her head on Leon's chest.

"Easy now, dear madam," he tried to calm her in Arabic. "Allah is great, He is the one you should be praising," he added and, in order to take her mind off the profound grief, he asked: "How old is Musa?"

"Ten, my lord," replied the woman, wiping away the tears on her face with her hands.

"Ten! Very nice. Give us your blessing so we can make him our student and teach him the doctor's craft, so he can turn into a man with honour, who will be helping others in the name of Allah."

The old woman opened her black eyes wide at that suggestion and started crying with joy. The hope she had been offered helped her regain her composure. She bowed in respect, kissed his hands yet again, and ran to her grandson.

Watching her leave, Leon thought back to his grandfather, Nicephorus Peleuses, and the period when he taught him medicine. He remembered his haughty attitude, his arrogance toward any master, even the emperors and bishops. "Nicephorus the Fearless" was how he was called by people who knew him.

"We are doctors, Leon!" he kept emphasising. "That's why you shouldn't be afraid of anyone."

Indeed, his grandfather feared no one. Once, when an epidemic struck the outskirts of Constantinople, the co-Emperor Romanus Lecapenus assigned him to handle the prevention and the control of the situation so that the plague would not spread inside the city. The measures he took to protect the citizens caused many reactions, but Nicephorus was neither daunted nor did he succumb. He forbade travel and the transport of goods, causing the merchants to protest; he administered a treatment he had found in one of the books belonging to the ancient doctor, Dioscurides, whose methods were considered heretical. However, what caused the utter rage of the clergymen against him was when he announced that the dead should be burnt.

At the patriarchate, at the churches, and at Constantinople's monasteries, a wave of protest broke out. His suggestion was un-Christian, heretical, and utterly satanic. If you burn the bodies of the dead, it means that they will not be resurrected on Doomsday and that their souls will never find peace inside the wondrous gardens of heaven.

Priests, monks, and hermits shrieked manically, incited the folks' superstition, and with their fiery words urged everyone to rise and capture the "heretical" doctor who condemned them to eternal punishment. The people were fanaticised and took to the streets in anger, heading toward Peleuses' mansion. However, once they were outside the gates, they quietly dispersed and every one of them took their way home, unable to decide on their actions.

They were governed by discord. They were angered by the thought that this obligatory measure would condemn their souls, but on the other hand, Peleuses was the only doctor in the city who never asked the poor for any money. To the people, he was a saint; to the rich he was a bloodsucker, whom they paid handsomely for treating them, but he was also the "only doctor who could heal." So, in spite of all the unruliness, the fear, and the superstition, they never crossed the gate of the mansion, nor did anyone lay a finger on him.

"We, doctors," his grandfather later told him, "possess great power. We are—let me put it to you this way so you understand—demigods. Living demigods!"

Leon was still young then and couldn't understand the world. His mind filtered the facts through teachings, not experience. He regarded his grandfather as a rough and rigid man, who always spoke arrogantly, boasting like a miracle-worker who could breathe fire.

"Don't look at me derisively," he demanded. "We doctors are indeed demigods to others. Listen to me carefully. Everyone knows that they are going to die eventually, but this fact doesn't keep them from trying to lengthen their lives.

"The philosopher Epicurus said that men always struggle to live, forgetting that with their birth they drank the poison of death. And this, my boy, is where we come in, we, the doctors, holding not the imaginary elixir of immortality, but something else, more real—the power to extend the living years.

"By treating the patients, all we manage is to add more oil to everyone's lamp of life so that it burns longer. We actually hold the key to the amount of time anyone can live for. If we want, we can close the gates of time and the patient dies. If, on the other hand, we wish to do it and are skilled enough, then we can keep them open for as long as our power and knowledge permits us, and thus the patient lives.

"So who can resist us? The master, the general, the rich man, the priest, the criminal? No one can! Not even the emperor!

"Always remember, my boy, that people only confess their inner thoughts to two kinds of people—the priests, so they can save their souls, and the doctors, so they can extend their lives."

Leon witnessed every word his grandfather told him when he worked by his side. He saw and felt all those displays of gratitude by the patients and their relatives, even displays of worship, which supported his argument. It was easier to him now to understand the overrated self-esteem in his words and deeds, but above all, his arrogant look.

And people everywhere, regardless of their origins or faith, are always grateful to doctors who fight to treat them or their beloved ones. That was why none of those who saw the old woman thanking Leon so conspicuously reacted or was surprised.

Bashar placed the cameleer's medallion on top of the central oak counter, next to the clay vessels with the substances, the several pots, and instruments for the preparation of the medicines. Because of the earthquake and the dozens of casualties, both on the floor as well as on the counters, there were vases overturned, dust, residue of herbs and dregs from the different medicines, which the students made every once in a while, following their two teachers' instructions. None of the three men noticed the mess.

Theodorus peered at the medallion without touching it and rubbed his short grey beard. The deep red colour with the dark shades left no doubt that Bashar was right. It was indeed the stone creature Mnizurin. Its features could be clearly seen: round eyes, no nose, wide lips, and two small lumps on the forehead, like horns.

Silently he recalled every little detail he knew about these odd entities; he tried to avoid reaching the threatening conclusion that some sorcerer had used it to induce the morning earthquake. He had heard rumours of such practices, but because he saw no logic in the situation, he simply regarded it as superstition. Besides, he had never met a real sorcerer.

Leon smirked, seeing his two friends being so silent and grim. He stooped over the counter and reached out to pick up the medallion.

Theodorus stopped him and looked stern. He said nothing, but Leon understood that he wasn't supposed to touch that stone. He took a step back and stood beside the wooden lectern, upon which was one of the medicine books of the ancient Greek doctor Galenus.

"What did the cameleer tell you?" Theodorus asked Bashar, not taking his eyes off the Mnizurin. At first, when Khalil brought him the message, he was planning on waiting till after sundown, but when he heard that someone had tried to kill his friend, he immediately ran to the clinic, in spite of the heat that caused him vertigo and burnt his eyes.

"I haven't spoken with him yet," Bashar replied. "I was waiting for you to come, so you can confirm it's a Mnizurin, and then we could talk to him together—"

"So is it really a magic stone?" interrupted Leon, who had neither seen nor known a lot about the Mnizurin.

"It's not a magic stone, boy. It's a petrified creature, which, in a way that some people consider magic, comes alive. Don't ask me how; I have no idea. And everything written about it is odd and questionable," Theodorus explained as he turned the Mnizurin upside down with a copper medical forceps.

The reverse side of the Mnizurin looked like snake's skin, consisting of small scales, and in the sunlight coming through the window you could clearly see its embossed surface. Its limbs were outlined, six thin tentacles that looked as though they had been carved by a dexterous sculptor.

"Some people say that the Mnizurin don't belong to our world, but are creatures coming from the sky," said Bashar, and added: "They are the notorious star-stones and the sorcerers sell their souls to the Devil to own them."

Leon almost laughed, but seeing Bashar's strict look, he became serious. He knew that his friends didn't believe in the superstitions of their religions, so the severity with which his Arab colleague had offered that piece of information seemed amusing to him.

"Don't let yourself be misled by the legends over a fact, but focus your attention on the fact itself," Leon muttered to himself, casting his scepticism away and keeping thoughtfully silent.

"Good. Now let us ask the cameleer how he found the stone or how he got it," said Theodorus in a hoarse voice and stood up from the stool he was sitting on.

Bashar took a metal basin, covered the Mnizurin, and, leaving the laboratory, closed the door shut. He ordered Khalil, who was waiting outside, not to let any of the other students enter and then led his friends to the mansion where he had transferred the man who had tried to kill him.

Husni was bound hand and foot in the corner of the guest room. Disoriented, he looked at the dead body of the bearded man on the bed opposite him. He had come to a little while before, gathered his thoughts, and settled his fears, but once he saw the corpse of the elderly man on the bed, he panicked.

He was no longer hallucinating and realised that the demon he thought had attacked him when he recovered his senses was nothing but an illusion. Otherwise, he wouldn't be lying there tied up like a sheep. That body, though, terrified him and brought back his recent memories of what he had witnessed at the reservation.

His situation was dire. Whenever he closed his eyes, he saw images of the slaughtered cameleers; whenever he opened them, his look was caught by the sutured, blood-caked wound that ran across the face of the dead man.

He eventually took a deep breath, gathered all the courage he had left, and peered at the body. He wanted to see if he could recognise his face, so he would understand which house he was in.

The dead man's beard was white from age, but soiled with blood and dust. His torn thobe was equally soiled. Husni recognised the city's cadi by his large nose and the mole on the cheek. He didn't know that there had been an earthquake, for at the time he was under the influence of the drug he had been given, and so he was surprised to see the dead man in such a bad state. He unsuccessfully tried to find an answer to who had killed him and mistreated his dead body. This morbid incident and his nightmares had affected him so much that it was impossible to think of any logical explanation.

At the sound of the door opening on his left, Husni pushed his back against the wall. The deaths at the reservation and the cadi's body along with the sedative that was wearing off frightened him greatly.

Three men appeared at the threshold. One was wearing a blue turban and the other two didn't seem like Arabs. He observed them in silence, and his heart started pounding when he thought that they might hurt him. He was unaware of the fact that the city guards had transferred him to Bashar's clinic; in his disoriented mind, those strangers seemed like killers.

"*Merhaba,*" they said and stood across from him.

Husni didn't respond. He only watched silently, his muscles tensing with fear.

"My name is Philetas," Theodorus said, introducing himself. "I am *Rum,* and a professor at the University of Damascus. This is Bashar ibn Fathi, and he's a doctor. And this is Leon Peleuses, also a doctor."

Husni raised his left eyebrow and looked at them, without his initial distrust. They looked calm and didn't seem to be ill-disposed toward him. Only the Arab doctor glowered at him.

"My name is Husni ibn Jaber and I'm a cameleer from Ma'arrat. Why have you tied me up? I didn't do anything! Believe me! It was the demons that killed them, not me! And I have nothing to do with your cadi's death."

Theodorus and Leon looked at the cadi's body on the bed and then gave Bashar a disapproving look. He winced, realising that putting Husni in the same room as the dead man was horrible. He spoke in Greek: "They told me he was insane . . . He acted crazy."

Husni didn't understand what the Arab doctor had said, but thinking he had accused him of something, he tried convincing them he wasn't a murderer: "I didn't kill him! In the name of Allah, I am no killer! I didn't kill the others either. I found them slaughtered when I woke up—"

"Don't you remember attacking me?" Bashar challenged him.

Husni gave up the excuses for the killings, looked at him in bewilderment, and, a few moments later, shook his head. He truthfully didn't remember, but at least the question helped him understand why he was tied up.

"It wasn't my fault, my lord. Forgive my doing so. I was given something to drink, I lost my mind, and I behaved badly. I am a peaceful cameleer, Allah's servant, and always faithful to the law of the Prophet: may His name be forever glorious."

"He doesn't seem insane to me," Theodorus whispered in Greek.

"Don't be fooled. Most insane people seem normal at first," Leon stated. "Talk to him, and if he starts his nonsense again, we'll know for sure."

"Who are these others you're talking about? Who else was killed?" asked Theodorus sullenly. "And why are you saying that demons killed them?"

Husni looked at the grey-haired man right in the eye. His face, his attitude, and the tone of his voice made Husni trust him. He also realised that the three men were cautious as a result of the previous misunderstanding, his attack on the doctor. In order to avoid any additional trouble, he drew in a deep breath and recounted everything that had happened at the reservation.

"We were ten men, all cameleers, and we were carrying merchandise from the South. The journey was uneventful, and two days ago we reached our last stop before Damascus. There we met with two more caravans: one was coming from Jerusalem and the other from Nablus. We all made a stop there, excited to sell our wares at the *souqs* and make a lot of profit.

"After the afternoon prayer, we relaxed a bit. We told a lot of funny stories and at night we went to bed, carefree and happy that Allah was protecting our journey—"

Husni's eyes opened wide and cut his narration short. The images were now crystal clear in his mind and caused him feelings that disheartened and upset him. The horror he had survived came rushing back with a greater intensity, just as when he woke up in his tent and realised everyone was dead.

"I woke up some time at dawn, I don't remember the details . . . and . . . they were all dead! Slaughtered! Their bodies dismembered, stomachs torn open . . . Blood everywhere; severed arms; smashed-in heads—" Tears started rolling down his cheeks. His lips had cracked from the heat and trembled as he spoke. His breathing was coming in short gasps in the wake of the sobs rising in his throat.

"Jelal . . . Jelal was killed and hung upside-down. They ripped his stomach open . . . His innards too. His face was covered in blood and fluids . . . They were all dead!"

Husni found it difficult to form a proper sentence. The words were lost within the memories, and revulsion shook every fibre in his body.

"Calm down," Leon said softly, approaching him. "Calm down. No one can hurt you now."

"I got out of the tent . . . Their footprints glistened in the sand . . . Wherever they had gone past, they had left slime trails, just like slugs . . . They were gone. They butchered them all, except for me, and left—"

Husni burst into tears. He slumped to the floor and curled up in the fetal position, while his sobs shook him.

The image of the collapsed houses and of the women sitting on fallen beams or smashed bricks, mourning over the crushed bodies of their relatives, intensified Leon's need to escape reality. Since the earthquake he hadn't left the clinic, and only now, as the shadows grew longer and the sun was setting behind the orange-purple clouds in the horizon, did he perceive the scale of the destruction.

Wails and cries of agony could be heard from every direction. The names of the Prophet and Allah were on everyone's lips, along with wishes and supplications for protection. The Damascenes' dismay still hadn't subsided, because it was augmented by the slighter tremors that followed throughout the day, and they all feared an even worse shock.

As he walked, he could feel death near him stooping over the ruins and smiling for all the prey it had taken in such a little time. However, Leon, unshaken, kept heading toward al-Mamun's den, impervious to the tragic scenes that took place along his path.

He was neither cruel nor callous before his fellow man's pain. He had simply witnessed so much death in his life that he had become inured to its presence.

"Only doctors can be indifferent to death," Leon remembered his grandfather saying. "That's how you should be, indifferent; otherwise, you'll lose your mind," Nicephorus had told him when he caught him crying over the lifeless body of his first patient. "If you're planning on crying and weeping for every person who dies, you'd better enter a monastery. You're not fit to be a doctor."

His harsh but truthful words rang once again in Leon's ears. He wanted to fight them, stifle them, but he couldn't. Nor was he able to defy them.

"Death is the only truth. Life is a lie, a fallacy," was his grandfather's philosophy. "Live the dream that is life, but never forget that death is on the lookout every step of your way."

Leon walked past a little boy who sat perched on the ruins of his home. He glanced at him, indecisive for a moment, and then continued toward the den with a heavy heart. The child, half-naked and dirty from all the filth that was stuck on his slender body, his eyes swollen from incessant crying, the dust caked on the snot covering his lips, was holding tightly the hand of his dead mother who had been crushed by a roof beam.

"If people ever beat death, they'll have doctors to thank." His grandfather always spoke in such an arrogant and cynical way that it got to his nerves. He had respect for nothing but medicine and he fought hard to pass this conviction onto Leon as well.

The moment he went round the corner, his thoughts vanished in the dark. The sight of al-Mamun's ruined mansion depressed him.

Only the wall around it had remained standing. The rest of the building was a pile of stones, bricks, roof tiles, wood, and crushed bodies.

He stood for a while, contemplating the rubble, and his mind was filled with images, blurry, dim, mystical, and sensual; the kind of images he always had every time he visited the den. The grand hall, with its colourful cushions and the semi-transparent silk partitions, was always covered in a thick haze of smoke. The air was heavy with smells—of hashish, of the courtesans' perfume, and of the various hallucinogenic herbs burning in silver vessels.

Inside the den, listening to music from instruments played by women's delicate fingers, light-headed with illusion, soaked in carnal pleasure, all men were one. There were no races, castes, religions; all this was saved for outside the wall surrounding the den. The dividing lines among the men, everything that differentiated them in life, seemed like waves on the surface of the sea, momentary ripples and random cracks on its infinite skin, while inside they were all present in the depth, alike, like children from the same womb.

He thought of the girl who kept him company during his last visit; he tried to remember what she looked like, but failed. He couldn't recall faces or names. They were all the same: beautiful, understanding, sensual, and attentive. They all loved him out of necessity, like servants, but he didn't love any of them.

He turned his back on the ruins and took the way that led to the temple of Damascus. He would go to Angelus Umbanes' pothouse, the only one near this area. Since he couldn't get high, he would get drunk in one of the city's pothouses, belonging to few of its Christian citizens.

He needed to feel giddy. He could no longer stand all the pain he had piled up inside him since that morning. His heart was aching. It did not matter how well his grandfather had armoured him by teaching him to be callous; in spite of Leon's impenetrable emotional walls, there were still cracks through which the tragedy before him stirred his soul.

Someone's pained groan interrupted his thinking. He searched in the gloom to find the source of the sound. Somewhere on his left, he heard someone screaming for help in a stifled voice and then some others swearing and groaning.

He listened closely one last time to make sure of the sound and rushed to the man who was calling for help. He turned to the dark alley on his left, and through the dimness he saw two men violently beating another man, who was now on his knees suffering the wild punches and kicks on his face and body.

"Stop!" Leon shouted. "What are you doing there? Let him go, in the name of the Prophet!"

The two men froze at the sound of his voice. They stopped beating their victim and looked at him in alarm.

"He's a faithless dog! A Jew! Go away and leave us alone!" one of them yelled.

"For goodness' sake, my man, help me—" The Jew didn't get a chance to end his sentence, because the man who had spoken before struck him sideways on the jaw and pushed him to the ground, making him spit blood and saliva.

"Stop it!" Leon shouted furiously.

"The infidel's got money, that son of a whore! And if he doesn't give it to us, we'll bury him along with it."

"I don't have—" The Jew was forcefully kicked in the ribs. He yelped in utter pain and crouched in a fetal position.

"Get out of here, or else I'll have the emir hang you by your balls!" Leon snarled, and the thieves, thinking instantaneously that he might be nobility, at first retreated to the shadows, and then walked toward him hanging their heads.

Leon moved aside to let them through, still glowering at them. He wanted to take them to the guards, but he knew he couldn't because he was an infidel.

"You're not an Arab!" one of the thieves exclaimed in surprise when he approached him and noticed the looks, the clothing, and the crucifix on his chest that sparkled in the dimness of the dusk.

Leon reacted with lightning speed. He knew that if he let them, they would hit him and mug him with no hesitation. They might even kill him for preventing them from killing the Jew and for speaking in a way not fitting to an infidel living in the caliphate. Without hesitation, he landed a heavy right blow on the face of the man who'd realised he wasn't Arab, and grabbed the other one by the throat.

The first man fell back with pain, whereas the other one, unable to breathe because of Leon's hold on his throat, tried to wrench himself free from the suffocating hold. Leon knew that if he didn't restrain one of them, it would be hard to deal with both at the same time, so he violently pulled the thief he was holding and thrust him onto the wall behind him. He hoped that if he knocked him on the head, he would immobilise him.

The Arab's eyes opened wide as he saw the wall coming toward him, but he didn't have the chance to react and knocked his head on the rocks. His forehead suffered an immediate gash and his face was instantly covered in blood. He didn't fall down, though. He stumbled, but remained standing.

In a stride, Leon was before the man he had punched. He pushed his averting hands aside, grabbed him by the hair, and, pulling his head hard, thrust it against his knee. The Arab's nose broke on impact, and his persistent moan could be heard along the alley.

"I'll kill you!" the second thief yelled, spitting out the blood that had dripped from his gashed forehead. "I'll—"

Leon turned fast, grabbed him by the throat again, and with his right hand hit him in the face twice—the first time on the jaw, and the second on the forehead, where his skin was torn. The thief, crippled by all the blows, sank onto the ground.

Leon remained hunched for a minute, panting, with his fists ready to strike. When he saw that his adversaries weren't going to get up, he turned to where the Jew was lying. In the semi-darkness, he couldn't discern his features, but the thick curls of his hair were grey with age.

"Are you all right?" he asked and took him by the shoulders.

"Thank you . . . thank you . . ." the breathless Jew murmured. He took Leon's hands in an effort to sit up, but a sharp pain in his ribs made him bend and crouch.

"Come on, get up," said Leon nervously. "Let's go, for if their gang gets us, there'll be no one to save us," he added and lifted the old man in his arms.

3. Dream and Nightmare

With slow and hesitant movements, Theodorus touched the Mnizurin and shuddered at once as he felt its slimy texture. Even though it was dry and appeared fossilised, its surface felt like mucus to the touch. He winced in disgust and quickly wrapped it in a linen cloth. He placed it in a special cupboard where Bashar kept the different pots containing poisonous substances, and quickly locked it.

He stood for a moment in front of the thick piece of furniture and looked at it, stunned. Several thoughts flitted through his mind and sank in, registering danger. He wondered whether what the cameleer had said about the demons and the massacre at the reservation was indeed just the ravings of a lunatic, as his friends had claimed. He wanted to believe them, but he had his doubts. His instincts were in a heightened state and that worried him, because he had learned to trust them. Knowing little about sorcerers or occult groups, he was afraid that the alchemists in Damascus would find out about the existence of the Mnizurin. He hadn't forgotten about the incident in Constantinople, where Andronicus Graeuses was found savagely butchered, after it was discovered that he had a starstone in his laboratory.

On recollecting his murdered colleague, he wasted no more time. He couldn't wait to find an answer to the questions that troubled him and he exited the laboratory in order to go to the University library. He wanted to look for books with information on those strange stone creatures, hoping to discover something that would help him cope with any unsuspected and perilous situation that might eventuate.

The names of three ancient writers came to his mind: Plutarch, Orpheus, and Theophrastus. Their books on stones and their properties would be the beginning and the foundation of his research.

Everything he knew about the Mnizurin stones mostly came from the writings of the Theurgists, that is, the ancient philosophers who tried to answer the questions of the existence of the soul, of the world, and of God. Even though he was familiar with their philosophical work, he used to question their teachings concerning the ways to communicate with the invisible forces. He changed his mind about their knowledge after Graeuses' tragic death and after reading his colleague's notes. The texts that Graeuses had left behind verified the Theurgists' theories about humans' contact with other worlds through logical arguments. This proof prompted him to be more receptive to doctrines he used to label as superstitions or even fantasies.

Most Theurgists were Plato's followers and developed their theories by including many mystical principles of Egypt and of the Mesopotamian peoples. The philosophical circles that were formed promoted a different view about God and the world, both the visible and the mystical one. They believed that our world communicates with others and is ruled by supernatural creatures. They separated and classified those alleged deities according to their powers and abilities, while recording the ways in which humans can not only communicate, but also achieve *henosis* (union) with them.

To Christians, Theurgists were nothing but sorcerers, instruments of Satan, and as a result they forbade people from reading their teachings and burnt most of their books. They announced that all those rituals, the glorification and genealogies of the deities, which their texts referred to, came from ancient devil-worshipping cults of the peoples that lived in that fertile land between the two biblical rivers, Tigris and Euphrates, specifically of the Chaldean people.

Thus, once the Christians prevailed over the Roman Empire, they launched a fierce hunt against the Theurgists, accusing them of sorcery. At the same time, they attempted to erase all memory of their existence. In the war they started, they used every real or spiritual weapon they could, and as a result, the name "Chaldean" ended up referring to a dreadful necromancer, a sorcerer who performs human sacrifices in order to rule the human soul.

But even though they weren't able to eradicate everything relating to the Theurgists, they successfully destroyed every copy of their most important book, the *Chaldean Oracles*. This work contained all the rituals and the doctrines concerning the contact of humans with the supernatural creatures and eventually became something of a legend, since most people believed it was just a myth, a book that never existed even though it was referred to in several writers' texts.

Regardless of the rumours, there was not a single professor in the Empire who didn't wish to find it and read its forbidden secrets. Theodorus was no exception. Being a worshipper of Plato, he had studied every extension or variation to the Athenian philosopher's doctrines and knew that the *Chaldean Oracles* was no fairy tale, as people claimed, but a real book that was wiped out by the fanatical and narrow-minded Christians. That is why he always hoped to find a surviving copy.

During his time in the Empire, he had lost all hope, just like other scholars. A copy could not be found anywhere in any private or public library. There were a few fake books in some secret circles and groups, but they were a mere fancy of their authors and had nothing to do with the original book. So he gave up searching, until he settled in the caliphate and his hopes were rekindled. Inside the libraries of the Arabs, he found many of the alleged lost books of the ancient Greeks, and this made him hope that he might also discover the *Chaldean Oracles*.

The like-minded al-Farabi, with whom he corresponded almost every week, had written him that he might find it in the library of Syria's Tripoli, which wasn't very far from Damascus. Theodorus took a leave of absence from the university and, for a whole month, scrutinised every cabinet of the caliphate's largest library, without success.

To soften his disappointment, al-Farabi had sent him some rare books of two philosophers who dealt with theurgy, Iamblichus and Plotinus, advising him that there was information in them about the contact with the otherworldly creatures. But he warned him that they didn't describe the specific rituals and methods.

Theodorus happily accepted this gesture and returned the favour by translating in Arabic the book of the astronomer and mathematician Sosigenis Alexandreas. It was about creatures who live on an unknown planet in the constellation Aries. He had found this book in the library of Tripoli, in its original language, abandoned to rot. His Arab colleagues considered it useless reading material. Apart from the astronomical puzzles and mathematical knowledge it contained, it also described the otherworldly creatures and the political situation of their society, which resembled Plato's *Republic*.

That was not all he discovered. Apart from some other "useless" works, like comedies and tragedies of the ancient Greeks, he also found the last book written by philosopher Damascius while in exile. (During the reign of Emperor Justinian, the Christians had closed down Plato's Academy and banished the philosophers of the ancient religion from the Empire.) In the book, the last philosopher of the Academy made a complete list of the contact humans had with celestial creatures. From his study, Theodorus gained some better insight into the god whom the Theurgists called *Bythos*, Depth, and whom they believed to be sleeping, not participating in the events but waiting for the right time to appear. He also learned about the unearthly demons Iynges, who come to the earth intending to restore the order that used to exist during the Old Ones' sovereignty.

He stayed at the university library until late at night, looking for facts about the Mnizurin. When he finished reading, he felt his head heavy and his thinking clouded. The information he gathered about the stone creatures offered no explanation for their existence, other than the fact that they were considered otherworldly and that they related to various constellations. The only interesting fact he read was a passage in which Chaldeans brought some Mnizurin to life with a ritual of fire and blood, in order to confront an opposing army; but because they couldn't subdue the creatures, the latter turned against them and vanquished them. The rest of the accounts were so preposterous and idiotic—such as that they aid sexual pleasure—that he paid no attention to them.

Exhausted and sleepy, he gathered up his notes and headed to the university guest house. He was too tired to return home and, thinking that both the injured people and their relatives would stay at the clinic, he decided to sleep at the school.

Leon arrived outside the house of Joel the Jew and knocked on the wooden gate. He glanced nervously over his shoulder, in case someone had followed them and knocked again impatiently.

"Open up, child," breathed Joel and passed out. He was in a really bad state. On the way, he had lost and regained consciousness several times. In his confusion, he eventually managed to introduce himself to Leon and tell him where he lived.

Leon was about to knock on the gate again, but seeing Joel unconscious in his arms, he kicked it really hard and opened it. He couldn't wait any longer, as he himself was exhausted and had already regretted helping him.

He entered the yard and with his last ounce of strength walked up to the wooden threshold. His arms were trembling with fatigue, and he was worried he might inadvertently drop the man.

The house door opened before he could lay Joel on the doorstep. A young woman holding an oil lamp appeared at the threshold.

"Father!" she cried, seeing Leon setting Joel in front of the door. "What's wrong with him? Are you all right, father?" she asked anxiously and rushed to them.

Leon sat on the steps and breathed a sigh of relief. He could barely stand from exhaustion, and his stomach rumbled with hunger.

The daughter kneeled down beside her father, saw the wounds on his face and, thinking he was dead, burst into tears. She placed the lamp on the floor and started kissing his hands, muttering a sad dirge.

"He's fine . . . he's just fainted," Leon whispered in Arabic. "They attacked and tried to mug him, and they beat him badly. Bring us some water and a piece of bread, please," he added and gave her a closer look.

The lamp flame didn't cast much light, but her features could be clearly seen: thin, arched eyebrows, big black eyes, thin, straight nose, and sensual lips. Her hair was hidden underneath a green kerchief, but a few black curls peeked out from the sides, revealing its colour.

The young woman looked at him with tears rolling down her face, puzzled by his accent. She didn't know him, and while at first she hadn't paid much attention to him, thinking he was a neighbour, she was now frightened at his sight. The idea that he was the one who hit her father and conjured up this lie to enter their house made her grip the lamp tighter, ready to throw it at him if he made any threatening move.

"Did you hear what I said? Don't be frightened, I'm the one who saved your father from the thieves."

Joel's daughter didn't move an inch. She had heard so many stories of how the Arabs entered the Jews' houses in order to rob them that she froze with fear. Of course, this man didn't look like an Arab, and his behaviour was completely calm, something that puzzled her even more.

"I am a doctor, I won't hurt you. My name is Leon, and I saved your father from two thieves," he explained in the calmest tone he could.

"Are you *Yavana*?"

Leon nodded. *Yavana* was an old name used by the people of the East and it meant Ionian, Greek.

"Yes, *Yavana*. Now, go bring some water—"

"What do you need the bread for?"

Leon heard the question, but as he was exhausted, he didn't realise it was in Greek, and so he replied in Arabic: "I am very tired and in order to take care your father's wounds I need something to eat."

Joel's daughter smiled and set the lamp on the floor. She stood to her feet and rushed home. She returned with a pitcher and a plate with cheese, olives, and bread.

Leon happily accepted them. He splashed a little water on Joel's face, dampened his lips, and, after bringing him to his senses, started eating greedily. He barely chewed down his food, all the while stealing glances at the woman's face. Enraptured, he was transfixed by her beautiful eyes. He felt euphoric but knew that this was not the right time to give in to his mood, so he turned back to his patient. All he told her, while eating, was that he would need a needle and some thread to suture the wounds.

She didn't see to his request, though. The moment her father opened his eyes, she fell into his arms sobbing both with joy and grief for what had happened to him.

Still in pain, Joel tried to reassure her and lift her spirits: "Don't cry, daughter, I'm fine. Leon is a doctor and he said that within a week I'll be able to walk same as before. . . . Isn't that what you said, doctor? Tell my Rebecca."

Leon finished his mouthful. "Joel," he smiled warmly, "in a month's time, you'll be leaping about like a baby goat," he commented humorously. His words brightened up the girl's tearful eyes.

"Are you sure?" Rebecca asked in Greek.

Leon was taken aback when he heard the question in his mother tongue. Dumbfounded, he stared at her. When you are in a strange land, surrounded by foreigners, and you hear people speaking in your language, it makes you feel as if they are your relatives.

"You speak Greek?" he asked. His eyes shone with a sparkle of familiarity and warmth.

"Father does, too," Rebecca said, making him turn his gaze to Joel's bloodied face in surprise.

"What? How?"

"My ancestors came from Alexandria, Egypt."

On Leon's face there was admiration but also something else, vague but quite visible. In fact, because he was conscious of how intense his look was, he turned his attention back to Joel. After a few awkward moments, he composed himself and asked Rebecca seriously: "Could you get me a needle and some thread so I can sew up his wounds?"

Rebecca kissed her father's hand again and rushed to her feet. Her fears had been dispelled, and the intensity of the Greek's gaze had struck an odd spark inside her heart.

Bashar was sleeping on his stomach, bare-chested, with nothing on but his underwear. He had gone to bed late, utterly exhausted. From the time Theodorus left for the university and Leon went to the infamous al-Mamun's house, Bashar attended to the wounds of five more people. After the fifth wounded person, his legs couldn't hold him any longer and his hands were shaking with fatigue. He had his students sleep in turns, and he headed to the mansion to relax a bit. But when he got out of the bathroom he didn't even have the strength to eat, so he went to his bedroom. He was so tired that he fell asleep as soon as he closed his eyes.

At some point, as the night moved to its darkest hour, in his sleep he felt something disturbingly heavy on him. He was dreaming that he was yelling, but, just like a deaf person, he couldn't hear himself—he only saw the movements of his hands and lips. His dream-self was distraught. He was shouting and gesturing, as if trying to warn himself about a great danger, and the desperation on his face revealed the threat that his body had already felt.

The discomfort he experienced was so intense that he woke up and opened his eyes. It was hard to breathe, and his limbs were trembling irregularly and for no apparent reason.

The clarity of his dream disappeared in the gloom of the actual darkness enveloping his bedroom. He tried to turn on his back and prop himself up, but he couldn't. Fear coursed through his mind. His heart beat fast as he tried again. None of his muscles obeyed his will. He gave another try and only then did he realise . . .

He stopped breathing, his eyelids opened wide, and his eyes almost popped out of their sockets. Something was sitting on his legs and back, a heavy creature that had paralysed him.

Bashar shivered. He breathed with difficulty, in short, almost choking gasps. His heart beat irregularly while his mind went dark from terror and his vision turned a dark shade of red. The ineffable horror that consumed him had left him speechless, because no matter how hard he tried, he couldn't scream.

He tried pulling up his legs, spreading them, bending them, but his body wouldn't obey. He was held in total captivity by the force of the creature sitting on top of him. He could feel it and, even though he couldn't see it, he knew that its mouth was open and its gaze was fixed on his neck. He could tell that it was a demon, not like those he had heard and read about on numerous occasions, but a creature even more powerful, more ancient, maybe even as old as darkness itself.

He tried his best to scream, but it was pointless. All he could hear was his own moaning—that forced, nervous moaning of a man striving with all his might to tear himself free from a crushing grip.

He pushed himself harder. He wanted to move, to turn around and fight back, but he couldn't. His inability to protect himself and the shocking realisation that he was a prey to the demon's appetite made him lose hope. His eyes welled up with the effort, his jaw ached with clenching, his heart was racing in his chest, but the worst of all was the horror that blurred his vision.

This supernatural, unprecedented threat he felt urged him to fight furiously for his life. He thought that if he didn't break free, the creature would kill him.

At some point, amidst his struggling efforts, he managed to turn his head a little to the right. From the window's opening, he could see a piece of the starry sky. On the bedside table there was a yellow candle, now burnt out, wedged in the portable candlestick. What he saw wasn't a dream, but reality. It wasn't even a nightmare, but a living horror.

Out of the corner of his eye, and in spite of the fear that had made his blood run cold, he looked over his shoulder and saw the creature. He saw it looking at him!

The creature's body was blacker than darkness and very heavy. But what was more unsettling and shattered his sense of reason were its yellow eyes that were fixed on him, ravenous before what would soon be its food. That look was fiercer than a lion's, more bloodthirsty than a wolf's . . .

His desperate screaming was heard all over the mansion, scaring all the slaves and servants. His continuous and desperate shouting propelled him to move and, using too much force, he fell off the bed.

He rushed to his feet, growling, with clenched fists. He looked around for the creature, but it was gone. The odd creature had vanished, as if it had never existed. No sooner had he realised it than he collapsed on the floor.

Three of his servants entered the bedroom yelling. Two of them ran to help him up when they saw him lying at the corner of the bed, and the third one ran to the open window, thinking that his master had been attacked by a thief.

Two more men stood at the door, but they stepped aside when they heard a woman's voice ordering them to move. Jasmine appeared behind them, with her hair loose, and she immediately ran to Bashar.

Mustafa al-Beidha's widow fell into his arms and tenderly kissed him on the lips. She didn't pay any heed to the servants' curious looks; she neither cared nor minded about the gossip that would spread as soon as the sun was up. She was worried about Bashar, and all she cared about was her love for him.

"What happened?" she asked and looked him in the eyes.

Bashar was too frightened and confused to feel happy about Jasmine's display of affection. Under different circumstances, he would hug her back and their kiss would be passionate, but now the sweat of fear stuck to his body and love was far from his mind; all he could think about was the horror he had experienced.

"I don't know. . . . Something—a demon was sitting on my back," he stammered and sat up at the edge of the bed.

Jasmine's beautiful eyes opened wide in bewilderment. Then, as if she were the lady of the house, she commanded the servants to exit the room and asked them for a pitcher of cool water.

"You had a nightmare," she told him as soon as the servants closed the door behind them. At the same time, she helped him rest against the head of the bed and stroked his face in compassion, like a mother soothing her frightened child. However, she didn't feel this way. Her gestures were not driven by motherly instincts but by passion; she was a woman in love taking care of her tired husband. Besides, Bashar's offer to put her up at his home because hers had collapsed was equal to a marriage proposal.

Jasmine had been a widow for two years now, ever since her husband, Mustafa, was killed after falling off his horse. She met Bashar when she called him to treat the stomach ache that troubled her. Love grew at first sight, but, because of the mourning period, they couldn't reveal it. However, the earthquake brought a solution to their problem and sped up the course of things.

"It wasn't a nightmare . . . and if it was, then it was a real nightmare," Bashar murmured and held his beloved Jasmine's hands in his own. "It was a dark creature, Jasmine. I felt it on my back and I saw it. I'm sure it was no dream."

With Rebecca's help, Leon took Joel home and laid him on the kitchen table. He sewed up the wounds that the two thieves' fists had made on the old man's face; on his right cheek, below his eye, on his left eyebrow, and on the left corner of his lips. At the same time, upon Leon's instructions, Rebecca prepared an antiseptic ointment that she later applied to her father's wounds.

Joel ached every time the needle pricked his skin, but when he noticed that if he tensed and moved, the pain became worse, he withstood every stitch by moaning weakly. What he couldn't endure was the doctor strapping him tightly on the table and trying to reposition his ribs. The unbearable pain made him lose consciousness.

"Let him sleep," Leon commanded Rebecca as soon as he was done, and he sat on the wooden chair beside the table. He was exhausted, sleepy, and ready to collapse. Nonetheless, as he wished to get to know her, he mustered all his remaining strength and remained alert.

"Were you taught Greek by a teacher?" he asked in order to break the heavy, sad silence that surrounded the kitchen.

"No, I wasn't. We use it at home. It has been a family tradition for many generations," Rebecca explained. Holding her father's hand, she told Leon the story of her family, whose relation to the Greeks dated forty-two generations back.

According to the family's stories, her first ancestor who met and loved Greeks was Iosaf ben Jova. Iosaf lived in a village in the valley of the River Jordan, when the Greek allied army, under the orders of Alexander the Great, freed Palestine from the Persians. Enchanted by the personality of the Greek commander, he followed them to India.

After the unexpected death of the great commander, the mercenary Jew chose to serve General Ptolemy, son of Lagus, the Pharaoh of Egypt, and settled in Alexandria. Ever since then, the members of Iosaf's family became Alexandrians and saw every change in history by being settled in the greatest city of the world. During the reign of both the Ptolemies and the Romans, many of the family's offspring served in administrative positions and were prominent citizens, until Alexandria was conquered by the Arabs, approximately three centuries earlier.

After the Arabs destroyed the city, most of the family members moved to Damascus, but never stopped thinking about their bonds with the Greeks; in honour of the glorious past, they kept learning the language at an early age. In addition to their Jewish descent, learning Greek was an exceptional and glorious legacy for them.

"But how did you manage to preserve the clarity of dialect for three centuries, with no teachers and no books?" Leon asked in disbelief. His eyelids were getting heavy and every now and then they half closed softly at the narration, but he insisted on staying awake, hoping for more time with her.

"Who said we have no books? We do, and rare ones for that matter. You wouldn't believe me if I told you."

"Like what?" In order to keep his head steady, he brought his palms underneath his chin and rested them upon the table on Joel's left.

"We have Homer's *Iliad*, the gift that Alexander the great offered to Ptolemy, the son of Lagus, with a handwritten inscription."

In spite of sleepiness and weakness, Leon's surprise was evident in his eyes. Such a book was more than a historical document, and he couldn't believe it existed.

"I don't believe you . . ." he mumbled, more out of surprise than doubt, but because of his sleepiness it wasn't apparent which.

Rebecca didn't reply. She got up from the stool she was sitting on and, smiling smugly, she left the kitchen. When she returned a few minutes later, she was holding a cylindrical book in her hands and her eyes sparkled with joy. But her bright smile was instantly gone when she saw that Leon had fallen asleep, resting on the table.

He woke up, soaked in sweat, and his head was heavy due to restless sleep. He didn't remember any of the dreams he had, but his physical fatigue and mental weakness attested to their stressful and menacing nature. For a few more minutes he remained lying on the narrow bed in the university guest house and tried to reorganise his thoughts so that he could change his mood.

Several images went through his mind, along with ideas and sayings, all tangled, disconnected, and incoherent. He thought about many things at once: the Mnizurin; his surprise when he heard that someone had disclosed the conspiracy to Constantine Porphyrogenitus; the earthquake and its victims; the Theurgists' theories on supernatural creatures; the ghastly murder of Andronicus Graeuses; the course of his exile, from Constantinople to the caliphate . . .

He pressed his palms against his temples and tried to concentrate. His mind was like a mill, grinding everything he had experienced, heard, or seen and entwining it with ideas, theories, and memories. This process caused him vertigo and, in order to stop it, he focused on her face; his wife's face, Eudoxia. Whenever he wanted to concentrate, he always recalled her shape, smile, and kind countenance, all those things that hadn't faded and would never be gone from his memory, no matter how many years went by.

This time, however, what came to his mind wasn't the look he had kept inside him so he could remember her with eternal love, but an awful image of hers when she was besieged by sickness. He closed his eyes to shut it out, but he was unable to shake away the memory of her.

The image of his beloved Eudoxia—with her skin rotting under dirty bandages, yellowed with pus, with her cracked lips and blood-soaked gums—wouldn't go away or be replaced with that exquisite image of her youth, when both their hearts pulsated with love. Despite his efforts to erase it, the memory of her decaying body stubbornly remained fixed in his mind, as if it wanted to torture him on purpose or warn him about an imminent danger.

He envisioned her just as she was last, before she was cremated; her sick body, dehydrated, shrivelled, full of sores and gaping wounds with dried pus and congealed black blood, lying on top of the other bodies, in the dim moonlight, through the orange flames of the greedy fire.

After the strong protests by the clergymen against the cremating of the deceased, Nicephorus Peleuses decided that the pyres should take place late at night so that the rest of the people wouldn't witness the burning of their relatives and loved ones. That's why Theodorus remembered her like this, inside the fiery shadows, like a hideous demon, cursed by unforgivable sins, blackened and charred.

He loved his wife and had cherished that same body which had turned to ashes. He couldn't stand the pain any longer, so he furiously headed to Nicephorus Peleuses' mansion and, once he found him, landed a heavy blow on his face. Ever since then, the only man that Leon's grandfather respected throughout the whole Empire was Theodorus.

The persistent knocking on the door chased away his bad memories, but still under their influence, dejected, he got up from his bed. In the corridor outside his room was one of his students, carrying an envelope with the wax seal on it still intact. It had been sent by al-Farabi, and Theodorus happily opened it and read it at once.

The look on his face changed as he absorbed the information his friend from Baghdad was sending him. "Something bizarre is happening at the caliphate," wrote al-Farabi. "Every day from all the country's corners come grim reports about brutal killings and bizarre phenomena." What impressed him was the similarity of the incidents, especially the way in which killers butchered innocent cameleers, whether the report came from the Gedrosian desert in the east or the Sahara desert in the west. However, the criminal attacks weren't limited to the caravans; they also occurred in reservations or local villages, suggesting that the perpetrators weren't thieves.

The caliph's advisers spoke of the onset of a revolution, even though the evidence didn't support such an assumption. The Bedouins, al-Farabi stressed, were terrified. Most of them abandoned their homes, which were near commercial routes or oases, in order to flee for safe havens, deep inside the deserts; places in which they hid only in cases of hostile raids.

In fact, throughout the caliphate, from India to the Atlantic coasts in Spain, an old poem could be heard, an invitation for the Arabs to raise their weapons against a fearsome and mighty enemy, whose intention is not to conquer the kingdom, but destroy humankind.

The expansive desert glistens under the life-giving sun.
The white feluccas in the sky sway to the hot winds of sand.
O sweet life, you splashed through the cracked pomegranate!

A dark shadow stretches out,
Slithering, mangling the melody of the stars.
Ancient threat gallops on a black multi-footed fiery horse.
O handsome sons of mother Arabia,
What evil lurks in your dreams?
Who stammered the hollow words calling on our enemies?
Who disturbed the desert, awakening the gods of devastation?
Quick, quick, hasten my brothers,
Arm yourselves, bare your weapons,
Mount your fearless steeds, the swift-footed mares and attack the enemies.
Vanquish them!
Before what sighs heavily in lethargy remembers it exists . . .

"This poem," al-Farabi said, "written approximately two centuries ago by a poet named Abdul Alhazred, is on everyone's lips, and though the Bedouins recite it to take courage, their eyes still brim with fear."

Theodorus didn't recognise the name, but judging from some of the lyrics in the poem, he could immediately tell that this poet was aware of the philosophy of the Chaldeans and the Pythagoreans, the ancient esoteric mathematicians. Otherwise he wouldn't have been able to write that life splashed through a cracked pomegranate, nor about the melody of the stars.

Frowning, his eyes remaining fixed on al-Farabi's short and worried sentences, Theodorus went into the guest house and closed the door behind him. The several odd celestial phenomena mentioned in the letter stirred his curiosity.

Al-Farabi, renowned for his inquisitiveness, listed a number of incidents that had happened in different areas of the caliphate and was asking Theodorus to help explain them. "In Basra," he wrote, "giant sea monsters washed ashore, half-eaten and severed in a way that couldn't have been inflicted by any known creature. Captains of the fleet sailing to or from India reported that for several days a thick layer of blood, greenish mucus, and dead fish covered the ocean. In Yemen and at the opposite coast of Ethiopia, terrified locals claimed that every night there was a loud noise, as if the sky shattered, while others said that they could see grotesque creatures with bat-like wings flying in the moonlight.

"In Tripoli, Libya," al-Farabi continued, recounting the strange events happening in the caliphate, "it rained pieces of frozen flesh; so many, in fact, that the citizens, petrified by the incident, locked themselves inside their homes. They had to get out and clean up eventually, though, due to the intolerable stench. The rotten pieces they collected were burned on the spot.

"And lastly, the emir of the far western al-Maghreb al-Aqsa, south of Spain, reported that he had arrested a group of sorcerers trying to summon the god who is sleeping at the bottom of the sea by performing a beastly human sacrifice with numerous victims. Prior to their arrest by his warriors, he corroborated, the horrible necromancers had sacrificed forty-five infant boys and girls, whom they had arranged in a circle around a Mnizurin."

Theodorus hastened when he read the last account. He slipped his friend's letter into the pocket of his cassock and hurried to the clinic. He absolutely needed to speak with Husni ibn Jaber, to find out what had happened at the reservation and where he had found the Mnizurin, because his piqued instinct was telling him that of all the things that had happened nothing was accidental, not even the earthquake.

Since the morning, there were continual funeral processions on the streets of Damascus. Those who had managed to dig their people out of the ruins the previous day were now taking them to the cemetery, inside sloppily built coffins. The enormity of the tragedy left no time for the living to mourn their beloved in the traditional Arabic way. The burials were so hasty and careless that dead relatives were mistakenly buried together.

On his way back to the clinic, Leon was not daunted by the death scene befallen on the Damascenes, nor was he moved by the guttural wailings of women who beat their chests in woe. The reek of death floating throughout the city did not break his stride. Of course he was sad, but as his mind was on Rebecca and his heart was beating merrily, the picture of the devastating reality almost leaving him indifferent. His mind was like a field in bloom, under a gloomy sky, and he looked like a dreamy poet who, even in hard and dark times, is optimistic enough to celebrate life and praise its wonders. Love had touched him, and he would neither deny nor prevent it. The dream of love flourished inside him, and the face of his beloved wouldn't leave his mind for a minute. . . .

Before meeting his friends at the mansion, he stayed at the clinic a little while longer to check on several seriously injured patients, and he instructed his students on the course of several treatments. Even though he hadn't rested fully, he didn't feel the least tired. On the contrary, he felt bursting with energy and power.

Leon entered the great hall in the mansion. He found Bashar and Theodorus sitting on low sofas with fluffy pillows, talking in hushed, almost conspiratorial tones. Leon ignored their secretive behaviour and cheerfully moved closer and sat opposite his Arab friend.

"I have a gift for you," he said and pulled out a cylindrical book made of papyrus from the bag Rebecca had given him.

Bashar, frowning, intrigued by Leon's happy face, looked at the book curiously, and without comment he untied the band that was keeping it closed. He read the title and the name of the author; impressed, he raised his left eyebrow and unrolled the cylinder wider to check the condition of the text.

"This looks genuine. Where did you get it?" he asked in controlled surprise after finishing the examination.

"You won't believe what happened to me last night!" Leon exclaimed joyfully, but his playful glance stopped on Theodorus' dejected expression. His stern look, his pursed lips, and that vertical wrinkle that stopped between his eyebrows made him wonder and ask: "What's the matter? Why so glum?"

Theodorus didn't reply. He was disappointed because he hadn't been able to speak with Husni ibn Jaber. The cameleer had yet to recover from the sunstroke he had suffered on the way to Damascus. He was delirious and unable to communicate with anyone. Bashar treated him with care, but he made clear that it probably wouldn't be for several days before Husni's state improved.

Sullenly, Theodorus handed Leon al-Farabi's letter without a word, and Leon started reading it in curiosity. He paused at intervals on certain portions of the letter and looked at his friends, at times wryly or in bewilderment. After he had read the last part that mentioned the star-stone, he held the piece of paper up and asked with a frozen smile, "Do you believe all this?"

"The thing isn't what we believe, but what exactly is going on," Bashar said pompously. "Something strange is happening, and we're in it."

"I don't understand. What kind of involvement could we have?"

Bashar related to Leon everything that had happened in his bedroom at dawn. The words "demon" and "threat" were ringing in his ears, but because of his euphoria, he couldn't sense his colleague's fears.

"It was a terrible nightmare," he commented when Bashar finished his narration. "The fatigue, the heat, and the exhaustion must have caused you—" Leon cut his offhand diagnosis short, seeing his friend lifting his linen shirt and showing his back to him.

"You think? Well, I didn't cause these marks and, of course, they can't be the result of a dream."

Bashar's back was covered with markings. There were two rows of red circular marks, clearly visible, from the end of his shoulder blade to the small of his back. The symmetry in which they were arranged and the distance between them were such that there was no chance they might have been done on purpose.

Leon went over to his friend to examine his wounds with more scrutiny. Every one of the round marks was red at the edges and black in the centre. They were similar to the marks caused by glasses for cupping therapy that doctors use to treat a cold, and it was obvious that Bashar couldn't have inflicted them on himself.

Theodorus looked at him gravely and shrugged, admitting that he knew nothing. His anxiety had increased ever since he heard about the dark creature that had attacked Bashar; after collating all the pieces of information to the facts, he had a hard time understanding what was happening. His mind fastened to the idea that there was a pattern, but no matter how hard he tried, he couldn't see it.

Leon leaned on the sofa pensively. He rubbed his unshaven chin with his left thumb and tried to reflect on the events, but it was difficult. His romantic mood was clouding his thinking. On the outside, he wanted to concentrate on the issues troubling his friends, but all he cared about was seeing Rebecca as soon as possible. Besides, with the pretence of treating Joel, he was planning on visiting them later in the afternoon. He would then talk to her, admire her bright eyes, her beautiful lips, her slender fingers . . .

"What are you thinking about?" Theodorus' voice brought him back to the present, shattering the dreamy picture of their rendezvous.

"Nothing. All this. It's all strange, but . . ." He didn't know what to say, so, in order to make his lie more plausible, he added: "My grandfather would have remarked that what the Bedouins say is senseless rubbish, simply added to logical facts. As for the marks on your back, they may have been caused by fleas. They tend to bite in this way, creating rows."

"I've never seen any flea bites as big as these!" said Bashar abruptly, offended that his friend belittled the terror of what he had experienced and narrated a little while ago in complete earnestness.

"They might have been infected." Leon stood by his assumption firmly and added sceptically: "As for the poor cameleer's Mnizurin and the one referred to in the letter, I can't see any connection. Nor in the looting attacks against the caravans; they're common in the caliphate. It's like associating random but similar incidents that took place in areas far apart and believing that the culprit is the same."

Processing Leon's words was like a cool breeze that relieved the heat and swept away the stale dust. Nevertheless, the two men didn't completely accept his simplistic justification. As far as Theodorus was concerned, the incidents occurring were far too many to be coincidental. Besides, the Mnizurin was real, locked in the laboratory, and was a danger to everyone. As for Bashar, he couldn't hide the horror he had experienced behind weak assumptions, just as he couldn't deny having seen the yellow, bloodthirsty eyes of the darkling creature sitting on his back. There could be a logical explanation to what had happened to him, but right now it was impossible to link them due to the heat, the fatigue and, of course . . . the fleas.

"By the way, don't presume that your grandfather was as much of a rationalist as you imagine," Bashar said and opened the book that Leon had handed to him. It was *On Nutrition of the Healthy,* by Acron of Acragas, a physician senior to Hippocrates. "If he had got this in his hands, he could have jumped for joy and performed experiments for the rest of his life, preparing divine foods."

"Why? Does Acron write about divine foods?" scoffed Leon.

"He's got a chapter on herbs," said Bashar, opening the book wider and pointing a finger at that specific passage, "where he lists the effect their composition has on certain illnesses with amazing therapeutic results. Because of their properties, he considers these herbs to be divine foods and reflects on the issue whether it is right to offer them to the ill or not, because curing the dying means that the world balance is disturbed. He also mentions that Asclepius re-animated that dying man by administering him one of those herbs, provoking Zeus' wrath."

Leon knew the myth of the healer Asclepius whom Zeus killed for reanimating the dead, and even though he didn't believe that there was any grain of truth to that story, he snatched the book from Bashar's hands and started scanning the text. He was curious to know more about the medicines that the ancient doctor was suggesting than about the herbs with the allegedly divine properties.

"Leon, Acron's chapter is packed with myths, so don't waste your time," Bashar said and looked at Theodorus, who had fallen silent. "Old Peleuses had turned everything upside down for this book. He couldn't accept that a medical book had been lost; a book that, apart from its various healing prescriptions, could also contain the secret to immortality—"

"My grandfather wasn't looking for the secret to immortality, but the herbs for longevity," Leon explained, without taking his eyes from the book. "He was convinced that with the proper combination of certain herbs, we can prepare foods that will extend our life. He had mentioned dozens of examples of nations and people well-known for their longevity."

"All the nations are mentioned in them, boy; the Indians, the Ethiopians, the Jews, the Persians, all of them, but this doesn't make it true," Bashar pointed out, making himself more comfortable on the sofa. "He didn't think that a medicine could make people immortal. He found such stories wishful thinking and nothing more than appealing fairy tales—"

"Nicephorus wasn't looking for the secret to immortality or longevity," Theodorus interrupted the dialogue between the two doctors. "He was seeking the way to bring back the dead."

Leon lifted his eyes from the book and stared right at Theodorus. What his friend was claiming about his grandfather did not sit well with him and seemed irrational. He had of course heard his grandfather mentioning the issue of the reanimation of the dead, in a reflecting mood, but he had never realised that he actually had any practice in it.

"Yes, he had confided it to me and on numerous occasions he had asked for my help on various experiments that he undertook." The look on Theodorus' face left no room for doubt, and the two doctors listened to him in silence.

"As he once told me, he was convinced that the reanimation of the dead wasn't associated only with God's intervention; there were several accounts in books revealing that it can also be achieved by humans, using specific methods. In Manethon's *Aegyptiaca*, in Berossus' *Babyloniaca*, and in Onesicritus' *Indica* and in many other texts, the testimonials on how to achieve the reanimation of the dead had convinced him that it was not an imaginary expectation, but a fact. Only all this had nothing to do with medicine—at least not in the way you two know it."

"What do you mean?" both doctors asked.

"The practice of reanimating the dead has to do with forces and energies that aren't visible—"

"Easy there, Theodorus. Next you're likely to tell us that my grandfather was a sorcerer who dealt with necromancy," scoffed Leon.

"If you wish to call your grandfather's research sorcery, go ahead; I'm not in the least bit interested in how you describe it. What is certain is that Nicephorus had reached various theoretical conclusions, but all his practical experiments failed due to the lack of data."

"Didn't he have this book?" Bashar pointed at the book Leon was holding.

"Not this. It was another one, the *Chaldean Oracles,* the book of the theurgy rituals."

"Nonsense!" Leon raised his voice and gave the book to Bashar, who held it in his lap while glancing at Theodorus.

"That's exactly how I reacted the first time he mentioned it. It was hard for me to believe not only that there were people who could raise the dead, but that they also managed to do it by the power of words and sounds. That is, there are certain words that, when uttered, can even change the nature of things."

Leon stooped over the low table and, pouring lemonade in his mug, mockingly said: "That's what happens when you read the Platonists! You envision the journey of the souls in the moonlight as they come from space in order to inhabit the bodies of the living, as Plato declared. Or, in this case, like Orpheus, whose music—his sounds—worked miracles."

Theodorus, offended by the nerve of his young friend, who mocked the philosophers' theories, looked straight at him. In many of their discussions, it was like hearing Nicephorus, but he knew that the grandfather was different from the grandson in that the former always left some room for doubt in his beliefs, whereas the latter was firm and absolute.

"I can refer to two incidents." Theodorus straightened his cassock and got comfortable back on the sofa, resting his elbows on his knees. "In the biography of Apollonius of Tyana, there is mention of the incident when he reanimated that dead girl. It is written that when Apollonius was in Rome, he happened upon the funeral procession of a girl. He felt deeply sorry seeing the grieving crowd, so he stopped the mourners, approached the coffin, leaned over the dead girl, and whispered something in her ear. The very next moment, she came back to life."

Leon was about to say something, but Theodorus silenced him by raising his hand. He knew that his friend was going to question that event and he didn't want to hear any comments before he was finished.

"And because you'll probably make fun of this and say that it's all pagan nonsense, I'll tell you what the bishop of Rome, Sylvester, did. Do you know anything about his life?"

Leon shook his head in response. He might have been a Christian, but he was not a zealot as to know the *Legends* or the *Gospels* by heart. Across from him, Bashar was silent and curious about what he was hearing.

"The church made him a saint because a group of Jews came to the emperor once, claiming that if they said the name of their god close to the ear of an ox, it would die. Indeed, the moment they whispered the name the animal dropped dead, and the emperor, amazed at that incident, prepared to embrace their faith, but Bishop Sylvester dissuaded him, saying that if he said the name of the real god, it would come alive. And it did. When saint Sylvester exclaimed 'Jesus Christ,' the animal came back to life."

Theodorus scrutinised the look of doubt on his young friend. During the last few years, their discussions about various philosophical matters were almost a daily occurrence, so he knew that Leon was sceptical about anything that was deemed supernatural and miraculous.

"Now don't stick to the analysis of the facts or the name they uttered, but to the evidence that three different religions claim that by saying specific words or names, it is possible for a man to kill or reanimate another. Don't forget that Jesus resurrected Lazarus by calling him."

Leon didn't have the chance to comment, because one of the house servants entered the hall and after curtseying, he announced to Bashar that madam Jasmine al-Beidha had called him up to her room.

The two Greeks, forgetting everything they had been discussing a minute before, looked at Bashar in surprise because, at that invitation, he jumped to his feet and rushed to meet Jasmine at the second floor room.

"I'll explain later," Bashar said before leaving the hall and gave them an impish grin.

"I don't think he told us everything that happened to him at dawn," Leon teased and wickedly added: "He could at least have told us that the demon which attacked him was female . . ."

For the umpteenth time since that morning, the cart transferring the dead to the cemetery parked outside the clinic. Two dusty, thin, and wiry slaves, with filthy hands, jumped out of the back of the vehicle, went through the clinic corridor, and reached the yard, where Bashar's servants had set the corpse of the Damascene cadi.

Theodorus, silent and pensive, stood aside, beneath the shadow cast by the shelter of the corridor connecting the clinic to the mansion. Next to him, just as pensive but in a different mood, was Leon, who leaned with his right shoulder against one of the pillars.

The servants had shrouded the unfortunate cadi's corpse in a white silk sheet and brought him down to the yard, placing it on a wooden surgical table. Anyone who saw this could understand that the dead man was a reputable person, and they would most likely assume it was a deceased lord.

Bashar hadn't announced the cadi's death either to the citizens or the ulama and the emir, because he had realised that the fear of the supernatural was growing instead of receding. But he couldn't hide the body any longer, so he decided to bury it.

"We're nothing but a bag of bones and flesh that's going to rot." Theodorus recalled Nicephorus Peleuses' cynical comment the day he had hit him, when he went to meet him after the burning of his wife's body. "Just a speck of dust vanishing in the infinity of time and space."

The next image he saw in his mind's eye was the first dead person he had ever seen—his grandmother. Theodorus was five years old at the time. Just an ordinary child, happy and curious about all the wondrous secrets of life that surrounded him, and he couldn't wait to discover them all. He knew nothing about death, the immortality of the soul, or the resurrection of the dead in the Second Coming, so none of this troubled his childish, lively mind. But when he saw his grandmother's still, pallid face, adorned with undying flowers inside the coffin, her crossed hands resting upon her rigid chest, he felt her loss in his hot tears and came to realise that there were more secrets beyond life.

As he grew older, he became better acquainted with death. As a teenager, he didn't pay so much attention to it, but he knew it was close to him, always around. Relatives, friends, and loved ones were all victims to the insatiable appetite of this most unrelenting beast. He wept many times, pained by the losses and the trauma caused by life's one and only enemy. Mental and spiritual wounds, unhealed, gaping, and bleeding, upset his thinking and darkened his eyes. At times he thought he could hear death laughing maliciously, laughing arrogantly, knowing its omnipotence all too well, since even gods fell victim to it.

The worst moment for Theodorus wasn't when he grasped death's supremacy over the world, but when he realised his own shortcomings as well as the weakness of all the living things against it. There was nothing he could do to stop it.

The cadi's corpse in Leon's line of vision was only an insignificant brushstroke on the painting of life—a drop in the vast expanse of the ocean. The young lover was not affected by death's macabre presence, nor did he let it trouble his thinking. His mind was dominated by Rebecca's form, and he was feverish with the desire to taste her kiss, breathe in the aroma of her hair, and feel her body against his. There was no place for death in his thoughts, only for life and love.

For an enamoured man, there is no death, only the flutter of life, full of beauty. His eyes are filled with colours, his ears are stroked by songs, and his heart turns lighter by the bright smile of his beloved. The only dark spot in his thoughts is that his love would be rejected, nothing more.

Theodorus watched the two slaves grab the table with shrouded remains by the edges and lift it in their hands. He looked in their eyes and failed to notice a sentiment in them; they were almost empty, filled with nothing but the task at hand. They didn't care about the lifeless body they were carrying, about matters of life and death. They were simply doing their job, mechanically and without complaint.

"We don't need to be interested in death; it is interested in us," he muttered, with his eyes still on the undertaker's slaves.

"What did you say?" asked Leon, crossing his arms over his chest, puzzled. He'd never heard that expression before. He didn't feel like going back to the clinic and deal with the casualties: that's why he was keeping his friend company as if he were some idle lord.

Theodorus repeated the phrase and added: "Thus said Hegesias Peisithanatos."

"Who was he?" Leon asked, wondering about that strange, grim name.

"He was a philosopher who lived in Alexandria. His name was Hegesias, but he was called Peisithanatos, the Death-Persuader, because through his philosophy, he persuaded people to kill themselves or, better said, seek redemption through dying." Theodorus guessed what his friend was about to ask him, so he explained: "The great philosophical question of his time, for himself and every philosopher, was how and in what way a man could achieve bliss. Every school of thought stood for a different view. Hegesias, as opposed to the rest, claimed that man can neither achieve nor know perfect bliss while living, because of the known and unsuspected factors that comprise it.

"According to his theory, perfect bliss is possible only after death. That is, when nothing can disturb the peace of the soul, because that is only when it doesn't sense any pain, desire, or need. Therefore, in order for humans to attain bliss, they first have to die—"

Leon urged him to go on. He wanted to hear the story of that odd philosopher, even if he wasn't actually very interested.

"As you can see, his theory caused a stir, and many were those who took it literally and committed suicide. As a matter of fact, it is said that the suicides were so frequent that King Ptolemy had to order the arrest of Hegesias.

"His texts were banned, and his students were pursued. We don't know if he was killed or if he also committed suicide. Some people believe that he banished himself to the desert of Arabia, where he set up a commune. No one knows for sure. His works have been lost or are likely to be heavily guarded inside secret libraries, forbidden to the eyes of the ignorant."

"Well, they'd better be! He was insane!" Leon exclaimed furiously.

"Insane? Why?"

"He instructed people to kill themselves."

"Teaching a philosophical view that only by being dead can we be blissful is one thing. But turning people to suicide is another. Hegesias was a philosopher who developed his theory to refute the rest. The deaths that occurred were caused by ignorant people who had twisted Hegesias' views. You see, it's unsafe to refer to philosophical issues openly before simple people, who lack a proper education and knowledge.

"However, since once again you've thoughtlessly labelled someone without testing or judging properly, tell me this: how are the deeds of the people who distorted Hegesias' theory different from those of the Christians who sought redemption through death? Remember all those Christian martyrs, whom you've heard so much about. In what way are they different?"

"They didn't commit suicide."

"Not fighting to survive or letting go without a fight are types of suicide," stressed Theodorus.

"Yes, but they suffered in order to save their souls—to earn a place in the Lord's heaven!" Leon passionately said, fed up by the violation of his Christian upbringing.

"So what you're actually saying is that all the Christian martyrs were killed willingly in order to achieve bliss posthumously," inferred Theodorus and headed toward the laboratory.

"Eh?"

Lying on a comfortable bed, Husni welcomed the care of the clinic students, who visited him every four hours. Sometimes he knew they were there and at other times he was lost in a maelstrom of darkness and didn't even register the coolness of the damp compresses they applied on his burning forehead. He was in and out of consciousness; he was so disoriented that sometimes he wasn't sure if he was dreaming or awake. Images flashed before him at great speed, shocking his brain. Colours alternated with darkness. Harsh and sudden movements shook his body, and he didn't understand whether he was making or receiving them. It was all jumbled, senses and sentiments, dream and reality. The only instinct still alert, never budging, was the one shouting at him that he was in danger.

Then at some point he started hearing a sound, strange and piercing, sharp and sudden, and every time it was repeated he shivered, whether he was awake or sleeping. Whenever he heard it he was startled, and a red flash covered his line of vision.

As time passed the sound changed tone; it turned deeper, igniting the sense of threat—a threat that encircled the room and reached his ears from afar, from an obscure place inside him.

He tried to determine if it was coming from an instrument, if it was natural or artificial, but he failed. It didn't sound natural, like the rustling of leaves or the splashing of waves, but neither was it artificial, for none of the musical instruments he knew of could produce that continuous, creepy sharpness.

A thought formed inside his head, something of an old saying, an indication and explanation of the sound in his ears: "The howling." His line of vision suddenly filled with grotesque images, of frightful colours and odd shapes.

He felt as if he were leaping forward, to the beyond. Floating over the world, over his body. He could see himself before him, as he was lying in bed, and his image got smaller and smaller, finally becoming a speck of dust, an imperceptible molecule within the vast, black universe.

He could also hear other sounds now, different but just as strange and threatening. New shapes and images came to his mind, different sentiments and colours enfolded him. He thought he could discern the murmuring of the darkness, the whispering of the space, and that he could explain their messages . . .

He re-entered his body faster than lightning, he sat up on the bed in alarm, and breathed in short gasps of air. Through the closed shutters the sunlight cast whitish yellow stripes, in which specks of dust were floating incessantly, a picture that reminded him of the dream he was having.

With the back of his left hand he wiped away the sweat that rolled down his face and wondered how long his "illness" would last. He was surprised at himself for having nightmares as if he were still a child.

That shrieking sound, the one he thought he had dreamt of, reached his ears clear as a bell, making him shudder. He was petrified and held his breath, completely still. He caught a glimpse of a shapeless black form moving fast toward him. He wanted to get up and run, but he couldn't. He wanted to shout for help with all his might, but the dread was such that it had literally paralysed him.

The only thing he felt that was still working on him was his brain, which kept saying pleadingly: "It's only a dream. It's only a dream." Wishful thinking, futile in this case.

The dark creature climbed on his back, landed on his right shoulder, and wrapped him up in its tentacle-like limbs, stifling him. It squeezed him hard, breaking his bones, and simultaneously choked him, acting like a snake.

The suffocation caused Husni's eyes to roll, and all that could be seen through his batting eyelids were the whites of his eyes. He was choking and could not scream. Only then did he realise that he was going to die, and that this was his last breathing moment.

4. The Manuscript of the Dead

The sun began its slow descent on the horizon. The well-known mystical veil adorned the sky over Damascus in shades of yellow, blue, and red. It is a sight that captures the spirit and nourishes the mind with images of a world beyond the limits of human vision. It is an everyday sight that goes unnoticed to locals but is majestic to foreigners and visitors. This natural condition affects the mentality of the residents without their realising it.

Theodorus took a deep breath and stretched his neck, listening to the crack of each vertebra. The day's stench had notably subsided and the scent of incense that burned in the copper pot on the bedside table filled the room. As it was more intense now, it pleased his sense of smell and lifted his spirits.

Drowsy from both the heat and his incessant musings, he was feeling rather tired while he considered the situation at hand. Earlier that afternoon, he had visited the bishop of Damascus and asked for the hymnbook of exorcisms by Saint Cyprianus. He was concerned about that strange being which had attacked Bashar, so he wanted to be prepared in case of its reappearance. He doubted the effectiveness of such a defence against it, but had no other choice. The power of the words used by the saint while composing his incantations had for centuries brought about positive results in similar cases, at least for the Christian world.

He didn't believe in magic, nor could he offer an answer to the mystery of the force that a spell can send forth, but he was aware of the result, and that was what mattered in this case. His colleague Andronicus Graeuses, who had experimented with the sounds of words and their effects on animals and humans, believed that the force lay in the way words are uttered and not in the words themselves. He might have been right, but Theodorus did not know how the phenomenon worked and, therefore, could not oppose or reject any view.

Before him, on the inclined surface of his lectern, was Plutarch's *On the Delays of Divine Vengeance*, which he had borrowed from the university two days before in order to study it, since the Arabic copy contained additional paragraphs as compared to the Christian equivalent. However, recent events played on his mind and he could not concentrate on examining the text.

He paused his reading when he noticed a comment on the margin of the papyrus. Actually, it was not a comment like the ones usually written by transcribers or scholars, but an addition irrelevant to the subject matter; a poem. He looked again to make sure he was not mistaken.

"I have seen the wealth of humans burn!
My dearest Allah, why?
Why do you banish your sons into darkness?
What fiendish demon was it
That the wise sons of desert led
To light torches, throw oil in the fire
And ruthlessly erase all memories of yore?
Eternal shame on the ignorant caliph!
Shame on the General of this holy war!
The glorious Prophet's devotees
Will forever bear this mark;

Of bright Alexandria brightly burning,
The cinders of Greeks!"

Beneath the last verse was the poet's name, which he encountered for a second time in a short while: Abdul Alhazred. This occurrence did not surprise him. It is not unusual in life to cross paths with people, names, or works. But remembering Alhazred's other poem, he was intrigued by the character of that man, who seemed to possess much knowledge and, at that time, a rare sensitivity toward education. He was not indifferent to these two conclusions. On the contrary, he thought of searching the university library for more of his compositions.

He tried to concentrate on the book again. He had borrowed it because he wished to discover whether the additional paragraphs really belonged to Plutarch or had been inserted by an unnamed scholar. Nevertheless, he lost his initial interest, despite the fact that this specific philosophical work had, in his opinion, tremendously affected the perception of Christians throughout the world, since what both laymen and clergymen called "divine retribution" was deeply rooted in the ideology of the pagan Greeks.

He smiled at the dogmatic fallacy that had been perpetuated for centuries inside and outside the walls of the church. Many times throughout his research, he had discovered similar ancient philosophical views, which later came to be called Christian. One time, during one of his lectures, he had even suggested to the audience that Plutarch be named "Father of the Church," because most doctrines, canons, and principles that the "saints" promised had been taken from his works.

The zealots of faith, for the most part crude and illiterate, were infuriated when they heard him. If it had been up to them, they would have dragged him out of the room, flogged him, and thrown him into a sunless dungeon until he repented. What rescued him from their predatory hands and sharp claws was the fact that he had a title, a position as well as friends in high places. Otherwise, he would still be dwelling in damp dark places, similar to the pitch darkness crowning his adversaries' heads.

Thinking has an odd habit, invisibly connected to a man's desire and temper, of being directed toward pieces of knowledge or memories that are seemingly unrelated to the previous ones, but they actually have discernible contact points, appearing like interconnected circles. Consequently, upon recalling that eventful day, one of the many he had had during his teaching career, his mind recreated the events in Adrianople.

It was a few days after the lecture when he and Bashar travelled to Thrace in order to visit the Duke Voreates. His dignitary friend had organised a three-day celebration in his hometown, in honour of his marriage to the emperor's cousin.

Adrianople was adorned in decorations, and celebratory lights shone everywhere. There were street parties in every neighbourhood. People shared food and wine and were all filled with joy for the future of their country's honourable child. Nothing could predict the tragedy that followed.

They stayed at a colleague's home, and on the first day they enjoyed themselves till late at night at the agora, where the tables had been set for the feast. The next morning they did not attend the equestrian races that were being held in favour of the Duke, but at noon they watched the poetry and singing contests.

The people were celebrating, Voreates and his wife eagerly took part in the dances, and the mirth and pleasure peaked in the afternoon, when a beauty pageant took place, where thirty shapely young maidens competed for the title of the city's most beautiful woman. Bashar felt as if he were in heaven and fervently chimed in with the wild displays of excitement by everyone present, who supported the local girls with hearty cheers and applause.

After the coronation of the most beautiful girl in Adrianople, the celebrations went on with singing and dancing, but after dinner Theodorus and Bashar opted for a tour of the city. Accompanied by his colleague, they strolled through the districts, marvelling at monuments and churches, while listening to the various stories behind each sight.

The sun had almost hidden behind the clouds, casting longer shadows that warmly embraced the world. There were few people still walking along the streets and roads, but most were exhausted from dancing and felt light-headed from all the wine that had been generously served at pavilions in the squares. The sound of instruments and off-key singing from the revellers at the central market indicated that the festivities were far from being over.

They had reached the city cemetery, when a loud cry of fear was heard on their left. They turned to the source of the sound and saw a man running toward them, frantically waving his hands and hollering in confusion. Theodorus couldn't make out his words and, puzzled, looked at his colleague, who also couldn't see why the man was running and yelling.

"Ghost! Evil has come out of the grave!" he was clearly saying now that he was much closer to them. They were about to ask him, but the stranger did not stop to offer any explanation. He simply went on his frenzied way, still shrieking piercingly and frightening his fellow townsmen.

Mothers, alarmed both by the terror their horrified neighbour was spreading as well as by the rest of the cries sounding from further afield, ordered their children to stop their games and return home. Scared old women shut their doors and windows. Only moments later, nothing in this part of town suggested that people had been celebrating. It now looked completely deserted.

Bashar was scared to death. A stranger in an unknown place, the menace scaring the locals threatened him twice as much, and he took a few steps back. His lead was followed by Theodorus' colleague, who had offered them a place to stay.

Two men and three women sprinted past them. Their faces were clearly marked with terror, and amid their inarticulate cries all that could be heard were words that crushed the sense of reason and stirred dark and ancient fears.

"Devil-stricken!"

"Ghost!"

"Demon!"

Theodorus smiled imperceptibly and almost made fun of them, but when he turned to Bashar and his colleague, he saw that they had hidden in a house yard behind him. However, he did not have the chance to insult them or even comment on their irrational fear.

An old man appeared on the street near the pine grove, gasping for breath. This is where the first frightened man had come running from, and the others had followed. Leaning on his cane, he walked hurriedly with all the physical and mental strength he could muster, muttering spells intertwined with swearing and cursing.

He fell on his knees a couple of feet away. His hands were trembling, and spittle was drooling down his bushy white beard.

"Help me, son . . . help me," he pleaded.

"What happened, old man?"

The elderly man collapsed on the ground without answering. His face was blue with the effort and his eyes bulged from their sockets as if he were choking.

Theodorus tried to see where in the dark Bashar had hidden. He called out to him in a strong, urgent voice, cursing him in Arabic, but his friend would not show his face. He had panicked and was not going to come out of his hiding place before the danger had passed.

"She came out of her grave," panted the old man and grabbed him by his tunic with his left hand. He crawled on the ground, pulling hard on the cloth, and tried to lean on his cane, but couldn't make it. "Yesterday we buried her. . . . Tonight she came back from the dead—" he said, leaving his sentence unfinished, and with a death rattle he took his last breath, right there in the middle of the dirt road, still holding tightly onto Theodorus' tunic.

A panicked screech from a woman who was watching the comings and goings through her window shutters made him turn his attention to the side of the road. The shadows were growing longer, the pines in the grove made everything within his vision darker, the little light cast by the outside lamps flickered and became stronger or weaker depending on the whiffs of the quiet spring night air, but what made him shiver was the sudden silence spreading around him. In the locked-down neighbourhood, not a single human sound could be heard, only the sizzling of the wicks inside the oil lamps.

From around the corner a female silhouette appeared, moving in a drunken step. Upon her head was the wreath her friends had made for her; a few of the flowers had fallen off while the rest hung loosely from the threads. The white veil that covered her long, dishevelled hair blew in the spring air in time to her wavering steps and was torn and filthy, most likely due to a fall she had taken. The girl's arms and knees were dirty as was her white wedding dress, which indicated that the girl had died unmarried and, according to the local customs, should be buried dressed as a bride.

The sight of her surely startled him and, even though he was familiar with cases of catalepsy, he was overwhelmed by phobic notions and tales emerging through centuries of superstition and ignorance. His heart ached, not only because of his sorrow for the poor girl, but also due to the dismay that was now making up for lost ground in his mind and called for immediate retreat before this unsuspected but likely terror.

His temples were throbbing, and his thoughts were fighting a losing battle with his instincts. As he tried to move, he was stopped by the old man's grip. Startled, he let out a breathless cry, wrenched himself free, and released his tunic from the dead man's fingers. The moment he heard the cloth tear, he felt his reason betray him. At once he took a step back, his gaze fixed on the girl who was approaching him in faltering steps.

"Help me," spluttered the girl and reached out to him.

His eyes burning with tension, he took a deep breath and willed any ugly and frightening thoughts to hide behind the reality of the situation. That poor thing had come back to life; she was no demon, nor ghost, as the thick-headed peasants had thought. He had to help her. He had heard of catalepsy before, so it was foolish to feel afraid.

"Bashar, come out of your hiding-hole, you useless blighter!" he called to his friend angrily. "The girl isn't dead, she's suffered catalepsy!"

The Arab cautiously peered his head from behind the wooden fence and looked at the reanimated girl first and then at Theodorus. He still shuddered at the thought of the supernatural, but seeing his fearless friend, he regained some of his courage.

"Are you certain?" he asked. The answer to his question was a curse word that made him stand up and approach the house gate.

Theodorus beckoned him to come near. He was angry at himself because he had almost drowned in despair like a superstitious person, and that was why he was so impatient toward the Arab, who was still doubtful. He took a step closer, but stopped. From behind him came an incomprehensible murmur.

In her effort to reach him, the girl tripped over a rock and fell on her knees, crying with pain. But as she went on cursing her misfortune, the words she was uttering altered. She was no longer speaking in Greek but in another language, unintelligible and coarse.

Theodorus was watching her curiously. He asked her if she was all right, but received no clear answer.

The young woman was down on her knees, hair covering her

face, the ruined wreath and the crumbled veil falling upon her shoulders. She was talking to herself in an unknown language, saying words that sounded like verses of an ill-sounding poem. Yet this was not what caused him awe. The incomprehensible whispers echoing around him spawned in his mind images of dark and vast stretches of land that were cracked by blazes of light. In their morbid luminosity, they revealed monstrous forms and hideous silhouettes, sharp fangs, scaly bodies, hungry yellow eyes, and membranous fins.

Bashar and Theodorus saw those unprecedented images very clearly. The same happened to all those who were hiding inside their homes, peering at the road through door cracks and skylights.

The hallucinating murmur upset them at once and was soon overshadowed by the residents' voices from within the houses. They were all shouting in fear, as if they were facing hell and all its demons.

When the maiden heard the frantic screaming she seemed to recover from her delirious state, looked around her in confusion, and stood up crying. Her reactions showed that she had no idea what was happening. Dizzy and agitated, she extended her arms and walked to the two men, begging for help and sympathy.

At her gesture the people's shouts multiplied, and Theodorus did not hear the other sound coming from behind him. He tried to yell and turned to his left to call for Bashar again; only then did he catch a glimpse of the two horsemen who galloped toward him.

"Stop!" he cried, trying to impede them by wildly flailing his arms, but they went ahead, forcing him to swerve to the side of the road so they wouldn't trample him.

The horsemen wielded their swords, their gaze fixed on the girl who was staggering before them. Their speed left Theodorus no choice, his screaming yielded no result, and the imminent disaster was unstoppable. It was already too late.

The first horseman thrust his sword into the girl's throat. Her blood gushed out and drenched her wedding gown; her body leaned right, her knees buckled, but she didn't fall. The second man's stroke hurled her head a few feet away from her body. Her veil and wreath, all bloody, fell somewhere in between, while her headless, lifeless body collapsed on the earth forming a dark pool of blood.

The wild cries of the two men drowned Theodorus' shouts, and what followed after the killing wiped away any wish he had to explain the error that had been committed. The townspeople came out of their houses, praising the horsemen with blessings and prayers chanted by all—men, women and children. Seeing all this, devastated by the unexpected outcome, Theodorus could not even swear at them although he was bursting with words of malediction.

He stood by, simply watching their reactions, disheartened and desperate. Besides, he could not prevent the raging crowd from dispelling their fears.

The townsfolk, armed with farm tools, pitchforks, spades, and pikes, pushed the dismembered body aside and covered it with wood and dry twigs. They doused it in oil and threw a burning torch on top of the heap.

The greedy flames, in accordance with the people's incessant hunger to avert this horror, ate up the unfortunate girl right there, in the middle of the street. It was an unholy pyre, which on the next day was purified through holy water and prayers chanted by the priests and monks who had been called to forever banish the soul of the "damned" woman.

He couldn't sleep that night. Sorrow kept him up. He and Bashar were longing for daybreak so they could go back to Constantinople. They did not want to spend another day in this place.

After hearing what had happened, Voreates paid him a visit and tried to change his mind, but Theodorus was firm in his decision. His joy over his friend's wedding had evaporated in the reek of the maiden's incinerated body. The image of her decapitation did not let him rest, and he couldn't pretend that nothing had happened.

Two knocks on his bedroom door brought him back to the present, in Damascus, on the day after the earthquake. One of the servants informed him that dinner had been served, but Theodorus was not hungry. The disturbing memories along with the premonition hovering over his head, the vague feeling of threat, suppressed every one of his physical needs. However, he got up and went to the dining room because at that moment he needed to be amidst people and not feel alone.

Even though his duty was to remain at the clinic, which never seemed to empty from the injured, when Leon heard the evening prayer he left for Joel's home in a hurry. The nature of love is such that it sweeps away every thought or need from a lover's mind. All he really cared about was seeing Rebecca. Death, pain, and weeping didn't belong to his world. All this was around him, but not inside him. He savoured and experienced the world shaped by his heart.

He walked briskly to Joel's rickety front door. He thought of fixing it, but kept on moving until he stood at the threshold. Just for a moment he was overcome with doubt that Rebecca might not return his love. But he immediately shook the thought away; he wasn't inexperienced in love, even though he knew that when someone falls in love, it always feels like the first time. . . .

He was greeted by a beautiful, refreshing smile and a pair of bright eyes, timidly wanton, which held him captive behind long, curled eyelashes. Seduction has its own ways, fixed, everlasting and sacred.

The momentary awkwardness between them, the flushing of the cheeks and the lump in the throat were soon overcome, wordlessly admitting to his own pulsating heart that the feelings are mutual. There are some tiny, subconscious messages that lovers get, simple indications of attraction and charm, which stick tightly to the rock of love like limpets.

Rebecca led him to the first floor bedroom, where they had moved Joel in the morning, before Leon returned to the clinic. She had followed all his instructions for her father's treatment to the letter and only left his side to prepare the balms and make dinner.

All those hours since Leon had left, his image was constantly on her mind. Her cheeks felt hot and her slender hands kept sweating whenever she caught herself daydreaming of his company.

In fact, her feelings were so strong that she looked at her father guiltily every time he awoke from his sleep. She dreaded that her ardour would show. She'd never thought that she would someday fall in love with a *goy*, a foreigner, someone different from her. She wondered what Joel's reaction would be if he found out or sensed it, so she feared the worst. That's why she felt guilty, because her heart longed for a man whom she wasn't allowed to love; the dream of sharing a life with him was forbidden and frowned upon.

Joel greeted him with a crooked smile and words of gratitude. He couldn't move and when he spoke his jaw hurt, but in a few hearty words he managed to show how thankful he was.

Leon firmly shook the old Jew's hand and sat beside him on the bed. He asked him about any discomfort he was experiencing, took a look at the swelling on his face and then, very gingerly, examined his broken ribs.

"Just be patient, Joel, and everything will be fine," Leon said with certainty after examining him and gave a hopeful smile to Rebecca, who was standing on the other side of the bed, very worried.

"Thank you, Leon. You're my saviour. I'm so grateful, and I don't know how I can ever repay your kindness."

"Well, God . . ." He didn't know how to respond and stared at Rebecca so intensely that her cheeks flushed. Then, realising that he might have disclosed his secret desire, he suddenly turned to Joel and lowered his eyes in embarrassment.

In spite of his bad state, after seeing Leon's behaviour Joel understood everything. He knew people well; being so agile, he understood their nature and passions early on. He grew up in a world that had shaped him through the knowledge of his people, the experience of the expulsions, immigration, and the fear that they might be repeated; that is, all the things that make you appreciate what's right and proper every time you witness what's unjust and wrong.

Therefore, he easily caught on to the feelings that infused Leon and smiled at the whims of fate; the man who had saved him was in love with his daughter. But then, as his reason overshadowed his heart's spontaneity and he remembered his "saviour's" origins and faith, he frowned and fell silent, conflicting thoughts filling his mind.

Once, when he was a teenager, he had fallen in love with Fatimah, his neighbour, but his father tried to prevent him from loving an infidel and sent him off to be a helper to his uncle, who wandered the fairs of the different cities in the caliphate, from Antioch to Libya's Tripoli.

He was away from Damascus for many years, working hard, learning about the world, but he could not forget. When he heard that Fatimah had married a scribbler from Jerusalem, he was devastated and cried pure tears of unfulfilled love. He might have been angry at God, who made up the world with both Jews and *goyim*. But he could no longer remember because it had been a long time ago. The only thing he couldn't forget, though, were her beautiful eyes, the first set of eyes he ever loved.

All too knowing, he stared at the Greek, as if trying to read his mind. His face, apart from being handsome, revealed power and gentility. It gave off a sense of trust and magnanimity. He would make an excellent son-in-law . . . if he were Jewish.

Mulling over his last thought, he decided to lessen his suspiciousness. He wasn't so young and inexperienced as to be led astray by stereotypical notions that tend to lead to dead-ends and traumatic situations. He therefore let himself ponder on the ways of life, shrugging away the instinctive feeling that Leon had fallen for Rebecca. However, no matter how far he banished it, the thought stayed with him.

A heavy silence filled the room. Everyone's gaze was lowered, their breathing was burdened with thoughts, and their movements were awkward. It was as if time stood still and the room was getting smaller and smaller.

"Would you like some tea?" Rebecca asked, breaking the silence.

Leon didn't reply; he only looked at her and got ready to leave. He knew he had revealed his feelings and felt uncomfortable, like a mischievous child who has been caught.

"Yes, child!" Joel agreed heartily. "Offer Leon something. Worrying too much about my health has made us forget our manners." Leon was about to decline and leave, but Joel insisted: "Treat him something, Rebecca, so he can see that ben Jova's offspring haven't forgotten their Greek upbringing. And show him our great collection of books. I've heard that you're interested in the books we own."

"Rebecca told me you have a lot of rare books," Leon said, encouraged by Joel's cheerful manner. "This morning she gave me a medical book. I'll give it back once I've copied it."

The pain on Joel's jaw kept him from smiling with pride. But his joy for the legacy his Alexandrian ancestors had left him was evident in the sparkle of his eyes.

"My last ancestor who lived in Alexandria," he began, holding Leon's hand in a friendly and somewhat fatherly way, "lived across from the library. Before that, during the Greek reign, some relatives of ours had worked there as librarians, before the Christians burnt it down. Knowledge was open to everyone then, yet there were still problems. But that's a different story," he said to himself and went on with his narration right away.

"After burning down the library, the Christians started collecting books again and founded a new library, which no Jewish employee was allowed to work in because of the clash of faith. Either way, they enriched the new library of Alexandria with thousands of books and it almost reached its original size. That was when the Arabs came, millions of illiterate goat-thieves, infesting our beautiful city like locusts, destroying everything."

As Joel was speaking, there was a glint of nostalgia in his eyes, and his voice faltered, as if he had witnessed the destruction of his ancestors' city himself, despite the fact that what he was narrating had been passed on from generation to generation for approximately three centuries now.

In the Jew's words and the lines on his face, Leon sensed the grief of uprooting, the sadness of emigration, and the fear of expulsion, but most of all the pain of loss, everything he himself felt five years ago when he left Constantinople.

"Those thieving brutes! They left nothing standing! They didn't even know what a book is, yet they burned down the building. My ancestor, seeing the library in flames, rushed with his children and started rescuing everything he could. Anxious to save as many books as they could, they threw them out the windows.

"Some of the Arabs saw them and started thinking. They thought that if the Jews are risking their lives to save those things of the *Nasraya*, it must have meant they were valuable. Thus, with an inkling, they started gathering and hiding them, thinking they were precious items that would yield profit."

Joel smiled imperceptibly and waved his hand in a "human stories of madness" way. Leon laughed at both the story and the Jew's look.

"After some time they banished us from Alexandria, and my ancestors decided to settle in Damascus, where there still were a lot of *Yavana*. That's why we possess dozens of books, some of which we rescued from the fire and others we collected through time—"

"How many are there? Have you counted them?" Leon interrupted him.

"They must be close to three hundred—"

"Three hundred eleven," Rebecca pointed out confidently.

Leon raised his left eyebrow in amazement. His grandfather, who was studious and a bookworm, had merely two hundred.

"Show him, Rebecca, and then come and join me."

Rebecca stretched out her hand to Leon, and he gave her his own. They both felt the warmth of each other's palm. They didn't look at each other, but the sense of touch bade their blood to surge inside their bodies. . . .

The beautiful Khalisah Fayuh, sister of Abbas Fayuh, sat restless beside the window of their modest house and stared out at the street, her eyes brimming with anticipation. Every now and then, if she saw a man walking hurriedly, she worriedly fixed her gaze on him, wondering whether it was her brother or not. But no matter how long she waited or prayed in silence, Abbas wouldn't show up, and her fear was all the more increasing.

On the second night after the earthquake, the city was almost silent. Once in a while you could hear sudden wailings and lamentations, which would stop just as suddenly, leaving Damascus with its body full of wounds, to find some peace under the starlight and the half-moon, amidst the chirping of the tireless crickets and the squawking of the nocturnal birds that paid no heed to the tragedy and the troubles of the humans.

Khalisah was really worried, and as time went by her concern grew deeper and her mind was overwhelmed by ominous thoughts.

Up to the day of the earthquake, Abbas had never before been away for more than ten hours. No matter how much work he had to do, he always returned home to keep an eye on things and bring food or money. He was a good brother, regardless of the poverty that had recently forced him to seek business with rogues such as Tariq and other small-time crooks who operated in the shadows of the city.

An owl hooted outside the window, and Khalisah shuddered, clenching her fist on her chest, near her heart; that kind of hooting is considered bad luck. Her large, beautiful eyes filled with images of death.

She knew that Abbas hadn't been killed in the earthquake because at that time they were having breakfast together. The house shook to the ground, all the crockery fell off the table, and they both instinctively darted outside. They heard the sound of other houses tumbling, the wailings of the casualties and the screams of the living, who saw their relatives under the ruins, and they remained in the garden, petrified.

Afterwards, when the tremor stopped and the dust from the crushed houses began to settle, Abbas left, dismissing her pleas. He wanted to see what had happened in the city, so he took to the streets, leaving her alone. But at noon he came back along with Tariq, whose cunning eyes were like those of a rat, predatory and starving.

As she was making them some lunch, she heard them talking about the damage and the victims. They said horrid things about the vast destruction and the people who got killed. Their descriptions were terrifying and saddened her so deeply that she dropped to her knees and prayed for the sake of the souls of all the people who had perished so unfairly.

"Tonight's our chance," Tariq said after the meal, and Abbas agreed with him. "We're going to catch that damn Jew and rip him off."

Khalisah had heard them many times that past week talking about that Jewish merchant and knew that they were planning to rob him. So, when they left home after the evening prayer, she knew where they were going and what their intention was. She therefore waited quietly for them to return, until the hours passed and her eyes grew heavy with sleepiness.

She hadn't seen him since then and now she worried about his life. At the same time, she cursed Tariq and silently hated the indecent path Abbas had taken ever since their parents had died.

Fearing the worst, she began pacing nervously up and down the kitchen. She sensed that something bad had happened. Her instinct was screaming and her imagination ran wild with the possibility of his death. As she waited for him, her fears increased and so did her relentless questions: *"What should I do now? Who should I call? Who should I turn to?"*

In the end, she sat on a stool and crouched over her knees, tears rolling down her cheeks. She couldn't imagine her future without Abbas, or rather *as* she was imagining it, she literally lost all her hopes, she shook with fear and felt light-headed. She felt as if she were about to faint, but a voice inside her convinced her to be strong and confront the situation bravely.

"Allah is great," she whispered and returned to the window. She looked at the empty street again and, stronger now as a result of the unexpected surge of courage that overwhelmed her, decided that the next morning she would ask for help from Harun al-Ghouta, the city's muezzin. A man of God would never leave a girl like her unprotected; an orphaned, poor, and—of course—beautiful girl.

In the light of the lamps, Leon examined the bookcase that stood before him like a plaster wall inside the visitors' hall. It was a five-row wooden structure with diamond-shaped cabinets, covered with thin, transparent cloth curtains. In each cabinet, there were five to six books, carefully arranged, while on either side of the bookcase, upon plates screwed to the wood, were two sayings: Solon's "I grow old ever learning many things" and Socrates' "I know that I know nothing."

Holding a silver candlestick in his left hand, he examined the row of cabinets at eye level, scanning the book titles, which were written on leather plates hanging by a string from the edge of each one of the cylindrical volumes. He stood before some books of medical content, read the names of some unfamiliar authors, and set apart only two that sparked his interest.

Later, after glancing toward the corridor to check if Rebecca was coming, he examined the bottom-row cabinets. The books weren't sorted according to subject, but age. In the cabinets of the third row from the bottom he read book titles about astronomy, tragedy, history, and philosophy.

He smirked at the thought that if Theodorus was with him right now, his heart would race in anticipation of finding any of the Greeks' lost books. The last four years, Leon had seen him several times, more than twenty, rushing into the clinic, happy as a child, announcing that he had found yet another book that was considered to have been destroyed by the fanatics' rage, either Christians or Arabs. His eyes were alight with joy and the flash of happiness made even the permanent worry lines on his face disappear. It was at those moments that he looked as if he had been reborn, or at least rejuvenated, forgetting the sorrow of immigration.

Leon singled out nine books whose authors' names he had never heard before. Except for the famous ancient authors and the doctors who had recorded their knowledge, experiences and experiments, he didn't know the rest and thought that their works might be among the lost ones.

Of the other two rows, he picked out twenty volumes more or less. He was so consumed by the search that he forgot about Rebecca for a time. He only thought that with the discovery of these books he would make his friend happy, a friend whom he loved like a father.

He heard the footsteps of his beloved as she was walking down the corridor while he was examining the fifth row, which was above his head. At once he dropped his search and turned to her.

The image of her entered through his eyes and was imprinted on his heart. Right there, in the half-lit corridor, as she paced quickly, holding a tray with mugs and a teapot, the flickering candle flames were reflected in her big black eyes, and the swaying, fine shadows gently stroked her face. She was a darling thing, seductive but also mystical and distant, almost like a vision, attracting him and filling his soul with a flush of first desire.

> *And love shook my mind*
> *Like a wind that buffets the mountain oaks.*
> *You came, I am so glad you did, for I was yearning for you.*
> *You cooled my heart that was burning with desire.*

He recited Sappho's poem aloud, needing to express his feeling as descriptively as possible. He could no longer stand the tidal wave swelling inside of him, and the poem offered him an emotional release and spared his mind from shattering.

Hearing those verses, Rebecca shyly lowered her eyes, blushing from the warmth they had caused her, and set the tray upon a small round table. She picked up the teapot and with trembling hands poured tea in the clay mugs.

Her embarrassment made Leon's heart flutter happily. She had neither reproached him nor refused, which meant that the same sun was shining inside her chest, just as in his.

"Beware of Greeks bearing gifts," the Jewish girl solemnly uttered the verse from Virgil's *Aeneid,* as she offered him the mug, composing herself.

Leon, surprised, blinked in bafflement at her intelligent response to his wooing. He admired her for her wit and knowledge, but at the same time he wondered whether that line meant a rejection to his courting. He stood there watching her, clouded by doubt, astounded by the quality of her character, light-headed by the ambiguity of her reaction. Wasting no time, he ended the short dialogue and expressed his appreciation instead.

"It's amazing that you're familiar with work that relates to Homer!" he managed to say and took the mug, unable to utter another appropriate sentence. The fear of rejection crept inside him, stifling his courage and experience; it is a normal state felt by anyone wishing to fulfil their most intense desires.

"I told you yesterday that the rarest book we have is Homer's *Iliad*, with a handwritten inscription from Alexander the Great to Ptolemy. It's a book we've been reading since we were infants, my family, I mean."

"Yes, I remember, but it wasn't among the rest," he said, pointing to the books in disarray.

"We don't have it in the library. It's a sacred heirloom, so we keep it locked. My grandfather used to say that if every book was destroyed and only *Iliad* survived, there would still be light in the world."

Leon raised an eyebrow, fascinated and excited at the way those Greek-speaking Jewish people cherished Homer's work. He even thought that if only half of the Empire's citizens felt the same, everything would have been different at home.

Rebecca padded toward the bookcase and pulled a silver chain that hung from her neck, revealing a key at the end of it. She stooped down in front of the stone wall and pushed the nightstand aside. Behind the piece of furniture, there was a square, built-in hiding place. The small iron hatch, as it was whitewashed and covered by clay, resembled a regular building stone.

Leon approached and watched her in curiosity. Inside the hiding place's narrow space, which was coated with leather in order to protect its contents, there were two books. Rebecca pulled one and gave it to him, grinning.

"Look at the inscription!" she told him, her eyes alight with pride.

Leon untied the string that held the cylinder closed, and in a serious, utterly devout way he silently read the words written by Alexander to his general and bodyguard. His eyes were moist with emotion and when he spoke, and his voice was hoarse.

"I've always heard and read about Alexander, his achievements and adventures . . . All those things—extravagant, strange, and legendary—his life that was like a fairy tale, like a made-up story, and yet here I am, reading his own words: 'Alexander, son of Philip, King of Macedonia, Commander of the Greeks.' In his own handwriting! I'm holding the same book he once held in his hands!"

Rebecca nodded, still smiling at the evident awe the book had caused him. "It's not a lie; it's a legend, which means that inside the exaggeration and the fantasy there is some truth to be found."

Leon pried the papyrus open, read the first twelve lines of the epic poem, and then locked eyes with her. "All about love," he stressed. "One woman, Helena, was the cause of the war and another, Briseis, was the one who prolonged it."

"Everything happens because of passion," argued Rebecca. "The passion of a man, Paris, was the reason for the war and the passion of another, Achilles, prolonged it."

"It's a matter of perspective," Leon said and laughed, delighted by her opinion. In the end, he rolled the papyrus again very carefully and handed it back to her, feeling thrilled both by the existence of the book and his acquaintance with her.

Rebecca took the book and crouched forward, putting it back inside the hiding place. Her heart was beating fast and her mind was like a spring garden. Her mood was galloping, happy and wild, toward a bright horizon.

"The other book you have in there—what is it?"

She stopped dead, as if she were made of stone. Her loving eyes were suddenly void of that dreamy shine and darkened, as they turned to the second cylindrical book inside the hiding place.

Leon couldn't help noticing her silence, her stillness, and the disappearance of her smile. Dying of curiosity, he repeated the question as the silence continued.

"It's . . . I don't know," she barely answered, and nervously closed the hatch and then locked it hastily.

"What is it?" Leon insisted nosily.

"I don't know. I haven't read it. Father has forbidden it." Rebecca pushed the nightstand in front of the hiding place and stood up. "It's cursed," she added without returning his gaze. Her face seemed completely different, as if she were sorry for something she had done, and she walked along the corridor, toward Joel's bedroom.

Leon followed her, terribly puzzled, not wishing to ask her any more pressing questions. However, her change of mood and the words "forbidden" and "cursed" piqued his curiosity, and his mind went wild from all the instinctive and irrelevant assumptions of his effort to determine what book it was.

"Have you seen our books?" Joel asked merrily, seeing Leon enter the room. "Did you find one that you liked?"

"I've seen them, yes. There are some I haven't heard before that I'd like to read . . ." he answered solemnly, with a hint of sadness in his voice. He looked at Rebecca, who kept avoiding his gaze, and with the audacity he had inherited from his grandfather he added: "Rebecca showed them all to me, even Homer's *Iliad,* but not that other one, the second book you're keeping hidden, the cursed one."

The Jew's warm smile faded and his look changed; it almost went dark. He glanced at his daughter sideways and then frowned at Leon.

"Believe me, Leon, it's best not to talk about it."

"Why? Because it's cursed?" the Greek scoffed.

"Because it's the *Manuscript of the Dead*," said Joel, looking at the young doctor with severity. "Because it was written by the dead for the dead."

Leon smiled derisively. He would have joked about it, but Joel's stern look stopped him. It was clear that the Jew believed every word he had said.

"And because whoever dares to read it meets a terrible death soon after."

Bashar found Theodorus sitting in the hall, sipping wine and reading through his notes. Ever since a party of Arabs captured a few papermakers in faraway China, reading and writing changed radically. The caliph put a ban on papyrus, and the use of paper spread all over the caliphate. It was easier to use than papyrus and the ink didn't fade easily on it. Also, the shape of the books wasn't cylindrical anymore, but square or rectangular.

The doctor made himself comfortable among the sofa cushions, cast a sideways glance at his friend, who was reading silently, and stretched his legs, letting out a loud sigh. Today was also exhausting. There hadn't been any new casualties since noon, but all those already under treatment were more than enough even after he divided them between him and Leon.

"What are you reading?" he asked, rubbing his right temple with his palm.

"I'm looking at the notes on the Mnizurin. In case I've missed something important."

"What do you think is going on?" he asked, placing his palm

over his warm forehead, and looked at Theodorus with misty, weary eyes. "I know that you've thought of something, and I want to hear it. I may not have the knowledge required, but what happened to me at dawn was unheard-of and extremely terrifying. Of course, that feeling of fear I had this morning is gone now. I just think it must have been some kind of dream, but the marks left on my back are telling me otherwise."

Theodorus rested the papers on his lap and tightened his lips in understanding. All this time he spent trying to explain the incidents, there was a great deal of conjecture in his mind, but he wasn't able to reach a conclusion. As a matter of fact, he only had one speculation, but he wasn't sure. He awaited Husni's recovery, so he could make a safe deduction and prove the notion that the events were indeed connected.

"I haven't decided yet," he replied apologetically. He first wanted to confirm his thinking and then speak.

"I want to hear . . ."

Bashar had known him for many years and knew his behaviour and mentality. It wasn't in his character to drivel or mislead his interlocutor. He had the ability to listen silently, which was very rare for the Mediterranean people; but above all, whenever he spoke he had a gift of charming his audience and leading them toward the core of the various concepts. Bashar therefore knew that Theodorus suspected something and he insisted on hearing what it was.

"All these phenomena and prophecies about the end of the world reminded me of one of Plutarch's theories, but I still cannot be sure," he said, trying to avoid unravelling his thought process, but Bashar urged him on. Theodorus knew that he would pressure him, so he continued: "According to that theory, there are certain times when humanity is altered. In general, old customs and habits die in order for new ones to appear; this process is due to the transformation of the individual.

"Plutarch never mentions exactly how often this transformation takes place, but he writes that it's accompanied by several other phenomena—natural or of a different kind. The last transformation he reports took place during the time of the Roman feneral and statesman Sulla, that is, almost eleven hundred years ago.

"What leads me to come to this conclusion is the nature of the different bizarre phenomena he records, which aren't like the current events, but are quite similar."

Bashar sat up on the sofa, pensive. That theory, which at first glance didn't sound alarming, had an element of threat. He was also worried about the future, since the doomsday prophecies were heard not only in the Empire, but also in the caliphate. The faith taught by the Prophet, once unified, had recently been divided, and most cults referred to the signs of the imminent catastrophe. Apart from a few differences in the details, the Arabs' predictions also spoke about the upcoming change and the violence that would take place.

"So you believe that the end of time is near?"

"The end of time for the transformation of humans maybe, but the end of the world, no. Personally, I don't think that God created our world in order to destroy it."

Bashar smiled. He knew that his friend's mind was on the opposite end of the dark prophecies of a total tragedy. Cheerful at the thought, he crouched forward and filled a silver mug with fruit juice.

"What about the Mnizurin? Any information about them?"

"Very little. Nothing useful. Many people mention them, but it's as if they are keeping their mouths shut. I wrote a letter to al-Farabi, asking him if he knows more, but I doubt that he has any extra information."

"What I don't understand is how they come into our world. Do they fall from the sky, like meteorites? Then again, I don't know how the unearthly creatures appear in our world either."

Theodorus took a swig of wine and placed his mug on the table. He entwined his hands and raised them horizontally in front of his lips. He had to speak of a subject that was hard for someone without the proper knowledge to comprehend. Not even his colleagues at Magnaura University could grasp that theory, not to mention accept its practical application. The only man who agreed with him was Andronicus Graeuses, whom they had killed in order to take away the Mnizurin.

"You know about the Pythagoreans, don't you?" he began, and Bashar nodded. "They were preoccupied with the nature of the world, and that is why they developed their insight on astronomy and mathematics. One of the many mysteries in Nature, which they dealt with, was the multilocation."

"What is that?"

"There are several reports that certain people appear simultaneously in different places. Picture me, talking to you right now, being able to appear before other people in Antioch, for instance—"

"I've never heard that before," Bashar interrupted him, but urged him on.

"As many people write, Pythagoras himself appeared in different places at the same time. That phenomenon was the reason many different theories were developed and why some philosophers speak of rifts in space. Later, others associated the multilocation with the skill of divination and talked about rifts in both time and space, saying that due to these, some people are able to foretell the future.

"As you know, the Pythagoreans were very secretive, and their theories never made it outside their members' circles in their entirety, but only in fragments. Plato came close to them, and several of his musings are rooted in what they had taught him. They told him about the different worlds on other planets, about the movement happening between them through these rifts, and so on.

"Of course, Plato brought morsels of those notions into his works, processing them according to his own personal views—"

"What are you two whispering about?" said Leon in a chirpy voice, interrupting the conversation. His face glowed, and his movements were light, indicating his inner euphoria.

"Well, well, if it isn't the lover-boy!" Bashar teased him, since he knew from Theodorus that the boy had fallen in love with a Jewish girl.

"Shut your mouth, you dirty old coot!" Leon retorted, acting offended. "When I met Rebecca, I didn't keep it to myself. I told Theodorus right away. You were secretly in love with Jasmine—and, in fact, brought her into the house—without telling us anything. You filthy Hagarene dog!"

Regardless the age difference, the two colleagues liked to tease each other by cursing or making fun of their origins, with no hard feelings. They developed that habit when they were still in Constantinople, when Leon, sensing Bashar's cheerful character, teased him with jokes the Christians told about Arabs and vice versa.

"I didn't say anything because it was all so sudden," Bashar explained but didn't finish his sentence, because Leon sat beside him and gave him a firm one-armed embrace.

"The professor is talking about Plato again," he said, shifting his teasing toward Philetas. "I'm only going to say this once, so listen carefully. We doctors will save the world. Not you philosophers, who keep wondering about this and that all the time. Who spoke about method? Hippocrates. Who spoke about reason? Aristotle. Luckily, Aristotle was a son of a doctor and turned philosophy toward reason, otherwise you'd still be saying that the world is flat, as the Christians of the West believe."

"What have you been drinking?" Theodorus asked him, amused at the cheerfulness of his young friend, whom he recently considered more like a son.

Leon bent forward, still holding Bashar firmly, gave them a conspiratorial look and said in a soft, mellow voice: "Love!"

The hall roared with the three men's laughter. The servants outside heard them clearly, but even though they were curious to know the reason why, they didn't eavesdrop, because they didn't speak Greek.

When, after a while, the hilarity was over, Leon poured some wine in a silver mug and asked: "No, seriously, what have you been talking about? Was there any new information about the supposedly strange things happening?"

"He was explaining the way the Iynges travel from their world to our own," Bashar said and freed himself from Leon's hold.

"How is that?" the young man asked, looking at Philetas straight in the eye.

Theodorus summed up everything he had told Bashar and added: "These are the theories I once tried to analyse with the help of Andronicus Graeuses, mostly in theory and partly in practice."

"The practical side of it isn't of much interest to us; we won't understand it anyway—"

"Oh, so you *can* understand the theoretical side?" Bashar teased Leon and laughed.

Leon laughed as well, but didn't go on with the teasing. He really wanted to know more about the rifts in time and space.

"What aroused my curiosity and made me want to examine the matter more closely was the story of Epimenides the Cretan. Have you heard of him?"

Both Leon and Bashar shook their heads.

"He was from Crete, a doctor-philosopher, and some people refer to him as one of the Seven Sages of Greece. We don't know a lot about his life, apart from three incidents such as rescuing Athens from a plague by uttering some words—"

"So what was he? A doctor or a sorcerer?" Leon interrupted ironically and elbowed Bashar.

"Remember yesterday, when I told you about the raising of the dead? It's the same thing. And, for heaven's sake, quit labelling everything as sorcery! You mentioned Aristotle before; I'm sure that if he were still alive, they would hunt him down and lock him up in a monastery accusing him of sorcery as well."

"All right, I'll try, but I can't promise anything," he smiled meaningfully.

"The other incident about Epimenides," said Theodorus after taking a deep breath, "is that one day he went into a cave and slept for almost sixty years. When he came out, he hadn't aged a bit—"

"Nonsense!" Leon cried out. "You are seriously pulling our leg! Do you really want me to fall for this folktale? How can you possibly believe that kind of story? Figure that . . . 'he went into a cave and came out sixty years later'!"

Theodorus locked eyes with him, a puzzling smile on his face. He knew that Leon would react in this way, just as he knew how to turn his thinking around.

"Fine. Let's assume you're right—that the story about Epimenides going into the cave and emerging after sixty years, not aged, is fake. Let's just say that it's yet another story crafted by the idiotic pagans. But what can you say about Maximilian, Exacustodianus, Iamblichus, Martinian, Dionysus, John, and Constantine?"

Leon was about to ask who they were, but Theodorus, guessing his question, beat him to it: "They are Christians and we honour their memory, because the Church has made them saints. They are the Seven Sleepers of Ephesus."

Leon raised his eyebrows. He had heard of the Seven Sleepers of Ephesus since he was a pupil, but he neither knew their names, nor did he remember their story.

"Those seven youths, in order to save themselves from the

Roman persecutors, when the Emperor Decius engaged in a hunt against the Christians, hid inside a cave and surrendered their souls to God. Two hundred years later, though, during the reign of Theodosius the Second, they reappeared, not having missed a single day since the day they had disappeared. For that miracle of their return, the Church proclaimed them saints."

"And what is the conclusion you have reached from these two stories?" Bashar asked impatiently, disregarding the surprised look on his young friend's face. He had heard similar stories being told by Arab heretics.

"That the rifts in time and space can also function in reverse. Just as the creatures can travel from their world to ours, so can we. What I think is that Epimenides and the Seven Sleepers travelled to other worlds and then they came back.

"This theory states that space is not concrete: that's why creatures from other worlds can pass through its rifts, or why a person can be present in different places, as long as this person is near one of these rifts. According to other philosophers, they're not rifts, but a passage in space, that is, a penetrable place—a gate, if you will."

"And why do you think that Epimenides and those seven children didn't age?" Bashar continued with his inquiry.

Next to him, Leon was sitting speechless and thoughtful. He silently admitted that the two stories had a lot in common, and the fact that the miracle of the Seven Sleepers was affirmed by the Church gave it the necessary validity for him to believe in them. At the same time, he wondered about the mysteries of the world and the big unknown, surrounding humankind . . .

"I don't know. Very possibly, since there are rifts in time as well, it's all due to some kind of a paradox. I can't be certain—"

Two heavy and insistent bangs on the door made Theodorus stop and look around. One of the servants came into the hall and took a bow. His face was ashen, and he revealed the reason for his intrusion with no delay.

"Master, something terrible has happened . . ."

His misty eyes, above his thin, hawkish nose, looked like those of a sick man, blurry and baffled. On his thin, bony face, wide cheekbones, tight fleshy lips, and round chin, his surprise was clear, while his long black hair was loose on his worry-laden shoulders.

He looked around the burnt surroundings in anguish. The place was foreign to him, and the picture of the catastrophe worried him. Shades of black and grey dominated the scene, morphing into fear, and despair agitated his mind and caused him heart palpitations. Seeing the charred remains of an extensive area always evokes many strong emotions, but above all it draws out a deep sorrow, due to the rising loss and almost palpable presence of death. That's why he observed every little detail, shattered, motionless, and disheartened.

He couldn't remember how he had got there, if perhaps he was a local resident or—worse—the area's destroyer. His chest tightened with that thought. He might not remember much about himself, but he was positive that he wasn't capable of such an inhuman and horrific deed.

He tried to remember who he was or how he had got there, but he failed. All he could remember about himself was his name, Husni ibn Jaber, but he couldn't be sure of that either.

Sweat rolled down his forehead and landed on the edge of his eyebrow. He wiped it away nervously with the back of his hand and fixed his gaze forward. The complete disaster, the tangible stillness of the air, and the scary twilight put his nerves on edge.

Suddenly he sensed that someone or something was watching him. He glanced over his shoulder a couple of times, without finding the cause of his disturbance. For some faint reason he felt something ominous slithering at the root of his mind, and his nervousness increased. His instinct was instantly alert. He frowned and looked at the scenery across from him, this time in suspicion.

The plain opposite and all around him was completely charred. An infinite stretch of land, covered in ashes and dirt.

In the east, near where he was, he could see clearly the thousands of burnt tree trunks framing the skeletal dry forest. It once brimmed with life, but now it was nothing more than a haunted, multi-tentacled ghost, inhabited by threatening ghastly shadows with long, thin limbs and dark grey mouths. The shadows swayed on the ground in blasphemy, turning longer or wider, abruptly and violently, as if they wished to wrench themselves free from their roots and cast off their shackles. That vision frightened him and made him look away.

To the west of the burnt region stood the ruins of a very ancient city. Remnants of some human presence, shattered and sooty, destroyed and crushed by the rage of fire and ravages of time.

All this was dwarfed by a dark sky that looked like a rickety and derelict shelter. The dirty yellow sheen of the massive black grey clouds hung low and looked like giants who had decided to stomp on the already devastated place.

Husni stood at the edge of a hillock's peak, an insignificant speck, against the backdrop of a collapsed horizon, powerless against the great masses that, under the gusts of wind, diffused the feeling of danger. Their movements were specific. Delicate. Purposeful. Skilled. Like a languid killer who toys with his victim.

A prolonged, piercing scream shattered the deadly silence. Husni was startled, almost jumping with fear, and fervently scanned the horizon. The grey plain surrounding the deserted city was empty. Not a trace of life could be seen—human, animal, or any kind of bird. Nonetheless, the screaming was repeated, making his heart race.

Pallid and startled, he turned his fearful gaze around, trying to locate the source of the sound. Nothing. Whoever or whatever was howling in the wilderness was invisible.

The intensity of the phantom threat galvanized him. He ran down the slope, his mind searching for answers. Fear and uncertainty challenged any kind of reasonable conclusion he might come to in order to explain what he was experiencing.

On his right, he heard wings fluttering and the sharp squawking of hundreds of birds. It was a frenzied uproar of bloodcurdling sounds, which surprised him and made him suddenly turn his head toward them.

His line of vision was filled with a pulsating black cloud, moving rapidly and menacingly near him. An enormous swarm of black crows was flying above his head ready to attack. He got scared and ran for cover.

He didn't make it. They caught up with him and started pecking at him, others pinching him with their nails, some with their beaks and most of them, due to their momentum, with their wings. He shrieked in despair. He tried to push them away with his arms and return their consecutive blows, but they weren't daunted. Most of them aimed at his head, but with their beaks and nails they pierced and scraped his arms. Tears of pain streamed down his face, and he felt that his end was near.

The crows were gnawing his flesh, pulling and ripping it. They nibbled on him and squawked triumphantly in his ears, like barbarian warriors who know that they are going to defeat their weak and cowardly enemy.

He struggled to save himself, but his winged enemies, fearless and full of hate, continued their rabid attack, until they shoved him to the ground, bleeding. Then, as if they had successfully accomplished their goal, they fled away toward the desolate city.

Husni closed his eyes, barely breathing, and curled up defeated, anticipating another attack. He remained lying a few moments longer, breathing and gasping rapidly; and then he timidly opened his eyelids. The horror he felt was indescribable, because he had never expected that birds would attack, overpower, and hurt him that badly.

Feeling shaky and disoriented, he staggered to his feet. His head was dripping with blood, forming tiny crimson rivulets down his forehead. His right eyebrow had suffered a severe gash. One of the crows had pecked him so hard that it cut open his flesh, revealing the bone. The blood from the wound was warm and dripped into his eye, making his vision blurry.

His sensitive ears caught an articulate sound, a word, a name, *his* name: "Husni!" The voice didn't sound human. It was more like an echo inside a cave, caused by the furious splashing of the water from an underground river on ancient stalagmites. He shivered and held himself so as not to faint with terror.

He looked around him in shock, cautiously, gasping with fear. He saw nothing. His hands were shaking and the veins on his temples throbbed furiously.

"Husni!"

The voice came from behind him, near him, ten feet away at most. He didn't turn around, afraid of what he would face. He began running with all his might. He was running while tears were rolling down his face. He could feel his persecutor close; he could hear thunderous strides. He wanted to see what the thing chasing him was, but no power in the world could make him look.

He didn't manage to go very far. He tripped over something and his thobe was tangled on a branch. At the sound of the cloth ripping, he fell on the ashes and began writhing and rolling like crazy, in despair . . .

He sat up on the bed, eyes wide open and face soaking with sweat. The gloom inside the room was thick, but he gradually started making out the outline of the furniture and the walls. His chest was heaving fast and rhythmically, as if he had just run a great distance. His breathing came out whistling through his nostrils.

He tried to calm down and figure out what was happening to him. He had constant nightmares of demons attacking him and black monsters with tentacles trying to kill him. While he was sleeping he thought he was awake, and when he was awake he thought he was asleep. He no longer had any sense of what was real. It was all so vague and confusing that it was impossible for him to tell truth from falsity.

He stared out into nowhere. His mind was on fire and his body trembled. He instinctively reached for his medallion, but he realised that it wasn't around his neck, and the panic made him remember.

Clear memories from the past sprang out, memories from a time buried under mental ruins. Images and sentiments he had forgotten and hoped never to remember again.

Husni saw his father along with other relatives and friends frantically dancing in a trance around a bonfire, uttering strange sounds that even Arabs would find hard to pronounce. They danced to the sound of tabors and sistrums, until the music was abruptly interrupted by a sonorous voice.

The dancers gathered round the fire, constantly repeating a phrase. "Iä iä k'le! Azathoth h'thag!" they kept yelling, falling on the ground frenzied, and then again jumping in the air, spread-eagled.

From the shadows behind them came a man dressed in a dark blue thobe. His features were barely visible in the half-light, and the shadows created by the flames looked as if they were crawling and sliding like living things on his clenched face. But what he could clearly see and what also haunted him was the little child he was holding by his right hand and violently dragging through the sand. A very young child, barely a toddler.

There was nothing visible in the man's gaze, no human feeling, except for the flames that swayed in the weakening breeze of the desert. His steady gaze was fixed on the fire and the strange pots arranged before him, pots that were filled to the brim with a thick black liquid—blood.

Without pausing, without looking away, he approached the fire, muttered a prayer, and in a sudden stroke of the sword beheaded the child. The body of the boy fell on the sand wiggling and painted it red.

The killer picked up the severed head by the hair, shook away the blood from the face, and signalled the people present to approach. Everyone obeyed. They went near him, he sprinkled the boy's blood on them, and they went away, muttering spells or prayers. His father did the same thing.

"You should never take it off," he heard his grandfather saying as he clasped the chain with the strange medallion around his neck. "Do you hear me? Never take it off, because there will come a time when it will save you. Wherever you go, no matter how far, you'll always bear the curse. You'll never get away, because the miasma runs in our blood. Only the Mnizurin can save you."

His grandfather didn't believe in the existence of the Old Ones. He was faithful to the Prophet's law, and that is why he helped Husni get away; when the boy was six years old, he sent him away from the desert, to the golden Mediterranean beaches. He implored him never to come back and to forget everything he had seen after he had secretly followed his father outside the settlement that night.

As time went by, he did forget everything; he buried the images in the sand deep inside the desert of his mind. He could no longer recall anything, not even the reason why he wore that slimy medallion. However, he never took it off.

He raised his eyes upwards and prayed to Allah. But praying didn't calm him, for in his mind's eye he could still see images of slaughter inside the tent. He clenched his teeth to stop the rushing memories from coming.

He could see it clearly now: he was the one to have caught Jelal in his sleep and cut his throat with a knife. Without hesitation or empathy, he tied him by the feet, hanged him upside down from the pillar, and with another stab ripped his stomach completely open. The intestines rolled down his dead friend's chest, the blood and the fluids filled his nostrils and the sockets of his eyes.

He was the one who had slaughtered him! He had ruthlessly killed him and then danced in a trance, stepping on the blood and the severed flesh. He danced and shouted the words he had heard at the ritual: "Iä iä k'le! Azathoth h'thag!"

Husni pulled the sweaty sheet that was tucked into the mattress and twisted it. He passed it through the horizontal roof beam and made a tight knot. In his mind he could see Jelal, his friend who had once saved his life when he fell in a raging torrent along with his camel.

He was the man who killed Jelal and the rest of the cameleers in their sleep! Of course, there were still those creatures that murmured their unspeakable language, but the medallion had protected him. It had protected his life, but not his spirit. The creatures didn't hurt him, but made him their accomplice.

He had slaughtered his best friend! Husni tied the sheet tightly around his neck and jumped off the bed.

5. The Poet of Demons

Before sunrise, Khalisah Fayuh headed toward the house of the muezzin, Harun al-Ghouta. She had spent all night waiting for Abbas to return, sitting on the stool beside the front door. Her eyelids drooped with sleepiness, and she was startled more often than not by everything she was hearing, whether it was street sounds or nightmares that disturbed her short sleep. Tormented both by sleeplessness and especially by her dark thoughts, she couldn't wait for dawn any longer and rushed to ask for help before it was too late.

Before leaving, she considered how she would present her problem. Although she remembered her father's words that "whoever speaks the truth can touch Allah," she opted for hiding the real reason why her brother had left to find the Jew. She was aware that if the townspeople found out about his intention to rob the man, they would think less of their family and, in the event of her brother being still alive, he would definitely beat her black and blue. So, in order to avoid the consequences of the truth, she thought it was better to lie; she would say that Abbas had lent the Jew some money and now, with the help of Tariq, he was looking for him.

Their neighbours and familiars would never believe her lie, since they all knew about the two siblings' poverty, but at this time she could not think of anything else. In fact, as she was thinking about what to say and what to do, she decided to appear in front of the holy man without the cover of her *burqa* and with loose hair, so that her agony and tragic state would be more evident.

Twenty feet away she burst into tears and, when she knocked on the door, her sobs were so loud they woke up the neighbours. Her tears weren't false; on the way there, she had been pondering on their terrible financial state and the indecent path her brother had taken. If it had been possible, she would have beaten him for everything he had done, but her kismet was to have been born a woman, weak and submissive.

At first, Harun al-Ghouta couldn't understand what had happened to the young woman who was sobbing at his threshold. He woke up to the sound of her yelling and tried to calm her first and then hear her problem, but as she dropped to her knees begging for his help, he let her vent, promising to do whatever needed to be done.

By the meagre light of the oil lamp, he contemplated her beauty in silence—not that if she were ugly he wouldn't help her; but those beautiful black eyes and her sensual lips were all the more reason for him to show sympathy.

The neighbours had woken up alarmed by all the wailing and came out to see what was going on. They weren't there out of curiosity, but real concern. They feared another earthquake, probably greater and more catastrophic, so any sound was likely to shatter their fragile state of calmness.

When they showed up, Harun led the woman to his yard. From the words that came out of her mouth, amidst her sobs, he knew that something had happened to her brother—something that had nothing to do with the earthquake.

With reassuring words, he led her to the garden, where the place was specially designed for rest and meditation: a spacious wooden gazebo, adorned with creepers and cages with exotic songbirds. He also ordered his servants to prepare a soothing beverage.

Khalisah continued crying, now caused by her shame and insecurity. She was afraid her lie wouldn't sound real. But as she observed the muezzin's placid countenance and patient gaze, she gained courage and related all the facts, according to the version she had practiced.

Harun's eyes shone at the sound of "Jew" and "merchant." With his temperament, it was like a spark on dry twigs. He saw an opportunity to prove his faith and diffuse his passion to his fellow townspeople, who had now turned slothful and sinful, forgetting what the Prophet dictated about the constant alertness and the spreading of his Law.

The fire in his chest didn't take long to ignite, and before his servant placed the brass tray upon the table, Harun gave him orders: "Take some men with you and go find out if Abbas Fayuh and Tariq Nabur are alive. Search the entire city and don't come back until you find them."

The servant bowed respectfully and got back into the house, calling out to four men. They all showed up at the hall with no time to waste. They listened to their master's demand and a few minutes later took to the streets, like hounds hunting for prey.

"Don't worry, sister," Harun said and looked at Khalisah in the eye. "Allah is great and every creature is protected inside His embrace."

Khalisah nodded, wiped her tears away and took a sip of the beverage she'd been offered. Her full lips touched the fine mug, and through her long eyelashes she looked at the holy man who comforted her.

Her appearance painted an image of eroticism in his mind. His heart fluttered from the beauty blossoming before his eyes, and his thought created love verses able to bring proud warriors to their knees. Overcome by desire for her, he compared Khalisah to an houri, one of the seventy-two virgins awaiting him in heaven. He was prepared to promise her the world and more than that in exchange for a single caress.

"If something has happened to your brother, all the filthy Jews in the city will pay with blood!" Harun al-Ghouta promised, puffing out his chest, determined to take her under his wing; for she was a gift Allah had generously offered him.

That night, the three friends slept badly, terrible nightmares disturbing their slumber. Husni's hanging, the recent tragedy that had struck Damascus, death that, unwavering in its path, kept its close proximity, and the surrounding mysterious threat affected them more that they would admit. They knew that something bad was coming; they couldn't determine what it was, but they instinctively felt its approach, its tentacles spreading around them.

The cameleer's demise saddened Theodorus the most, because he lost all hope for ever finding an answer to his questions. Bashar felt badly because a man had ended his own life under his roof. He thought of it as derisive and insulting toward him. All the while, Leon had to step out of the blossoming garden of his personal happiness and face the real world, which was still violent, vain, and unjust.

The sight of the tanned man dangling from the ceiling, tied to a sheet from the roof beam, his dead, still eyes gaping out into space and his tongue hanging out the corner of his blue lips, was an image that disturbed them psychically. They were perplexed more by the deed than by the dead body. Suicide was beyond their sense of reason and mentality. They couldn't imagine what had led that man to kill himself. What evil or what problem could have been so great as to force him to make such a desperate decision for a way out of his dead-end?

The servants' superstitious attitude agitated the thoughts of the three men. Low-spirited and disappointed, they exchanged a few brief, reassuring words and retreated to their respective bedrooms. The two doctors managed to fall asleep sooner, and their nightmares weren't as intense as Philetas'. For Bashar, Jasmine's kisses and caresses were like a balsam to a patient, while Leon calmed his sorrow in the imaginary arms of his beloved Rebecca.

Theodorus, however, was up till late, failing to understand the reason for Husni's suicide. His friends, wanting to set his mind at ease, explained that Husni's deed was the result of insanity. However, he wasn't convinced. He suspected that his suicide was directly related to the Mnizurin, only he couldn't prove it.

The image of his friend Andronicus Graeuses came to his mind, and the memories of the past emerged, reconstructed according to the latest events, but also with the additional knowledge he had gained after his tragic murder. The memories were crystal-clear, but also shrouded by the fog of mystery and shady activity.

The events in Adrianople had scarred him. Apart from the slaughter of the poor girl and the burning of her body, he couldn't possibly forget her sinister mumbling, which incited hellish delusions in anyone who heard it.

At first he thought that it had only affected him, stirring primitive memories inside his mind or opening up gates of communication with other worlds, dark and fearsome. But when they discussed their shared experience, Theodorus realised that those words had a force capable of distorting time, taming the winds, and altering the nature of things, just as Empedocles, the ancient philosopher, told his students about the knowledge he possessed.

He heard what Empedocles boasted about from Andronicus, whom he immediately went to visit as soon as he was back in Constantinople. He longed to reveal his testimony of the events, and he visited him in order to reach a sensible conclusion after analysing what he had witnessed. He went to his laboratory at noon and stayed there until the next morning. That's when he found out about the experiments Andronicus was working on and about his theory on the properties of sound.

During their long talk, they were concerned about the relation of catalepsy to sounds and, in the end, to the possibility of prophecy. They tried to discover, even theoretically at first, the connections and the different aspects of the matter.

There were many examples, but the ones that determined the course of their research were the Sibyls and Emperor Zeno's tomb. The texts on famous female prophets of antiquity mentioned that these women acquired the power of prophecy after their catalepsy. Their predictions weren't about near events, but distant, future events, in ages that not even the present imagination could have reached, revealing that time, even if it is endless, is not compact.

The discussion moved to the association between the rifts in time and the powers of sound. The question posed was whether something expressed verbally can sooner or later become real, not because of the desire of the individual who uttered it, but because the sound triggered an activity creating the conditions that would yield the desired outcome.

Andronicus didn't exclude the possibility of the existence of an activity through sound, even though he couldn't confirm it through an experiment. To him it seemed logical, and he claimed that even time, or perhaps space as well, can be affected by sounds. But there was definitely a connection between them.

When Zeno's case came up, Andronicus' eyes shone with a cunning glint. It had almost been five centuries since the death of that former emperor, but everyone in Constantinople knew about the incident, and the dark, frightening stories that went around still caused trembling and gave them nightmares.

Zeno was a bad king and the people hated him. As a result of his politics, he lost the throne, but a few years later he regained the reign and his power transformed from tyrannical to brutal, until he finally died.

Nobody shed a tear at his funeral. On the contrary, they were all

happy. Their happiness, however, didn't last long. The next morning, all the townsfolk heard that Zeno had suffered catalepsy and
from within his sarcophagus he was calling people to let him out.
There was not a single person in Constantinople at that time who
hadn't visited the imperial tomb. The curiosity about that incredible
incident didn't leave anyone indifferent, and of course superstition
overshadowed reason. It was said that the king had come back to
life with Satan's help in order to torture his subjects even more,
steal their souls, and drink their blood.

For three days Zeno begged to be let out, either by promising
gold and titles, or by insulting and shouting horrendous curses at
everyone. No one opened the sarcophagus; they left him there to
die of starvation and thirst.

"Did you happen to hear that he was thought to have predicted
the future of the Empire while speaking in an incomprehensible
language? I didn't believe it myself, until I was called to build the
mausoleum for Porphyrogenitus' father. That's when I thought I
should try to discover the truth," Andronicus had confessed to him
that night.

"One day I dismissed my workers and, with a crowbar, pried
Zeno's sarcophagus open. His skeleton was there, intact, and its po-
sition indicated that all the stories about his catalepsy had been real.
He was lying in the fetal position.

"I was about to close the tomb when I noticed that in his right
hand he was holding his *chiton* buckle, golden and adorned with
gems. Then, intrigued, I lifted the marble lid a little more and saw
that he had carved some symbols and letters."

Theodorus' reaction to his friend's words was immediate and
critical. But then he thought it wasn't a matter of sacrilege but a way
to document the truth. Since he, too, would have done the same, he
changed his attitude toward him.

"It might have been helpful if we had them," he said finally.

"I do have them," Andronicus said with a mischievous smile. "I wrote them down on a papyrus and tried to decipher them, but without success." He took the papyrus out of a wooden chest and showed Theodorus everything Zeno had carved inside his sarcophagus.

Theodorus examined the symbols, which resembled hieroglyphics, and uttered the two names that were written in Greek: "Dagon" and "Yog-Sothoth." He frowned in disappointment. He couldn't understand the meaning of that strange writing, and the two names were unknown to him.

"They are deities. Dagon was a god of the sea, a reformer of the world. The Chaldeans associated him with the constellation Pisces. Yog-Sothoth might have also been worshipped in Egypt, as the guardian of the gate leading to the world beyond death," said Andronicus, revealing everything he had discovered during his research.

Theodorus could still picture him sitting in front of the four lecterns in his laboratory, his eyes sparkling, analysing every single piece of information. Andronicus Graeuses wasn't an ordinary professor or some idle wealthy person who meditated and performed purposeless experiments. His amazing artefacts decorate the imperial palace and cause awe to everyone who sees them.

Any man who visits the Throne Room can see with his very eyes the mechanical structures of the "second Heron," as they used to call him. On either side of the entrance there were artificial trees with simulated birds that chirped like real, metallic butterflies that flew from branch to branch, and leaves made of cloth that fluttered as if a real breeze swept through them. On the stairs that led to the royal pedestal stood the brass roaring lions, and at the sides of the throne the motorized eagles that with the press of a button spread their wings, fluttering them and lifting the heavy seat along with the emperor high, almost at the height of three grown men.

That was Andronicus Graeuses, the man who always kept a geometry, biology, astronomy, and engineering book open on each of the lecterns in his laboratory. Among those lecterns was where they had found him six days after their all-night discussion.

Two days before his murder, Andronicus had announced to the university that he had discovered a Mnizurin, which Theodorus and Bashar went to see. That was the last time he saw him alive.

When Harun al-Ghouta was done with the purification of the house, he sat on a stool across from Bashar and gladly accepted the lemonade that they offered him. Dressed in his green priestly vestments, he smugly listened to the thanks of the servants, Jasmine, and also the doctor himself, who had invited him to bless the house because of the miasma they thought Husni's suicide had brought.

The muezzin waited for the others to leave the room and then, when he was alone with Bashar, spoke clearly and strictly. He wasn't like all the other priests of Damascus; he was younger and lacked the wisdom that comes with age. His words and his eyes shone brightly, and he explained the Sharia with all the drive that was reflected by his age.

"Bashar, my brother, you have two infidels inside your home," said Harun, raising his hand confidently, demanding that Bashar, who was about to defend his friends, let him finish.

"I know you have the emir and the cadi's blessings, but I have to remind you that Allah watches and knows of our sins. Your heart has been affected by the ways of the infidels—you must admit that. The practical knowledge they possess is one thing; the Prophet's Law is another. The Law is above all, and you disregard it, acting like a sinner or a heretic—"

"What do you mean, reverend brother? Where did I go wrong?" interrupted Bashar, who had begun flushing at what he heard.

"In a different case, a modest man like you would have never behaved with such disobedience, taking the widow of the unfortunate al-Beidha into your home. This isn't the way for a faithful man to behave: that's why I want you to return to the right path as soon as possible and set a date for the wedding."

Bashar breathed a sigh of relief. At first he had thought that the muezzin would lecture him about his friends and get him to try and convince them to embrace his faith, but once he heard that it was about Jasmine he relaxed.

"Don't worry, my brother, I was meaning to do it, but after the terrible earthquake I've been waiting for the right moment. As you understand, it's not the time to be merry, with all this grief around us."

Harun finished his lemonade in one gulp and got up suddenly, showing that he accepted the answer. Clemency was not one of his traits, but at that moment he was thinking of other matters that tempered his severity and his strong urge to return home and be there when Khalisah would wake up. He wished to see her blooming in the sunbeams, like a rare Damascene flower. He felt the intensity of love sweeping away every other thought or duty. Ever since he first clapped eyes on her, all he wanted to do was taste her kiss and feel the warmth of her body. Nothing else.

He had also started to get irritated thinking that none of his servants had come back from the search for the two men, even if it had already been four hours since they had left. He longed for the moment he would tell her the news and receive her thanks and gratitude.

Bashar accompanied him to the yard. He intended to go to the clinic to pray for the injured people and give courage to their families, but before they had the chance to enter the building, one of his subordinates stopped them. The news he was bearing was terrible for Khalisah, but not for him and his intentions.

Abbas Fayuh was found dead in an alley, and the neighbours had left him there along with other dead bodies, in case one of his relatives recognised him. Tariq Nabur was nowhere to be found; no one knew where he was, if he was alive or dead.

"That Jew or his friends must have killed him," concluded the servant, instigating his master's thoughts.

Harun weighed the facts silently. He resented having to give the bad news to Khalisah himself; on the other hand, though, he was certain that this recent development would bring them closer. He was given the chance to comfort her and help her with her immediate needs. What mattered was to be there for her and prove that he could protect her. With that specific thought on his mind, he linked his wish to the bidding of the Sharia. It was apparent that the Jew had killed Abbas, most likely Tariq as well. That was why the punishment had to be not just exemplary but sweeping.

"Those sorcerers, the spawns of Satan! And we let them live in our sacred land! The thieves! They only care about making a profit and destroy everything like locusts. They will pay for their deed. They will pay!" he thundered, red-faced, and clenched his fists.

"What happened, brother?" asked Bashar curiously. The muezzin's good-natured countenance had altered, and his words dripped with poison. But what frightened him more were his eyes, which revealed sacred wrath and indignation.

"A Jew killed two innocent brothers of ours. They suffered in the hands of that unfaithful dog, and I'm not going to let this insult go by unpunished. They are all going to pay for this! All those demon spawns that are also responsible for . . . the earthquake. That's right! They were the ones who caused the earthquake, with all their sins and errors!"

Bashar tried to appease the furious priest's spirit and recommended prudence. He knew that all that naming and swearing was but an excuse to incite the idiots and the adventurous, who would in turn cause fanaticism among the innocent and the naïve. He had on many occasions heard the angry, fiery sermons delivered by his fellow countrymen, and since he had lived for some time among the Christians, where he witnessed similar expressions of intolerance, he knew that it was a common trait among people in general.

"I'm not expecting a corrupted man, living under the same roof as infidels, to have a proper view of the Sharia," Harun erupted when he heard Bashar suggesting calmness and restraint. His fragile peace was gone forever. "You're impure, and as soon as I'm done with the rotten spawn that taints our city, I'll come looking for you. Remember that!"

Harun turned around and strode toward the clinic exit. When he reached the gate, he stopped and turned to face the astounded Bashar. His black eyes glowed with hatred and rage.

"The infidels shall be gone, and any Arab that falls in the battle will be a glorious martyr expected in heaven," he snorted and took to the street.

He reached Joel's house without even realising it. The moment Bashar told him about al-Ghouta's intentions, he dropped whatever he was doing and hastened to protect Rebecca.

The memory of the expulsion of Jews from Constantinople gave him enough courage and strength to cover the distance without stopping. All he thought about was preventing a tragedy similar to the one he had witnessed a few years before.

At that time, co-Emperor Lecapenus was on the throne and all the reckless spending on luxuries had emptied the city treasury. Simultaneously, even though the taxes were high, the public needs increased; the army, the public works, and especially the pointless spending of the noblemen leading the easy life had drained every fund. There was no money left, and during the council meetings the councillors ruled out the imposition of any new tax, because there was risk of a revolt by the citizens in the province, even desertion. One of the suggested solutions, the most appealing and inexpensive, was to banish the Jews from Constantinople and confiscate their property. The plan was put into action, and the events that followed darkened the soul of every prudent and sensible person.

Leon could never forget the hordes of those scoundrels that barged into his neighbour's mansion and, in the name of Jesus, raped the women, beat the men, and dragged everyone out to the Golden Gate, naked, bleeding, and molested, so they could expel them from Constantinople. Those indelible violent images, filling him with fear over the life of his beloved, urged him to move and act immediately.

Rebecca was perplexed when she saw him standing at the door, out of breath and flushed. She had expected him to come, of course, but not that early. His countenance and his eyes told her that he hadn't come for a good reason.

"What happened? Is something wrong?" she asked, her heart pounding in her chest, her instinct howling ominously.

"Get your things ready—" said Leon, taking a deep breath to ease the burning sensation in his chest as a result of the sprint. He rested his left hand on the door frame. "You must come with me," he added and made his way to Joel's bedroom.

"What for? What happened?" His behaviour alarmed her, and fear wrapped its cold fingers around her thin throat.

Leon looked her in the eye. He wanted to kiss her, hug her, but the latest events and their rapid development curbed his desires and set his logic into motion.

"The Damascenes are ready to expel the Jews . . ."

Rebecca froze at the news. Her eyes widened with bewilderment, and she raised her palm on her chest. When she was a little girl she had heard about the expulsion her people had to suffer through, the slaughtering, the uprooting, the rapes, but she never thought that she would ever experience a situation like that. Apart from the derelictions of some fanatics and exploiters, the small Jewish community led a peaceful life in Damascus. Of course there were some incidents of theft, but such cases could be overcome.

"You two must come with me so I can hide you in the clinic," he added and took her hand, showing her that he was there for her, that she could count on him.

"Are you telling the truth? What happened?" She couldn't believe her ears. Her mind was overwhelmed by many images, black and red, images of agony and loss, terrible and bloodcurdling scenes related by old people, whose memory carried the misfortunes of their forefathers.

Leon didn't reply. He himself wasn't sure about what had happened. The only thing that was clear in his mind was Bashar saying that the muezzin Harun al-Ghouta intended to raise the Damascenes against the Jews. He didn't need to hear more. He dropped the medicine he was preparing and ran to get to them first. He could clearly remember the misdeeds in Constantinople, so he left as soon as he heard the news, without asking for details or confirmation.

"How are you feeling, Joel?" he asked in a mellow voice, trying to relieve the tension inside him. He didn't want to alarm him.

Joel gave him a shaky smile and motioned him to sit next to him. He took his hands and held them tightly, thanking him yet again.

"We have to move you," he said, looking into his eyes and then glancing at Rebecca, who was standing across from him, silent and pale. "We'll take you to the clinic, so I can monitor your health."

"Is something wrong?" Joel asked, surprised at Leon's suggestion.

"It's just better you are near me so I can step in whenever necessary."

Joel examined his face. He immediately understood that something terrible was happening, but he couldn't think of anything beyond his personal issue. He figured that the state of his health had deteriorated, even if he didn't feel any different.

"All right. Rebecca—" He was about to give her instructions but stopped in midsentence because the moment he turned to her, he noticed tears rolling down her face.

"What's the matter?" he demanded. "Daughter, why are you crying? Somebody tell me!"

"A muezzin is instigating the Arabs against the Jews," confessed Leon, who couldn't keep the truth from him any longer. "You'll both come to the clinic with me, and when things calm down you can return. Just get what's necessary and some money, in case we need to bribe someone. A carriage will be here shortly to take us there. I'll go to the yard and wait for it."

Desperate, Joel fell into deep thought. As he lay there wounded, he couldn't do what he wanted to do, not even protect Rebecca. Sad, with worry lines on his face, he remained pensive for a while. He only spoke when Leon went to the gate to wait for the carriage. His instructions were short and precise.

Rebecca, crying softly, followed every single order obediently. She wrote a letter to her relatives and gave it to one of the neighbours' children, telling him to deliver it immediately; she also prepared the clothes they were going to take with them and in one of the bundles put all the valuables in the house.

When the carriage arrived, two students carried him out in a stretcher. Joel looked at his home, tears in his eyes. Although he hated thinking pessimistically, he feared he might never see it again, at least as it was right now. He was certain that the pillagers would strip it bare, and he shivered at the thought that they would eventually burn it down in the frenzy of their rage.

"Leon, if there's enough room, take as many books as you can," he said in Greek when they put him in the carriage. "Those barbarians are capable of destroying them all."

Leon nodded and along with Rebecca rushed to carry out his instructions. They stood before the bookcase and looked at the cylindrical volumes in the cabinets. Once again, those books were in danger of destruction.

"Take only the rare ones," Leon advised and added: "Including the ones you keep in the hiding place."

"I already took those, along with all the valuables."

Leon looked at her passionately. He wanted to tell her something encouraging, tell her about the beauty of life, but no word came out of his mouth. He only moved closer to her, hugged her, and then kissed her right there, in front of the bookcase. The world around them disappeared, the upcoming disaster lost its momentum, the fears melted away, and the only thing that remained in the world was their hearts connecting, that sweet feeling of erotic giddiness.

Joel relaxed a bit when they transferred him to the second-floor bedroom. He was worried and felt sad about what could happen, but as he was observing the Arab students who looked after him affectionately, not treating him hatefully or with displeasure, he thought that maybe there wasn't an actual problem. He had heard about the expulsion on numerous occasions, and the threat was always present, but it had never come true. Thus, he hoped that maybe the upcoming menace was nothing but yet another rumour.

He squeezed Rebecca's hand. She was sitting beside him in silence, and he gave her an encouraging smile. The care Leon showed to both of them made him happy, especially when he thought that at such a perilous time they had someone to help and comfort them. He wasn't so much worried about himself, but he didn't want anything to happen to his daughter.

"Don't worry. You'll see, everything will be fine." He was addressing Rebecca, but he himself felt better when he uttered those words.

Rebecca smiled with difficulty. She was afraid. Her mind was constantly bombarded with violent images, and she shuddered at the torture she would suffer at the hands of the Arabs. Simultaneously, in her confused thoughts she also remembered the kiss she and Leon had shared, the beauty she felt in her body, and that alternating feeling gave her vertigo. Tension made her unsteady; she felt smothered. She wanted to go out, walk in the city streets, sit on the lawn of a garden alley and relax.

Bashar entered the bedroom holding a jar containing some ointment. He first greeted Joel and then Rebecca in Arabic. From the quick glance he gave her, he could immediately tell why his friend had fallen for her. The Jewish girl was more than gorgeous.

"This ointment is a salve we made according to the instructions Leon found in the book you gave him," Bashar said, placing the jar on the nightstand and giving Joel a warm smile. "How are you feeling?"

Joel didn't answer; he just nodded. Two Arabs had broken his ribs with the intention of robbing him, others were pursuing him, and he had left his home because of them. He didn't intend to strike a conversation with one of them now.

Rebecca stood up to assist Bashar, but the doctor stopped her. Her beautiful eyes were filled with grief and glittered in the early afternoon sunlight.

"No, you can sit. If I need your help, I'll ask you." Bashar lifted Joel's undershirt and examined his ribs. Leon had readjusted them properly. He took the jar and poured some of the thick substance on Joel's chest and began to apply it.

Leon appeared at the threshold and next to him stood Theodorus, who had woken up late. As soon as he'd been informed that Rebecca and her father were in the house, he wanted to meet them.

"Joel, meet my friend, Theodorus Philetas," a smiling Leon said, his fears hiding behind the deceptive safety with which his profession and their house provided him. "This man has the library of Alexandria stored inside his head," he continued in Greek, in a teasing mood. He wanted to dispel all the dark thoughts hovering above their heads.

Theodorus frowned in disappointment at the exaggeration the boy had uttered and extended his hand for a handshake. Joel was pleased to meet him, but his mind was troubled by something else.

"Leon, my boy, can you please apply the salve? I don't trust this Hagarene dog."

"This dog is a doctor, so watch your mouth because you're in my hands now," Bashar said in Greek, shocking both Joel and Rebecca.

Joel flushed with embarrassment and felt badly, both for insulting him and for the threat against him. He gaped at Bashar and then lowered his eyes in humility.

Leon and Theodorus, after the initial surprise of hearing Bashar's empty threat, started roaring with laughter, breaking the momentary awkwardness.

"I'm sorry," Joel apologised to Bashar, hearing the laughter.

"I don't blame you." The Arab doctor smiled and kept spreading the salve on the body of his patient, who was now looking at him in regret. "I would also blame all the Jews in general if one of them had broken my bones."

"It's not only that. They also want to kill us all," added Joel, reminding him of current events.

"My dear man, we learnt this fanaticism from you," Bashar pointed out. "You consider yourselves to be the chosen ones; we, too, adopted this thinking."

Joel shot a look at Bashar, ready to defend his people's tradition. He wouldn't allow any Arab to lecture him, even if his life depended on it.

"That's what the Christians say as well." Theodorus seized the opportunity to calm everyone down. "But the problem doesn't lie in religion, but in people. They are accustomed to fear everything different and unknown."

"Oh, those Greeks and their witticisms . . ." scoffed Bashar, winking at the Jew, who, realising that he was among people who knew the conventions that defined life, continued the teasing.

"That's right. Not like us, who can come to blows over nothing. When *they* get the chance, they immediately start moralising!"

Their laughter shook the room. The dividing lines were smoothed out and for a moment they all forgot the danger that was coming toward them.

The commotion from outside woke him up and flustered him. Being in the house these last few days, he cared about nothing but when his bruises would go and his broken nose would heal. He felt ashamed and didn't want to go out, so that he wouldn't have to explain his mishap. Apart from that, it could ruin his image if it was found out that Tariq Nabur, the "four-handed thief," was beaten up by an infidel.

Tariq got up from his cot and moved toward the windows of his bedroom. The shutters were closed, but he became increasingly curious about the cries he could hear outside. They didn't sound anguished but angry, which meant they had nothing to do with the earthquake. Something else was happening in Damascus and he had to know what that was.

He stood by the window and strained to make out what the gathered crowd was yelling. At first, when he heard the words, he was taken aback and thought that he had heard wrong. But then, as the meaning of the words became clearer in his mind, he was astounded.

Outside his door, some people had assembled and were shouting: "Tariq, our brother, you became a martyr in the name of Allah, and we will avenge your murder. Death on the Jews!"

Tariq was stunned. He couldn't fathom what was happening. He looked through the shutters and saw people, familiar and unfamiliar, shrieking hysterically and waving their fists in the air. Some of them held knives, while others carried tools and wooden bats.

An acquaintance of his, his neighbour from across the street, who hated him because Tariq had once stolen a bronze platter and a silk scarf from him, stood before the crowd and started making a speech in favour of Tariq, calling him humble and good.

Tariq couldn't believe his eyes or his ears. He stood there, dumbfounded, and heard words he never imagined someone would say over his worthless existence. His bafflement came to an end when he heard about Abbas Fayuh's death. Only then did he realise what had happened.

"Let's banish the Jews!"

"Death on the murderers!"

"Tariq, Abbas, your brothers will avenge for you!"

If Tariq was known for something in the alleys and shady joints of Damascus, it was his agility and wit. Both were immediately set into motion.

He was saddened by Abbas's death. He hadn't known, because after that infidel had beaten them, he didn't stay and see what happened to his companion. Instead, he took to his heels, bleeding. So now he understood that his friend had succumbed to his injuries and that his fellow citizens thought the same had happened to him.

He had no way of knowing how they had associated the Jews with the killing. He suspected that Abbas had told someone about it; he never trusted him much anyway. Or his sister may have betrayed him.

But all this was insignificant. Everyone outside was asking for blood and revenge, and he had a chance to take advantage of the situation. He could show up, lie, and add more fuel to the fire. He could say that Jews had tried to rob them, that Abbas became a martyr for his faith, while Tariq himself was saved at the last minute thanks to merciful Allah. He could turn the Damascenes' rage toward the Jews and enjoy unimaginable gains.

The image of the man that broke his nose and gave him bruises came to his mind. He knew who it was. He recognised him by the golden crucifix that hung on his chest. It was that Christian doctor who had treated his cousin Ismael's burns the previous year. Tariq himself had taken Ismael to the clinic, and that was when he noticed the doctor's gold. He never forgot something he had seen, especially if it was valuable.

The idea of revenge was planted inside him. The Jews would pay, and so would the doctor. He took in a deep breath, grabbed his staff, and, pretending to be crippled, opened the door with a deeply grieved look. He was positive that he would profit from this situation.

Theodorus sat on the stool next to Joel's bed. Bashar and Leon had gone to the clinic, and Rebecca was in the kitchen with Jasmine, supervising the preparation of lunch. The young Jewish woman was gloomy and terrified. That's why Jasmine had urged her to leave the bedroom and busy herself with something else, so she wouldn't think about what was happening to her friends and relatives.

Theodorus stayed back to keep her bedridden father company. He didn't wish to leave him alone under these circumstances. He knew that the old man was frightened, even though he didn't show it. He also knew that in his state, he needed someone to stand by him and give him courage. It was something he would do for any fellow man, but in the case of Joel he had all the more reason to do so.

He smiled at the thought of love-stricken Leon and recalled the young man's anxiety when he was looking at him earlier; Leon was trying to detect some kind of approval of his feeling for Rebecca in his facial expressions. Theodorus left him wondering for quite a while before he finally nodded that he approved of his choice. The boy's eyes shone with joy, and Theodorus felt as if he was giving his own son his blessing.

A lump came to his throat that moment. He and his wife had had four children, three boys and a girl, but he had lost them all when they were still very young, from diseases the doctors couldn't treat. In fact, when Eudoxia died during the epidemic, she was almost four months pregnant. The unbearable pain and deep-seated grief for the loss of his beloved had drained every last piece of hope for a domestic happiness. All he was left with, because he had decided so, was to fight for a better future for his fellow men.

Many people had tried to convince him to start over, because there's no point in living alone without the joyous union with another person, but he had dismissed every suggestion, remaining firm to his beliefs. It would have been easier to become a monk than remarry. He loved Eudoxia with all his heart. He felt that she was his soulmate and that any other woman would be a mere shadow, a bandage on an open wound, the body of a stranger that would never truly unite with his own. Yes, even on the matters of love he remained an unrepentant believer in Platonic philosophy.

"Leon tells me you were a professor at the University of Constantinople," Joel began the conversation. The sounds coming from afar were like indistinct clamour; rabid voices, enraged shouts, intertwined with pained screams and heart-breaking pleas.

Theodorus noticed the black clouds covering Joel's eyes. A couple of neighbourhoods away, a tragedy was unfolding; they couldn't see it, but the mere idea of it caused grief and fear. His

wrinkles, nervous glances, and pursed lips attested to the spiritual
pain he was feeling.

"I hear that you possess Homer's *Iliad*, signed by Alexander
himself," said Theodorus, switching the topic of the conversation to
the Jew. He thought it would be better if he put him in the place of
the speaker instead of the listener: when people talk, they concentrate on what they want to express, while if they listen, their minds
can wander.

Joel nodded cheerfully and repeated the story of how the book
came to his family. But as he was talking about the banishment his
ancestors from Alexandria suffered before they ended up in Damascus, his eyes became even darker.

"Can I see it?" asked Theodorus, feeling bad that he had failed
to relieve his sorrow.

"It's inside that box," he said, pointing at the box with his chin.

Theodorus opened the box and reverently took out the cylindrical book. In his hands he was holding Homer and Alexander the
Great and King Ptolemy of Egypt. At that moment, he felt as if he
was holding the whole of Greek history.

He closed his eyes and immersed himself in the momentum of
time, in the maze of historical events, in the deeds of innumerable
people who lived, loved, were hurt, and died in the ocean of time.
Very gingerly, he untied the string and devoutly opened the book.

His astonished eyes were filled with the Arabic writing. He read
the book title and the author's name: *al-Azif* by Abdul Alhazred.
Perplexed, he glanced at Joel sideways and, while he was closing the
book, he remembered that he had seen that name again, in the letter
al-Farabi had sent him, and also in Plutarch's text.

"This isn't the *Iliad*, but Abdul Alhazred's *al-Azif*," he said and
looked at Joel in puzzlement. When he uttered the words, he shuddered suddenly and unreasonably, as if something cold had touched
him. He felt the hair on the back of his neck rising. And he sensed

that someone or something was watching him intensely or perhaps maliciously.

Joel jerked at the sound of that name. The pain for his fellow Jews' expulsion was gone from his eyes and was replaced by a dark cloud of terror. He instinctively reached for the book, but because of his broken ribs he was unable to do so and slumped back to the mattress. His face looked like a horror mask. He was white as sheet, as if he had seen all the ghosts in the world.

"Close it!" he demanded and winced at the pang of pain in his chest.

Theodorus closed it, not out of obedience, but because he was overwhelmed by a ghastly wave of negative thoughts. He couldn't specify this feeling, and though it was extremely unpleasant, he didn't take the time to analyse it.

"Why so anxious?" he asked and shuddered as he placed the book back in the box.

"It's dangerous . . ." Joel examined the Greek's face and added: "It contains knowledge that is better left in there."

Theodorus raised an eyebrow. Once again in his life, he heard someone forbidding him to read a book.

"What is it about?"

"I don't know. I really haven't read it—"

"Then why do you assume that it's not good?"

Joel frowned in distrust. He wondered if he should reveal what he knew or if it was better to end the conversation.

"There are certain instructions, and all the people in my family who have had this book in their possession have taken vows that bind us," he said finally, looking at him straight in the face.

Theodorus didn't react. He knew that prejudice against many doctrines made ignorant believers behave with hostility and unjustified fanaticism. He pursed his lips and waited for further explanation.

"It's a sorcery book. Real sorcery! And it's cursed—"

"Meaning what?" Under different circumstances he would have smirked, but the look on Joel's face, the tension in his eyes, and the lines on his forehead revealed that his fear wasn't the result of mere superstition, but had a real basis.

"Whoever read it met a tragic death."

"Is that a rumour dictated by the book or are you familiar with a certain incident?"

Joel fell silent and closed his eyes. It was obvious that he had difficulty deciding whether he should answer or not. Apart from the vows that restrained him, he couldn't trust a stranger.

"I don't want to upset you," conceded Theodorus. "Since you have taken a vow, I don't want to be the reason for your breaking it. I simply wanted to know, because the author's name has lately been associated with several bizarre incidents—"

"What do you mean?" Joel interrupted him, breaking his silence.

"There is information about gruesome killings and necromantic rituals taking place all over the kingdom." Theodorus noticed Joel's surprise and went on. It was obvious that the Jew knew things that he mentally associated with what was happening in the caliphate. "In the letter I received, there was the name of this author, Abdul Alhazred, whose name and work I know nothing about."

"What kind of rituals? Where?"

"Summoning of gods, I think."

The moment he heard the reason, Joel opened his eyes wide and then started thinking hard, his lips forming a line of displeasure. This affirmed Theodorus' guess.

"A few days ago, there was a massacre at the caravan station, south of Damascus, a day's travel from here," he added and could instantly recognise the panic his statement had caused his interlocutor.

Joel tried to get up, but the pain kept him in bed. He grasped at the sheets for a moment and then let go, disappointed at his weakness.

"What's wrong? Why are you upset? I think you should tell me."

Joel closed his eyes and remained still, as if he were praying. When he opened them again, he began talking slowly, with difficulty. He explained that the vows he had taken had to do with preserving the book, forbidding anyone from reading it, but also from the carrying out of the rituals it contains. He therefore didn't have a problem talking about the book and its author.

"Abdul Alhazred was a poet from Yemen, one of those dreamers who wish to change the world, make it more beautiful, and give it the fire of pure love, which appeases hatred. However, he bore a heavy curse since birth. According to what he has written, he was born dead. The midwife who delivered him was ready to bury him. Luckily for him, though, there was a wise man from Egypt in the city and he knew of an ancient practice for reanimation. That was how he survived.

"From a young age he was guided by the whim and fancy of lyrical verses; he embraced bewitching mirages and got drunk on the bittersweet taste of his desires. But at the same time, he was possessed by another power that had nothing to do with the Muses' gift: he had the ability to hear the voices of invisible creatures and see into the future.

"That ability made his fellow citizens in Sana'a expel him, even though they appreciated his poetry. Abdul was exiled and, troubled by the people's treatment toward him, decided to search for the reasons for his unusual gift. He longed to be normal, just like all the common people, and that need led him to learning, the pursuit of knowledge."

When Joel started his narration, despite the fact that he didn't go into much detail, it was as if he were confessing his own experiences and not those of a man who had lived centuries ago. Theodorus listened carefully, without interrupting him, but mentally forming some questions as Joel spoke.

The young poet began his search from Egypt. He headed to Cairo, where he conversed with omniscient white-haired ulamas in the shadow cast by the Pyramids. He went to Alexandria hoping to find lost relics of the Ptolemaic alchemists; he went up the Nile, in the regions of the Copts, to read the blasphemous books of the heretical Christians. He lived in the Sinai Peninsula, at the monastery that lay at the foot of the mountain where the god of the Jews appeared before Moses. At the great library of Saint Catherine he studied the Greek writings. He then took the road to the Persian plateaus, spoke with the few priests of Zoroaster, found ancestors of the Magi who sent him to the famous—but decadent—Babylon to meet the remaining Chaldeans, from whom he learnt about the stars and their secrets.

The knowledge he accumulated brought him even greater thirst, so he continued travelling and eventually ended up in India, with its many and strange deities, studying the writings of the Brahmans and indulging in the wisdom of Buddha's followers.

He wandered for many years and by the time he started to feel homesick, his hair had turned grey. That was when he decided that the time had come to perform his duty and go to Mecca for his pilgrimage.

One night during his trip to the sacred city, thieving slave-traders attacked his caravan. He was miraculously saved. Alone, with the little food and water he had managed to scavenge on the day after the raid, he went on his way.

When he ran out of water on the fourth day, he realised that he would die in the desert. He didn't know where the wells were or how far the oases were. His death was certain, but at night, when he stopped to rest, he saw a light glowing before him. With all the strength he had left and with the hope of survival resurfacing, he headed toward that bright place. His only concern was to survive, and he didn't even care if he met those unscrupulous Bedouin thieves again.

He proceeded, delirious, praying, staggering on the sand, until he reached the corner of a road where he fell on the paved road, dizzy and exhausted. When he woke up in the morning, before the hot Arabian sun came up, he noticed the pure white buildings that stood before him and knew that he was in the white City of the Pillars—the famous city of ancient demons, Iram, which is older than Atlantis, and whose name the Arabs whisper only in fairy tales, out of fear.

Abdul quenched his thirst with its water, satisfied his hunger with its food, and regained his strength, walked about its wondrous streets, thrilled to have been saved and also because he had discovered the secret mythical city where the knowledge of all the centuries is stored.

The City of the Pillars is deserted, dead, but at the same time alive. The Arabs say that it is inhabited by cursed genies, but Abdul did not meet any. He didn't see them, but he heard them. He heard the speech of demons, their howling, as he called it, and learnt all their secrets.

He didn't register how long he stayed in the City of the Pillars; time there doesn't move according to human terms. It could have been months or maybe years.

He was found wandering half-mad in the streets of Medina, reciting blasphemous verses, drinking animal blood, and foretelling indecencies and disasters. They called him the "poet of demons."

A compassionate old Bedouin took pity on him, brought him home, and cured him with exorcisms and salves. Abdul recovered from his "madness," but not entirely. Every once in a while he fell into trance, spoke with demons, and predicted what would happen to people.

The peaceful inhabitants of Medina, terrified by his words, decided to send him away from their city. It wasn't only because they feared his threats, but also because many hideous crimes had been committed. Children disappeared, adults were found brutally butchered, animals died for no apparent reason, and, worst of all, at night the fluttering of demons' wings could be heard.

Once again, Abdul was exiled in his own country. Wherever he went, they chased him away. In every city he looked for shelter, ghastly killings and catastrophes occurred. In Gaza the indignant citizens cut off his left arm, and in Jerusalem they threw him into the fire. He was saved at the last minute, but the burns on his face and body never healed.

His vagrancy took him to Damascus, the capital of the caliphate. That was when he finished his book, *al-Azif,* the *Howling.* In a stroke of reason, realising the evil he was committing by writing down all the secrets that demons had whispered to him and the details he had collected on his journeys, he left the basement where he was hiding and took to the streets, heading toward the only temple of Zoroaster not destroyed by Arabs when they took over the city. He believed that the pure, ancient fire would destroy the book, and the secrets it held would be gone forever.

He threw it in the sacred fire of the temple, but the book didn't burn. The eternal fire went out and the temple shook to the ground so intensely that the pillars cracked and the roof collapsed. The priests who tended to the fire of God, furious and terrified by the incredible incident, threw him out.

Abdul, devastated for not having been able to destroy his blasphemous work, found his way back to the city. When he reached the central market, right there, before the very eyes of dozens of people, the air was lacerated. Out of nowhere appeared spiky tentacles, scaly limbs ending in claws, and crooked beaks of black-coloured creatures. He didn't scream at their sight: the screams that were heard belonged to the people present. He didn't get a chance to scream. The demons attacked him and pulled him to pieces.

They tore him apart and devoured him in front of the panicked Damascenes. After they had finished their bloody task and disappeared again in the ether, all that was left to remind people that there was once a man named Abdul Alhazred were the black drops of blood on the dusty street and the book.

"Nathan ben Yova the rabbi," Joel pointed out, taking the narration to a more personal level, "my ancestor, who was at the *souq* that day, saw everything that happened with his own eyes. He was the one who picked up the book from the street, and he was the first person in my family who met with a tragic death.

"After that, the cursed book came into the hands of his brother, Elijah. Prudently, without yielding to the temptation of repeating the rituals, he wrote down the instructions and bequeathed it to his son. But Samuel didn't follow the rules his father had set. One night he disappeared as he summoned the guardian of the gate . . .

"The book was passed on to his cousin Isaac, who in turn left it to his son, Daniel. Daniel was found dismembered in his house basement, among strange hieroglyphics that he had drawn on the floor with blood. Once again, someone had tried to contact the demons . . .

"Daniel's son, Aaron, fearing that his children might read it, gave it to his cousin Benjamin, my great-grandfather. My grandfather was the last to read it. My father found him burnt in our cottage outside the city. In the notes he had kept, he wrote that he had renounced the god of our ancestors in order to embrace an Old One named Nyarlathotep."

Theodorus scratched his bristly chin, considering the information he learnt both about Abdul Alhazred and about Joel's family. The story of the Arab poet, even if wildly exaggerated, caught his interest, not in terms of the superstitious aspect, as he had expected, but the philosophical one. The idea of such a journey for the pursuit of knowledge had crossed his mind numerous times, but he had never attempted it. Thus, in his mind, Abdul was equal to a philosopher.

"He wasn't mad," he said pensively. "He was *salós*."

Joel didn't understand and looked at him in bewilderment. "What do you mean?"

"Abdul was *salós*. That is Greek for the 'sacred fool,' as the Christian call this; he's a man who can communicate with the divine. The laymen think of them as stupid or insane, but they're individuals with heightened senses and who can capture what we normal people don't have the ability to see or hear. Not knowing the meaning of *salós*, the Arabs called him 'mad.'"

Joel raised his left eyebrow. He wasn't much interested in the name the people give to such individuals. All he cared about was the bizarre and inhuman incidents that were happening.

"And what are those demons?" asked Theodorus, understanding that now was not a good time to analyse the facts. "I don't quite understand."

"My ancestor, Elijah, the one who left the instructions for the book, wrote few things. He hadn't read it himself and only recorded what he remembered from what his brother had told him. They are creatures of the stars, frightening and incredibly powerful. They can somehow travel here; and when they do, it's because they have been summoned by the ones who have the knowledge—that is, their subordinates, the sorcerers.

"They call them the Old Ones. Some of the names I can recall are Dagon, Nyarlathotep, as I told you earlier, Hastur, and Yog-Sothoth. Their great god Cthulhu is away, sleeping somewhere in the depths of the sea, waiting to return."

The words rang a bell in Theodorus' mind. Not the strange names, some of which he already knew, but those that defined the state in which their great god is. The similarity this report had with the surviving passages from the cursed Chaldean book was evident.

The god described in the *Chaldean Oracles* was named *Bythos,* the ocean bottom, and was sleeping far away, waiting for the right time to come back.

Theodorus was thunderstruck. His heart was beating so fast that he thought it would jump out of his chest. He opened his eyes wide, looked at Joel speechless, and then turned his gaze toward the box in which he had left the Arab's book.

Was it possible that he had earlier been holding the book that all the Empire's philosophers were looking for? Had he found the *Chaldean Oracles*? Was it there, in front of him?

Doubt kept him from believing that, and he first examined the facts. If he stripped Joel's story from its layers of superstition and utter exaggeration, the image of the *salós* Alhazred changed radically. The Arab wasn't a mysterious and strange man, but a philosopher who travelled through the world searching for wisdom. Eventually, in one of the places he visited, he found the forbidden book written by the Chaldeans in a dusty old library. All the evidence pointed to that version; even the words that the Jew used in order to prevent people from reading it were the same ones the Christians used.

The strong feelings that came over him made him stand and pace up and down the room. Joel was watching him without realising what had happened. He figured that those terrible events had disturbed him.

Theodorus' mind went to all those names he knew, the ones in the text and the ones Zeno had carved inside his sarcophagus. At the same time, the form of his colleague Andronicus Graeuses appeared like the ghost of a messenger. He recalled his research about the properties of sounds and associated it with the *Howling,* the title Abdul had given his book.

He felt dizzy. His head filled with colours, his temples started throbbing intensely, and his heart was pounding. There was no doubt; he was close to the book of his dreams.

Overcome by his thoughts, he didn't hear the footsteps on the stairs. Neither did he understand what Bashar was shouting at him in fear. It took him a few moments of disorientation, embarrassment, and selective deafness, before he took in his friend's words.

"Theodorus! They're coming for you!"

Bashar was adamant. He offered no option but escape. Ever since he heard that Harun al-Ghouta was leading his party of fanatics to the clinic, aiming to catch the Greek doctor who did business with the Jewish merchant, he had no doubt about what would follow.

"They'll kill you! Even if they don't, the new cadi will charge Leon with murder. You must leave now!"

They had very little time to spare. Everything had to be done fast and cautiously, just as in Constantinople, when they had heard that the guards had orders to arrest them. Nevertheless, there was some delay.

Rebecca didn't want to leave her father. She lay next to him, held him in her arms, and, teary-eyed, refused to abandon him.

"Daughter . . ." Joel suppressed the knot of sadness in his throat with great difficulty. If he hadn't, he would have burst into tears over their cruel fate. He didn't want Rebecca to despair or see him yielding at that moment. "I'm bedridden. If I come with you, you won't have enough time to exit the gate. They'll recognise us, arrest us, and kill us all. You have to go. You must be saved."

Rebecca refused. She hugged him tightly, wailing, her tears dampening his traditional Jewish clothes.

"Let me die in peace, child. Don't deprive me of the joy of knowing you'll be safe and alive. What kind of father will I be if, instead of saving my daughter, I let her die with me?"

His eyes were filled with tears, his voice breaking. He had dreams for Rebecca: he imagined her married to a gallant and righteous Jewish man, the grandchildren she would make him, his old age in her care, all those things a tired man desires before closing his eyes.

He gently kissed her on the head and gave her an encouraging pat on the back. "You've always been an obedient daughter; don't ruin this now. Deep inside, you know I'm right. There is no other choice. Besides, God is great and merciful. Perhaps nothing will happen; and when I am well, I can come find you, wherever you go."

"Our only choice is Cyprus. It's near and the journey will not be hard on us." Leon held Rebecca by the shoulders and pulled her away softly. His eyes were blurry. On the one hand, he felt guilty for all this, since he had caused this display of fanaticism; and on the other hand, he was worried about what might happen next. Their future was uncertain. If they stayed here, they would be captured, at least Rebecca, Joel, and himself. In their frenzy for revenge, the fanatics might even arrest Theodorus; it was a possibility he couldn't overlook.

But even their escape would be hard. They first had to get past the guards, which was only possible if they bribed them. Then, with one of the western harbours as their only way out, their journey seemed extremely difficult, especially if there was a searching party after them.

He tried to persuade Theodorus to remain in Damascus, not bind his destiny with his own, but his friend was adamant. As soon as he heard what had happened, he gave instructions and suggested solutions, as if he had had an escape plan ready for a long time. Leon thought it was likely, since they had discussed the possibility of their banishment from the city because they were Christians.

Of course, what Theodorus hadn't thought about was that they would have to travel with a woman. He came up with a solution to that issue as well. He asked Bashar to bring them one of Jasmine's dresses. When they were banished from Constantinople, they were dressed as monks; now, they would be disguised as Arabs.

"You must get dressed," Leon told Rebecca as he gave her the traditional attire of the women in Damascus and the burqa. He had already put on a thobe and a turban on his head.

He was left alone in the room with Joel, as soon as Rebecca went to the next room to get ready. He felt bad and he needed to apologise, to ask for forgiveness.

"It's not your fault, Leon," said Joel, guessing the doctor's intention. "This was bound to happen, sooner or later. They had been whispering it for years, and now it was time they put it into action. They were simply given a motive. The reason lies elsewhere. What worries me right now is—"

"I'll look after her," Leon interrupted him, knowing what he was about to say. "I'll respect whatever you command and I swear I will never do anything that could insult her."

"You're an honourable man, Leon. I owe you my life. I'm sure those two men would have killed me, but there are some things that separate us, chasms and walls. Under different circumstances—" He didn't finish his sentence because Theodorus entered the room.

"Are you ready? We don't have any more time," he said and looked worried. In the turban and thobe he didn't look at all like the professor monk of Damascus. He approached Joel and shook his hand.

"You pray for our fate and I'll be praying for yours."

"God is in favour of the modest and pious," smiled Joel nervously and squeezed his palm with both hands. "Go; hurry. Leon, don't let her come in. I don't want to see her in Arabic clothes. I've always been haunted by this thought: an Arab taking her away from me. I hated that. I wish to remember her . . . Go."

Leon shook his hand and then went to the door. He stood there a little before leaving, looked at him one last time, and shut the door. He had seen tears in his eyes, but his face was bright with a hopeful smile.

"Let's go!" he called to Rebecca, who was putting on the burqa. Her face was red with crying and tension. Her hot tears were rolling down her eyes and her soft sobs shook her chest.

He took her hand and led her to the stairs, but Rebecca fainted. He lifted her in his arms and took her to the yard, where Bashar had prepared a carriage for their escape.

"You still have time, Bashar," he heard Theodorus saying to their friend. "Just get some money."

Bashar smiled and shook his head. "I'm not going anywhere, Theodorus. No more moving for me. Besides, I'm not in any danger; I'm in my homeland, with my people. If I go back to the Empire, I'll be a foreigner again, an enemy. Swear that you'll write to me and let me know you're all right. Who knows? We might even meet again."

"You can count on that, my friend." Theodorus hugged Bashar and kissed him on the cheek. His eyes were filled with tears. He always thought he would leave Damascus and go back home, but he had never imagined the parting. He was losing his best friend and he knew it was virtually impossible to see him again.

Leon put Rebecca in the back seat of the carriage, helped Theodorus inside, and looked at Bashar. Without a word, they neared each other and hugged firmly.

"Thank God you came to Constantinople and became a real doctor," Leon teased him.

"I might not be as good as your grandfather, but I'm definitely better than you," Bashar said laughing and gave him a friendly slap on the back. They stood there hugging tightly, as if they didn't want to separate, but relentless time was pressing them and poisoned their thinking.

"Go," said Bashar hoarsely, pushing Leon away.

Leon jumped to the coach driver's seat and took hold of the horses' reins. He looked at his Arab friend one last time and then cracked the whip in the air. The two horses started moving, the carriage axles creaked, and the wheels started rolling on the paved ground.

"Till we meet again," he called as the carriage left the yard.

Bashar wiped away a tear on his cheek. He knew that he'd never see them again and it was hard for him to believe that they had parted so quickly. He stood there for a few moments, considering the sudden turn of events, remembered the happier times they had had together, and then, with his head low, went to Joel's bedroom. They both needed to talk and exchange positive thoughts about the future.

The raving Damascenes, thirsty for blood, revenge, and apparent justice, guided by the bigotry their muezzin had poisoned them with, wielding makeshift and real weapons, surged in the streets in front of the entrance of the clinic and mansion. With resonant and wild cries they demanded to get their hands on the Christian doctor who had killed Abbas and with the Jew's help injured poor Tariq. Their fervent voices shook the neighbourhood buildings and scared the bystanders to death.

In charge of the raging party, Harun was holding the green silk flag with the Prophet's words embroidered in golden thread. All the rapes, tortures, and killings that had happened earlier hadn't shaken him in the least; on the contrary, the craving for more violence was clear in his eyes, which were glassy with excitement.

Beside him, in a makeshift stretcher, carried by two strong men, was Tariq, who made a perfect impersonation of being heavily injured and about to die. He had no turban on his head, but a green kerchief with the phrase "death on the infidels" on it.

Hassan, one of the doctor's apprentices, got out of the clinic and carefully approached the raging crowd. Even though he had no reason to be afraid, those threats, rhythmically reiterated by hundreds of mouths, and the blood that was visible on some of their weapons haunted him.

Humbly he went near the muezzin, curtseyed, and in a trembling voice informed him that Leon had left Damascus an hour before. Inside the clinic there were only the doctor, the earthquake victims, and the patients.

Harun al-Ghouta opened his eyes wide at the news. The rage that stirred up his thoughts and actions blurred his vision. He found it disgraceful that the culpable had escaped, and the face of the person who had insulted him came to his mind. He turned abruptly to his docile followers and raised his hands high, asking them to be quiet.

At once, a fragile silence spread all over. All that could be heard was heavy breathing. They all stood and listened to their leader, clenching their teeth and fists.

"The Christian has escaped!" Harun cried, and an angry whisper, like a dragon slithering, rose through the air. "We'll catch him! Be sure of that! We'll catch him and hang him on the wall above the gate, so that every infidel can see that we follow the Sharia to the letter!"

Barbarous and festive clamour, mixed with prayers and wishes, shook the whole neighbourhood. Some people shouted something about a war against the *Nasraya,* others swore at and cursed them, but all of them stopped when they saw Harun signalling to them.

"I didn't want to believe it. You see, I'm but a humble man, a true descendant of this land and pious, just like you. I didn't want to believe that among us there was a snake, a traitor."

Bashar was behind the gate, listening to the muezzin's words clearly. When he looked through the window and saw the raging crowd approaching, he went to the yard to prevent anyone from entering the clinic. It hadn't occurred to him that Harun's insanity could ever turn against him. But when he heard the words "snake" and "traitor," he instantly knew.

"In our honoured city, tucked in its bosom, we've long been keeping a tainted man, a heretic, someone who loves Christians more than the people sharing his own faith. A rotten man who helped the killer escape. A corruptor who leads a sinful life, misleading prostitutes, offering fake services, deceiving us. Bashar ibn Fathi—"

"What kind of lies are you spreading, you ungodly man!" shouted Bashar in indignation, coming out to the street. "Have you lost your mind?"

Harun turned to Bashar and stared at him hard. His eyes glowed with rage and had a malicious glint of joy.

"That's the traitor!" he said, pointing at Bashar. "He loves Christians more than he does his own brothers!"

Bashar opened his mouth, but he made no sound. He felt an acute pain in his head, and everything turned red. All he managed to see was the rock that had hit him, rolling on the dirt.

He touched his forehead in surprise, as if he couldn't believe what was happening. His sleeve was soaked and his palm was filled with blood.

"Harun, you blasphemous—" he tried to speak, swear at him, curse him, but a second rock hit him on his chest and another one got him on his head.

Bashar dropped to his knees. Behind him a woman's cry was heard. Jasmine ran screaming, trying to protect her beloved.

"There's his whore!" shouted the ardent muezzin.

Jasmine held her beloved, kissed him on his bleeding head, and amidst her sobbing cursed at the muezzin for unjustly blaming an innocent man. The tears rolled hot down her cheeks and blended with Bashar's blood.

Right then, a group of ten bat-wielding Damascenes, yelling in frenzy, flung themselves upon the couple and began beating them furiously. Their angry roars overshadowed the pained groans of their victims' death rattle.

When they were done bashing them and stomping on the blood-stained bodies, they rushed to the yard. Others followed them. They all knew that there was another Christian inside and wished to get him.

Shouting and pushing, the apprentices tried to prevent the invaders from entering the clinic, but they barged inside the house. They hit, smashed, and shattered any object they found in their way. When they failed to find the Christian on the ground floor, they went upstairs, proceeding with their appalling work.

Two of them went into the room where Joel was resting. Judging from his hair and clothes, they knew immediately that he was Jewish.

They didn't hesitate for a moment. Their eyes throbbed with hatred, and they stabbed him repeatedly with their knives. Then, in their holy frenzy, they lifted his body and threw it on the street through the window.

6. Necronomicon

The persistent, hacking cough of the bishop of Adrianople interrupted Demetrius Meligrates' narration and brought him back to the patriarchate's boardroom of Constantinople. For a few moments, he stood there looking at the old high priest in confusion, lost in time and space, somewhere between the facts and the intensity of his emotions; but then, as his mind returned to the present, aware of the situation, he curiously waited for any reactions.

The bishops, also startled by the sudden interruption, turned to assist their colleague, ignoring the monk. Only Patriarch Theophylactus cast him a quick, indistinct look before calling to one of the servants.

"Are you all right? Do you want us to call a doctor?" asked the bishop of Nice with genuine interest.

The old white-haired priest shook his head. The stubble around his mouth was dripping with drool, and his forehead glowed with beads of sweat. He looked sick or at least overcome by exhaustion. He wiped his mouth with a white silk handkerchief and passed the back of his trembling left hand over his forehead.

His peer priests, concerned about the state of his health, asked him if he wished to retire to the guest room and have some rest, but he said no. He only asked for a warm, soothing beverage and looked at the bandaged Meligrates straight in the eye.

He wished to stay and hear everything that followed after the escape from Damascus. During the monk's recounting of Theodorus Philetas and Leon Peleuses' story, he had been carefully listening, without reacting. Twice he raised an averting hand when he noticed the rage bubbling within the bishop of Thessalonica, who, on hearing all those preposterous and distorted notions, had become enraged.

Once, when he was young, he was no different from his peers, where impulse and passion were concerned. Yes, there were times when he chased down any cult and distortion of faith, like a fanatic, a blinded zealot and fierce advocate of faith. As time went by, however, he realised that each individual has a personal view of God. Even the most faithful ones, his friends and relatives, processed theological matters differently. He was troubled by that discovery, being unable to comprehend the differences that lay inside every person, but he finally understood that if he kept pursuing those who were different from him, he would have to proclaim them all as heretical and blasphemous. Only the sycophants, who feared his power and would benefit from his help, embraced his religious point of view, without really adopting it—he was certain of that.

Since then, he had been lenient toward anything odd he heard, and instead of punishing, he learnt to advise people and make them see reason. After all, that was his purpose. This is how Jesus taught people to act. Not with swords and fire, nor with fear and threats.

Many times in his life he had regretted the mistakes of his youth. He had punished and condemned hundreds of heretics; he didn't have them killed, but he gave them pain, a lot of cruel pain, both physical and spiritual. He was guilty and felt sorry for his mistakes, and that's why he was more conciliatory now, in his old age.

Of course, all the things the monk had related about Philetas' beliefs were extremely heretical; there was no doubt about that. Nonetheless, he wanted to hear the rest of the story and how the disaster at Patmos took place, so he could form a complete picture of the two exiled Constantinopolitans' actions, as well as of the details recorded in the Arab's book.

In his understanding of theological matters, he remembered several of the cults of the first Christians, who had almost the same notion about God, demons, and man. And of course he was keenly aware of the Chaldeans and the Platonists, who tried to hinder the Word of Jesus with their pretty and unintelligible oratory. He had already thought of certain books by the Church Fathers which he would suggest that poor Meligrates read, so that he would be freed from deception.

"Do you wish we stop for a moment?" the bishop of Philadelphia, Justin, asked again. "Should we hear him another day when you won't be feverish?"

"No, don't worry. It's nothing serious. It's probably just a cold," he answered and stared at them, in a feeble attempt to show them he still had his strength.

The bishops and the patriarch obeyed and, reassured, sat back in their seats. Their demeanour was unreadable and their foreheads were not creased with any worry lines to suggest concern.

Meligrates was the only one seriously worried. That interruption for the bishop's health and the suggestion to resume the meeting another day troubled him. He thought that if they interrupted him one more time, he might never again have the chance to finish the story. Only he knew the urgency of time pressed upon him. The fear that they would lock him in a dark cell with the accusation of heresy made him nervous.

He realised that he shouldn't speak at such a great length and he needed to focus on the facts. Also, in order not to waste time, he would skip the details and stick to his purpose. All these thoughts stressed him even more.

"It's very obvious," said the Patriarch Theophylactus, addressing Meligrates, "that what you've recounted so far you only know by ear. You haven't referred to yourself at all."

At that realisation, the monk's eyelashes fluttered, and he looked at the patriarch in mistrust. They exchanged searching glances, since Theophylactus was also staring at him.

"That's right. I wasn't in Damascus. Leon told me all this when I met him in Patmos. I'm narrating everything he told me. I have no way of knowing if something is untrue or not."

The servants placed before the bishops three small tables on which they set platters with assorted fruit and nuts. One of them served mugs with beverages. But when he got to the monk, he kept his distance, shaken by his appearance, and handed him the mug carefully, so as not to touch his gloved hand.

Meligrates took the mug, but he didn't drink. He placed it next to him on the floor. He was nervous, and his instinct kept telling him that he didn't have much time.

"You may continue," said the old bishop after his fourth sip, feeling his chest getting warmer.

Meligrates examined the faces of everyone present, stopped jerking his right foot nervously, and took a deep breath. He knew that if the things they had heard so far had sounded heretical, the rest would definitely be considered satanic and infernal.

Escaping the squad that was after them was easier than they had thought. They only changed their course during their journey and instead of heading toward Beirut to the west, they took the road that led north to Homs and from there went to Latakia. But they didn't stay there either; instead, they headed further north, planning to reach a marine settlement where they could engage a fisherman to help them go across to Cyprus.

The fact that Cyprus didn't belong either to the Arabs or to the Empire was the main reason they chose it as their destination. The second reason was that the inhabitants were mostly Christians, so they wouldn't run the risk of yet another expulsion. And lastly, it was closest to the caliphate, even though they had trouble reaching it because of the many days of rough sea.

They were staying at a fishing village when they heard about the deaths of Joel, Bashar, and Jasmine. The news about the earthquake that hit Damascus and all the events after that had spread before they even got there, and so they heard about everything that went on in the city after their escape.

The rumour, according to the uneducated and biased fishermen, was that the Jews had caused the earthquake by casting spells, and as a result, the Damascenes sent them into exile. The Jewish sorcerer and his Arab accomplice, an evil doctor living with Christians for years, were both killed by the maniacal crowd at the clinic.

The news shocked Theodorus and Leon. Rebecca, devastated by deep sorrow, fell into depression and became ill. Later, when she had slightly overcome her mental anguish, she couldn't recall much of their stay at the fishing village.

Her grief was so deep that she forgot most events until they settled in Cyprus. But she could still remember Theodorus' paternal treatment and Leon's kind and protective behaviour.

After the continuous storms subsided, they sailed off in a felucca and disembarked on the eastern coast of Cyprus, which belonged to the Arabs. There they bought a carriage and headed toward the northern part of the island, which was controlled by local Roman lords. They only felt safe when they reached Kyrenia and changed attire, three weeks after their escape from Damascus.

They stayed at an inn outside the city's castle and relaxed with no one after them now. Since Cyprus wasn't under the emperor's reign but divided in provinces and ruled by Arab and Christian local elders, they sought out a place to settle. They hadn't yet decided if they would stay in Kyrenia.

The innkeeper informed them that, even though the island was neutral to the agreements between the caliph and the emperor, usually during the summer months the Hagarenes launch pirate raids on the outskirts and, more often than not, they reach the walls of the gate in an attempt to take over the city. None of them wanted to face such an unstable and dangerous situation.

From the information they gathered, they concluded that of the thirteen cities on the island, Paphos in the west was the most appropriate for them to settle in. On the third day they got ready to leave, but didn't.

The lord of Kyrenia, Nicolaus Kalligenis, upon hearing that one of the newcomers was a doctor, asked to meet them and pleaded with them to stay, generously offering them many things in exchange: a home inside the castle, servants, land, and animals. Tearfully he asked for their help, because both his sons needed immediate medical care.

Theodorus convinced Leon to stay and live in the safe and majestic castle, near the port. Kalligenis let them use a three-storey stone mansion and did everything he could to make their stay pleasant and comfortable. Simply by being in Cyprus, their mood changed for the better, especially Rebecca's and Leon's. The beauty of this island is so enviable and seductive that anyone who visits it falls in love with it; it is no coincidence that Aphrodite the Goddess of Love was born in its warm waters.

Cyprus, the enchanting Mediterranean island, had always been the most coveted trophy to any conqueror. Dressed in green, adorned in a myriad colours and shades, surrounded by that blue colour of the playful sea and the jolly sky, with high mountains, fertile valleys, fruitful plains, full of trees and with gurgling cool waters, it resembles a precious gem that every king wishes to have on his crown. This is the island's curse—its beauty. Like a gorgeous woman, whom many men desire and fervently fight for her love, all the people, even pirates, want to possess it. Its vast expanse, its natural richness, and its location entice the appetite of every aspiring suitor, making it seem almost like Odysseus' Penelope, whose love and fortune were coveted by all those men with their greedy and predatory instincts.

A week after they settled in Kyrenia, Theodorus moved to a farm near a fishing village, two hours away from the city. His excuse was that he needed an open and relatively isolated place, in order to prepare the siege engines for the city's defence.

Indeed, when Duke Kalligenis met with him, he asked him to supervise the defensive works and equip them properly. When the imperial army left Cyprus, the mechanics took the siege engines with them, as well as the projectors of the Greek fire, the ever-burning fire invented by one of the Empire's alchemists. Both the composition of the Greek fire and the construction of the pressurised projection siphons are secrets known by neither lords nor generals.

Leon didn't object to Theodorus' moving out. After all, he wished to be alone with Rebecca, whom they had presented as his wife, in order to avoid malevolent comments and the intervention of the zealous priests, who would rush to cause trouble and stir the citizens against the sinful and immoral foreigners who had come to their city. He didn't know that his friend had removed the forbidden book from the box, so he didn't suspect anything.

Theodorus didn't tell Rebecca that he'd taken it so as to avoid any objections. Nor did he mention it to Leon, because he knew the whims of a heart in love. Indubitably, his young friend would share the opinion of his beloved and would oppose him, so he chose not to disclose his deed until he was done reading it. He wanted to read it in peace, just as a grand philosophical work deserves to be read, and he wouldn't let anyone stand in his way.

During their time at the coast north of Latakia, he was burning with the desire to read it, but forced himself to be patient. He mourned Bashar while at the same time supporting Rebecca and Leon. They were both in a bad emotional state. Rebecca was sud-

denly left alone, with no relatives in a strange land with two technically strange men, while Leon blamed himself for the loss of Bashar
and Joel. When he had finally managed to lead them to safety, away
from danger, and when his spirit was calmer and saw them recovering, breathing in the daily rhythms of Kyrenia, he jumped at the opportunity that Kalligenis offered him and rushed to withdraw to the
fishing village.

Every morning for a long period of time, he oversaw the mechanics' work in the construction of the siege engines, and he occupied himself with the book only in the afternoons. He refused to
accept any kept servants, except two women who came in the
morning to do the housework and left with the workers at noon.

Also, every two or three days he visited the young couple at the
castle, had dinner with them, discussed daily matters, and left before
sundown. He tried not to raise any suspicions among both the
Kyrenians and Leon and Rebecca.

Only when he was all alone did he sit in his specially arranged
room and dedicate himself to the book, with no other thoughts
troubling his mind but reading and translating it. Even from its introduction, he knew it needed to be translated. In order to examine
it, to uncover the real ancient passages, the influences and the additional elements recorded by Abdul Alhazred, he had to translate it
in Greek.

He also considered its form. In the years he lived in Damascus,
he had comprehended the benefits and usefulness of paper in com-
parison to papyrus or parchment, and that's why he taught the
workers he supervised how to make it.

He believed that the *Chaldean Oracles,* that forbidden and long-
lost philosophical book, like the phoenix that rises from its ashes,
would be reborn in a new form and belong to every professor in the
Empire. However, from Arabic writing to Greek writing, from papyrus to paper, something new was born.

When he had obtained *al-Azif*, at a time when Joel wasn't watching, he did so in order to rescue a valuable work, where the meaningful Chaldean knowledge lay. A legendary book for scholars and a dream for the mystics; a piece of writing that contained the brilliance of Platonic philosophy together with the most secret doctrines of the Mesopotamian people: that's what he originally thought he had rescued from Damascus; the realisation that it was a different book came later.

He didn't read it hastily, but took his time to examine it meticulously, so he could comprehend and accurately translate the meanings. This painful process was completed nine months later. Nevertheless, he didn't give up on it, not even when he realised that it wasn't the Chaldeans' book.

From the very first verses, he was hooked on Abdul's writing skill, the direct and appealing way in which he passed on his knowledge and experiences, without complicating the sentences and meanings with secondary philosophical notions. In fact, the more he read on and translated, the more he probed into revealing secrets; as a result, in the seventh month, he stopped work altogether on the weapon construction he had promised.

Up till then everything moved in deceptive peacefulness. No one could tell that at night, when the workers left the farm to go back home, he not only read and translated, but also started performing some of the rituals recorded in the book.

The first to suspect that something bad was going on were the fishermen of the nearby settlement. But even they, reassured by the duke, most of them with innocent intentions and judgment, didn't act aggressively, except when it was already too late.

The storm broke out suddenly. In the last hour, nothing in the sky indicated that such havoc would follow. The expert eyes and knowledge of the locals didn't leave any room for error. They could tell that this phenomenon wasn't due to climate change, but to something else, which the most courageous of them could barely whisper, causing fear to the rest. "Curse," "sorcery," "demons" were the words, and everywhere were glassy eyes, frightened gasps, clenched teeth, terrified heartbeats, big, insecure hugs by the weak and at the same time protective ones by the brave.

Above the fishing village there was a blanket of threatening clouds, black, light grey, and deep purple. Their huge mass quaked and was torn by the consecutive thunders, which looked as if they wanted to tear apart their throbbing nest and burn down the whole world. Every thunderbolt caused fear, every lightning caused praying.

The cold wind roared, conquering everything in its passing; it wrenched straw roofs from the fishermen's huts, lifted them up, and twirled them around in the alleys or maniacally thrust them on the walls, along with all the branches and trees its wild fury had snapped. At the same time, heavy rain fell hard, as if wanting to pulverise the earth, and the waves tore through the angry sea, crashing into the coast with great force, as if planning to swallow it whole.

The marine village seemed ready to collapse, its streets were filled with water, and the house yards looked sunken. The occupants, shut in their typical two-storey houses with the outdoor wooden stairwell, astounded by the rage released upon them, knew that something bizarre was going on. They could sense it, their instinct was shouting it, but they kept silent. The justified fear above their heads held them captive, subdued. They were merely fishermen, illiterate and poor, tired from the whims of life, the daily struggle for a living and the blood-stained wars. On top of all the old troubles of these last few months, the fear of the supernatural came to be added.

At first, when Theodorus Philetas set up his house near their village, they were happy and felt safe having him as their neighbour. The lord of the castle had come in person and explained to them that the professor was going to assist in the area's defence by building machines that would protect them from the Hagarenes' raids. In addition, he knew the secret of the Greek fire, which they took to mean peace and progress, since the enemies would cower in fear, without venturing any more attacks against them.

Thus, in a short time, their sea-beaten village was transformed into a worksite. Every day, different men came from Kyrenia: ironmongers, builders, carpenters, and all kinds of professionals, who worked according to the plans of their new, educated fellow villager. It was a new situation that altered the boredom of their daily life, and during their spare time they had more things to talk about other than their everyday catch, the weather, or their rotten boats.

Pretty soon, though, almost three months later, many odd things started happening. At first it was the sounds. Every night, deafening raps disturbed the sky and tore through the air, like a thunderstorm. The thunders were angry and tremendous, as if suddenly the Devil had decided to ravage the world.

Naturally, the poor villagers jumped out of their beds and went to their yards to see the uncoiling disaster, but there was nothing to be seen. They could hear things, of course, but could see nothing alarming. In the end, they figured that all those sounds were coming from the works that probably went on at night as well. Even though the workers left at noon, they imagined that the professor kept experimenting on his own.

Then after the fifth month, there also appeared luminous displays in the sky. Weird iridescence, reflections of colours, mostly shades of red, took on several different forms above Theodorus' residence and moved or remained still, in a way that terrified anyone who saw them.

The villagers, though scared by what they witnessed, as they were ignorant, thought that all this had to do with the weapons that were being secretly built. They had heard of the Greek fire, that undying fire used by the imperial army and the navy to blaze ships and people. They also knew about the projection devices, those gigantic siphons that spew fiery jets at a great distance. However, they had never laid eyes on them, since both the secret weapon's composition and the designs for the machinery were unknown to all citizens, including the officials.

One of the reasons they couldn't tell the difference was that Cypriots, in general, hadn't seen Greek fire ever since the emperors gave up every attempt to retake control of the island—that is, about forty years earlier. So, even though they quivered at the events, they were also filled with amazement and courage that with such a weapon in their possession, the Hagarenes would forever cease the fighting.

The mysterious incidents went on, but as time passed, and as a result of their repetition, the horror they caused lessened, and the locals went ahead with their hard reality, their daily struggle for survival. Then a third phenomenon awoke their fears again and dispelled every doubt and dissent they had, since it was in no way justified by the works of their so-called saviour.

In the beginning of the tenth month since Theodorus' arrival, late in the afternoon, most of the villagers rested in their yards, as they usually did during summer evenings, discussing the daily news, with no suspicion of the events that would follow. The villagers who lived near Theodorus' farm heard a strange murmuring emerging, like a repetitive chant—a monotonous, deep sound, like well-water gurgling, making them shiver.

An odd feeling of threat enveloped them. Even the farm animals, dogs, hens, donkeys, and cats behaved nervously, terrified by an invisible, imperceptible danger. This lasted for as long as the anomalous chant could be heard.

Then, as soon as that stressful whisper stopped, above Theodorus' farm the sky began to tear, as if by the violent thrust of a divine sword; where the colour was dark blue from the sunset, the tear revealed an intense blackness. Simultaneously, the whole area was shaken by consecutive tremors.

The people who were near and had visibility could see, through that rift in the sky, dozens of black shapes darting out, like large raindrops, most of which fell into the sea. At the same time, an appalling smell flooded the area—the reeking stench of decomposing flesh.

The animals bolted. The ones that weren't tied to something ran away and vanished in the fields; many others were injured and some of them were killed trying to get out of their cages or break free from the ropes they were tied with.

In less than two heartbeats, the rift closed again and the sky was once again whole, but that is when the first panicked cries were heard. Those who were facing the sea were the first to view the chilling sight. It was very clear, and at once the men were naked of all bravery that defines a seaman. Not wasting any more time, they grabbed the women, the children, and their elder parents and took to their heels, toward the plains, to the hillock outside the village, where stood the small church of the patron saint of seamen, Saint Nicolaus.

They didn't pause for a minute to think or examine what had happened. They left panicked, dragging along those who were unaware of the incident. Those who witnessed the sight reported that the black shadow-like creatures emerged out of the dark green waters the way the sea caresses the shore—just as the waves sweep and roll the pebbles away.

Indeed, the creatures, polymorphous and multi-limbed—if, indeed, those things were limbs—left the sunless depths of the sea and, unruffled, crawled to the shore. They didn't technically have a body; they looked like real shadows, only they moved autonomously, sometimes quickly, sometimes slowly, like skilled hunters looking for a certain prey.

Scores of shadowy entities swarmed through the village, stealthily and threateningly. They slithered across the ground, undeterred, not minding the men, animals, or other obstacles in their way. They crept up the fences, the low walls, past the ditches, crawled under the door cracks, and all together headed toward Philetas' farmstead.

Some people felt their touch, an icy and slimy feeling, like touching an eel or limpets on the rocks. The dumfounded villagers quickly realised that when those shadowmorphs came in contact with living things, either pets or humans, a sort of stinky mucus was left on them, like a mark, causing them even more horror.

From the hillock where they had gathered, petrified and silent, they noticed that the crawling black shapes went up to Theodorus' farm boundary, stood for a few minutes looking for a way in, and then, as if something had prevented them, they all went to the village cemetery, where they disappeared behind the low picket fence surrounding the graves.

That night they all stayed up inside the church. No one was brave enough to return home; even the children, despite their needs, sensing the threat, didn't complain for having to sleep outdoors with empty stomachs.

In the sunlight of the next day they went back to the village; the horror of what they had seen was written on their faces, and their hearts were beating erratically. They knew that the danger was not over, thus many of them packed their belongings and hastily moved to the city. The ones who stayed behind demanded that the community priest order Kalligenis to send away his favoured guest, who was probably the culprit for all those incidents.

The priest and all those who escorted him to Kyrenia met with the duke at noon. Even though they expressed themselves flamboyantly, using words like "sorcery," "demons," "ghosts," and "damned souls," they refrained from depicting Theodorus in such a way as to appear biased against him. They did, however, demand vehemently that he leave in order for the tragedy to be prevented.

The reply they received wasn't the one they had expected. Kalligenis didn't believe a word his boorish subjects said. In a stern voice, he stated that they had to suffer through the noises and the flashes, because the professor was at the final stage of his project. He didn't refer to the shadowmorphs; he disregarded them as if they were but mere fantasies, even though they had appeared twice in the village; both times it was at six o'clock in the afternoon.

From that day forward, the desperate villagers shut themselves at home and avoided the "sorcerer's farmstead," as they called it among themselves. They filled the streets with makeshift wooden crucifixes; they burnt incense daily on every crossroad and wrote spells on the walls, the doors, and windows of every building to ward off evil.

The most courageous decided to take the law into their hands, but wavered to put their plan into action. They stalled both out of fear and because they were waiting for the bishop to return from a pilgrimage to a monastery in southern Cyprus. They had laid all hopes upon him. They knew that he would sympathise with them and oppose the duke, who had worked with a heretic and necromancer.

But as long as the bishop was away, few had the courage to live under that daily fear, fatalistically waiting the attack of the demons who often appeared in the village. Even the most natural things— simple sounds, ordinary human or animal actions—were now reasons for panic.

The storm that broke out in the morning wouldn't normally terrify them; they would of course wonder, but they wouldn't be startled at its cause. But now it was clear to everyone that the village was surrounded by demonic forces and that the only defence in case of an attack, apart from flight, was prayer.

Amidst the sound of the thunderstorm, from inside barricaded houses, there could be heard loud supplications to the Virgin Mary, the Saints, and Jesus' angels. They pleaded for protection and, at the same time, proof of faith and repentance.

She stood in front of the window and looked at the threatening black masses covering the sky. Surprised, she watched the lightning, which wasn't vertical, but stretched out and branched away in the clouds horizontally. That odd sight impressed her but also frightened her. Instinctively, she raised her right hand over her chest and shuddered at the thought that something bad could happen to Leon. She still wasn't over her father's death and she was certain that one more fatal blow would finish her off.

Rebecca closed her eyes in sorrow and begged God to protect her beloved. Her intuition told her that something bad would definitely happen to Leon. She sensed the danger, could see it, and her instinct throbbed with it, which is why she couldn't rest.

From the moment she had heard about Theodorus' deeds, her thinking focused solely on hideous outcomes. She had sworn never to read that cursed manuscript, ever since she had learnt to write, when she was still a little girl and her mother and siblings were still alive. In fact, her father often asked her if she had broken her vow; she always said no, and every time he kissed her on the forehead affectionately, glowing with the joy that all parents have when they see that their child is obedient.

Of course, she had thought of reading it, but she stifled her desire, recalling the example of the first created woman, Eve. Not only would she commit a sin by reading it, but she also worried that her action, a pure result of her curiosity, might bring harm upon her family.

She considered the matter, the irritating internal voice that every day whispered, "read it, read it," as practice for forbearance and self-discipline. She had emerged victorious from that, and that's why she was so angry at Theodorus. She couldn't conceive his action, understand the reasons why he not only had read and translated that book but also performed all those unholy necromantic rituals.

It was impossible for her to explain why the otherwise prudent professor, disregarding the dangers and taking nothing into consideration, was overcome by temptation and surrendered to a temporary desire. For her, even touching the cylindrical manuscript was enough to make her quiver and refrain from reading it.

Such was her fear and revulsion that in time she decided to leave it there, buried inside that hiding place so that her children would never find it when she would eventually inherit it. Even the status of a mere keeper was like a curse to her, an infectious disease that had to be eliminated once and for all. She could only explain all those deaths of her family members through curse and disease. So she thought that the best solution, since she couldn't destroy it, was to leave it hidden so that its existence would be forgotten. Maybe not in the same place, for she knew the filthy tricks of fate, but somewhere she would put it herself. She didn't intend to possess it nor keep it. But now she blamed herself for taking it along with all those other rare books when she left home and forgot about its existence all this time, as if she hadn't seen or heard about it in all her life.

She went to shut the window, but paused. Her glance stopped on a guard at the walls who, leaning against a turret, watched the turmoil in the sky, that grand destruction of Nature.

The incredible storm that broke out west of Kyrenia caught everyone's attention. The sky seemed divided in two; on the one side it was grey-black and shattered by orange flashes, while the other, over the city, was calm and white-blue, since it neither rained nor was there a harsh wind blowing.

That odd antithesis—the horizontal lightning and the guard on the walls, resting his spear on his thigh—made her realise that she had seen that image again in one of her dreams. Instantly, her mind flared up with dark thoughts.

From the first month they had settled in the city, weird dreams disturbed her sleep and terrible nightmares frequently woke her up. At first, she hid her torture from Leon and tried to overcome her problem on her own. She believed that it all had to do with her recent tragic experiences, so she often cried over her bad fortune, the banishment of the other Jews, the escape from her homeland, and the death of her father.

During the time of that severe depression, Leon comforted her in every possible way, winning her heart. Even when they settled in the castle, under the same roof, like a married couple, he respected her mourning. His every move, his words, and the warmth in his eyes indicated that he sympathised with her and understood her agony.

They made love for the first time after four months. She was the one to request it, because she needed to be loved, to experience a connection and enjoy life in spite of its ugliness. And she did feel all that.

Her life was refreshed by a new, joyful wind, the world lost the grey hue that surrounded it, and another, more optimistic future began to appear before her. Everything pointed toward a happier outcome, foreshadowed something beautiful and blooming, like a blossoming field in the springtime. It was love, of course, that developed day after day by cultivating a strong bond, always in harmony with the place and the people.

Her eyes didn't sink into the golden sand anymore, or the colourless sky and surroundings that dominated Damascus, but swam in bright blue and green, the lively colours of Cyprus. *Khamsin,* the hot, dusty desert wind, didn't blow here, sweeping everything away with its sickening, dry force, but cool and refreshing gentle winds, carrying the sea breeze and the rich smells of thriving Nature. All this urged her, in spite of the pain for her loss, the sorrow of her uprooting, and the grief of loneliness, to dream and start breathing freely. But once again the landscape was altering; it began changing and the dream was transforming into a nightmare.

During that whole time, entirely surrendered to her personal desires, her love, she hadn't noticed the changes in Theodorus, nor his movements. She hadn't suspected anything alarming, but now, aware of his deeds, she was convinced that the bad ending to all the joys she had experienced was coming toward her forcefully and revengefully. This always happens to people when they think they have finally found peace in life: they dread the moment when a sudden, yet imminent, storm breaks out.

Her fears were not unfounded. Especially not after that dark occurrence two nights before, when she woke up drenched in sweat, feeling that she was drowning, and saw that living horror sitting on her back. Everything she had heard or read about demons, the fright she had while sleeping or when she was awake, was nothing compared to what she underwent when she noticed the shape on her, paralysing and suffocating her with fear. She thought she was drowning, but this feeling was not the worst of it. The worst for her was that she was unable to move, do something to save herself, or even call for help.

When the black creature left her and vanished, she got up in panic and woke Leon up. She needed his protective arms around her. His soothing words and reassuring caresses soon calmed her down; but when she recounted what had happened, she saw the fear in his eyes, because, as he explained, that same shadowy creature had also appeared to Bashar, in Damascus. Several thoughts crossed their minds, and they all had to do with the rumours circulating throughout the city about Theodorus' witchcraft ceremonies or his unholy alchemistic experiments.

She couldn't know the truth, but her worry gushed out like lava from a volcano. She was positive that it was all because of the book, and that the terrified villagers coming to the city were right to have asked for help.

With hasty, nervous movements, she shut the windows closed. She regretted letting Leon leave alone. She too wanted to hear everything that had happened or that *would* happen. But most of all, she shivered at the thought that something bad would happen to her beloved. She couldn't bear to think that, and she couldn't sit and do nothing. That's why she decided she should act and show courage, in order to prevent any bad outcome.

Little Vasiliki packed her few toys inside a makeshift bundle and looked at them, frowning. She was sure that something was missing, but she couldn't remember what. She turned to the window, where her nightstand was, and at once her eyes gleamed with joy. She had forgotten her talisman.

She rushed there, opened the small door, and happily took the little cloth icon with the golden-red thread. She kissed it reverently and wore it around her neck with pleasure. Reassured now, she looked through the skylight at the flooded street, and her peace was disrupted: a dark silhouette was slowly moving outside the house.

Seeing that big creature, she screamed at once and, holding tightly to her talisman, she crouched in the corner on her right. She too had seen those mysterious shadowmorphs that had shown up in the village lately. In fact, one of them had moved over her left foot, covering it with foetid, greenish mucus. Her mother, terrified by the rumours, took off her clog and sock and threw both in the fireplace. Since then, she burned incense six times a day in front of the icon stand, loudly reciting the Lord's Prayer.

When her father heard her screams, he ran from the kitchen and lifted her up in his arms. Perplexed, cold sweat dripping down his forehead, he carefully peered through the shutters. It was still morning; noon was two hours away; so he wondered whether those black spirits had changed habits and started appearing in the light of day.

He couldn't see very clearly, because of the heavy rainfall and thick fog enveloping the village. Despite that, the experienced fisherman knew that the shape in the street wasn't an evil creature, but a horseman, covered in a dark-coloured leather greatcoat.

His guess was confirmed as soon as he heard the animal's shaky whinnying. Relieved, he turned to Vasiliki, who was shivering in his arms, and kissed her fondly.

"It's a human, my daughter, don't be afraid," he said soothingly and put her down on the floor. "Go pack your things and don't dawdle. We're leaving for the city this afternoon."

Vasiliki did as she was told. She too longed to leave the village. Besides, out of the fifty families living there a few days ago, there were now only twenty left.

Leon turned his head to the house from where a girl's scream had been vaguely heard and, with his left hand, lowered his hood to his nose. He didn't see anything alarming and continued on his way. The heavy rain had already soaked his overcoat, drenching his hair and soaking his skin. All he cared about was reaching Theodorus' house as soon as possible, so he spurred his horse onward. The restless animal waded through the mud. It acted scared. Its eyes bulged, and it snorted constantly and moved with difficulty as if it could sense some unseen threat.

He clenched the reins in his right hand and forced the horse to follow the path he had ordered. He could tell that the storm had caused the animal to fear, but he didn't want to stall for more time. He was already late and also very cold.

The raging stormwater dragged a poorly constructed wooden crucifix before him, while another one, lodged in the ground, had been knocked sideways by the force of the wind and would soon fall in the middle of the street. On the walls, the spells written by the villagers, either in coal or in whitewash paint, had faded and the paint dripped as it was washed away by the raindrops.

He mentally cursed Theodorus for choosing to stay away from the city. At the same time he felt angry at himself for allowing it, even though he couldn't possibly know nor foresee the future.

When they had arrived in Cyprus, everything seemed auspicious. Nothing could prepare him for these developments. He wasn't aware then of the fact that Theodorus had taken the bag of books with him and that the real reason he wished to live in isolation was to study *al-Azif*. Also, he didn't know that before leaving Bashar's clinic he had also packed the Mnizurin along with his things. He learnt all that when he paid a visit to his friend and pressured him to confess his doings, because the gossip and the rumours circulating the city and the village about unholy rituals and strange phenomena were no longer discussed in silence, but aloud, supported by the priests and also by Kalligenis' political adversaries, who looked for an opportunity to take over the power. The whispers he had once ignored had now been transformed into roaring shouts, war trumpets, calling the people to fight.

Even though he didn't believe a word that the Kyrenians accused Theodorus of, he unsuccessfully tried to chase away their fears. However, suspicious of his unusually long isolation, he decided to visit him and force him to speak to him. Thus, only yesterday did he find out about the truth.

"What is the truth, Theodorus?"

On the second floor of his home, in the room he had transformed into a study, he was sitting in an armchair with his face buried in his hands. The windows were shut, but the sounds of the storm could be heard clearly, and the trembling shadows of the candles moved on his forehead like living things; a play of the light, like a battle for prevalence.

His face had changed a lot: it was now marked by deeper lines than the ones he had in Damascus, and his hair was whiter, as if he had aged suddenly during the months he spent in Cyprus. But what was completely different was the look in his eyes. Anyone who had known him before could tell the difference, the change that had occurred, the burden of the worry that was crushing him. He used to be known by that mature glow of someone who has lived a full life; but now he showed the fear of the weak initiate, who had just discovered secret disastrous truths. Before, anyone could clearly see innocent optimism in his eyes; but now whoever looked at him could see that he was saddened by impending catastrophe.

Theodorus shut his eyes in annoyance. The corners of his lips lowered and his fingers pressed his cheeks. He couldn't escape the question he was posing to himself, nor avoid hearing it over and over again; that monotonous, compulsive, and demanding question. It was impossible to lie, mislead, and divert his own conscience. Although he knew the answer, he didn't have the nerve to admit it, or even accept it. Miserable, he pressed his temples hard and clenched his teeth.

Instead of an answer to the burning issue posed, other questions intruded his internal dialogue. Questions of self-criticism lanced his thinking, sometimes defensively, other times aggressively, in an attempt to justify and blunt his deeds and intentions. But that question was constantly posed with torturing punctuality.

"What is the truth, Theodorus?"

Everything is relevant, but also different in the end. Similar, but also dissimilar. It was obvious that Abdul knew the philosophers' theories, their deceit and their false view on the subjects they developed. They tried to approach the truth using their fanciful reason, while he already possessed it. He didn't lightly touch it with his fingertips; but, holding it in his hands like a doctor holding his patient's heart, he revealed its workings and its purpose.

Indeed, the poet of demons, the Mad Arab, could see and hear things that Nature had kept from ordinary people. That was, after all, the difference between him and the philosophers; he had died and come back to life, thus learning the secrets of life and death, while the others were breathing people who simply guessed, imagined, and conjectured.

Abdul knew the laws of the dead, the essence of life and the workings of the darkness. He had come back from the dead twice, gaining knowledge of the stream of existence; the first time was right after his birth, since he'd been born dead, and the second time he died and then was reanimated in the streets of legendary Iram, the City of the Pillars.

A thunder interrupted Theodorus' course of thinking. He glowered at the window and then observed the position of the furniture.

On his left was the lectern on which was the cylindrical papyrus of *al-Azif*, open and kept in place with wooden pincers. Next was the small table with the inkwells, the quills, the pounce and blotting paper, the pins for the perforation of the sheets, and the rulers for writing in a straight line. Next to the table, on the second lectern, the breeze that entered from under the door ruffled the pages of the translated text.

The flames on the candleholders swayed irregularly and persistently, like orange creatures trying incessantly and tirelessly to free their tail and go up in the air. That image reminded him of humans, who struggle to live and survive, yet knowing that they are held captive by death.

"What is the truth, Theodorus?"

The question rattled him, like a twinge, deliberately reiterated to disconcert his soul and force him to confess—a type of self-punishment or revenge for his actions.

At first, as he was translating Abdul's records, he doubted their veracity. Having studied at the University of Magnaura, with knowledge of philosophy and theology, with views as solid as a granite rock, he found it impossible to believe what he read.

The poet from Yemen's Sana'a didn't record a philosophical theory, nor did he confide unholy—for the religious—ceremonies; but in an almost blasphemous mood, he uprooted every empirical principle established by people since the beginning of time. Not even divine rules were undisturbed by the whirlwind of information mentioned; on the contrary, they were altered, doubted, and brought down by a single touch, like sand castles, collapsing after the water reaches them. Even the nature of reality was transformed through the rituals he dictated.

Al-Azif provided answers to the questions of philosophers, theologians, and alchemists. But the answers were such that anyone would have trouble believing or wouldn't believe until verifying them. And that's exactly what he did.

He started experimenting with sounds and their properties. He shuddered at the thought of a mistake, was nervous about the outcome, but he wasn't intimidated or diverted by fear of the unknown. He got out of the house in the evenings, performed the rituals, and confirmed the truth about everything he had heard and once believed to be fairytales or legends. Using certain sounds, he managed to make flower buds bloom or make trees grow; he changed the course of the clouds and finally contacted creatures that lie in the dark and listened to that ill-sounding "howling of demons," just like Abdul.

There was truth in the stories about Orpheus, "the father of song," and about Pythagoras, who revealed the secret doings of the stars. These stories had been slightly altered, but they were still true.

Many times, as he read it, he had wished for Nicephorus Peleuses and Andronicus Graeuses to be there with him. Perhaps because his thoughts lingered on their theories, he insisted on reading and translating the text because the mystery of time, the properties of sound, the rifts in space, the gift of prophecy, the gods and the demons, everything, but above all the issue of the raising of the dead and what follows death were all connected, analysed, and explained in the book.

Al-Azif wasn't the *Chaldean Oracles;* but he knew, he was certain now, that if he ever found the real book by the Theurgists, it would be a miniature, almost a bad copy of the Arab's work. Even so, he didn't know if he was lucky to have discovered it or not. Assuming there are many worlds in the universe is one thing; having proof of it is another. Referring to demons abstractly is different from actually meeting and controlling them. Likewise, living with a faint idea of coming back from the dead is completely different from being able to *bring* back the dead!

The laws of the dead didn't derive from the *salós* poet's morbid imagination. Most people talked about their existence, undoubtedly accepting them, while many used them both in theory and practice, letting them define their daily routine.

Everybody in the world knows about life after death. It's a conviction found everywhere, from faraway and mystical India to the Christian and Arabic kingdoms in the west, where Africa and Europe border with the infinite ocean. All peoples and nations, all cults and religions have referred to the human soul and the resurrection. An unshakeable, ancient certainty, which is shrouded by many dissimilar local beliefs, religious doctrines, and philosophical theories that, despite sharing the same root, are transformed and blended according to the perception and knowledge of those making these claims.

Abdul, however, with what he recorded, cleared the disarray of theories, shed light to the darkness of mystery, solved the enigma of life, and clarified the faults in the approach to the issue. Of course, to the devotees of any religion or philosophical doctrine, especially the ignorant and God-fearing folk, his work seems blasphemous, heretical, and maliciously supernatural, because on the one hand it refutes all current knowledge and, on the other hand, it offers all those macabre details for the confirmation of its claims through hideous and inhuman ceremonies. He wasn't the one who thought of them, but they were enforced by the otherworldly overlords of humanity.

Before Theodorus read *al-Azif,* reality had seemed simple, almost monolithic, like two separate pieces, one painted black and the other white. But now, just like confirming the alchemic rule of the combination of the elements, it looked more complex, like a painting with no image, but whose two halves are painted in blue and yellow and in the middle, where the colours blend, green emerges.

Without realising it, totally unexpectedly, word for word, paragraph after paragraph, enraptured, he walked into worldly secrets; and although his mind was alight with the influx of knowledge, at the same time the knowledge darkened his reality and threw him into a sunless abyss.

Abdul, the "traveller of the two worlds" as he called himself, the traverser of life and death, according to what people think is true, recorded everything he saw, did, and heard being whispered by the dark-dwelling creatures of infinite space, what the fearing people call "demons." Only they aren't demons, but living things that possess power and knowledge beyond any reason and natural law.

The simple folk, deep in ignorance, prisoners in a world of enforced limitations and regulations, insignificant and weak before the creatures of other planets, from that distant time when they contacted them, called them gods, became their pawns, and worshipped them, because of their superior powers. It was only natural for primitive man, who lacked special skills and gifts apart from his uncontrollable mind, with fire as his only weapon and a few wooden and stone tools assisting him; he couldn't confront the otherworldly visitors that had come to conquer his world, and therefore, he became their slave.

Luckily for humanity, those senior gods once battled with some other creatures, which the mystics named the Old Ones. The reverberation of their terrible conflict left its mark on the people's memory, and so, in the several national mythologies, this is referred to as the great war of the gods of antiquity.

These creatures, knowing about the rifts in time and space, travelled from their distant astral worlds using their superior technology, which, in the eyes of humans, seems like witchcraft. It might be that, since its meaning is inconceivable.

After their titanic clash, some of them retreated, hid in secret places, away from people, while others went back to the stars, planning on returning when the time was right. The relative lull that followed offered humanity the chance to develop and evolve.

People never forgot their overlords, whom they took for gods, especially some groups of faithful worshippers. These latter, because they have hopes for the return and dominance of these overlords, try to summon them again, open up the gates of the rifts in space, and fight night and day to make their dreams come true. All over the world, these unholy subordinates struggle for their masters' comeback and perform rituals with that exact goal in mind.

Similarly, many of these ethereal entities long to return and take over the world again. They choose individuals to communicate with them through dreams and manipulate them so that the right circumstances are formed for their comeback.

Abdul stresses that death is not the end, but a mere gate to other worlds. That element, which the philosophers called "soul," that immortal part of our body, ruptures natural laws, surpasses their limits, and travels in space in order to transform into other realities. This condition is only known by those who have come back from the dead.

By knowing this detail and also the science of astral creatures, any mystic can raise the dead. The method may strike one as magical, but it is actually based on natural laws that ordinary people fail to grasp, either because they haven't discovered them yet or because they haven't studied them properly.

All religious and philosophical doctrines are aware of this truth, that is, the continuation of existence after death and the possibility of resurrection; even Theodorus' favourites, the Platonic philosophers, talked about the soul's detachment from the body at the moment of death and the journey it makes. They just offer this knowledge to common people in fragments and in an unclear way—not only because all those who mention it haven't experienced death, but also because the stream of existence must not be disrupted. The mystics themselves don't disturb the worldly balance, unless they intend to rupture it in order to impose their own power.

According to Abdul, the stream of existence has a purpose, and whoever artificially restores the soul in a dead body creates a chain of anomaly in the universe of the creatures. The Old Ones, desiring to cause chaos, passed their knowledge on to their subordinates, in order to inflict a complete disaster and put an end to the current harmony. That is when the prophecy of doomsday shall be fulfilled.

"What's the truth, Theodorus?"

The truth, what his own self demanded to know, was that while reading and translating *al-Azif—The Manuscript of the Dead*, as Joel's ancestors called it—he didn't confine himself to the philosophical examination of the text but, fervently wishing to confirm Abdul Alhazred's sayings, performed some of the rituals. He didn't just re-animate a dead creature, but also did something even worse: he opened a rift in time and space, by unlocking a gate through which the astral creatures managed to come into our world.

The raindrops fell heavily on Leon's head and shoulders as his lips and skin were blue with a cold wind that was anomalous for the time of year. The previous night, due to the summer heat, he and Rebecca had slept on the stone floor, with every window in the house open, and now he was shivering with the winter cold.

Of course, he knew the reason for this sudden change in weather. When Theodorus had confided in him what he had been doing these last few months, Leon didn't believe him. He couldn't accept all the outrageous and incredible things he was telling him, and as a result Theodorus made a "little" demonstration of the forces described in the book he had translated.

Now, as he was facing the angry wind and the heavy rain, with his frightened horse stopping every now and then, disobeying him, Leon tried to remember all his friend's insane and completely heretical words, which sounded more like a madman's delirium than the words of a sane, educated man.

As a matter of fact, he hadn't forgotten them; on the contrary, he remembered every word, even though he showed suspicion. Ever since he was a little boy, he had learnt that the thinking process should walk hand in hand with reason, and that he had to explain the facts through their causes. That's why he insisted, like a Doubting Thomas, on "putting his finger into the print of the nails." As a result, Theodorus proved everything he had claimed.

Leon had mockingly asked for a demonstration, maybe as a joke, because of the impossibility of the situation, but inside he could already feel his view being contradicted. He could still remember clearly Joel's look when he had spoken about the book, that combination of fear, despair, and sternness, but his beliefs were even more shaken when he saw his friend's look yesterday; there was a glint, a dark and omnivorous force that unsettled him. Even his words had a tone of stability and a calm vibration that excluded the possibility of a lie. And Leon knew very well when somebody was lying. He had learnt it all those years working with people as a doctor and understood when someone alters or conceals the truth.

"Tomorrow, after you exit the walls of Kyrenia to come here and by the time you get inside, I'll have changed the weather to a winter storm," Theodorus had told him with absolute certainty, adding that this demonstration was the most harmless he could give without any cost in human lives or property.

Leon shuddered when he heard it, but he also shuddered now, below the rain that had transformed to sleet. Only the word "witch-craft" could describe the wondrous aspect of the phenomenon. However, since he was used to their talks all these years, having practised investigation and method, he constrained himself and didn't let himself be lost in superstition. Besides, Theodorus himself had told him that "everything looks like magic, but it's not."

It was impossible to grasp what he had heard, erase any knowledge he had about the world, either by experience or in spirit, shatter every standard and on top of the ruins to place the likely figment of an Arab poet's imagination. On the other hand, every-thing that seemed incoherent and unconnected was now united and blended in harmony; this condition provided the book with, if not originality or unprocessed truth, at least authenticity.

Leon was definitely confused and silently admitted that he was afraid of everything he had learnt. Not so much of the astral crea-tures that aim to rule the world as of knowing how to raise the dead and the anomaly in balance this would bring.

All the years he had been helping people not to die and live long lives, he saw the different forms of death many times and had pon-dered on it. He understood the difference between life and death, but also the imbalance that resurrection presupposes. His grandfa-ther may not have had the same opinion and he indeed might have been looking ways to revive the dead, but to him such a perspective seemed unholy and disastrous for the laws of life.

This internal mental struggle continued even as Leon left the narrow village streets heading toward the farm. The sleet kept falling, and his fingers were blue with cold. The first snowflakes started dropping on his cape sleeves, and his teeth clattered unintentionally because of the freezing cold.

The questions and the dubious realisations attacked his mind with the same intensity, but one of them differed from the rest: "If the blizzard is indeed due to the knowledge Theodorus has gained, then this means that all the rest that the Arab claims is also true."

He didn't want to think that, nor accept it. He continued the effort to use reason over the doubts emerging, but he failed. As much as he wanted the Arab's assertions to be proven wrong—to be simply frivolous talk, the result of Theodorus' mental disorder—when he matched it with what was said by the villagers who had fled to the city in great fear, he resented the appearance of the parasitical idea that they could be true.

"They are true, Leon! But they are not connected to the black and white, good and evil, as we learn to view the world from an early age. The nature of reality is different and we can't grasp it because we're alive," Theodorus had explained the previous afternoon, when he showed him the book. "In order to comprehend life, we first have to die."

That dogmatic statement throbbed inside his head. He wished to understand the meaning of the words, touch their essence; but death, which he himself had seen all those years, was so unrelenting, so unchangeable, regardless of its cause, that every theory seemed at least childish. Yes, he had been raised in a strictly Christian environment, he knew about the resurrection of the dead during the Second Coming, but all this had faded within him through time; observing and analysing the evidence led him to conclusions that lay contrary to any faith.

"I'm not talking about faith; it has nothing to do with that," Theodorus had stressed repeatedly, seeing his disbelief. "Religious myths are nothing but altered historical facts, instilled with theological elements, just as legends are instilled with supernatural ones."

Leon couldn't agree with his friend's words without raising an objection. Even at that time, when the unnatural winter storm turned into a blizzard, he doubted the Arab poet's incomprehensible beliefs. There was a huge possibility that Abdul had drawn all those fancies from an heretical old text, which he had discovered on a library shelf. It was so huge, in fact, that if he chose to disregard it, he would go against the principles of his science.

Thoughtlessly accepting that the living can raise the dead was immensely difficult for him. As a doctor, in spite of some of his imaginative colleagues' prayer books, he knew that such a thing was against the causality of life. Theodorus, however, argued that even life is something different from what the theologians and philosophers professed.

"I've told you about the Theurgists," insisted Theodorus. "One of them was the philosopher Iamblichus, who wrote about the Old Ones, the demons Iynges travelling to our world, and the great god who is away sleeping. Abdul calls him Cthulhu and reports that he is sleeping at the bottom of the sea in an old, ruined city called R'lyeh, in the ocean beyond India.

"He also records the way in which the opening of the rift in time is achieved. He describes every detail of the technique and explains the Mnizurin and their function.

"In the ancient texts it is written that one day Iamblichus conjured two creatures through two potholes, but it's not exactly clear how he did it. But the important thing is that he actually took out two living things through the liquid.

"Do you remember the letter I received from al-Farabi? Somewhere he mentioned that some necromancers performed a blood ritual by killing children and using a Mnizurin in order to summon a demon.

"Abdul explains that the Mnizurin is indeed a star-stone—not a living thing as many sorcerers believe, but the gate through which the star-creatures can come through to our world. It's an artificial mechanism, made in such a way that when it is operated, it expands space, and through it the otherworldly intruders can enter. In order to pass from their world to our own, they somehow manage not to have a body; they consist of matter, but are bodiless, like ghosts. In fact, they look like shadows, just as Plato describes them when he refers to their journey from the sky to the earth.

"The Mnizurin is what makes it possible for them to come, to appear, but not to materialise. In order for that to happen, they need blood, and that's why the necromancers perform human sacrifices; they supply the shadows with blood so that they can take form, with flesh and bones. Only the Immortals, whom we called gods, are able to travel from one world to another without changing their form."

Theodorus tried fervently to instil in him all the things he had read and understood. He referred to several issues and insisted on the alteration of the facts and how, when they are being recounted, they are completely distorted. In a nutshell, he helped him understand that whatever he had learnt through theology and philosophy was wrong—real, but distorted.

In order to convince him, he offered as an example the battle that Christians claim that occurred between the angels of Good and the demons of Evil. And in order to prove how the real facts are distorted, he read a passage from Abdul's book. A blasphemous version, a mad delirium that swept the divine and standard laws, everything that people accept and are familiar with:

"Myth old, ancient, from the fogs of time, the old man of the holy mountain narrated to me, the venerable white-bearded Omar. Inside the sacred kitabs of the swarthy followers of the disobedient Hastur, he said he read the true story, which is now known only by those who whisper in the darkness.

"And I am recording everything truthfully.

"On the evergreen, multi-coloured plain that stretches out between the life-giving rivers Tigris and Euphrates, two almighty generals assembled their armies.

"The fruitful, wheat-giving earth was swamped by the hordes of troops. Silky flags blossomed, and inventive and artistic coats of arms fluttered in the wind; weaponry of every type, sharpened and shiny, made for giving death, shimmered in the sunlight. Legions of the valiant stood on the earth. There were twenty thousand of them on one side and twice as many on the other, their war cries rattling the world.

"They had no good purpose, these legions of men. Their sole purpose was the unadulterated need to conquer.

"They sought victory, wealth, and women, everything that was promised by the two bloodthirsty kings, who held the reigns over the sea of men before them with clenched fists.

"The leader of the north encampment was fearless Sabaoth, the horned. Highlander, son of a jackal, from Khaldu tribe, the feral and dynamic Akkadians. He had a jewel-adorned horn atop his helmet. A magical, finely crafted horn, taken from a black unicorn. It was a gift from Eni, the sorcerer, who lived high atop a peak with other necroscopes. They were the fearless ancestors of the Chaldeans, who under holy decree by the heavens recorded the navigation of the stars.

"Brave master of the south encampment was the guileless Neflus, the first-born of Tamas, from the nation of Sumer. Ancient residents of the heavens between the two holy rivers were the Sumerians, and Neflus, the chosen winged leader, wise and brave. The unselfish Tamas' son wore a tightly woven chain mail, adorned with copper plates that the imams had etched spells on. The tireless lord designed the combat with great tactical precision.

"It was a dark time in the house of the ignoble Scorpion when the horn of the maniacal Taurus shone. The priests whispered it from everywhere. Murmurs of rage and fear. Secret words that had been revealed only to the two kings.

"The human war was a bad omen. Something stirred slowly from afar. Something insidious and covetous, harsh and callous, more so than the futile

need that makes humans perish. An elder of the Old Ones, the sorcerers whis-
pered, had awoken, and had promised his children the gift of the fields.

"Such bleak tidings the two masters heard in the leather rooms of their
tents, in secret from their men. The stars foretell evil. The omens are bad for all;
no hope is left.

"The melody of the calamity could be heard from the depths of the desert.
Here is the great pronouncement of the judicious sorcerers: 'Fearsome Gods were
roused from their slumber in the meteors' place. Ancient sovereigns of the earth,
once lost, now return, to condemn us to beggarly slaves. Demonic armies seek the
earth to conquer.'

"Neflus, the winged, when he heard this, bellowed with laughter, untimely,
the poor man. In an insipid manner he dismissed the diviners. The descendant of
Sumer possessed the heart of a lion, but his reasoning was lacking, as he vainly
doubted the knowledge of those who held keys of all that is unseen.

"The oracle of the necromancers, Sabaoth the horned king, did not over-
look, he merely appointed them to elect a protector. And these unholy men vio-
lated their oath.

"They had knowledge of the secret; the ancestors of the Chaldeans, sorcerers
of Sorcerers, knew the words that could reanimate the dead. Alas, they took a
solemn oath, all of them, once they were initiated into the indissoluble bonds of
the priesthood, not to utter them in vain, not even if there was a worldly need.

"O, the wretched! Their oath made them quake to avoid violation. They
feared punishment, so they deliberated and came upon a solution. To invite the
sacrilegious one, the sorcerer, the renegade. In exile they had him banished, atop
the mountain peak, Satenoth, the heresiarch, who was once in conflict with his
peers. Evil they named him, the worst kind of corruptor, once they heard him
propose not to believe in Gods. 'Believe in man, in his will. All these gods, the
fakes, beings such as us, stronger, with knowledge grand and considerable virtue.
Do not fear, then, but proclaim that man write his own fate.'

"To this atheist, a messenger they sent with great speed to the mountain to
bear the invitation. And he hastened, for two days he rode his swift mare to
meet him before battle.

"Satenoth, a true idol, bigger than eternity, awaited this moment to prove his worth. Wrongfully, he said, he lost the primacy, because he was the Great Sorcerer, the Grand, the only one of experience. Without thinking, he accepted silently. He knew of the future, the titan of time, and without ado mapped a cunning and sly plan. The unholy man performed funereal predictions, uttering names, birthday years, and star signs of the rotten dead. And once he weighed up everything, conversing with souls; he drank human blood of a three-month-old infant and the menses of a childless sixteen-year-old girl.

"Ready now, he stood before the horned master and, smiling vaingloriously, unravelled his plans. To concede defeat, he dictated to the king regardless of the ill-omened end. He commanded him to accept the fall, a blessed baptism in blood, by the merciless sword of Neflus, to meet his death so he could invoke his return.

"Silently, Sabaoth accepted the plan and called upon the trumpeter to herald the army to awaken. The battle thus commenced.

"Neflus answered the enemies' declaration with speed, arraying his troops. Broadly smiling, the lionhearted led his men, certain of victory.

"The sky darkened in the east, dense clouds dimmed the sun. On the far horizon, there on the sacred earth of the swarthy Indians, where old knowledge proclaims Adam the first man was born, an unwholesome anthropomorphic bastard race, crossbred children of humans and demons, called upon their forefathers to rise from the depths of the ocean. These crossbred beings were ugly, mucus concealed. They had bulbous eyes, flattened noses, fat and flabby lips, and sharp teeth. Scales shot up on their backbone and their tentacles slithered like snakes, membranes conjoined their fingers and spiny thorns popped out of their chests.

"Vile beings washed up on shore, of ghastly appearance and fearful acts; they fed on human flesh, quenched their thirst with blood. An entire nation incited the fertile land to conquer, upon the spot where aeons later the humans built the holy city of Babylon.

"These incurable, repugnant germs called upon the multi-tentacled god from the sunless depths, to ascend and reign, to bless the dawn of an era anew. The entreaty had commenced.

"Such is the ceremony, a phonetic psalm. Words and lyrics uttered in accordance with the pulsing of the stars, with every two breaths, a long-winded intonation belonging to the blasphemous common language of the Old Gods who dream in the fog-shrouded abyss.

"'Hastur iae! Iae h'thog drath'h. Ee nyar dag'f. Ee fthah zag'h.'

"'O, sons of Adam! What unnatural beings answered the call of the bastards! Fishlike offspring, inhuman and beastly, almost gods, entirely demonic, washed upon the river banks and estuaries.

"Horror magnificent! Ancient fear that persecutes memory and humans barely remember, immortalised in images and in statues taken shape, now bubbled in the sea foam, free.

"The battle between the two enemies commenced, hard, unscrupulous, unmerciful. The third enemy, the most fearsome, approached with stealth, without a word.

"The kings stood off like gladiators. They stared each other down, swore, snickered, and brandished their weapons. In the end, they each attacked the other, to deal a deathly blow.

"Neflus the winged and Sabaoth the horned began their battle, mighty and virulent. Blow by blow, war cries, terrifying clash, sweat, and blood dripped with each step of their battle dance.

"Ten times Neflus attempted to bring about Sabaoth's demise. Nine times their blades duelled; on the tenth, Sabaoth plunged into his side. The blade cut into flesh, blood spurted forth, and with a deathly bellow he fell to his death.

"Victorious Neflus cheered over bowed heads. Fearful, the descendants of Akkad watched their king fall. Before they could avenge the death they were confronted with the unexpected. Neflus the winged, the triumphant, threw his weapons down and danced a maniacal dance. With tears, lamentations, leapt and swayed, insanely danced over the lifeless body of Sabaoth.

"Fiery combat flared. Better to have a dead leader than to see him go mad. Thus the Sumerians turned their backs and began their retreat.

"Indescribable carnage resulted from the frenzied retreat, and the mad king found himself headless. In that moment of evil, an invisible harness, 'magical' one might say, held the Sumerians, strengthened their nerve, and armed their hearts with last minute courage.

"The battle rekindled, as if dry twigs were thrown on embers. The din of war held for another hour, the freakish slaughter. The first minute of the second hour saw no man alive. All were dead. One had slaughtered the other, to the last man standing.

"And then there could be heard, silently, the ancient incantation. The dark-blue lips of the old sorcerer scattered words amid the wind's elements. The perjurer, Death's seducer, Satenoth the impure, murmured in his blood-soaked palms words that mortals had never heard before. He entreated Sabaoth's soul to return from the ether, the moment the fishlike demons appeared on the border of the field.

"At the sight of the dead, the slimy descendants of Hastur, the Old One from the depths of stars, who lived in sunken cities, flapped their membranous limbs in relief. Even they love the life they have. The dead corpses of Adam's sons evoked gratitude. In vain they celebrated, unaware of the necromancer's plan. For Sabaoth the horned opened his eyes. He jumped up, grabbed his sword, and raised his hand high up over his head and with a wild cheer cried out.

"'Arise, men, children of humans! Rise! Hear my command! Ye that were once living enemies, reconcile now, become brothers of the same womb. Here is the enemy! Here is the calamity! Follow me, against him.'

"The blasphemous psalm continued and the rigid bodies of the dead men slowly stirred, reanimating. A freakish sight for the innocents! The dead rose and, under command to the power of Sabaoth, like marionettes, surged against the demonic beings. Never had the sun witnessed, since the dawn of time, such bloodthirsty soldiers. You must know, my brothers, that only the dead do not fear death.

"This was the plan of the malevolent Satenoth, to reanimate the dead and turn them against the demons. Evil can only be won by evil, the sorcerers claim.

'O, what a sight!

"The army of the dead surged. Many were headless, some without arms, and few had hands. There were many who limped; some slithered along without legs. *There were dead whose chests were torn open, their innards gaping; and for others, with each step they took, their intestines followed behind them like a bridal train.*

"*Macabre was this sight of the dead soldiers, repulsive, but there was no pain. Breathless, the undead advanced to the battle of the fiends.*

"*The old sorcerer Satenoth, dauntless, sage of all that is invisible, knew what he evoked. There is one weakness of the sea demons, the aroma of blood, just as the smoke of hashish entices its users, enthrals them. This is how blood, a sweet unadulterated wine, drives them to insobriety.*

"*And this is what happened. Once the bastard children of Hastur smelt the blood, they did not pause to fight, but, betrayed by their inexhaustible need for raw flesh, the fiends hastened to quench their hunger.*

"*They attacked to satisfy their hunger and their thirst not to command with their presence. They grabbed, cut, tore at the bodies of the dead people. Their tongues lapped at the gaping wounds, sucking, licking, and swallowing blood. They ripped the soft juicy flesh from the bone; with flabby lips they chewed on it.*

"*The demons had a veritable feast, a true orgy, like locusts on a sown field; a gruesome feast of saprophagous birds of prey.*

"*The dead feel no pain. The murdered do not fear death. Thus, the bites, the tearing of flesh did not affect the army of the horned king. Senselessly they marched on toward the pleasure of the fiends, but carried out their commands with discipline. Their swords and javelins plunged into fiends feasting on them. They slaughtered, relentless, in their search for others, until the sky darkened and no one remained . . .*"

Necronomicon, Theodorus read the calligraphic title on the first page silently. Abdul named his work *al-Azif*—that is, the "howling," since the speech of the astral creatures reminded him of the creepy sound that the demons of the desert made. The Jewish men of the ben Yova family who took it into their possession described it as *The Manuscript of the Dead,* more in theory than in essence, since the book had been written by a dead man and addressed those who

would die after reading it. But to Theodorus, the most appropriate
title, the one that represented the essence of the information in the
text, was the combination of the Greek words *nekros*, dead, and *nomos*, law: the law of the dead.

So he decided to name the Mad Poet's book *Necronomicon*, because everything recorded inside is connected to the laws of existence, which we can only grasp once we're dead. In his opinion, the
reanimated Arab didn't write a book of demonology, as any theologian or superstitious reader would call it, affected by the reference
to all the demonic creatures that try to dominate and destroy the
world. No, Abdul, despite presenting the invisible notions, classify-
ing them, and revealing their secrets, actually clarified the laws of
death, overturning every current theory or dogma.

Necronomicon, the laws of the dead, was just like the *Chaldean Oracles*, that is, what the Chaldeans foresee. A dreadful title, subversive,
but at the same time succinct, timely, and indeed malevolent, since
the knowledge it contains must be forbidden to the ignorant. That
knowledge is fearsome to their eyes, scary to their ears, disastrous in
their hands.

Andronicus Graeuses' image came to his mind's eye. If he had
been living and heard the title, he would definitely have commented
on many things. His preoccupation with the properties of sound
urged him even to examine the words under a different perspective,
looking for meanings or forces each one holds. Acoustically, apart
from the words *nekros* and *nomos*, the title contained other notions
like *onoma, icon, chronos,* and *on:* the Greek words for "name," "image," "time," and "being," respectively.

Theodorus rubbed his forehead with his fingers, feeling tired.
He was now aware of the secrets of sounds and knew that they had
nothing to do with acoustic similarities, but with the rhythm and intensity in combination to the knowledge of time and the appropri-
ateness of space.

He went to the window and looked through the shutters. Snow was falling heavily now and the treetops were white. He knew that Leon was near and wondered whether he had overcome his doubts and was ready to listen and believe.

Theodorus cursed in a quiet voice and raised his head, closing his eyes. He kept swearing at himself mentally. He judged himself for his deeds, but he had no other choice; he had to try, to see for himself if what Abdul had written was the truth and not inspired lies or fancies of his sick mind.

His titles and qualities influenced him; but most of all, what compelled him to move from reading to performing the rituals was the philosopher's "divine curiosity," as Plato called it—that is, the insurmountable spiritual need that gives man the urge to attempt the impossible and comprehend the unknown. That's what threw him from the ethereal essence, the theory, to infernal sin, the practice.

With his mind on Plato's sayings, Theodorus remembered how much the Athenian philosopher was opposed to all sorts of practical applications. He was certainly aware of the risks, and that is why he belittled the practical verification of the theorems. He wanted every student to grasp the meaning in theory, but not to go experimenting and, therefore, causing problems.

Along with everything else, Theodorus had disobeyed the advice of his favourite philosopher, at the most inopportune time. Perhaps if he had been a scholar, a mere theorist, he wouldn't be at all interested in verification, but only focus on the literary examination or the dogmatic analysis of the text—in which he didn't believe at all, because he knew that if he had simply been a craftsman or even a farmer, he would eventually try to perform the rituals described in the book with so much detail. This outcome was obvious even from the history of the ben Yova family. The only relatives of Joel's who had resisted the temptation were the ones who were very close to the people killed. So he now knew that he too would not have the valour to constrain himself and not perform the ritual of the reanimation. Of course he didn't have it, because no matter how many excuses he offered to himself, he finally performed it.

He had, of course, taken precautions, fearing a surprising outcome, and that's why after he brought back the dead dog, he immediately killed it again, cutting off its head. He decapitated it the moment he reanimated it. He didn't waste a single minute; the instant the dead animal came back to life and wagged its tail, he fiercely brought down the axe, cruelly and irreversibly. He heard it yelping once, and at the second stroke the animal's head was separated from the rest of its body and rolled to the side, soaking the straws on the stable floor in blood.

He took the same precautions when he activated the Mnizurin and opened up the gate. Even so, he had no luck there, and he blamed himself for that. The creatures came through the rift and, even though they were bodiless, he feared the worst, devastated by the idea that he would be responsible for the end of the world.

7. The Attack of the Demons

Gregorius and his three sons, along with four other villagers, were sitting around the table in his mansion deep in discussion. The bizarre storm that had struck the village, almost covering it in ice and snow, had stopped a little while before, and now the eight men were wondering whether this was the right time to act and put their plan into effect: banish the "magician." They all agreed that they couldn't wait any longer, for the morning snowstorm was yet another sign of an imminent catastrophe.

Gregorius Andriotes was a grey-haired middle-aged man, a brave skipper who had become a man at sea, shaped by salt and unstoppable winds, fighting against the Hagarenes and the pirates with perseverance and enviable bravery in the name of Jesus and his country. Both the sea and his enemies had left their war marks on him; a scar ran down the left side of his face, from his cheekbone to his chin, an indelible reminder made by a pirate during a deadly onslaught, his last act before falling to the stout captain's sword.

Since the strange phenomena started occurring, Gregorius had tried to persuade his fellow villagers to deal with the issue themselves and not wait for the bishop and, most of all, beg for Duke Kalligenis' help. However, the rest of the villagers didn't agree with his bold strategy. They were afraid of the lord, but also of Philetas' magical powers. They were no cowards, but they were scared of fighting a sorcerer, or if he really wasn't one, someone who could defend himself with the Greek fire he had hidden in his storeroom. Both cases were dissuasive for the naïve Kyrenian fishermen.

As a matter of fact, what prevented them from making any kind of move was superstition, a typical trait among seamen. Only, in their case, it wasn't about mere rumours or fairy tales narrated around a fire, but about true events they had witnessed themselves. What the courageous captain asked from them was beyond their ability.

Nonetheless, with the help of his sons, Gregorius managed to band together four men with the goal of sending the "magician" away. He was more than certain that when they went outside, all armed, heading toward Philetas' farmstead, the other villagers would eventually find the mettle to follow them. Under his guidance, the whole matter would be settled in a short time, less than what it took them to plan the attack.

Indeed, Gregorius was annoyed at the men, who only drank wine and quarrelled over trivialities. They had come to his home so they could discuss it before the storm started, and they yet had to reach an agreement, even though it was almost noon.

The issue that had come up was whether they would kill the "magician" or simply send him away. The answers were a source of discord to the men present. His sons agreed with his opinion, that is, kill him on the spot like a dog, but the other four men wished to send him away. But even among themselves they couldn't agree on one thing, for two of them suggested sending him to Kyrenia, and the other two thought it best to take him away from Cyprus, having him board a ship for the opposite coast of Asia Minor.

Gregorius was inflamed with rage by the dispute. He was well aware of this particular trait of his people—that is, if Greeks are given a reason to disagree, they are going to talk about it till the end of time. So he had to interfere, otherwise they ran the risk of falling out with one another, and the discussion could end up in a dead end.

"Enough!" he shouted and banged his fist on the table. "We must raise the rest of the men. Now is our chance. The snowstorm has frightened everyone, so if they see that we're determined to take action on our own, they will side with us. If we let today go to waste, I'm afraid that in a little while we'll be burying one another or we too will have to abandon our homes.

"Kalimeris is leaving for Kyrenia this afternoon. He's not worried about his life, but about his children. I know him well; he worked for me for two years. He's a sturdy fellow; if he sees us armed, he'll follow. The others too, but previously we weren't able to organise ourselves. But now, since we have finally reached an understanding, let's not spoil it. Let's go get that heretical dog, Philetas, and then see what we'll do with him, whether kill him or send him away. The point is to get our hands on him—"

You won't even have a chance to blink when I cut his throat, he added silently, still retaining his stern and serious look. "Unless you want to wait until those black ghosts show up again."

His fellow villagers shook their heads. His words had convinced them. They feared that this was their last chance and didn't want to miss it by arguing with each other, so they agreed to act quickly.

"Arise, Georgius," he addressed his second and his youngest son. "Go fetch the swords and bows from the case. Nicolaus, my son, go tell the servants to get the horses ready," he ordered his eldest son, who was sitting on his right.

Everything had to be done rapidly, and he wouldn't let time go to waste. If he truly wished for the attack to be successful, it had to be done in daylight; otherwise, when night came, most of them would lose their nerve and back out. No one would dare go near the farmstead at night, with all the shadows spreading around, and the torchlight playing tricks on them in the darkness. He knew that courage vanishes when superstition and fear take roots inside a person's mind.

Even now the sky looked terrifying. The storm may have stopped, but the black clouds still hovered above the village, foreshadowing a threat. This situation, in combination with the freezing cold all over the place, incited hideous, bloodcurdling thoughts.

He examined the pale white faces across from him and saw that he was right. Even the men who possessed the slightest courage and agreed to the attack trembled at the idea that the time of confronting the "magician" was near.

"Drink!" he barked and raised his wine mug in salute. "Drink, in the name of Jesus Christ and Holy Mother Mary. With their help and Saint Nicolas' guidance, we'll succeed!"

The four men made the sign of the cross, raised their mugs, and shouted in unison: "With Saint Nicolas' help, in the name of Jesus Christ and Holy Mother!"

Leon, dressed in the dry clothes that his friend had given him and covered in a thick fleece, was sitting in the armchair across from the fireplace and absentmindedly looked at the flames scorching the twigs. His brown hair stuck on his face and cold droplets dripped on his shoulders. He held the mug with the hot beverage Theodorus had made for him. He didn't look at him, he avoided eye contact; he simply watched the fire, deep in thoughts and fears that came over him when he saw the storm end abruptly as soon as he had entered the farmyard.

Everything went according to prediction or, better yet, according to plan, since Theodorus hadn't predicted the snowstorm but had caused it at will, using the knowledge he had gained from the Arab's book. That realisation pierced his mind like a ruthless conqueror, barging through the once impenetrable gate and, with a victor's arrogance, burning down every building, house or hovel, with the sole purpose of tearing it to the ground.

That's how he felt inside his mind, like a deserted place; a burnt-out area, full of ashes and debris. That was the reason why he hesitated to look his friend in the eyes. He didn't know whether he hated him, despised him, or feared him.

"If you read it, you'll see."

"I won't read it, Theodorus. What's the point? I don't want to," he said, turning to him without raising his eyes. His gaze was fixed on his feet.

"You choose ignorance?" asked Theodorus in surprise. His friend's attitude seemed unreasonable, but justified all the same. He had expected him to display a certain freedom of mind and accept the facts. On the contrary, he acted like a snail that, sensing danger, had withdrawn inside its shell. "Since you were a child, you've been taught so many lies, twisted theories, and inconsistent doctrines that you doubt everything. I completely understand. What I cannot accept, though, is that now that the truth is handed to you, you choose to close your eyes and ears. Don't you really want to know what's happening?"

"No! Besides, what happens after death doesn't affect our lives here. Apart from that, I won't only learn facts and stories, or theories and proofs, but I'll also be taught ways to destroy the world. Didn't that cross your mind while translating that book?"

"Those two are bound together . . ." faltered Theodorus. The boy was right. The *Necronomicon* did not contain only knowledge, it did not simply record mere facts; it also described in detail rituals for achieving circumstances that, in the hands of an immoral, sick, or selfish person, could turn into instruments of pain and, even worse, a means for the world's utter destruction.

He closed his eyes in disappointment. He understood Abdul Alhazred and his effort to record all those secret and invisible things, the pain he had suffered, his will and the reasons why he had done what he had. The Arab hadn't written all this in order to deliver to his fellow men a textbook for calamity, but to give them knowledge of reality and offer them the truth. The *Necronomicon* wasn't simply a weapon for attack, but also for defence against the insurmountable and invincible astral intruders, the monsters lurking and wishing to destroy God's creation.

While translating it, Theodorus suffered from the same thoughts that were now troubling Leon. He wondered whether his deed was right and prudent, aware that people acted according to their needs, always with an interest in mind, and thus, they at times behaved with kindness and at times with deadly cunning. However, being optimistic and well-intentioned by nature, he went on with his translation, aiming to spread the truth and help the world find balance and harmony in the face of the common great enemy that was threatening it.

He didn't disregard the fact, of course, that Abdul himself had tried to destroy his own work in the end, but he could see that it was just the hopeless deed of a desperate man. During the last years of his life, he was more like a scrawny animal than a human being: no one stood by him or sympathised with him; no one reached out to him; nowhere was there hope for an end to his hardships; he walked about among the crowd like a damned soul, all alone, hurt and persecuted; he felt like a reject, tainted and completely abandoned. He wasn't insane, but in the end he did turn mad. He himself had performed the ritual and cast the spell that would protect the book through time and, in his desolation and his unbearable grief, forgetting about his own actions, he attempted to destroy it, as a punishment to his unfaithful fellow countrymen.

Theodorus didn't feel the same way, as his own experiences were different. But above all, there were people he could count on and have his hopes rekindled. Leon was there and, even though he looked scared, Theodorus was positive that in the end his friend would support and help him.

"Leon, don't be so childish. Indeed, this book can be used for destruction, but don't forget that it's our only means of defence against the otherworldly creatures wishing to subdue us. That's the reason I've translated it, not for people to learn yet another written story or to have a new philosophical issue to ponder on.

"*Necronomicon* is neither a divine nor a satanic book; it's the bible of reality, whether we accept it or not. We live on a planet and there are more surrounding us. We already know of Mars, Jupiter, and Venus, but there are plenty more, countless and distant; and just as we inhabit our own, similarly other creatures, strange and hideous-looking, inhabit them. Just as we struggle to dominate one another here, fight one another, that's how they also battle and want to make us their subjects. You should know that."

"I know that this book, which you cleverly have named *Necronomicon,* includes the way to raise the dead. What you claim that we have to avoid is described in graphic detail. You yourself admitted that fear made you kill that dog instantly, after you performed the necromantic ritual for reanimation. If you're so certain of its usefulness, then why were you so scared? What could have happened?"

"The shorter time a being stays alive after reanimation, the less disruption there is to the continuum. Abdul mentions this. He himself was an anomaly to the flow of existence. Even though he died, he managed to come back and survive for so long that he set other powers in motion against him."

"I don't want to hear that. It seems unreasonable that you would indulge in all this . . . witchery, but actually hearing you supporting it is even worse. Do you know that in Kyrenia they are preparing to take action against you? The priests are incited, thinking that you're planning on bringing forth the Antichrist. When I got back yesterday, Kalligenis' advisor met with me and asked if everything that is rumoured about you is true. I told him that they had just misunderstood your experiments for the construction of a new weapon. Nonetheless, it was clear by his attitude that the Duke isn't going to resist the pressures for long. And they are not asking him to send you away, but to kill you."

Theodorus blinked in surprise at Leon's news. Having been inside the house these last few months, he had no idea of what was happening outside. In order to keep working without any distraction, he stopped calling the workers and the housekeepers, for fear of frightening them. He didn't even know that the villagers had gradually abandoned the fishing village, as if it had been struck by a deadly epidemic.

His instinct lurched in frenzy. He shouldn't waste any more time. Even though Leon refused to believe him, he still needed his assistance in chasing away the creatures that had gone through the rift. Otherwise, they could take shape by means of random incidents.

He could imagine the destruction they would cause if the Kyrenians imprisoned him before he had the chance to perform the banishing ritual. He had opened up the gate of the world where Yog-Sothoth ruled, and the guards Iynges had come through before he managed to shut it again. It was as if they had been waiting for that exact moment, or they were simply sucked in by the vortex created when the rift appeared.

With Leon's help, he believed that he could send the Iynges back to their planet. If not, then they had to find other ways to make them go away.

"The pressing matter now is that I need you. As I told you earlier, I tried to open up a gate in time and space. But before I could close it, many creatures passed through it, shapeless creatures; the shadowmorphs you heard the villagers mention. That's why I've invited you here, because I need your assistance in banishing them. Because, if they manage to take form, then we're going to need a whole army to beat them."

Leon looked him straight in the eye. His own eyes flashed with anger but also with pain. He was like a boy finding out about a terrible mistake his beloved father had made. He wanted to curse at him, shout and reprimand him, but he knew that he had to stand by his side.

Gregorius' shouts raised the whole village. The few villagers who were left and heard him calling out to them to come to his assistance went to their doors or windows and looked outside in curiosity.

On his horse, like a general going to battle, the resourceful captain wielded his sword while at the same time shouting at every household, calling his fellow villagers by their first names.

"Come on out, brothers! Let's go get that heretic, the Constantinopolitan! Come with us, Apostolus! What are you afraid of? If we don't catch him now, everything you're scared of will come true.

"Where are you hiding, Sergius? Stop clinging to your wife and grab your sword. Are you forgetting that three years ago you thrashed those pirates all alone, like a lion? Where's your bravery now, eh?

"Angelus! You're a disgrace to Cyprus! You lazy Kyrenian dog, come along with us and I'll give you all the wine barrels we'll find inside the heretic's cellar. Come on, you bloody drunkard!

"Sotirius, you lousy, stingy man! Come outside and follow us! Two golden coins will be yours if you help us . . ."

He steered clear of using the word sorcerer or magician, because he didn't want to frighten them while asking for their help. They were too terrified by all that had happened, so he was extremely careful with his every word. He was scared too, just like any man in the face of the supernatural; he didn't deny that to himself, but he knew of one rule he had learnt through experience, by fighting waves or men: no enemy is invincible, not even the sea . . .

The village fishermen, some from decency and others from shame, and still others with frozen smiles, grabbed any sharp tool or weapon they could find and took to the streets. Fear made their blood run faster through their veins, but since the situation couldn't go on like this anymore, they were forced to join the others. As soon as they did, they felt lighter, less worried.

They watched Gregorius sitting straight on top of his horse, in a leather breastplate with embroidered talismans, wielding his Damascene sword—his loot from a duel he had fought with a Hagarene intruder—and they felt heartened. They smiled with ease at his every taunting or saucy calling and added similar commands, like the members of a Greek chorus.

Once they had reached the centre of the village, the captain's small party increased by ten more men. On the face of each one of them there was no sign of fear or worry. They were all excited by the heat of the moment and by the rage they had been stifling inside because of procrastination or dead-end pondering.

Gregorius kept shouting toward all the houses, swearing, mocking and promising. He knew that the more men assembled, the easier their success would be. Being greater in numbers always provides men with an edge against their enemies and also helps boost their morale.

"Vasilius, get your bow and come join us! Bring along your dogs—"

The sound of a carriage axle, the clattering of its wheels on the wet, cobbled road, caught the captain's attention. A roofed horse-drawn vehicle was moving slowly toward the villagers.

The carriage driver directed the two horses and, perplexed, noticed the weapons in the villagers' arms. When he was near them, he halted and asked in clear curiosity:

"What is going on here, Christians?"

The villagers didn't reply, but only examined him carefully with a hint of suspicion. Ever since the strange phenomena had begun, the people had lost their former sense of hospitality and friendliness. They treated any stranger in a measured and unwelcoming way.

"First, you tell us why you've come to our village," Gregorius snarled at him.

When the driver met the captain's gaze, he got quite a fright. He immediately knew that the man was not well-intentioned and wouldn't think twice to use his bare sword for any reason or pretext.

"I'm driving Doctor Peleuses' wife to Professor Philetas' farmstead," he said at once, hoping to avoid worsening the villagers' fury.

Rebecca drew the small curtain on the cabin door and peered at the men, who were clenching several weapons and sharp tools. At the sight of their wild, warlike faces, her heart started racing and her mind immediately formed horrendous violent images.

The whole time she had spent in Kyrenia, she realised that the Greeks were peaceful and pleasant people, but also quite god-fearing and superstitious folk. Leon had told her that they should keep her Jewish descent a secret, along with the fact that they lived together unmarried, so as not to ignite the common sentiment or the priests, who always sought for someone to call a sinner, despite what they preached. That's why up to this moment she hadn't had a problem with them. Even these last few days, when the rumours about Theodorus were said in the open, no one had associated the young couple with their elder friend's doings.

Even so, now that she was in the village, seeing their faces craggy from the salt and sun, their clenched teeth, the pitchforks and the bows, she was swamped by fear, and her instinct sent out an ominous call.

Hearing that name and the carriage destination, Gregorius' eyes opened wide with a malicious joy. His face was alight, as if he had just discovered a hidden treasure. He smiled, made the sign of the cross with a tinge of satisfaction, and raised his sword decisively.

"See, brothers? God is with us," he shouted and signalled his men to surround the carriage.

The farm that the Duke of Kyrenia had given to Theodorus was near the sea, surrounded by a vast vineyard. Stretching from the right of the two-storey building was an orchard with citrus trees; at its end, almost two hundred feet from the house, were two rectangular storerooms.

The house was similar to many other houses that any traveller might come upon in several areas of the Empire or of its former domain. The high-ceilinged ground floor served as an area for the keeping of domestic animals, like a shed, while an outdoor wooden stairwell led upstairs, into the spacious gallery and the guest rooms.

In the front, almost in the middle of the paved yard, there was the well and a small, stone-built trough for the animals. Ten feet from the well, next to a firewood shed, there stood the dome-shaped, wood-fired oven and next to that, underneath a shelter formed by the vine branches with their wide leaves and hanging fruits, there was a long table with several seats on either side; a space similar to the lords' pavilions for family banquets during the summer months.

Nevertheless, ever since he had settled there, Theodorus had made a number of changes. Behind the oven where the vineyards once stretched, he had the workers build a smithy for the processing of metals, and in the space on the left of the house he had them set up the laboratories. Finally, beside them, the men built the two-storey storerooms where Theodorus could keep the Greek fire, the metal projection siphons, and the rest of the mechanical weapons, such as ballistas, wheeled catapults, and portable field pieces.

Near the ammunition magazine was the building used for the processing and production of paper. Inside there were presses, a pulping tub, a metal-piped tank that kept channelling water, and much other sophisticated machinery. Right there, outside the paper mill, fifty feet from where the beach started, there was a bare stretch of land.

The two friends stood in the middle. The sand was wet and shuffled by the rain, snow, and gale that had swept the area a couple of hours before. The white-crested sea waves, filthy and angry, kept lashing at the shore maniacally.

Theodorus set up a metal tripod that reached his waist. On the top he placed a flat basin. Then, slowly, he took the Mnizurin out of his sack and nervously glanced over his shoulder.

Leon watched his friend's every move feverishly. By his feet, he had laid the bundle of six spears that he had carried in the farmstead just in case. Theodorus had told him that they would be useless in case one of the shadowmorphs took form, but he wouldn't listen. He felt much safer with the weapons by his side.

Even so, his heart was throbbing with agitation. Although he didn't want to, he would participate in a magic blood ritual. The mere idea made the hairs on his neck rise, and he could hear his internal voice screaming hysterically, trying to dissuade him.

The notorious book was in his hands. Theodorus had given it to him until he completed all the preparations for the ritual.

A fierce battle was taking place inside of him. On the one hand, he felt the urge to read a passage or two, but on the other hand his survival instinct shouted no.

He managed to distract his mind for a while, observing his friend. But then, against all warnings, he bit his lower lip and slowly opened the thick, leather-bound volume.

The word *Necronomicon,* written in ink on the first page, was impressed in his mind painfully. He tried hard not to let himself be swept by fears and superstition. His heart was beating fast and his hands were shaking. His clammy fingers leafed through the book, glancing at chunks of the text.

Judging from the few sentences he read, he knew that the original text was written in metre, something common among the authors in the Empire. The chosen words conveyed the meaning coherently and literally, but the phonetic gaps during reading made him realise that it was difficult to maintain the poetic metre in the translation form Arabic to Greek.

Another thing he noticed was that his friend had divided the volume in books, a now lost practice from the time of the Alexandrian philologists. The books had no separate titles but were numbered in Greek letters.

"Hand me that vessel."

Leon, startled and flushed, picked up the container in question and approached the tripod. Theodorus poured the contents into the basin, and the liquid almost covered the Mnizurin.

An acid smell pierced the doctor's nostrils, and he instinctively held his breath. He curiously observed the bizarre, thick liquid.

"It's an alchemistic mixture," said Theodorus. "According to Abdul's instructions, it activates the mechanism in a way unknown to me, perhaps like a sort of fuel."

The next moment Leon gasped in surprise. The star-stone, the machine belonging to those ethereal creatures, started creaking and throbbing. Momentarily, a blinding flash of light made him cover his eyes with his left forearm.

Theodorus grabbed him by the shoulder and pulled him away from the tripod. Underneath them, the ground began to quake and the wind grew stronger, forming small eddies on the beach sand.

They stopped twenty feet away from the tripod, where Theodorus had left a leather sack filled with the blood he had collected from the animals in the shed. In order to conserve it in liquid form, he had made a herbal mix, which prevented the blood from congealing.

"Don't you worry," he tried to encourage his shaken friend, whose bulging eyes were watching the alternations in the colours of the aura rising from the tripod and into the air. "Everything will be all right. Just do what I've told you and don't be afraid."

Leon nodded. He couldn't speak; his breath faltered with agitation. The strangest phenomenon he had ever witnessed was now taking place before his eyes. The aura turned into a green-red mist that spread sideways, launching bright shades of colour. Simultaneously, the air was torn, cut, as if having been slashed by an invisible knife, and a black emptiness spread out in every direction, forming a breach in the sky.

He wasn't sure what was happening, nor could he explain it. The image before him reminded him of the opening of a dark cave at the foot of a mountain. Theodorus' words about Epimenides and the Seven Sleepers of Ephesus came to his mind.

"Give me the book."

Theodorus opened the *Necronomicon* to a specific page he had marked with a cloth strip. He cleared his throat, took a deep breath, and started reading aloud.

Hidden within the vineyard, the Kyrenian fishermen, holding their breath, kept watch at the house, the storerooms, and the laboratories. For most of them, this was the first time they had visited the farmstead, and they were unaware of the function of all the buildings, tools, and machinery they saw. Their gaze was impelled by suspense and anxiety as well as curiosity.

After making sure there was no guard, Gregorius and his sons moved first and ran to the stairs of the house. Four more men followed, one of whom held Rebecca tightly. Before they got to the farm, they had gagged her with a handkerchief and tied her hands behind her back with a rope. They had also sent the carriage driver away, warning him that if he told the lord about any of this, they would brutally punish him.

Unable to do anything to warn her beloved, Rebecca looked at her kidnappers in utter terror. She watched their every move as they barged into the house. She could neither scream nor break her bonds. The fierce, monotonous beating of her heart was throbbing in her temples, and tears welled up in her eyes. She feared that she would be the reason for Leon's demise. She was certain that he would try to free her and attack the men, disregarding the weapons they had in their hands.

Gregorius stood at the gallery of that floor and signalled to the men on the stairs to go down. Next to him, his eldest son indicated to the rest, who were hiding behind the wood oven and the smithy, to leave their hiding places.

"They're not in. Search the buildings. They must be somewhere near. Vasilius, let your dogs free!" he shouted angrily. He was disappointed that he hadn't found them inside; he was the first to go upstairs because he wanted to kill the "magician," before his men had a chance to stop him. The doctor didn't interest him much, but if he tried to save his friend, he would thrust his sword into him as well, with no hesitation whatsoever.

He thought it was stupid to let such a dangerous man go to the city or to banish him to another place, not caring whether he'd continue his devilish deeds. No, his logic dictated that Theodorus had to die, and Gregorius was determined to kill him himself.

"Aris, Georgius," he addressed his two sons, who were halfway up the stairs, "take a look at the beach. If you see them, holler."

The young men nodded, smiling, and rushed to the buildings overlooking the sea. They were no more than twenty years old, but they both could handle a sword and a bow since they were little; their father believed that they first had to learn how to use a weapon before they could learn anything else.

Two of Vasilius' ten dogs also ran to the sea. The rest, with their tails held high, not barking pointlessly, sniffed the air and searched the laboratories, the storerooms, and the orchard behind the house.

"Do you know where they are?" the captain asked, coming down the stairs.

Rebecca didn't move an inch. She closed her eyes and tried to remain calm. She didn't know where the two men were, but even if she did, she would never say, no matter how much they tortured her.

"I won't hurt them, especially not your husband. He has done nothing wrong. All I want is to have Philetas board the first ship heading to the Empire and bid him farewell. We just don't want him here. He's dangerous. We won't even allow him in the city.

"If you two want to stay in Kyrenia, that's fine by me. Actually, it'll be good for us. Everyone has only nice things to say about the doctor; he's a good man. So don't worry. I've already told you, we gagged you so you won't warn Philetas."

Rebecca straightened her back proudly and looked him straight in the eye. The tone of his voice, despite the meaning of his words, betrayed his lie. From his gaze, she could discern the violence he was trying to conceal. Or if she hadn't grasped that with her senses, her heightened instinct was telling her so.

A squawking noise came from the sea. Gregorius turned around and looked toward the source of the sound in suspicion.

A second squawking reaffirmed his hope. It was the secret code he had taught his sons so they could communicate between them without their enemies knowing.

"They found him!" he said in a loud whisper, and ran to where Aris was with one of Vasilius' dogs. His face shone with the joy of the discovery.

"He's at the beach, and the doctor's with him," stated the young man nervously when his father approached him. "They're doing something."

Gregorius raised his left eyebrow, smirked arrogantly, and walked to the paper mill, from where they could watch their movements clearly. He first wanted to check the area and then give any orders.

But the moment he took the first step, the earth shook underneath his feet. He stopped for a moment, waiting for the tremors to pass, but he realised that they were persisting and growing bigger.

"They're doing a ritual!" he muttered to himself and turned to see the men accompanying him.

Behind him were Sergius and Angelus, white as sheets, eyes bulging. A little further away, a terrified Apostolus tugged hard at the rope holding Rebecca. Next to him, Sotirius was about to take to his heels.

"Don't move, you dogs!" the captain cried out. "Don't you dare quail now, or I'll slaughter you like lambs! This is our chance. Their minds are on the ritual and they won't know we're here. Follow me!"

With slow, frightened steps, the Kyrenians gathered at the area between the ammunition magazines and the paper mill. Most of them were sweating with tension. They stood there speechless, not daring to meet the eyes of the others, feeling ashamed of their fear—and it was evident on their faces. They simply watched the captain and awaited his commands.

Gregorius peered from the corner of the wall and scanned the area. Philetas and the doctor were standing near the shore. The distance between them wasn't so great for him to be afraid of an assault, but at the same time it was long enough to prevent a surprise attack, and might provide the "magician" with enough time to make use of his powers.

What caught the attention of the fearless captain, though, was the empty space that vibrated in the sky in front of the two men. At once, he froze at the sight, every intention for attack suddenly vanishing from his mind; he stood there observing the phenomenon, thunderstruck. He had no idea what was going on, and he felt fear creeping up his spine.

He unconsciously gripped his sword so tight that his knuckles turned white. The thought of postponing the attack and returning to the village chimed in his mind. The agonised command "go away now" was reiterated inside him, and he was about to do so without hesitation.

He drew in a deep breath and hid behind the wall. He cast a quick glance at the men crouching by his side, awaiting his orders. Even though they couldn't see what was happening at the shore, they were all pale with fear. The earthquake had scared them to death, and their terrified looks were turned toward him.

He noticed exactly where their eyes were aimed at and saw that they were looking at his sword, wavering in his trembling hand. In an instant, he pulled his hand back and lowered the sword to hide his confusion. He also tried to regain his composure. He had to remain calm and decide wisely whether they'd attack or retreat with their tails between their legs.

He risked another look from the corner of the wall for one last time. He didn't have the attack in mind; he had no way of knowing what would come through that gaping hole in the sky; so his only choice was to retreat.

That's what he decided they should do: leave. But he wouldn't return to the village. No, he would stay there. He'd go to the house and wait for the "magician" to come home. Having Rebecca as his hostage gave him an edge for negotiation.

His senses heightened, he observed every move the two men made, the way the dark void fluctuated in size, and the greenish mist that was spreading and which the wind carried in the opposite direction. He saw that the doctor was carrying a big leather water-carrier, while Philetas was holding a thick book, like the ones the Hagarenes used. He had seen such books in his various journeys to different emirates, so he recognised the similarity.

A whisper came from the spot they were at. The whisper turned to a murmur and then to an ill-sounding chanting.

Gregorius felt a shiver rising up his spine. Everything he had heard in his life about the doings of sorcerers and necromancers flashed before his eyes, and his head went numb with all those consecutive thoughts. As soon as he realised that he was at a place of witchcraft and that at any moment dozens of hungry demons would spring from that black opening, he lost every last drop of nerve, bravery, or calmness.

They had to withdraw; it was the only coherent and comprehensible thought he managed to form in the havoc inside his mind. However, the cry of horror that reached him from behind shattered his heart and blurred his vision.

Startled, extremely terrified, he turned around to see what had happened. In front of him, an inch away from his face, a shadowmorph was swaying. It was one of the airy, black creatures that had swarmed the village lately.

Everything happened with such speed that he couldn't register all the details. Staggered, he fell on his back upon the muddy ground and, as a reflex, raised his armed hand to cut the black creature with his sword. At the same time, panicked voices reached his ears; they came from his men, who, being surrounded by dozens of shadowmorphs, started running to the shore, pushing one another away, piercing the darkling creatures with their weapons and fighting them off.

The sword's elaborated, sharp metal blade penetrated the immaterial body of the shadowmorph, which, unrestrained and unhindered, went on its course to where Philetas stood, chanting. Gregorius' fist, on the hilt of his weapon, filled with a thin, green liquid.

Another shadowmorph crawled indiscernibly across his face, leaving behind that same slimy secretion on his cheek. Simultaneously, one of his fellow villagers stepped on the captain's left hand as he made to go past him and run to the open space near on the beach. The captain cried out with pain, but mostly with fear, because in his confusion he thought that the pressure on his hand was caused by one of the spectral creatures. Instinctively, in order to protect himself, he hopelessly thrust his sword in the air blindly.

Sergius felt a sudden burning sensation on his leg. His line of vision took on a crimson hue, and tears filled his eyes. The next moment, unable to control his staggering, he fell into the mire, writhing in agony. One of the shadowmorphs ground to a halt at the level of the wound, wrapped its spectral limbs around his body, as if hugging him, and began pulsating.

The unfortunate seaman felt an unbearable pressure where the captain's sword had cut him. He immediately realised that the black ghost was sucking his blood, like a leech. Scared to death, he clenched his teeth and tried to get it off himself with all his might. He struggled furiously, growling and moaning, because he knew that if he didn't break free he would die.

At first he couldn't get hold of anything; he only fought the air. But then, as his blood filled the stomach of the shadowmorph, he sensed it being materialised and, at the same time, he felt his wound expanding, as if a sharp object were tearing his flesh.

Desperate, he rolled on the ground, jerked his legs, pushed with his hands, and did his best to wrench himself free from that deadly grip, but failed. The creature's strength was overpowering.

Exhausted, at his last gasp, his throat shaking with an involuntary tremble, he noticed the demon's features. Four tentacle-like limbs, covered by thick, firm scales, were wrapped around him like a clamp, squeezing him.

Left with no strength or a drop of blood in his body, he leaned his head on the side and breathed his last tortured breath through his blue lips. The very last image that was impressed on his dehydrated eyes was the shocked face of the captain, who, lying on his stomach, was watching the fatal wrestling, thunderstruck . . .

Amid the bloodcurdling cries, the pushing and haphazard shoving, Apostolus left Rebecca unattended and ran to save his life from the attack of the demons. He didn't know what had happened; he had only heard a scream of terror behind him, saw the shadowmorphs that moved past them, leaving secretions with their every touch, and took to his heels. He almost collided with Angelus, who was staggering because someone must have shoved him, went past Vasilius, who was cutting the air with his sword, and ran to the beach, driven by the momentum of his survival instinct.

All he thought about was getting away as far as possible, crawling inside the rows of vines and from there, after going around the farmstead, going back to the safety of his home. Afterwards, no power in the world could hold him in the village. He would leave; go to a different city, even one of those the Hagarenes owned, as long as he was far from Kyrenia.

In front of him, also running, were Georgius, the captain's son, and Lucas, the cobbler, who was holding a pitchfork like the ones used for feeding animals. A little further and on their right was the "magician" with the doctor, watching them in confusion, while behind them, a few inches above the ground, a huge, roundish opening was clearly visible in the sky—a black hole that throbbed and swayed.

He didn't pause to think what it was. His mind immediately provided him with an answer: "the gate to Hell"; and that made him even more scared and quickened his strides. His lungs ached with the effort, and his ears filled with the continuous screaming he himself was letting out. Yet he kept running with all his might.

He heard the doctor shouting from the shore: "Come here, don't be afraid! We're trying to send them away—" but at that moment there was no force or logic strong enough to make Apostolus stop his frenzied scuttle.

A shadowmorph sped past him, as if it were chasing after Lucas and Georgius. It twisted its way across the ground with great ease, without touching it. Its shape was indistinct, but it looked flat on top, where its head probably was, and had a narrow torso and a wider lower limb.

"Lucas!" he yelled, as the next moment the darkling creature went near his neighbour.

Lucas heard his name being called, turned around, and was terrified at the sight of the creature after him. All of a sudden he stumbled, lost his balance, and, after taking a few clumsy and unsteady steps, sprawled on the ground. Being so anxious to protect himself, he immediately jerked his pitchfork forward, wishing to pierce his ethereal opponent.

The two prongs tore the air and were thrust in the stomach of Apostolus, who was close behind. The blood drenched his linen shirt and, as Lucas pulled back the pitchfork, terribly upset at the harm he had involuntarily caused, the ground and the shadowmorph were sprayed with blood.

Wounded, Apostolus cowered and instinctively raised his hands over his wounds. He first whimpered in pain and felt utterly desperate; then he started cursing, but stopped suddenly as he saw the shadowy spectre moving. The moment it felt the blood spray, the shadowmorph halted, turned to him, and stood straight, showing its aggressive mood. It was twice as tall and three times as wide as him.

Apostolus' knees buckled. In front of him, right behind the shadowmorph, Lucas threw the pitchfork and crawled on his back to get away, while Georgius, who had seen the unfortunate incident, ran to his rescue.

With a sudden move, the shadowmorph wrapped itself around Apostolus, stifling him. The blood from his twin wounds dripped on the creature, which started feeding on it, letting it course through its body and give it substance.

Georgius grabbed Lucas by the shoulders, but both of them, despite their fear, watched the demon taking shape. They could see the six limbs being formed, covered by hard scales, as well as its long and narrow head with a thin neck and a stooped back, in the middle of which there rose a spiky fin, similar to that of a fish.

Captive inside the death grip, Apostolus tried to free himself but with no luck. Out of breath and completely hopeless, his blood being sucked through his veins and feeling his flesh being torn, he lost consciousness and dived into the deepest darkness of his mind, until he stopped breathing.

"Hit it!" Lucas commanded as he rose to his feet.

Georgius was unable to react. He could see the demon taking form by sucking his friend's vital fluids and was totally astounded. The likelihood of striking flesh instead of air with his sword was reasonable. However, he lacked the nerve to go near and attack. His knees were shaking, and so were his hands.

"Hit it!" Lucas repeated and tried to snatch the sword from him. But he stopped dead on his feet, seeing the demon turning toward them.

It hadn't taken its final form yet, but its features were clearly visible. It looked like a fish; long, without lips, and with bulging eyes and no eyebrows. Its head was crowned by a curved bone crest, with fine, sharp spikes, looking like a spiky collar.

Georgius didn't realise how the sword slipped through his nerveless fingers. His heart was banging in his chest and his will to fight had been shattered by the unbelievable horror he was witnessing. The next moment, within his disorganised thoughts, amidst the screams of his instinct and the cries of his friends, he heard a hissing sound, saw a fleeting movement, and felt his chest burning. The almost fully formed demon had jerked its three-clawed tentacle incredibly fast and had torn out his thorax.

Before Georgius could lower his head and see the gaping wound in his chest, one of the shadowmorphs hurried on top of him and began sucking away his blood and flesh. The shadowmorph's frenzied swaying and its sudden jerks revealed its ravenous appetite for food.

Lucas grabbed the sword that lay on the ground, cast a horrified glance at the demon that had attacked the captain's son, and flew at the one that had already killed Apostolus. He barely took three steps, for on his fourth stride his head was separated from his torso and dropped on the ground, soaking it with blood. The monster had struck his throat with both its upper tentacles. The next moment, the cobbler's lifeless body became a prey to the appetites of another shadowmorph that was nearby.

Theodorus started casting the spell that was written in the language spoken by the Iynges, Yog-Sothoth's followers. His plan was to open the gate in time and space, perform the summoning ritual, and lure the otherworldly creatures with animal blood, which he would throw into the rift. Then, as their need to take shape urged them to enter the opening, he would shut it and get rid of their existence once and for all.

While reading the *Necronomicon*, apart from his many philosophical questions being answered, he had also seen the errors committed in the rituals by the aspiring necromancers. As a matter of fact, most of them did nothing but repeat the erroneous bloody rite of each tradition and, as a result, their efforts continuously resulted in failure.

The necromancers who had not come back from the dead (that is, most of them), but also those unaware of the secret of how to open the rift in time and space, were unable to make contact with their bloodthirsty, dark gods. Nevertheless, in spite of their constant failures, they went along with their malicious conduct, causing all those macabre and bloodstained incidents, like the beastly human sacrifices and the inhuman blood rituals. Their deeds, in combination with the twisted image of reality spread by the devotional

groups and the utter terror spread out due to their murderous rituals, distorted the truth even more, hurling it deep into the abyss of
oblivion.

Of course, there were also those who had been reanimated and
knew the secret of the flow of existence; but even among them, most
ignored the necessary details. Very few searched in dusty texts, in old
myths and dark traditions for the elements that would offer them the
possibility of successful contact. In fact, they longed for the rituals to
be realised because these sorcerers belonged to those very ancient
sects that promise the coming or the awakening of the Old Ones.

The rest of those who escaped death and came back to life were
mostly occupied with theology and created new devotional groups,
connecting the existing religious tradition of their respective homelands with their personal experiences and estimates.

Abdul Alhazred was explicit. He recorded all the names of
those who had distorted reality and whose teachings resulted in the
truth being misunderstood in most of the world's nations, by reiterating that his testimonial shouldn't be received as a new gospel or
become the seed of a new cult.

Theodorus understood him. Abdul had been to every corner of
the world, become acquainted with almost all the cults there existed,
met the people of every race and comprehended their shortcomings, their fear of death and their need for a safe haven. Their
weaknesses made them worship and deify their astral conquerors.
Those same weaknesses that can lead anyone to intolerance, physical assault, and harm.

Abdul renounced the religion of the Prophet, Jesus, and any
cult or theological belief, but not Allah, God himself. Besides, the
continuation of the flow of existence made His presence and power
evident. Abdul wrote the *Necronomicon* with the desire and passion
of a pure and unbiased witness, not with the rhetorical persuasion
of a preacher or a fanatical believer. His purpose for revealing the

truth was to join people together, not set them further apart, because the threat hovering above humanity—the imminent catastrophe that will take place once the inhuman, astral creatures dominate the world—will be the same for everyone.

Theodorus also understood Leon, who was standing beside him, holding the leather sack of blood. The ancient Greeks found it natural for other living things and thinking creatures to exist on other planets, but the predominance of Christians inside the Empire had a decisive effect. The illiteracy they enforced shrouded the nations in a superstitious darkness. Moreover, the belief that only the Gospels contain the truth about the world doomed most of them to ignorance and executed them with the noose of dogmatism. Thus, despite the fact that Leon was an educated and open-minded young man, he was having difficulty accepting the reality Theodorus had presented to him, as a result of long misunderstanding and distortion of the truth.

Nonetheless, Theodorus didn't lose his patience with him. He was certain that, as time went by and after reading the book, Leon would eventually accept the correct knowledge. He believed that the same thing would happen with the rest of people once they read the *Necronomicon*. Besides, that was his goal; as soon as he had taken care of the Iynges issue, he would hire transcribers so that he could disseminate the book all over the Empire.

The frightened voices coming from behind him interrupted his reading and his thinking. He turned his head around perplexed, glanced at Leon, and then turned his eyes toward the paper mill.

From behind the building appeared some of the village fishermen, running and screaming. Along with them were also the spectral bodies of the Iynges.

"What's happening?" Leon asked, startled.

Theodorus didn't reply. He kept watching the panicked men who scattered all around the beach and the shadowmorphs that headed toward the rift at great speed.

"Leon! Go and stand near the gate," he finally ordered him when he spotted the danger, but his friend didn't obey. He was petrified by the materialisation of a creature, which was feeding on the blood and flesh of an ill-fated man.

"Look! It's eating him!"

Theodorus was stunned at the sight. The creature had stuck on the man's body and was draining, probably from an open wound, all the vital fluids it needed in order to take form. Simultaneously, four dogs stood around it and, barking furiously, tried to make it scurry away.

It was obvious from the monster's reaction that the wild barks didn't scare it. It quickly shot one of its tentacles at a brown-furred dog, pierced its body, and lifted it in the air. As the dog was about to die, whimpering, the rest of the dogs retreated, realising that the distance wasn't enough to protect them. Even so, after a second attack they scampered even further.

The Iynx's movements were steady and well-timed. It threw away the dead animal carcass and, with incredible agility, jumped onto another dog, breaking its spine with its weight. At the same time, whipping one of its tentacles, it cut the throat of a villager who was running for his life.

Theodorus' heart sank as he saw that the dead dogs and the man were swarmed by shadowmorphs. He knew that it was a matter of time before everyone was killed and the soon-to-be materialised Iynges went on with their destructive work, first demolishing the village and then the city. He had to act now!

"Leon! Go to the rift and open the sack!" he told his friend. But he was calling to three men, running to the vineyard, to come near them.

"Leon, don't be late!" he shouted in dismay. "Go to the rift! Now!"

Leon, numb from everything he was witnessing, Apostolus' accident and the Iynx's attack against Georgius and Lucas, turned to Theodorus in shock. His eyes opened wide and he cowered in fear.

Before him, all over the area between Theodorus, himself, and the rift, the space looked as if it were boiling. Dozens of shadowmorphs jostled, one close to the other, pulsating and quaking, like tadpoles around their food, giving out the impression of a dark, rough lake.

He unconsciously held to the sack tight in his arms, stood and stared at the otherworldly creatures. He was frozen with fear, and his instinct was ordering him to leave at once.

"Leon, son," Theodorus spoke quietly, "they can't hurt us in that form." He had to ease his young friend's mind, help him keep his calmness, and prevent him from going insane, so they could manage to achieve their goal. "Don't be afraid. Go near the rift and do as I told you. We have to send them away fast and then kill the ones that have taken form, otherwise they'll destroy us."

As if waking from deep sleep, Leon took a frightened step forward. His foot went through a shadowmorph and, seeing that he hadn't caused any aggressive reaction, he moved ahead. In the end, recovering his courage, he quickly went to the breach.

Simultaneously, Theodorus ran and stood in front of the tripod. He took a wide clamp from his belt and took hold of the Mnizurin. Then he gave the signal: "Now."

Leon carefully tore the sack with his knife. The acrid smell of the blood wafted through the place, upsetting the shadowmorphs, which began swaying impatiently and hopping onto one another. With no delay, and with his mind fully alert, he threw the blood inside the breach with a semi-circular move upwards.

The red liquid spread all over and then vanished inside the dark hole, which resembled a cave's opening. At once, all the shadowmorphs, as if magnetised by the vital fluid, dived into the opening; when Theodorus saw the last one of them gone inside, he deactivated the Mnizurin, removing it from the basin.

The two men exchanged looks. Leon's chiton, from his waist to his feet, was soaked in the shadowmorphs' secretions, while Theodorus' chest rose and fell with intensity, as if he had run too long a distance for his age. In their eyes there was a hint of satisfaction, but the horror was deeply impressed on their faces. Despite having sent the spectral Iynges away, at least six of them had taken shape and were now killing the villagers. The animals' moans, the wounded men's wailing, and the barking of the dogs were a testament to the critical situation.

Leon ran to where he had placed the spears and took two from the bundle. Theodorus put the Mnizurin in a leather pouch, tied it to his belt, and examined the commotion taking place.

He counted seven Iynges. Each one had six limbs and a crouched back with a spiky membranous fin, which rose every time they were threatened; but its purpose was obviously navigational, since Yog-Sothoth's followers, according to the information in the *Necronomicon*, were amphibians and could easily move both in sea and on land.

His gaze turned to where the pack of dogs had surrounded one of the creatures; yelping persistently and growling, they lured it away from the men. They didn't go near, but from a safe distance they irritated it with their barking and made it chase them.

An arrow whistled through the air and hit the monster in the back. The arrowhead glanced off the beast, while the shaft snapped and fell on the ground. A second dart was wedged in its ribs, between its two right upper tentacles, but it didn't seem to cause any damage.

"Line up!" yelled a young man, no more than twenty-five years old. Five fishermen, holding spears and pitchforks, ran and stood beside him.

"Vasilius! Keep attacking it to draw its attention!" shouted the young man with the leadership skills. His tense features showed that he meant to attack, without fear of his opponent or of losing his life.

The men with the bows, following his orders, kept firing and managed to lead the beast close to the one that the dogs had immobilised. At the same time, the six seamen rushed at them and, when they received the order to scatter, ten feet away from the two multi-tentacled creatures, they scattered, while hurling their weapons at the same time. It was a war tactic generally used by skirmishers, in order to draw the enemy fire and then, as they swiftly changed places, confuse the opponents.

Four spears and two pitchforks fell near the Iynges. One spear went between them and pierced the ground behind them, while one pitchfork fell into the mire near one of the dogs, startling it. Another pitchfork was flung, but it was snapped by a successfully executed defensive stroke of a tentacle. However, the other three spears found their target and were wedged into the body of the monster on the right.

To everyone's amazement, the demon was shaken by the blows; it staggered and fell into the mire with a great thud. While lying on its back, it looked like a turned-over insect as it clumsily moved all six limbs.

"They can be killed!" yelled the young man in excitement. "Those bastards can be killed! Don't—"

He couldn't finish his sentence. His chest was punctured, and a blood-stained tentacle appeared through the wound. One of the monsters had attacked him from behind and had rammed his back.

Blood filled his mouth. The second spear in his hand slipped away, and dying spasms rattled his body. Before he could take his last breath, one more strike smashed his head.

The monster lifted the lifeless body up and jerked its tentacles. The dead man plummeted into the mire and the bloodthirsty, astral killer attacked the nearest man, cutting through the air with its long and thin limbs.

"Nicolaus!" a loud, grieving shout was heard. "My boy!"

Gregorius crouched in the corner formed by the wall and the ground as he saw the demon standing, having a complete form now and dropping Sergius' totally drained corpse. All that was left of his friend was the skin on the bones—a bony, shrivelled effigy that only remotely looked human.

One of Vasilius' dying dogs whimpered and caught his attention. The speed of the events had paralysed him. He looked on all those unforeseen and incredible phenomena in astonishment, unable to react. He completely lost control of the situation and also of himself.

He watched the demon kill every living creature nearby. Its upper tentacles ended in claws, sharp and strong as knives, while its middle ones looked like hands with three bony fingers. Its exterior was hideous, repulsive, and it didn't look like any of the creatures he had seen on his travels. Some of its characteristics partially reminded him of existing animals, but overall it was something totally different. Its black, slick body brought to his mind the way demons are portrayed in religious paintings, but it didn't have a tail or horns, only a spiky crest on its head.

Before he could take a second breath, the monster killed one more dog and at the same time it tore Angelus' throat apart. Three shadowmorphs rushed to the dead bodies and started feeding.

His head was aching with tension. He knew he had to stand on his feet. If he wanted to live, he had to act now. He had to protect his sons.

Armed with fear for his sons' lives, he rushed to his feet, sword in hand, and, indifferent to the shadowmorphs going past him, yelled to everyone who had gone to the farmstead. If he was to die, he'd rather do so in battle, on his feet, as a man, an honoured descendant of glorious ancestors.

"Come back, you cowards! Where are you off to? Come and fight them here, or once they're in the village they'll slaughter everyone. Stop it right there, you lazy bastards!"

His cursing made some of them stop their frenzied scuttle. Only four of them, scared to their very soul, kept running, listening to what their terrified selves were commanding them.

"Raise your weapons! Now! Follow me!" he shouted and kicked a spear that was lying on the ground. The mud he splashed on sprayed Rebecca's face. She was kneeling, petrified by the shadowmorphs' appearance and Sergius' death.

Gregorius grabbed her harshly by the hair and lifted her on her feet. His eyes were burning with rage and hatred. He wanted to jab his knife in her stomach, but he restrained himself.

"See what your man and his friend did? D'you see that, witch? I'll slay you all!" he barked and slapped her hard across the face.

Rebecca's nostrils filled with blood. Her vision turned blurry with pain, and her eyes instantly welled up. She didn't know what to think, and all she wanted was to pray. The image of that creature, the sighting of the dozens shadowmorphs that passed by her, covering her dress in their foul-smelling fluids, in combination with the thought that they would kill her, made her shudder and feel dizzy.

The captain pushed her forward, and she staggered. She looked ahead with bulging eyes, hypnotised. The dogs barked maniacally; some Kyrenians were running like mad to save themselves; others readied their bows and hurled their arrows at the demons. Rebecca felt sick. She struggled not to throw up, but a second nudging threw her face-down in the mire.

"Get up, you devil's whore!" rumbled Gregorius and, bending forward, grabbed her by the hair and by the kerchief knot, a little above her neck. His hand gripped at his sword and he got ready to slash her throat.

"Father! It's Georgius, Father!" His son's cries stopped him dead. He raised his eyes and saw Aris standing behind Vasilius. With his bow in his hand, he was pointing somewhere near the black gaping gate in the sky.

Aris' face was covered in tears and the brave captain felt a cold grasp over his heart. He dropped Rebecca and, utterly enraged, almost out of his mind, he ran to his son, not minding the demons that were taking form or the ones that were already fighting his men.

"Oh, hell! Jesus Christ, no! Not my poor Georgius!"

Rebecca felt a hand propping her up from the ground. The kerchief over her mouth had come loose, and as she was kneeling, she threw up. Her body rocked, her breath was cut short, and her chest shook with pressure. She thought that she'd choke, but the man who had lifted her pulled away the cloth and all the vomit jettisoned on her chest and on the ground.

She remained like that for a few moments, disoriented, almost suffocating. Eventually she took a deep breath and, with blurry vision, looked ahead, past the demons, where a black hole could be seen in the air. And she saw him. She instantly knew it was him. She tried calling his name, but she couldn't, for she gasped again and doubled forward, expelling the rest of the fluids that rose to her throat.

"Leon . . ." she whispered once the stomach spasms ceased.

The man propped her up roughly and ran to join the others who were under a young man's command. Speechless, she stood and watched the development of the battle. The Kyrenians formed a line in order to confront the demons, while some others fervently shot at them with their bows. Further away, the captain, his son, and three other men attacked other demons and behind them all, she saw Leon running, holding spears in his hands.

Rebecca screamed the name of her beloved. Her voice evaporated amidst the mad barking of the dogs, the men's shouting, and the wailings of the wounded men, who fell on the ground, crippled by the tentacles of the demons.

Her internal voice was urging her to flee, telling her to run and hide inside the house, break free from her shackles, and pray for Leon's life. She turned her head around to see if any of the villagers were behind her. There was no one there.

She set to go, but a shadow rose at the corner of the ammunition magazines. It didn't look like the ones she had seen go past her a little earlier. This one was different: it looked more massive and wasn't spectral, but compact.

Horror grasped her heart when she recognised it. It was that same shadow that had sat on her body two nights before, and now it was heading toward her.

Her initial shock was gone as she wrapped her mind around the danger she was in. Her frozen limbs suddenly were loose and, with her head throbbing with pressure, she ran to where the captain was, yelling the name of his eldest son, who was lying dead in the mire.

"Leon!" she screamed at the top of her lungs and ran to meet him.

Leon stood about twenty feet away from the three demons over the dead bodies of Apostolus, Georgius, and Lucas. Their posture didn't reveal that they planned on attacking; they looked as if they were talking to one another. He tried to listen, but couldn't; the sounds of the battle covered their incomprehensible murmur.

Out of the corner of his eye he saw three men approaching quickly. He shot a glance at them and lifted the spear over his shoulder. It had been years since he had used weapons, but the distance and the massive volume of the demons provided him with the confidence that he wouldn't miss.

He waited for the Kyrenians to come closer, so that the demons would turn to them, and at the most opportune moment he hurled the spear with all his strength. The point of the spear went through the upright, membranous fin of a monster, and it was lodged in the ribs of another. The third demon, on the other side, jumped on the three men and effortlessly killed two of them, impaling their chests with its deadly tentacles.

Leon was astounded—not by the men's tragic death, but because the two monsters he had injured turned against him. Having witnessed their agility in long jumps, he threw the second spear at them and cowered back.

The spear got the Iynx on the left straight on the chest. With a strike like that, any human would be instantly killed, but the monster grabbed the weapon by its wooden shaft, pulled it out, and snapped it in half, continuing to move forward aggressively.

By the way their backs were hunched, he knew they were about to pounce. Instantly, mentally calculating the length of their tentacles, he rushed and jumped to one side, in an effort to avoid them.

He fell face first on the ground, knocked his jaw against a stone, and felt his palms being scraped on the beach pebbles. Wasting no more time, moaning with pain, he crawled on the sand. His eyes caught the leather shoes that Theodorus wore, and a strange sound reached his ears. He raised his gaze and saw his friend holding the *Necronomicon* and reading.

The next moment, he heard two thuds on the ground and felt a heavy blow in the middle of his back. He immediately turned on his back, scared to death, thinking that he was being attacked by the

Iynges. He saw the tentacle on top of him and the two monsters lying motionless, dead.

At once, the yelps of the dogs, the whistling of the arrows, and the screams of the people all stopped. He turned to where the other Kyrenians were battling and saw that those astral creatures had also dropped on the sand.

"It was about to kill you," said Theodorus, closing the book and helping him get up. He was sweaty, but in his eyes the happiness of success was evident.

"But how? How did you kill them?" mumbled Leon in confusion. His legs were trembling with tension and fear. He had been certain he would be killed, and he still couldn't believe his unexpected rescue.

"Do you remember when I told you that there are certain words that can kill or reanimate?"

Leon stood up and wiped the sand from his clothes. He gave his friend a grateful look and then turned to look at the monsters.

"It was really going to kill me," he muttered to himself, staring at the motionless tentacle.

"It's over," said Theodorus, then stood beside him and gave him a friendly slap on the back. His momentary joy turned to grief as he saw the fleshless corpses lying all around them. He had succeeded in banishing the Iynges, but the unanticipated losses crushed him.

Leon began to speak, but he stopped at the sound of a woman's voice calling his name. He looked toward the source of the sound and recognised the silhouette of his beloved running among the monster carcasses and human remains.

"Re—Rebecca!" he shouted. The expression on his facie when he realised that Rebecca was among the men changed abruptly the moment he saw a man grabbing her, pushing her down to her knees, and placing a sword over her throat.

Without thinking twice and avoiding Theodorus, who tried to stop him, he rushed to where she was. His eyes were fixed upon the man who held Rebecca, and when he went closer he could see a large scar running along his face.

"Don't come any closer, magician!" Gregorius barked and pulled Rebecca's head back so that the sword on her exposed throat was visible. "I'll slash her, you son of a whore! I'll slice her just as the demons killed my sons!"

Leon stood next to the dead body of a fisherman. He saw the sword on the sand and with a swift move took it and aimed its point at the captain.

"Let go of her! She didn't do anything!" he roared and crouched, ready to attack.

"Stop it! Calm down!" called Theodorus, who ran in front of Leon and stood between him and the captain. "Calm down, brother—"

"Hell, I'm no brother of yours! I don't even know you! My sons! My pride and joy! You killed them!"

Theodorus fell silent, saddened by the disastrous incidents, and stretched out his hand in appeasement, searching through his crushing guilt for the proper words to say, to console the father who had lost his children.

"It's not the girl's fault. I—"

"That whore! You're all to blame!" Gregorius, blinded by spiritual agony. With a swift and dexterous move of his wrist, he ran the blade of his sword over Rebecca's exposed throat.

Rebecca didn't sense the cut, but she felt the blood running down her neck, along with the pain and the difficulty in breathing properly. She gasped, her eyes rolled, and her sliced throat filled with blood. Involuntary spasms rocked her body; she let out some unintelligible sounds, and the last image that froze inside her vision was the beach sand as Gregorius pushed her on the ground. Leon's desperate scream that reached her ears vanished inside a maze of incoherent moans, growls, and monotonous sounds that faded away, just like the light from her eyes.

Theodorus froze at the sight of Rebecca's slaughter. His mind was disoriented, his thoughts were gone, time stood still, and he was lost in another dimension, sunk in a chilling abyss. He felt his knees give way and his heart clenching hard. The next moment, realising what had happened, he heard Leon screaming and saw him going past him rapidly, rushing at Gregorius.

The captain, his stare sharp as knives from the desire for revenge, strode over Rebecca's dead body and raised his sword. He would kill them all, even his fellow villagers if they tried to stop him.

The blow he suffered shook his arm violently. He was instantly aware of the doctor's strength and, as he was experienced in fencing, he considered that in order to defeat him, he would need a ruse.

The clanging of the weapons was heard across the beach. Everyone, both dogs and humans, dizzily looked at the two men fighting with rage. They had just been saved from those supernatural monsters, and some of them still wanted to kill each other.

Leon attacked, blinded by avenging wrath. He cared about nothing else except to kill that man, to see him blood-soaked, crawling and begging for his pathetic life. Leon would stab his body a thousand times with the sharp blade and slice him, armed with all the savagery and inhumanity that every enraged person has.

He had no experience in battle, but like every lord in Constantinople and the whole Empire, he was taught to fence by the most skilful and experienced masters. Perhaps if he considered the matter carefully, he'd hesitate, but at that moment, when hatred filled his soul, all he wanted was to cause death, even his own. He didn't care about life any more. He had no reason to keep living if he didn't have Rebecca; that's why he fought fearlessly and aggressively, constantly attempting risky moves.

Gregorius was on the defence from the beginning. His opponent was at least fifteen years younger and his valour was evident in every thrust of the sword that Gregorius fended off. He only managed to do so five times, because the sixth thrust hit him on the face, from his cheekbone to the chin. He sensed the blood running on his cheek and beard, letting out a long moan and cowering back to protect himself from a new stroke, but he was too late. His opponent's blade impaled the skin on his thorax, cut into his body between two ribs, piercing his right lung, and it was then pulled out of his chest, cutting his breathing short. The final stroke sliced his throat.

Leon saw Rebecca's killer kneeling down and falling on his face, drenching the sand with his blood. His body was shaking with tremors, as he was struggling to hold on to life. However, Leon neither felt nor showed mercy. He stood above his antagonist and plunged a thrust of his sword in the man's throat, finishing him off.

"Father!" he heard someone's voice shout from afar, but he paid no heed. If he looked carefully, he might have seen the captain's second son raising his bow and aiming at him. Instead, with his back turned to the young man, he dropped the sword and ran to the dead body of his beloved. He kneeled by her side and took her in his arms.

"Leon, watch out!"

His friend's voice made him turn his teary eyes around. He saw Theodorus standing before him with his back turned to him. His mind was in turmoil and he was too shaken emotionally to know what had happened. He instinctively held Rebecca tighter in his arms and kept looking.

Theodorus let out a muffled moan, took two unsteady steps and slumped down on his side. The wooden shaft and the feathered fletching of an arrow peeked through his chest.

Leon turned his blurred gaze toward the Kyrenian fishermen and saw someone bashing an archer on the head with the butt of his sword. He looked at his friend's unmoving body one more time and noticed that the garment around the arrow wound was soaked in blood.

"Theodorus!" he breathed and held on to Rebecca even tighter.

The moment Leon saw Theodorus falling dead before him, he instantly knew what he had to do. He made up his mind as soon as the *Necronomicon* fell next to his friend's body.

He remained still for a long time, between the dead bodies of his loved ones, in a haze, lost in agony, depression, and an array of questions, unable to grasp all that had happened. Kneeling and with tear-filled eyes, he watched with an empty stare the Kyrenian fishermen collect the dead and the injured and then, after having set the monsters' carcasses on fire, leave for the village, hunched with grief.

They didn't trouble themselves with him; they even avoided his eyes. They had fought an incredible battle with real demons, the "magician" was now dead, and each side counted its losses. All they cared about was to return home to their families, mourn their dead, lick their physical or mental wounds, and soothe their mind's tempest inside the affectionate embraces of their loved ones. The evil was gone now, and they believed that no other danger was threatening them.

Leon wasn't fooled by the apparent peace around him. He knew that once those devastated men went home, they would lose the calmness imposed by the facts, because the friends and relatives of the dead would demand explanations. Especially when the news reached Kyrenia, on the priests' signal, the need for revenge and fanaticism would turn them against him.

Despite the pain, the shattering of his heart, and the burning sensation in his chest and eyes, he had to act fast and effectively. He had no time to lose. He waited for them to leave and then stood up, planning on putting his thoughts into action as soon as possible.

He ran home, harnessed two horses on the carriage he found outside the shed, collected any valuables he could see while going over the rooms, anything that could be sold or exchanged, took the Arab's manuscript, and headed toward the beach again. Silent, crying, his chest heaving with quiet gasps, he loaded the carriage with the remains of his loved ones and covered them with sheepskins.

He felt alone, weak, and devastated. He sat in the driver's seat and was still for a few minutes, almost transfixed, deep in pain, and overwhelmed with agony. His whole world had been destroyed and shattered, to such an extent that he couldn't accept the facts. In his mind's eye, he saw the images repeating and he had the feeling that he was having a dream from which he'd soon wake up, high on hashish, next to a courtesan in al-Mamun's den in Damascus.

He failed to grasp the enormity of the destruction of his reality. In a short time he realised that some stories he had thought imaginary were indeed real, while all the things he thought he knew were completely unknown and distinct. Under different circumstances, he might have been scared, but the mental agony that crushed him, due to the emptiness the losses had created inside his heart, was ruthless and, oddly, soothing.

If he heard anyone relating everything he had just lived through, he wouldn't believe them and he would think they were crazy. Yet he didn't hear the facts—he actually saw them with his very eyes, he felt them. He saw a gateway to other worlds opening up in the sky, supernatural shadows taking form before his eyes, sucking human blood and flesh, but above all, he witnessed mankind's hatred, by losing his beloved and his friend.

He fixed his gaze on the sack where he had put the original text and the translated book. He realised that in there he would find all the answers, but also the way to transform the overwhelming pain into utter bliss. He would definitely read it, learn all the recorded secrets, and perform the reanimating ritual with no second thoughts.

Decisively he cracked the whip on the rump of the horse on the right, and the carriage wheels creaked forward. He had to hasten, go to Kyrenia, find any ship, and leave the island. He had no preference as to where; all he cared about was to get away from the city that very night, otherwise the Kyrenians would kill him.

As he took the way back, thousands of thoughts crossed his mind. Two were the images, though, that kept flashing in his eyes, torturing him, making him crazy. He kept recalling Rebecca being slaughtered and the way Theodorus' body fell in the sand.

He drove the carriage absentmindedly, not looking around, with his gaze fixed ahead, on a deep, dark emptiness. Once in a while, tears rolled down his cheeks, but his touch fumbled for the book in the sack beside him and his fleeting sense of reason came back.

At some point along his way, he tried to calm down and plan his next moves. He had to remain calm and act in the usual way so that whoever met him wouldn't suspect anything.

The street was empty. It was a sign that reaffirmed his guess that the villagers wouldn't rush to deliver the news to the townsfolk. This provided him with the necessary time to leave Kyrenia. On the next day, before noon, he was certain that the events would spread as quickly as a fire, and he could imagine what the reactions would be.

He caught himself wishing to be lucky. He prayed for a seagoing ship at the harbour heading toward an island or any other place away from Cyprus. Otherwise, if his streak of bad luck continued and he didn't find one, he would have to ask the Kyrenian ship-owners one by one to take him across to the coast of Asia Minor, which would definitely cause suspicion if he couldn't come up with a plausible lie.

Thinking all this and keeping his hopes up, he stopped the carriage at the dockyard of the Kyrenian harbour. He took a look at the covered-up remains and, taking the sack with the books, he ran to the quay.

The three moored ships in the port seemed to his stressed mind like angels sent from God, a proof that He was by his side. Without further ado, he ran to the port office and was informed that one was coming from Chios and headed to Alexandria, the second one had travelled from Tarsos to Paphos, and the third one had left Gaza in order to reach Rhodes.

His eyes gleamed at hearing the name Rhodes. He took a boat and approached the anchored ship and, after convincing the captain to set sail in the next few hours by offering him almost half the gold he had earned in those ten months in Kyrenia, he returned to the harbour and then went to his clinic at the castle.

Four hours later, as the sun began to sink visibly, he was leaning against the ship's prow and, relieved, gazed at the deep blue sea. In his arms he was holding the leather sack with the books. Underneath him, inside the ship's hold, there were his belongings, a wooden case with clothes and valuables, as well as two big earthen pots for olive oil; within these he had placed the bodies of his loved ones after drenching them with antiseptic, whose composition had been known since the ancient Egyptians mummified their dead.

His only concern was to read the *Necronomicon* and learn every detail about the reanimating ritual; once he was in Rhodes, he would bring Theodorus and Rebecca back from the dead. Nothing in his mind predicted anything bad or catastrophic. No, the clear air that filled his lungs eased his pain, wiped away his misgivings, and gave an optimistic, reviving breath of spring to the ruined foundations of his reality, scattering the ashes in a distant corner where all his grim memories were piled up.

8. Reanimation of the Dead

His surroundings were grey, dull and foggy. He couldn't remember how he had got there, whether he had taken a wrong turn, or which path he had faltered on. All he could sense was that he was in pain and he felt lost, alone, and miserable. He took another look and failed to determine if all that haziness was due to fire smoke or thick, ashy mist.

He trod clumsily along the uneven ground, which was covered with cinders and debris. He slipped at every step he took, kept losing his balance, but didn't fall. He went on his way with arduous steps. Sometimes he felt as if he were stepping in baskets of ripe figs, which were squished under his weight and stuck to the soles of his shoes. Whatever the thick layer of ash covered wasn't visible, and as a result he felt even more insecure.

Disgusted, astounded, and confused, he tried to step over a high pile of debris, but he missed his footing and rolled down the slope that lay ahead. The inclined ground impelled him into a dizzying, unstoppable drop. He kept falling and falling, wriggling, knocking on several obstacles along the way, in a wild tumble that seemed endless, until he finally came to a grinding halt against a big rock.

He remained there, writhing in agony, amidst the cinders, atop squashed masses, his feet punctured and his palms scraped from several sharp objects he crashed into during his fall. He made no effort to get up. His breathing was slow and his chest was aching. His vision turned even more blurry with the vertigo his fall had caused. His heart was beating tiredly, almost funereally.

At some point, some centuries or a few heartbeats later—it wasn't clear which—he propped himself up. He stood on all fours and blinked in an effort to see more clearly. There was no light. Complete blackness spread all around him, caressing him, touching him, gripping him. In his disoriented mind, the murk surrounding him seemed to breathe with life.

He groped his way up and turned to move, but he stopped at once. His name echoed in his ears, terrifying him: "Leon!"

He shuddered. The tone of the voice didn't sound human, but animal, a blend of growling and guttural death-rattle.

"Leon!"

He hunched in defence. The sense of a threat took over his mind and body.

Unexpected lightning violently cut through the pitch darkness and provided him with enough light to see where he was. He had fallen in what looked like a natural chasm, but it might as well have been a deep, wide well, whose walls were no longer steep because of the ash and the charred objects underneath it.

He turned to the source of the voice and, under the light of the flashes that shattered the sky, saw a short creature standing beside him, silent. It looked like a child, but Leon couldn't discern its features. It was motionless, and all that he could make out in the dark was its outline.

At the momentary lucidity offered by the next bolt of lightning, he jumped to his feet, letting out a loud scream of horror. He had been startled not only by the presence before him, but also by its bizarre and chilling appearance, visible under the grey-yellow light.

The creature didn't have a face. Its head was completely smooth, without contours, eyes, lips, or nose—a formless mass, with no distinctive feature to prove that it was a face apart from the fact that it was on top of a body and supported by a thin neck.

What had seemed in the darkness like hair was just thin, dark-coloured shadows that coiled like snakes.

The creature extended one of its limbs and touched him right on the middle knuckle of his middle finger. Leon yelled with the sudden pain he felt spreading all over his body. The blood in his temples started pumping feverishly, and he instinctively ground his teeth. With the last tinge of strength that his survival instinct offered, he rushed to escape.

Overhead, an ethereal war was taking place. The lightning and thunder shook the world, and the first fat raindrops thudded fiercely into the chasm he was in.

His breathing whistled through his chest and his temples throbbed. Fear conquered him like an unprotected city. His eyes opened wide and his resonant, bloodcurdling screaming rang in his ears.

The torrents began to clear up the cinders and carried them away, creating hundreds of glittering brooks, which flowed together forming black, viscous waters like the waters of the poisonous river Styx and the damned river Acheron. It was a river surging with debris and charred remains, oppressively rising in the limited space around him.

The angry rainfall flushed out the terrain, and the spot where the sloping ground was covered in the thick layer of ash could be gradually seen. Before his surprised eyes, under scores of lightning flashes that disturbed the sky, everything that was concealed a few minutes earlier was now in the open.

In front of him were dozens of mangled human skeletons. Smashed skulls, shattered jaws, crushed bones, pointy and sharp, severed spinal cords and broken ribs; a bone stairwell with steps made of rotten flesh . . .

The moment he realised that what he had been stepping on, thinking it was stones, pieces of wood, and pebbles, was nothing but human remains, he lost his mind. Frenzied, he climbed up the corpses and tried to get out of the pit. His long chiton would get caught in broken bones, his feet would sink into maggoty flesh, and his fingers would cram into slimy, sticky entrails.

In his hurry, he slipped and fell back down; he fell chin-first onto the open chest of a slaughtered man, and black liquids covered his face. He pressed his hands on the flaccid bodies and propped himself up, queasy with disgust and fear.

His unhinged mind wasn't able to give an answer to his torturing question about what was happening or where he was. There was no logic; it all felt like a nightmare. Yet this nightmare had a realness about it that he could not define.

He forced himself to wake up. He didn't want to see that faceless creature again, which was approaching him from behind. He could hear its footsteps, its soles splashing on the water, the hissing of the shadows on its head. He knew it was some kind of a demon, not the ones described by various religions, but an entity that had come from the stars.

His chiton was drenched, his hair stuck on his face and neck, and his feet had sunk into the decomposing body of a gutted woman. He made an attempt to pull his shoes out of the decaying flesh, but he failed. It was as if that charred woman, with her bare, bruised breasts, had trapped him in her slimy innards.

Panicked, he began wrenching himself away and stepping on the mouldy, burnt intestines of the corpse. His brusque movements made the woman's scorched skull disconnect from the rest of her body and roll to the left. It stopped next to a stone, and her thin jaws, with the crooked incisors, opened wide, showing an image of devious and malicious joy.

At that exact moment, the creature stood in front of him. The coiling shadows on its head moved swiftly, threateningly, like living things that had just sniffed food. One of them separated from the rest and entered the creature's amorphous face, through the spot where its mouth was supposed to be. It got into the flesh and left a gaping wound behind, on which small white and yellow maggots slithered and started feasting on the skin greedily.

Leon tried to shout, call out for help, pray, but with no luck. In desperation, he attempted to climb up the pit again, but now the murky water flowed in a faster rhythm, sweeping away any resistance and drifting him to the bottom. He tried to swim, but the muck created by the putrid, stringy flesh, the maggoty intestines, and the numerous small and big bones didn't let him move or float. Instead, it pulled him down, like that thick liquid in the well that swelled and roared like a living creature.

Indeed it was one. The faceless demon showed two thin suckered tentacles, which bent, coiled, and smacked the air. Simultaneously, the rest of its body joined the muck, forming a slimy mass, which lagged and swayed like soft clay.

Leon tried to escape, weakened by all this horror. One of the tentacles snatched him by his torso and lifted him high, squeezing hard. He felt his skin burning, his bones breaking, and his soul being bound to eternal, tormenting shackles. He tried to scream, but the sound of his voice vanished inside his crushed chest. The last thing he saw, before he breathed his last breath, were two sick, yellow eyes staring at him malevolently, enviously.

Most people have an optimistic attitude toward life. They don't perform or do everything thinking that death is on the lookout for them; but, hoping that they can live pleasantly or feel happy, they move and act, urged on by the dream of a better future. Of course, they are defined by fear, that dark, disturbing feeling that makes the heart throb anxiously, but it doesn't dominate their thoughts. No, no man expects something bad to happen when he goes around the corner, when he lies in bed, or even when he makes a point of achieving something that everyone else considers dangerous.

The abbot of St. John's holy monastic community in Patmos, John Lambrinus, revered by the faithful Christians, was no exception. A descendant of the Lambrinus family of Naples, famous for its accomplishments in war going back to ancient times, he had grown up in a family environment where life's creed was encompassed in the martial saying: "Do as you desire, and God will bless you once you achieve it."

He reached manhood in battles against the Langobards, who had for years tried to part with the Empire and establish their own independent kingdom. He gained much experience during the pursuit of the Saracen pirates who coveted the islands' wealth and ended up as a monk, after his wife and two children had drowned in a shipwreck outside Rhodes as they travelled to meet with him.

His knowledge and noble descent helped him to become the abbot of the hermit community on the "island of the Revelation," after the death of his elder predecessor, three years later. However, John had already begun to feel confined inside the boundaries of small Patmos and the stifling monastic life. Accustomed to the joys of battle, when the gale either kissed or lashed his face, either along plains riding a horse or on sea-beaten ship decks, he knew that the era of his isolation was over.

He hadn't lost his faith. On the contrary, he shaped it more, he breathed and behaved according to Christian teachings, but he simply couldn't stand being locked inside a poorly constructed cloister and pray without contributing anything to his fellow men—or at least preaching the Lord's Word to the unfaithful and the ones who went astray. He could picture himself as a preacher, a dynamic defender of faith, and not as a plain monk who, through self-examination, tries to earn a place in Heaven, detached from the problems of his brothers in cities and villages. He had given himself wholeheartedly to religious duties, even though he still maintained his former military arrogance and dreamed of the eternal glory of holiness.

He was well aware that ambition isn't one of the Christian virtues; but no matter how hard he tried, his passion never waned. He was definitely not humble; that was something he well knew, but he believed that his charity work tempered his sin, leaving him room to dream of having his name written in ecclesiastical books, with the world commemorating him. Of course, he didn't imagine his future in this way, but he harboured the faint hope that his deeds would someday be acknowledged by all Christians.

In order to ease the suffocation that tormented him, to give a new meaning to his passive life, heavy with the smell of incense, and to relieve the tedium of a monk's daily toil, he planned a voyage of pilgrimage to the Holy Land. He hoped for a wondrous adventure, longed for the search for unknown pitfalls in order to reaffirm his faith, and prayed for anything his fate had in store for him.

The rest of the monks were angered at his decision at first, but he convinced them easily with the rhetoric his education had provided him with. Thus, unhindered, he took the way toward the kingdom of the Hagarenes, leaving a much-loved monk in his place for as long as he'd be away.

Four more monks accompanied him on his pilgrimage. One died on board before they even reached the shore, while two of them remained—with his blessing—in Jerusalem, at the Church of the Holy Sepulchre.

He had spent a year on the holy grounds before he took the way back home. The pilgrimage, the wakes, and the praying didn't in the least affect his desire to act and further help the unfortunate, nor did they make the bonds with the monastic life tighter in his heart.

He confessed his desire to the only brother who was also returning with him, Demetrius Meligrates. He even told him that the next journey he'd like to make was toward the kingdoms of the West. He wished to meet fellow Christians who lived in the countries where the fog meets the ocean.

His intentions changed when Leon got on the ship. The doctor's strange, almost misanthropic attitude intrigued him, and within the ten days they journeyed from Cyprus to Patmos they struck up a friendship.

Leon was taciturn, lost in painful mazes, with a vacant gaze and a subdued countenance. He wasn't interested in making friends or making small talk with the sailors, as most travellers do. It was clear that he was avoiding any social interaction and meeting new people.

He didn't even look like a doctor but more like a mountain brute, whose long separation from humans caused him to behave like a wild animal. The details that revealed his noble descent and his higher education were his clothes and that big, leather-bound arabesque book, which he read every morning sitting at the ship's stern.

The inquisitive John Lambrinus had met many people in his adventurous life and could instantly tell that the young man, on top of the heavy burden on his shoulders, also suffered in silence due to an unbearable pain. In his expressions he saw the same angst that he himself felt, when they informed him that his family had been lost in the Aegean waters. So their meeting each other was only a matter of time.

Leon's words, though, perplexed him. In their conversations, he stated that his wife, Rebecca, and her father, Theodorus Philetas, would stay in Kyrenia until he could find a quiet and proper place for them to settle. All this didn't harmonise with his behaviour, especially with his words, because on many occasions when he spoke about his loved ones he used the past tense and involuntarily heaved heavy sighs.

As he was so perceptive, he knew that for some reason Leon was concealing the fact that his family was dead, perhaps out of guilt, perhaps because he wouldn't accept the tormenting truth. John himself had a similar reaction; that's why he compassionately suggested that he not disembark in Rhodes, but follow them to Patmos instead.

In order to convince him, John promised him land, livestock, and a house in exchange for the medical services he would offer the wretched islanders and the poor pilgrims. Leon didn't say yes right away. But later, after he had considered the circumstances and got to know the abbot and the monk Meligrates, he finally decided to accompany them.

Six days after they had set sail from Kyrenia, John opened the *Necronomicon* at a time when Leon had inadvertently left it unattended. Apart from the title, he also managed to read a few paragraphs from the introduction. A shiver ran through his body as he read the verses. He immediately understood that it was a demonological book, and his first reaction was to shut it closed, thinking that he should have the captain arrest Leon as a sorcerer and a heretic.

But on second thought, he considered it wiser not to betray Leon's darkest secrets. The reason for this decision was a sentence he read in the *Necronomicon* out of curiosity: *"The Mnizurin press atop and the gate will open with screeching sounds and grey, foul smoke and dark-coloured mists. Fear not the earthquake, for it is an omen for the rift that tears the air."*

When he was young, just like all the adolescents in his circle of friends who got a better education than laymen, John had engaged in alchemy and mechanics, experimenting with substances and metals, in an effort to invent or create anything useful and handy. Despite the fact that he was frustrated by his constant failures, he still remembered much information about the elements the alchemists used or searched. He knew of the rumours around those strange star-stones.

But what really drove him to show interest in Leon and his book of magic was that, as a monastery abbot, he possessed the keys to the cave where his namesake saint had lived; and it was also there, inside an oak cabinet, that he kept his sacred relics, among which was a red-black star-stone.

The elder monk who served as a secretary, with the duty to report to every abbot about the legacy of the Apostle and to supervise their safekeeping, informed him that the author of the Book of Revelation witnessed all that he had written about by using that stone. He also heard that few were the monks who had not been tempted to use it based on information they had found in alchemical manuals, but with no success whatsoever.

In fact, one of them, understanding the danger of the Mnizurin being stolen by treacherous necromancers, forbade its depiction on the holy icons. The early artists used to paint the stone in front of the evangelist, below the opening where his vision could be seen, but now they simply had to paint the cave in the star-stone colours. From that moment on, the "Cave of the Apocalypse," as it was called, was always depicted in shades of red and black.

It wasn't at all difficult for John Lambrinus to have an idea. On the contrary, as if that were what was missing in his life, he instantly thought he could activate the Mnizurin; that is why he didn't mention anything about the evil book to the captain or Meligrates. He forced Leon to become his friend, and at every chance he got, whenever the doctor got lost within the maelstrom of his mind, pondering on his spiritual wounds, he took the *Necronomicon* and secretly read its forbidden secrets.

When they reached Rhodes, John ordered the ingredients for the preparation of the mixture from a local alchemist, planning on opening the gate to time and space. He would fulfil this dream once he knew all the information about the Mnizurin. With that goal in mind, during the time they were in Patmos, he went to Leon's house pretending to be ill. Every time the doctor left to tend to other patients, John sneaked into Leon's room and received the knowledge in small quantities.

Of course, these last days, he constantly doubted everything he read, unable to decide whether it was true or a mere compilation of an intelligent madman. It wasn't easy for him to accept the blasphemous doctrines that Abdul Alhazred maintained. However, doubt had seeped into his thinking and he had a hard time concentrating on his devotional Christian duties. In truth, his only concern was the ritual.

He was more interested in contacting God and seeing the future than anything else. He wholeheartedly believed in the Maker's existence and didn't care if some of the doctrines of faith were false or altered. Besides, if he was given the chance to see Him, talk with Him, or at least hear Him, just as his namesake did, he was positive that every question he had would eventually be answered.

Nonetheless, doubt riddled his convictions, gnawing away at them and dispelling them. Ever since he began reading, he hadn't believed a thing. He labelled the text anti-Christian, penned by some heretical and imaginative author who knew the theological doctrines and wished to refute them, aiming to present another religious point of view. But this pursuit couldn't be successful, since it was lacking a moralistic element.

Even though he hadn't read the entire book, he knew that the Arab wasn't moralising, but merely recorded, explained, and presented facts, rituals, information about creatures, gods, machines, and distant planets, artificial magical phenomena, and scientific knowledge beyond human perception, such as the rift in time and space that looks like a giant worm-shaped tunnel and offers the possibility to link the two worlds.

He didn't understand all the doctrines, nor did he believe them, because they weren't of any theological value to preoccupy him; that is why he skipped them mechanically and with indifference. He only paused where the text mentioned the Mnizurin and the reanimation of the dead. He wondered about the theory concerning the properties of sounds. He laughed heartily when he read that there are sounds that cannot be heard or others that come from the future or the past.

Only reading about the instance when Jesus used that specific sound to resurrect Lazarus was enough to enrage him against the author and pay no more heed to his conjectures. As for the human sacrifices and the blood rituals mentioned, they were more than enough chilling proof to arrest and sentence Leon to death, but for the moment he wasn't thrilled about that outcome. He first wished to take a glimpse of the future, hear God's mandates, speak with Him; and then he would deal with the persecution.

He wasn't afraid of using the Mnizurin, nor of the fact that he had found its activation method inside an anti-Christian book. Since John the Apostle himself had used it, it must have meant that he wouldn't be committing a punishable sin; on the contrary, he thought it would earn him a place in Heaven.

He didn't exclude the possibility that even the ingredients for the mixture could be fake and imaginary, but such an instance didn't worry him. When he would see the wickedness of the *Necronomicon* and its messages for himself, he would better enjoy the arrest of Leon, who, based on fabricated theories, planned on killing people and performing brutal barbaric rituals of an irrational and nonexistent faith.

Pain! The axe, the sword, the fire; the heart is torn apart, the soul is punctured, the eyes inflamed, the chest ablaze. We know it, we can feel it, experience it, and never forget it. We might bury the most precious moment of our lives, but never the worst one, when the brain is marked by life's most indelible emotion.

The pain caused by the loss of loved ones, parents, children, siblings, friends, or lovers is due to the breaking of life's bonds. It is then that we grasp how weak and lonely we are, the fragility of the conditions we think are eternal, while the hot tears that trickle down the face, the great lump in the throat, the heaviness in the chest, the breaking of the heart, all these disintegrate our personal world and destroy our reality.

As a doctor, he had built a wall between himself and the pain of loss; he had fortified it with sympathetic indifference to the tragedy of others. He was saddened by the death of people and could understand their relatives' agony, but he was also unperturbed by their deep sorrow and went on with his life as before, without the heavy burden of experience.

But when he lost his own people, he sank deep into his personal anguish, drowned inside the bottomless pit of spiritual pain and, having realised that he was a lonely bystander in an irrational world, considered his fate, his misery, and his happiness more profoundly.

During the voyage from Cyprus to Rhodes, everyone on board was baffled by his severe and sad look. No one, either sailor or passenger, knew what troubled him, and they often wondered what the cause of his depression was. They saw him sitting in isolation every day, holding the Arabic book and reading. Other times, usually in the afternoon, he leaned against the wooden rail of the prow, from where he gazed at the dark, breaking waters silently and absent-mindedly, as if he didn't know where he was or where he was going. He sat alone; he even ate alone, like a wild animal. He avoided all the others, as if he despised them. Only the two monks had approached him, talked to him, and kept him company.

In time, the good-humoured sailors got used to his distant, almost invisible presence. One of them justified Leon's behaviour by saying that it was probably because of a family tragedy; and from that moment on, thinking about his pain and sympathising with him, they left him in peace, in his silent isolation.

Leon understood them. He used to behave with the same sympathetic indifference as well; he wanted to know the other man's problem, to show compassion, but all he actually cared about was to satisfy his natural curiosity and feel the momentary relief that he himself had been spared from such a tragedy. Consequently, he avoided socialising, simply because he wouldn't have to speak. Besides, what did he have to say? Describe how his beloved was slaughtered? Confess that his best friend saved his life by giving his own? Mention how the monsters from the dark worlds of the skies came alive? Or confide to them that he owned the book that held the secrets of life and death?

No, he didn't have many things to talk about. He was hurting. His heart had been ripped out from his chest. He couldn't endure recalling the events; he could still see them in his dreams. Every night, after he had closed his eyes and drifted into the depths of slumber, nightmares upset his body and soul. Again and again, he dreamt of Rebecca's smile fading away in an outpouring of blood, while Theodorus' shining, wise eyes perished inside the darkness.

He also saw many other things, bizarre things. He dreamt about the worlds of the stars, while the more of the *Necronomicon* he read, the more details and images he observed: planets surrounded by grey-green fog, multi-tentacled beasts, almost divine, with an octopus quality, huge, malevolent, and bloodthirsty, travelling along with him, following his own personal course, like authorised torturers.

But what unsettled and startled him awake, soaking him with sweat on the hammock he was sleeping in, inside the hull of the ship, was that in every single dream he was chased by the same hideous-looking shadowy beast. He couldn't see it clearly, but he knew that it was coming closer intending to harm him, and no matter how fast Leon ran to avoid it, no matter how far, it always caught up with him and eventually seized him.

When John Lambrinus suggested that he should settle in Patmos, Leon first considered the offer before making his decision. He reflected it was better and wiser to settle there instead of Rhodes, which many lords usually visited, and where the risk he ran of someone recognising him was great.

The risk wasn't insignificant, since the island of Rhodes is one of the naval bases of the droungarios of the seamen, the admiral who controls the vulnerable side of the Empire from raids by Cretan and Arab pirates. The imperial fleet patrolled the area, and he personally knew many of the officers, including the admiral himself, Theodosius Moschinus.

Thus, having no prejudice against the place where John the Apostle wrote his prophetical text about the end of the world and the resurrection of the dead, he decided to settle in that small island of the Aegean Sea. He didn't think it was an omen, nor did he have a hidden agenda. Besides, he had read the *Necronomicon* and learned about the nature of reality, the misleading theories and doctrines that, once spread, distorted the truth.

He didn't doubt what he had read in the least. Theodorus had accepted every sentence with great ease, simply due to its plausibility, with no tangible proof, urged only by his theoretical knowledge. Leon, who had seen that rift in time and space, the shadowmorphs and the Iynges, Yog-Sothoth's followers, was not the one to judge the violation of all those things he once thought as the mighty explanations for the creation and the existence of the world.

All he worried about was the issue of reanimation. He had started having second thoughts, and the doubts gnawed away at his mind like maggots. He longed to see his loved ones alive again, but he was afraid of raising them.

Abdul was clear in his words: *"The dead men's journey does not offend. Let the soul be; do not attempt any pauses or returns. Ghastly and dreadful is the mistake to decide in the throes of grief."*

It was not only that, but also a veiled threat that *"Evil awaits whoever tries to be the Maker. Melanus is lurking, that shadow-tentacled judge, spawn of the darkest night, sucking the human breath, as a ruthless pursuer of sinners. In many and multiple forms, all over the world, he steps on the body; he cuts the breath short; bitter taste of death gives he, the Darkness-walker."*

Consequently, deep in sorrow and tormenting thoughts, daunted by the dead-end, he tried to shut himself inside the house John had offered him, in an effort to weigh up the deed and its results, having as sole companions the two dead bodies inside the pots. He didn't succeed.

When he took the abbot's offer, Leon had forgotten that Patmos, because of its sacredness, was a popular destination for dozens of suffering people from the islands and the western coast of Asia Minor. Before he had a chance to rest from his long voyage, the first sick people had already appeared at his front door, begging for help, despite the fact that they had come to the island hoping for a miracle by the saint.

He was weary and tortured by his thoughts, yet he couldn't turn them away. His morals and his conscientiousness toward his fellow humans' physical pain didn't allow him to remain passive. He evaluated the circumstances and asked Lambrinus to send him three monks every day, including Meligrates. He also had him assign at least five teenage islanders as his assistants.

Thanks to the great help Meligrates offered him, in only four days he managed to organise everything necessary for the clinic to be operational, while he also spent time treating the patients in a critical state. He wasn't pursued by time, nor did he try to catch up with it. By lying that Rebecca and Theodorus would come and find him, he had also set the day he would perform the reanimation ritual. He had to wait at least two weeks for the lie to seem plausible. So, even though he was irritated by the situation he was facing, he endured it patiently and at times accepted it stoically, since it helped him forget his misery.

The other thing he had also failed to take into account, when he thought about the future, was John's unforeseen secret doings.

Since the day they met, he hadn't detected anything strange in his behaviour, nor had he suspected a ruse. He thought he was taking all the necessary precautions, but most of the time he was actually absentminded, lost in pain and memories, but also in the information he had learnt from that book, which was the reason his loved ones had perished. The world he knew had collapsed, and the radical change in his life threw him hard inside sunless pits; that is why he hadn't realised how or when the abbot had started reading the book.

Leon himself read it every day, fearlessly and thoughtlessly, in plain sight, since he knew that most of the men were illiterate seamen, but also because he believed that few of those who could read would be in the mood to pore over a medical textbook with unintelligible words and concepts, as the *Necronomicon* would seem to them.

He didn't even become suspicious of Lambrinus' daily visits after he had settled on the island. He thought they had to do with his ailment and kept welcoming him in a friendly mood. Only when he caught him secretly reading did he realise that he had behaved with foolish naïveté.

As usual, after he had examined him, Leon left him alone and went downstairs to tend to the patients who were assembled in his home yard. But at some point he needed to go back and pick up some medical instruments, and he found John sitting in front of the lectern, engrossed in reading.

He didn't react. On the contrary, he feared that this was the first time John had read the *Necronomicon*, and he shivered at the thought that the monk would have him arrested and accused of sorcery. His original alarm subsided when the supposedly ailing abbot left for the cloister community and said goodbye to him as politely as he had done on the previous days.

The suspicion that entered his mind only made him think of bad and tragic outcomes. Even if John was a heretic, Leon still ran the risk of the monk betraying him to others, because it was impossible to know his intentions. In addition, he wouldn't like for some heretical group to obtain the power the book had to offer, because, as opposed to Theodorus, he was convinced that the *Necronomicon* should never belong to humans—except, perhaps, only the passages that referred to the ways of protection against creatures from other planets.

The next day, he had tangible proof of John's secret game, watching him reading the book yet again, at a time when Leon wasn't supposed to be in the room. He neither knew nor could understand why John hadn't turned him in yet. He practically didn't care that much, because all he was interested in was to hasten the reanimation of his two loved ones and take them west, to Italy, maybe even further than that.

Neophytus Vuketes wasn't from Rhodes. He came from Chandax, an Arab-occupied region of Crete. He had lived in his beautiful homeland until he was thirty, when the city cadi accused him of sorcery and asked the island's lord to kill him in an exemplary manner. This would have entailed decapitating him, hanging him from the city walls, and burning his body in the centre of the market.

Such a decision left him no choice but to leave Crete and seek salvation in the free land of the Empire. So he settled in Rhodes, where he could now practise his darkest secrets; for the cadi's accusations had not been false but true.

Vuketes was indeed a sorcerer. To everyone else he pretended to be an alchemist and a devout Christian, but he actually belonged to the Esoteric Order of Dagon, whose members secretly worshipped the Old One, Dagon, who had once come from the stars.

The Order of Father Dagon in Crete had been formed in the mists of time. Not even its own members knew exactly when His ancestors had begun worshipping Him; but they knew from the antiquated records they kept that there were followers of His since the time of Minos, the King of olden Crete, whose memory is lost within the labyrinths of legends.

Ever since those ancient times, the Dagonists always acted secretly and founded other branches of the order in many other places in the Mediterranean, where they joined the local groups of the same denomination. They were never numerous, and in every historical era they ended up being pursued by the followers of different religions, who were opposed to their human sacrifices and their blood rituals. Especially after Christianity prevailed and after the ruthless banishment they suffered, the members of the order were reduced to merely ten families; as a result, they rarely performed their rituals and, in order to avoid pursuits, they ended up sacrificing their own kin, and then made their deaths look like an accident to the Christian prefect of Crete.

But after the Arabs conquered the island and transformed it into a stronghold for pirates, their small community started to feel more relaxed inside the lawless regime. Even though they still worked in the dark, secretly and quietly, performing what other people believed to be their unholy rituals, they weren't so afraid as they had been when Crete belonged to the Empire, since they now could buy off someone's silence, support, and even the collaboration of the unprincipled and eternally corrupted pirates. Apart from that, they performed their blood-stained human sacrifices more easily, without running the risk of provoking the rage of the victim's family, since at the monthly slave market in Chandax they could now buy the poor Christians that the slave traders brought from every corner of the Mediterranean Christian Europe.

Even in such a corrupted regime, there are still those honest and righteous people who will confront paranoid and inhuman actions. The benevolent cadi sought the sorcerer's death, but gold is always a most efficient assistant; thus, by bribing the lieutenant of the master arch-pirate, Vuketes managed to flee to Rhodes.

For ten years he posed as a law-abiding citizen of the Empire, but he continued his secret, blood-quenched acts. Whenever he was given the chance, he killed an unsuspicious Rhodian or kidnapped a girl from one of the villages and performed his dark rituals, offering his victims' blood to Dagon, hoping that He would grant his wishes.

Just like every believer of any god, he too was convinced that he would eventually be able to contact Him, and he never doubted this belief, not even when he came so close to being arrested in Crete. So, when he saw the monk entering his laboratory and then heard him listing all the ingredients needed for the mixture of the star-stone activation, he knew that the long-awaited moment had finally arrived.

On the previous night, he sacrificed a three-year-old girl, drank her blood, and ate her heart as an offering, which strengthened and refreshed him. The exultation he felt and the awakening of his senses puzzled him, and he later understood that it was a sign, an omen that God fully accepted the devotion he showed to him.

He knew the ingredients from the holy grimoire all the members of the Order owned, just as he knew the method to prepare the mixture; yet he had never managed to find and activate a real Mnizurin, at least not until he met John Lambrinus. Even though he didn't get any information, he read in his face and eyes the secret he was hiding. He was certain that the monk from Patmos had what he desired.

In order to make sure whether he belonged to the Order of Dagon, he asked him a few recondite questions, but John was unaware of the right answers. This meant that he was acting on his own, so it was easy to kill him and steal the coveted object. In fact, he put this plan into action on that very day, considering every possible detail.

Wasting no more time, he sent an encoded message to the other Dagon worshippers of Chandax, with a seaman who cooperated with the pirates, setting the date and their course of action. He needed the help of his like-minded colleagues not only to steal the Mnizurin, but also to summon Father Dagon. So, when he met with them, he announced most emphatically that the great moment they were hoping for, the day they would set eyes on their God descending from the torn skies, was near . . .

The house John Lambrinus had offered Leon wasn't a luxurious or sturdy structure, but meagre and made of wood. Generally in Patmos most edifices were built of wood and brick, apart from the church that stood in the centre of the village.

The small Aegean island had never been a very appealing place to settle in, and so, ever since it became Roman property, it was turned into a place of exile. Arid, with little vegetation, few olive trees and vineyards, it couldn't possibly attract people to choose it for permanent residence. At times, the island had seen some increase to its population, but soon the youth left for other islands that offered better living conditions. In Patmos, one had to struggle simply to survive.

People came and went. Only the old fishermen remained and a few dozen hermits, who lived in dispersed cloisters at the foot of the mountain, where the "Cave of the Apocalypse" was located. Not even the pilgrims stayed more than one week; except for the destitute and the sick; the rest returned to their respective homelands. One reason for this was that the island lacked the necessary resources to support them; another was that because of its few inhabitants it was also unprotected, becoming an easy prey for the pirates.

There were two things that the Patmians were most afraid of: fires and pirates—the former because the island, due to the dry climate, could turn to ashes within minutes; the latter because of their misdeeds and the kidnappings. There was not a single family on the island that hadn't lost a family member to a pirate raid. The rapes, the beatings, and the stealing could be endured; but not the kidnappings.

The pirates rarely killed, especially those who didn't fight back. They usually beat or injured whoever resisted. Other than that, they raped and stole food and valuables. But the worst thing they did was to snatch the prettiest girls and the well-formed boys in order to sell them at the slave market. They sold the maidens for more money than the rest, and kept for themselves all the young men they hadn't castrated, so they would teach them pirating.

The parents were always left behind, beaten up, raped, devastated, and distraught, because there is nothing worse for a parent, apart from death, than their child being taken from them. All the Patmians, without exception, had experienced this particular pain; and because they didn't want to lose more children, they built basements in their houses so that they could hide their offspring along with their meagre belongings.

In the basement of his own house, Leon had placed the two earthen pots he had brought from Kyrenia. None of the locals or the sailors on board suspected that the pots contained human bodies; instead, they thought they were filled with olive oil or wine.

With Meligrates' help, he wedged them deep inside the basement, in a small space that resembled a room. He didn't go down there often, so that he wouldn't attract any suspicions, but also because he couldn't bear the thought that inside were Theodorus and Rebecca.

But on the day he had decided to bring them back from the dead, he performed as a doctor should—with apathy. He lined up all the ingredients he would need, lit oil lamps and candles to shed light to the place, and laid two makeshift straw cots with sheets.

Only when he opened the lids and the pungent smell of disinfectant hit him did he begin worrying. He stayed there for a few moments, sad and haggard, plagued by the macabre image of his two loved ones' corpses; then, taking a deep breath, he first took out Rebecca. He clenched his teeth when he saw the greenish-yellow colour of her skin, and his knees gave way when his eyes went to the grey-coloured slash on her throat. Her skin was creased at the ends of the cut, and her flesh had the dark colour or decomposition.

His heart beat sadly, but he wasn't disgusted as anyone would be if they had to look at the dead body of their beloved. However, he felt woeful, and he was overwhelmed by all the memories of her smiles, her kisses, her orgasms. With bated breath, he carefully removed her from the pot and laid her gingerly, almost devoutly, upon the cot. He stood by her pillow, affectionately caressed her wet hair, and, thinking that he might soon be able to feel her breath on his face again, he took courage.

He moved trance-like, mechanically. The shadows formed by the flames on the walls of the underground room, the nauseating stench of the disinfectant, the slime on the two bodies, and the yellowish shades on their skins might prevent someone else from proceeding. But he continued, disregarding the colour and the smell of death. He shuddered at the thought, yes, but he stuck to his goal, and hope gleamed in his eyes.

The hole on Theodorus' chest made by the arrow looked as if it had closed up; it was just a black spot, and around it there was wrinkled skin. Leon never met his parents; for this reason he always treated his elder friend like a father, especially when his grandfather was still alive and they all sat on the terrace of their houses in Constantinople with Bashar, talking about the current situation and the events in the Empire.

That is how the future he dreamt about looked like when they were in Kyrenia. He longed to have children with Rebecca, and Theodorus would be their grandpa, who would offer them his wisdom and talk to them about Plato.

A teardrop clung to his eyelashes. He grimaced and covered up the dead bodies in white sheets. He still had the chance to live all he dreamt about, and so he began the ritual with confidence and high spirits. All he thought about was that in a few hours he could again hold them in his arms, alive . . .

The technique of raising a recently deceased person is different from the one applied for someone who has crossed to the other side a long time before. Abdul had recorded the details with great clarity in his grand work. The difference lies in the time needed for the ritual and for the revival of the flesh, which can be reconstructed artificially by simply having one of the dead person's hairs.

But the return of the soul to the body is also based on the same principle. Both for the recently departed and for the long-dead, the power of a certain sound is used. This sound is attuned to the soul's pulse and leads its way to the body.

What Leon had to do was to perform a special ceremonial healing operation to restore the preserved bodies of his loved ones to their former state and then spend many hours reiterating the sound to achieve reanimation. It is much easier to summon back a soul that has just left the body than one that has already been through the process of reformulation in the beyond.

Even laymen instinctively know this process, so it is forbidden for the relatives to speak in a loud voice around the deceased; consequently, the mourning period is forced on them for the first nine days, because during this time, before the soul sets off for other worlds and the body is still in a good condition, there is a chance of return.

The arduous procedure lasted three hours, and when first Rebecca, then Theodorus opened their eyes, Leon slumped on the floor completely exhausted. He was so tired that he couldn't even feel happy when he saw them alive, writhing under the sheets. He had been so wearied by the repetition of the sound that he was too weak to take a normal breath, hug them, or express his happiness in any way.

He curled up on the floor, sweaty, almost breathless, and stayed there, even when they sat up, looking at him in confusion. All he managed to notice was that there wasn't any mark from Gregorius' sword on Rebecca's throat, and that the arrow wound on Theodorus' chest was nowhere to be seen. Then he closed his eyes and was lost within the darkness of a deep sleep.

When he opened his eyes and saw the familiar images of his world again, Theodorus couldn't grasp what had happened. Until a short while ago, he had been following a sound that was pulling him back, enchanted. He wasn't conscious of the situation, but simply sensed the pull, a great power calling him back, telling him to change his course and return, which he did instinctively but unwillingly. He sensed the calling of birth or rebirth and, enticed by the exquisite pulse, obeyed just like Odysseus, who had been tempted by the song of the Sirens.

Theodorus didn't have senses during his journey to the beyond, at least not in the way he knew them in the human world. He didn't hear or see, but he could sense everything. He was deaf and blind, but he "heard" and "saw" everything through the pulses and vibrations his soul received. It even felt as if he "smelled" the sounds, those oscillations of time and space.

He couldn't describe the circumstances, whether they were lovely or ugly, good or bad, or anything like that; he just headed toward a specific destination and "observed" the stirring of life around him, continuous vibrations and endless palpitations, knowledge and information entering him without leaving any trace, marks, or feelings. If he could describe his experience at all, he'd say that he was like a drop of water travelling in oceans of eternity, until it was ready to detach.

When he took his first breath for the second time in his life, it was painful; he was uncomfortable and aware of the limitations his human body imposed on him. He could recall a few scattered experiences, but for an indeterminable amount of time he was unable to grasp reality. When he revived completely, Leon told him that he had been in a state of aphasia for five hours. So had Rebecca.

He crouched outside the wooden cloister and listened to the sounds carefully. A murmuring reached his ears, and he could tell that the abbot was praying. He eyed his companions derogatorily, almost in disgust. Their eyes gleamed with intensity and greed at the thought of the looting. They had swords and knives in their hands, and they stank of sweat and onions. Of course, he couldn't have expected much from pirates.

Neophytus Vuketes had been extremely angry the previous night when he saw the other members of the order arrive at the deserted beach of Rhodes under the custody of pirates. The plan he had devised to steal the Mnizurin and perform the summoning ritual didn't include all those filthy and iconoclastic men whose only concern was what they could fill their stomachs with, what they could carry in their hands, and what they could stick their dirty penises in.

But no matter how angry he got and how much he swore at his brothers of the order, he didn't show his revulsion to that sea rabble. He knew that if he tried to send them away they would get angry, and if he didn't pay them he would have to fight them. So he accepted them silently, even though he was worried that their unruliness might cause trouble and he might miss the chance of a lifetime.

Of course, as they travelled from Rhodes to Patmos, he thought that his brothers may have acted wisely for bringing them into play, because he didn't know if there were any guards on the island for the visit of an official, and also he could make use of them in case of a probable resistance by the islanders.

Even so, every time he looked at them he was appalled, especially the two who had accompanied him to John Lambrinus' cloister. The rest of the pirates along with the Dagonists had scattered around the village, waiting for the signal to attack.

His only true concern was whether the imperial army had taken notice of them, even though the pirate leader had assured him they hadn't, offering a coaxing smile. But he knew that it was easy to spot six ships in the small sea, and especially if they were pirate biremes, with their colourful hulls and sails.

He took a deep breath and buried his concerns. He was about to accomplish the most significant mission of his life and shouldn't waste time thinking pessimistically. So he knocked on the cloister door decisively. The wooden hut where John lived at the foot of the mountain was no different from the rest; it was a small building, plain and stable, constructed simply to protect its occupant from the elements of Nature.

"Brother John Lambrinus, I come from Rhodes. I have a parcel from Neophytus Vuketes, the alchemist, addressed to you," he said in a steady, somewhat altered voice as soon as he heard the abbot responding to the knocking.

John interrupted his praying and with a face alight with joy, stood up, and went to answer the door. He longed for this moment and pictured it every day in anticipation, because he knew that once he had the ingredients for the mixture, his dream of seeing his Maker would finally come true.

He was so excited when he heard he was going to have the parcel that he was out of breath with nervousness. His heart was beating insanely and his palms were sweating as he reached for the door handle.

He didn't have time to react when he saw the alchemist before him. Someone grappled the door and opened it wider, distracting him, while Vuketes swiftly hit him hard on his head with the bat he was holding.

John's head was covered in blood. He felt dizzy and stumbled, but didn't fall. He had been hurt numerous times in the battles he had fought in his youth, and this specific hit hadn't been so hard as to immobilise him.

He instantly retreated inside the cloister and picked up the first stool he could find. He didn't know what was going on, but he knew he wouldn't give up without a fight. With fiery eyes, he scanned his surroundings and observed his opponents. The fighter within him made the pious monk disappear and let out a deafening cry, providing him with the necessary courage to confront the situation.

He wasn't concerned with the reason for that unexpected attack; all he cared about was to survive, and in order to do that he had to fight. Provided he emerged victorious, he would ask questions later.

A second pirate appeared at the threshold, with a bared sword in hand. John cowered, examining him. He could beat them, but the space wasn't sufficient to move the way he wanted to.

"It's no use, John. Don't fight back," said Vuketes with a smirk. "Hand me the Mnizurin and we'll let you live."

The alchemist's voice had all those characteristics that proved he was lying: a mocking and derogatory tone. John didn't stall for time; with a swift move, he smashed the stool on the face of the pirate closer to him, while another move brought him face to face with the one behind.

The stool was reduced to smithereens and the pirate's forehead was covered in blood. The dark-skinned man let out a short moan and fell to his knees. However, the other pirate jabbed his knife in the defiant monk's belly. He wouldn't have been able to do that if Lambrinus had his metal breastplate on, as he usually did when he fought.

Despite his wound and the pain that shook him, John wrapped his hands around his opponent's throat and saw him turn red, but he didn't manage to put him out of action. Vuketes gave him a mighty blow on his head again and brought him to his knees.

"You lousy dog! Filthy Christian!" Vuketes grabbed the kneeling monk by the hair and pushed him on the dirt floor. "Keep an eye on him!" he shouted in the face of the pirate who was gaping at him, still unable to realise that the old man had almost choked him.

The Cretan sorcerer didn't have to ask where the Mnizurin was. The moment he asked for it, he had his eyes fixed upon John and saw the imperceptible flicker of his gaze to the left.

With rapid movements, he opened the wooden wardrobe and at the bottom, below an old, rusty copper pot, inside a similarly crafted mug, he found the much craved-for red-black stone. His eyes shone; he threw the sacred relics once used by John the Apostle on the floor and turned the Mnizurin toward the light of the oil lamp on the shabby nightstand.

"We got it!" he cried, smiling in delight, addressing the pirate who had recovered from the monk's blow. "Signal them to begin," he ordered, his eyes still screwed on the red-black star-stone.

"Ia Dagon h'am k'let. Iä iä h'thag!" he exclaimed triumphantly, kissing the Mnizurin gently and placing it on his forehead. "God of the dark sea depths, your followers will soon welcome You. Your throne will be adorned with the skulls of the faithless and the carpet You will walk on will be crimson with blood, laid with carcasses."

Vuketes' face glowed with joy and his eyes sparkled with longing. He covered the star-stone in his palms and turned to the pirate who was guarding the queasy John.

"What do I do with this one?" the pirate asked in Arabic, not minding the tone and the gibberish of the alchemist.

"Get him up, I'll offer him to our God. Tonight we're welcoming Dagon!"

For almost five hours they were like bad copies of themselves. They moved and spoke clumsily, like toddlers who had just learned to walk and talk. Sometimes they looked like people who had suffered brain damage, as their movements were awkward and careless. Their speech was slurry, with gaps between words, and their utterances were mixed and incomprehensible. Many times they spoke in unknown languages and, generally, acted oddly; sometimes they spoke languidly and at still other times they wouldn't stop.

Slowly and steadily, they began regaining their lost kinaesthesia, until the blur was gone from their eyes and the facial expressions revealed that they were conscious of their surroundings and circumstances. The first to recover was Rebecca, who, after recognising Leon, hugged him tightly.

They remained like this for a while, holding each other, lips locked together, their hearts beating fast with emotion. Their fervour was great and their faces glowed. They said nothing, only stared into each other's eyes, holding each other tightly and taking in each other's existence.

Their reunion wasn't like that of the couples that are away from each other because of life circumstances or because their selfishness forces them to stay apart for a while. No; their reunion had all the characteristics of tragic loss, the awareness of the eternal parting imposed by death.

All couples in love, when they are at the peak of their emotional charge, take vows of reunion and exchange hearty promises for the imminent tragedy that will someday irreversibly shatter their bond: death. It's in love's nature to smooth space and time, to bind the souls in ardour, and to offer the mind a way out. The ultimate beauty of life makes them believe in the power of their love and consider it so pure and grand that it will unite them even in the afterlife.

That is what was different in their own exultation. They had managed, despite the unexpected ending, to find each other and be together again. It was something that not even Orpheus, "the father of song," as Abdul named him, who knew sounds and their properties, had been able to accomplish when he attempted to bring his beloved Eurydice back from the beyond.

The moment they realised they were back together again, everything was lost around them. There were no outside noises, smells, lights, or shadows, only the pulse of their love, creating a world much more beautiful than the real one, more perfect and ideal only for them. If they could stop time and freeze space, they would, so they could stay like this, forever united, a love sculpture, a drop of life in the ocean of death.

Nonetheless, Theodorus' moaning brought them back to present time, in the basement, on the damp cot, filthy and reeking, but alive and ready to rebuild their lives.

Demetrius Meligrates was sitting at a bay at the southwestern side of the island and prayed in time with the repetitive sounds created by the combination of the sea, the land, and the wind. He liked secluding himself, staying away from the church and losing himself within the mazes of his thoughts. Alone, in nature, staring at the sea and the sky, he felt that he came closer to God, that he was united with Him, especially during the time when the colours changed and the light blue gradually turned to orange and then to violet. He immersed himself in visual grandeur and read the cloud shapes, considering them heavenly messages.

Many a time he had imagined himself being able to fly and nestle against those white clouds that, when approaching the sun, are tinted like vain women, seeking to attract and seduce. During those hours, almost enchanted by an array of sounds and colours, he wondered about the ethereal world, Heaven. He longed to go to Heaven, climb on the clouds, and cohabitate with angels, but also with the honest, modest, and pure souls of the humans whose deeds had earned them a place within merciful God's kingdom.

That was the reason why he left the village at dusk, on serene nights, so as to cherish that stolen feeling of happiness. Long ago, he used to think that by doing this he sinned, because he didn't attend the evening mass. He had also heard that only heretics prayed outside of church and feared for his soul, wondering whether he might end up in Hell, and he confessed his transgression to the priest. When the priest told him that St. Vasilius wrote that we can and must pray whenever possible, he was relieved.

A thousand thoughts crossed his mind during that meditation time and, lately, almost all had to do with Doctor Peleuses. From the day Leon had chosen him as his assistant and put him in charge of the patients, something was different inside him. The contact with the sick, the concern about the state of their health, the examination of the symptoms, the preparation of the medicines, but above all that charitable feeling of sympathy, made him care more about medicine and feel more energetic and dynamic.

That was why he had found himself closer to Leon, regarding him as a friend and a teacher. He was also the reason he neglected his religious duties, something he once dreaded out of fear for sin; but now that he helped the poor and wretched, the thought that he was doing something wrong didn't even cross his mind.

He stared at the sea hopefully and stood up from the sand to go back to his cloister. But what he saw terrified him, and he cowered behind a spiky bush.

A group of armed men headed toward the village. His mind shook with the realisation: "Pirates!" He looked again to make sure. The men wore no uniforms and were disorderly; half of them had Arabic features.

He didn't waste any more time. With his heart racing, his knees trembling, he went toward the sea. He had to inform the monks and the Patmians about the attack as soon as possible. In order to go unnoticed by the intruders, he thought he should follow the coastline to the path leading to the village.

He could still remember the last time they had been attacked. His stomach was instantly tied to a knot by the unpleasant past memories. They had hurt him badly and had shaved off his beard, not because they wanted him to reveal a hiding place for valuables or to give them money, but simply because they wanted to have fun.

He ran as fast as he could. He knew he could beat them to the village. If he failed, he would try to climb to the top of the mountain and light the beacon fire. He had heard a fisherman saying that the imperial fleet was near. They might not be able to arrive fast enough to prevent the intrusion, but it was certain that they would catch up with the pirates at sea and rescue any kidnapped victims.

Thinking all this, he decided to drop by Leon's house. The doctor wasn't feeling very well, and that morning he had asked not to be disturbed for any reason, so that he could recover. Meligrates had to inform him and alert him of the danger.

The flow of life is such that it is always determined by unsuspected and unforeseen factors. A wrong step, an inconsiderate turn from our routine way, even a simple word we say or hear could lead us to unique, unexpected situations. The Arabs call this kismet, the Greeks *moira,* and the Christians destiny, but all three have the same meaning: our path is predetermined. Even those insignificant, random incidents, the actions and reactions in our daily lives eventually seem to have been defined by something or someone beyond the limits of our perception. We can grasp this awareness and realisation of reality once we consider the result.

Everything in our lives looks like a mathematical process, as the Pythagoreans used to claim; something is added to something else and they all add up to a total. What Theodorus didn't know beforehand, when he thought about the meaning of life, was whether the events that make up our lives are random or just their outcome. He couldn't possibly know the truth, because like most people he also considered the course of events after they happened and not during.

When he read the *Necronomicon* and reflected on what he had learnt, he wondered if it was inevitable that he had found and translated it or it had just got to his hands accidentally, as a result of a combination of unforeseen incidents. He wondered how far back in time he had to go in order to find the first moment in the order of events: the conspiracy against Porphyrogenitus? his love of Plato? Eudoxia's death? Earlier, when he was a student? Or later in Damascus, in the mere fact that Leon saved someone from danger by accidentally killing someone else and then everything taking its course? Which one was it? Fate or chance?

These were the kinds of questions that probably occupied his mind before he died and then came back to life. But at that moment, with the knowledge of the situation beating inside him, with the experience of death and the flow of existence, he didn't consider nor stop to ponder on ill-timed philosophical matters.

He had little memory of his journey to the beyond. He could still recall some fragments, though, random ones, like sudden flashes, but generally, he couldn't recall his experience totally. The only things he understood now in their entirety were Plato's words on the journey of the soul and also the verse by the poet Pindar, that man is a dream of shadow. The rest was hazy and vague.

He probably needed more time to remember, or he had to stay calm and relax. But he didn't have the time or the calmness. When he managed to be himself again, before he had a chance to wash that disinfectant stench off his drenched skin, developments brought him face to face with another threat.

The moment he and Leon sat down to talk, while Rebecca was in the kitchen boiling water for their bath, their words were interrupted by loud, harsh sounds, women screaming, scary dog barks, and pirates' wild cries. They got to their feet and darted to the window.

In the street and across from them, in the house yards, armed pirates were dragging women and children along, beating men, and grabbing old people by their chitons. Others, completely surrendered to violence and looting, carried any valuables they found in makeshift bundles; still others undressed women, tore off their clothes, hit them without mercy, and raped them moaning with pleasure, exhilarated by the pain they were causing, delighted by the pleas and the sad cries.

Theodorus and Leon didn't have time to react. The very next moment, the door on their right was smashed open and at the threshold were two bare-chested men wielding their swords.

Leon tried to move, but Theodorus held him. Two more pirates sneaked into the house and started searching through the rooms, growling.

"Gold!" one of them yelled in broken Greek and grabbed Leon by the throat. "Give me, quick!"

"A wench!" someone exclaimed happily after finding Rebecca in the kitchen. The next moment, he dragged her by the hair to the living room and thrust her in front of the table. Leon grunted and tried to break free from the pirate's hold, but the point of the sword was gently pressed against his throat and immobilised him.

The pirate, who had Rebecca lifted her dress but froze when he pushed himself against her, softly moaning with lust. He slapped her hard, spat on her face and, disgusted, he shoved her on the floor.

"You dirty whore! Skunk!" he shouted and spat on her again. The stench of the disinfectant nauseated him.

"We're friends of the Damascene emir," said Theodorus in Arabic, trying to draw their attention. Out of the corner of his eye he noticed Rebecca's movements.

"Who gives a shit?" the pirate holding Leon shouted, but his companion tried to calm him down and looked at him in the eye.

"Give us all the money you got," he said in a studied calmness. "We'll take you with us to Crete, and if you're lying and we don't get a single gold coin, we'll butcher you, but after we torture you so much you'll wish you had never fooled us. Yusuf, let that woman alone."

"I did leave her, that filthy cunt. Not even a badger would fuck her," he said and laughed loudly, causing his companions to roar with laughter, too.

Rebecca, scared and desperate, tears in her eyes, ran to Leon's arms. She was so shocked and disheartened, not believing her hideous fate, that she was about to collapse. No sooner had she come back to life than she was already experiencing another violent incident.

"Hurry! You, give us all the money you have. Woman, you pack a change of clothes for all of you and we're off!" shouted the pirate, whose cunning black eyes glittered at the thought that the emir of Damascus would offer him gifts and a title for rescuing his friends.

Leon looked at Rebecca, who ran up the stairs and opened the crypt that he had made on the wooden floor. The pirate stooped over him, eyes wide open, thirsty for gold. He pushed him aside and took all the coins he found.

"Why are you hiding these books? What are you? Heretics?" he asked and opened the *Necronomicon*. He didn't know how to read Greek and tossed it aside. "What's this?" he asked and picked up the Mnizurin.

"It's a pebble," said Theodorus calmly. "My wife carved it."

"Disgusting!" The pirate winced, appalled by its slimy texture, and threw it at Theodorus' feet.

"Muammar! Move your stinky ass over here!"

The third pirate came down from upstairs holding silk clothes in his hands. In front of him was Rebecca with a leather sack, in which Leon quickly shoved the two books.

"Out!" the pirate shouted and pushed him through the door.

In the streets, all that could be heard was the wailing of children and the moans of women. The most discouraging sound, though, was the silence of the men, who were weak, beaten up, and wounded, with their heads low, deep in sorrow, as they hadn't managed to protect their loved ones. Their appearance was such that they looked more like living corpses than humans.

"Stop it!" a man in a red cloak shouted. He repeated his order both in Greek and Arabic. He was accompanied by three women and four men, all of whom had a similar cloak on and were dressed in the typical local costume, distinguishing themselves from the gang of pirates.

"Take them all and go to the clearing outside the village. Hurry, we don't have much time." Theodorus discerned from his accent that he was Cretan.

At once the pirates ceased the rapes, the beatings, and the pillaging, obediently following his command. Shouting and pushing, they lined up all the hostages of the area and led them through the streets to a specific place. More pirates joined them, dragging along other captured Patmians.

Neither the pilgrims nor the hermits were spared captivity. All of them, over seven hundred people, men, women, and children of all ages, crying and moaning, walked under their captors' angry eyes. The attack had been so sudden and unexpected that not even one of them had the time to ring the church bell and sound the alarm, or even light the beacon fire to alert the imperial fleet. They were inconsolable, since they realised that they would spend the rest of their lives as slaves.

That's what they thought until they arrived at the clearing and saw approximately sixty men and women in red cloaks. That's when they realised that their fate would be even worse than they had imagined.

9. The God from the Stars

The pirates led the Patmians to an open space with low vegetation and no trees and ordered them to sit on the ground. There was nothing but grey rocks and sun-scorched pebbles. In front of them was a pile of wood and next to that there were several objects.

Neither the cool lapping of the waves nor the gentle breeze could ease the tension in the least. The Patmians knew that the pirates normally attacked, did what they had to do, and left within an hour. This particular group didn't seem to be in a hurry. On the contrary, they meekly obeyed their oddly dressed masters and procrastinated, calm and carefree.

But what really frightened the hostages were the Cretans, who didn't look like slave traders and whose manner didn't betray their intentions. They simply gathered at one side of the clearing and talked in hushed voices. Their behaviour increased the Patmians' apprehension even more, since the idea of death flooded their minds. They couldn't think of anything but the worst.

Theodorus was sitting at the edge of that miserable sea of people. He silently watched what was happening, just like everyone else, in order to grasp the situation. Strangely enough, his instinct wasn't alerting him as it used to, signalling danger, but spoke to him and showed him macabre images and bloody scenes, as if offering him a glimpse of the future. The intensity of those projections was such that it brought him vertigo and disoriented him.

There were moments when he sensed invisible presences, heard voices, and saw buildings that weren't there. Not even the rustling of dry weeds or the lapping of the water affected him now; he didn't process them as natural sounds, but had the impression that he could understand Nature's language itself.

From the moment of his reanimation he realised that something was different in the way he understood reality. Not only did his every breath have the taste and scent of life, but each move, word, or colour also seemed to make a different impression inside him, sharper and at the same time more emotional.

Had he more time, he would undoubtedly have considered it thoroughly, but the rapid succession of events left him no room to think of anything but their outcome. And so he was silent while examining the Cretans, his temples throbbing with concern.

The same thing was happening in Rebecca's mind. She saw movements, heard voices, and felt things that weren't happening at the time. A red-black layer of mist sporadically concealed her line of vision, and unconnected events appeared before her in momentary flashes.

She would lose track of time every now and then, tiny moments that disappeared from her memory as if they had never existed or never happened. She was holding Leon's hand and suddenly realised that he was holding her inside his arms and her hands weren't touching him. She could see one of the pirates standing in front of her and then, without registering how, he was behind her. Even her thoughts betrayed these interruptions in time.

Terrified, seeking an answer, she looked at Theodorus and could see the same feelings reflected in his eyes. In fact, she thought she heard his voice, talking straight to her inside her head; but as she was so worried and light-headed by the pandemonium of the hallucinations, she paid no attention.

But the thing that scared them both was a bizarre and disparate howling, like a distant whisper. It was a chilling and persisting sound, which sometimes was like a vague word, and even though they looked for the source of it, they failed. This situation had them on edge.

Leon, extremely concerned, attempted to talk to the pirate guarding them. His intention was to extract some information from him, but the man put him off, poking him hard. Leon was annoyed by his violent behaviour, but he didn't react. He knew he couldn't do anything without risking his or his loved ones' lives. The pirates were impulsive and, even though they only had profit in mind, they had no control over their actions. If they got angry, they would kill him first and regret spilling his blood later. So he clenched his jaw and pinned his eyes on the Cretans.

The darkness had unfolded its black starlit veil and the intruders, without any feeling of dread, lit their torches. Only the sound of the children crying disturbed the deadly quiet of the place. The wounded men and the abused women had stopped wailing and moaning, in case they caused more violent reactions. The fear was palpable.

Suddenly, a great fire brightened the night and its light flickered on the Patmians' desolate faces. The Cretans devoutly formed a circle around it and started chanting in a soft voice. Their rhythmical murmuring caused shivers in the others, even the mighty pirates.

John Lambrinus was sitting in the front row, where Vuketes had assigned him, so he could have the chance to see the coming of the "real God," as he had sarcastically told him. He was applying pressure on the wound in his stomach, blaming himself for the pirate raid and the assembly of the demon-worshippers.

He kept his eyes fixed on the movements of the strange group, like a spectator at a play whose ending he already knew, in contrast to the rest of the hostages, who didn't. He could sense the danger spreading around him like an invisible noose and stifling him.

At one point, as the disturbing psalm continued to scrape his ears, he decided to act and warn the unfortunate islanders. He couldn't bear the responsibility that, because of his personal ambition, those hundreds of Christians would be sacrificed at the altar of a bloodthirsty beast. He stood up bravely and shouted that the Cretans were sorcerers and were summoning Satan.

A new wave of horror swept over the kidnapped people as soon as they heard the abbot revealing the intentions of the pirates and the group leading them. Many women fainted at the thought that they would end up in Hell, being constantly raped by hideous fiends, while the men attempted to resist one last time. But the pirates' swords, glistening in the light of the torches and the fire, brought death to some of them. The rest crouched down disheartened, refusing to witness the ritual that was taking place.

"Pray, my brothers!" John yelled, wincing with pain. "God's love will embrace us and no harm will ever come to our souls. Pray with me."

He no sooner had started praying than he fell unconscious to the ground. One of the pirates had run and hit him hard on the nape of his neck with a bat, and another monk who tried to protect him was severely beaten on the back.

"If anyone tries to stand or speak, we'll kill 'em!" the pirate shouted, flaunting his bat in the air. He was one of the Cretans who had converted to Islam, and that made him more dangerous than his companions because he constantly wanted to prove that he didn't feel a drop of mercy for the believers of his former religion.

The hostages ceased their every move and sank into a deep, fatalistic silence. Their frightened eyes mirrored the steps of death, just as every one of them pictured them. One thing was certain for all: there was no hope for salvation.

Once the whispered chanting had stopped, Neophytus Vuketes broke the circle formed by the Dagonists and put on a black tiara. His companions had bestowed upon him the honour of being the ritual leader, even though he wasn't the eldest or the master of the order. His face was alight with happiness and his constant smirk made his satisfaction evident.

In slow and studied movements, he stood before the fire, raised his hands toward the dark sky, and took a few small, almost dancing steps, as if he were trying to stand on smooth ground or use a specific star to find his bearings.

Theodorus and Rebecca craned their necks to see better. They had no doubt that the man was performing a magic ritual. The confirmation came with the hymn the other members started chanting, this time loudly and clearly.

Leon also watched in curiosity. The words of the psalm came from a rough, guttural language with many consonants, like those he encountered while reading the *Necronomicon*. He shuddered at the realisation and instinctively squeezed Rebecca's hand. From the way the Cretans uttered the words, it was clear that they didn't know the language, but simply tried to imitate its sounds, just as when someone tries to mimic the chirping of the birds, the barking of the wild animals, or the whistling of the wind.

However, those sounds were perfectly clear and comprehensible to the ears of Rebecca and Theodorus. It was as if they could hear the hymn of Dagon, the god from the stars, in their respective languages.

"They're sorcerers!" stated Theodorus to the pirate behind him. "They're going to hurt—"

He couldn't finish his sentence because he fell to the ground, bleeding. His lips were torn by a sudden and heavy punch. The eyes of the pirate who had hit him shone wildly with joy, and his sadistic smile reminded him of the grin of a ravenous wolf.

"Stay put and don't you talk or I'll kill you. We know what they are, we're no fools," the pirate growled, and Theodorus looked at the ritual site frowning.

The blow hadn't hurt him much, and he didn't mind the pain or the metallic taste of blood in his mouth. His only concern was to find a way to save as many Patmians as he could and of course to come out of this macabre adventure alive.

He hated people's stupidity—hated the fact that in order to satisfy their needs, they behaved cruelly and inhumanly. The pirates killed, raped, and stole for their material pleasure, and those Cretan charlatans, as he believed them to be, did the same for their supposed spiritual pleasure. The thought that the Dagonists may own a Mnizurin never crossed his mind, so he believed that this histrionic ritual would end in failure—a failure that would leave dozens of dead behind . . .

From far on the left, some monks who found the courage to express what they believed called out: "You're anti-Christian! Damned! We will never betray our God!"

"Pray, Christians! Don't let the demons enter you!"

A few pirates squeezed into the rows of people and started hitting the monks who shouted. Some Patmians found the courage to chant the Credo, but they stopped dead when they saw two severed heads thrown behind the Dagonists.

As soon as the hostages realised that the pirates were determined to impose order and silence with their swords, new crying and sobbing was heard ascending into the air. The mothers hugged their children tightly, the husbands hugged their wives, siblings hugged each other, letting out wailing and cries of pain.

Vuketes, completely uninterested in the hostages, lifted the Mnizurin he was holding and prayed in a loud voice. The members of the order, also indifferent to the islanders' tragedy, kneeled piously in total devotion, focused on their sacred ritual.

When the hymn was over, ten Dagonists got up and walked toward the crowd, snatched six Patmians, both men and women, led them near the fire, and forced them to kneel. Expressionless and focused, they looked at their high-priest, oblivious of the heartbreaking pleas that addressed them.

Vuketes walked on erect, followed by six women of the order who were holding silver goblets. His lean and angular face was unreadable; only the flickering shadows created by the fire swayed on it, like living creatures, alternating between long and short in an effort to embrace and even dominate him.

Unruffled and unaffected, he stood before each one of the hostages and offered a short incantation. Then, with a silver knife, ruthlessly and coldly, in studied moves that revealed his experience, he cut the throat of each victim. His companions next to him held their goblets below the fatal wound and filled them with hot blood.

Except for a few shouts of horror, the assembled crowd didn't react much to the slaughter. They were all so scared and haggard from the events that couldn't think clearly. Most of them seemed to have accepted their fate and prayed in silence.

When Vuketes killed the last of the women he stood between two of his companions, and the rest of the Dagonists started going in front of him one by one. They drank a sip of blood from the goblet of the priestess on the left and kissed the Mnizurin the master was holding. Then they dipped their thumbs in the right-hand priestess' goblet and marked their foreheads with three parallel vertical lines.

The hideous, barbaric ritual made the pirates exchange disgusted glances. Violence and brutality may run through their veins, but they weren't totally inhumane. However, apart from wincing and looking appalled, they didn't do anything, staying true to the deal they had made with the necromancers.

When the blood-drinking came to an end, three Dagonists set a deep metal basin before the master of ceremonies and poured the mixture for the activation of the Mnizurin inside. Vuketes kneeled and with devout gestures placed the star-stone in the centre. At the same time, the rest of the members started uttering their God's name rhythmically.

Demetrius Meligrates ran as fast as he could, but didn't manage to warn the Patmians about the danger they were in. He knew that the pirates had launched an attack, and that the group he had seen at the beach was just scouting the area for any fishermen who happened to be at the village at that time. So, shaken by the violent incidents taking place at the streets, he didn't go by Leon's house; instead, he ran to the mountain, with the intention of lighting the beacon fire.

He was able to cross the village, concealed by the shadows, and reach the foot of the mountain. Luckily, the mound he had to climb wasn't big, and was practically a hillock compared to real mountains. Nevertheless, when he reached the top landing, he was about to collapse with exhaustion. He wished to light the beacon fire right away, but he first stopped and tried to catch his breath beside the shabby columns of the ruined temple of the goddess Artemis, where a church had been built some centuries before.

He checked to see if anyone had followed him and then he scanned the village. In spite of the dusk, he could tell that the houses and streets were empty; no cries or wailing could be heard anymore, as when he had been halfway there. He was baffled and tried to understand what was going on; nothing made any sense. Only when he saw the fire lit by the Dagonists at the clearing did he realise what was happening; but still, new questions were formed inside him by the inexplicable delay of the pirates.

He wasted no more time thinking about it, however. He rushed to the small outpost where there was an oil lamp, which the village verger lit every afternoon. With nervous moves, he immediately lit the torch, poured oil over the wood, and ignited the beacon fire from every side. As soon as he saw the flames rising, he took some steps backwards and made the sign of the cross.

"Dear God, have mercy. Please, may someone see the fire and come quickly," he prayed aloud and turned around to see the men's reactions.

Surprised, he saw that no one at the clearing had noticed the beacon fire's bright light, since they all had their attention fixed on some other flashes shooting out in front of the fire. The very next moment, the whole island was shaken by a huge tremor and, simultaneously, a greenish mist spread across the clearing, reaching the seashore.

What mostly impressed him was that the darkness above the clearing had turned even gloomier, so pitch-black that neither the flashes nor the flames from the fire and the torches could brighten it. In order to see better, he ran to the edge of the mountaintop and lowered the torch in his hand.

He couldn't see much. He was hindered by the night and the mist that had covered the area. Yet he could clearly hear the shouts and the screams of the people who were facing death, the townsfolk who were being slaughtered. . . .

The admiral, Theodosius Moschinus, scratched his left cheek while gazing at the dark sea. He was a little tired, but still alert. Since morning, he had been looking for a pirate convoy, which had been seen sailing off the shore of Rhodes, heading north, and in spite of all his efforts he hadn't managed to locate it. In order to facilitate the search and prevent any raid to the nearby islands, he had divided his fleet into two squadrons. He sent one to the northwest and directed the second between the islands and the Ionian coast to the northeast.

He plied the sea without any results, and his worry had him constantly on edge. He was afraid he had missed the pirates or that they had fooled him with a ruse and were already pillaging the islands or the Greek coast. He didn't want to tarnish his name like the droungarios of the seamen who, forty years before, had missed the pirates who had captured Thessalonica. He could never stand such a disgrace, nor could he bury it underneath countless prayers for forgiveness, locked in some monastery. He'd rather die, drown himself, than live with the shame and the heavy burden knowing that due to his incompetence or neglect innocent Christians were killed, while others were dragged to the slave markets of Crete and Egypt. For that reason, he was not sleepy and walked about the deck like a wild animal in a cage.

The last of the fishermen he found at sea hadn't seen any pirates, and that piece of information made him turn back again to the south. He thought that those six ships didn't carry enough men to besiege a large wall-enclosed continental city, but only an island or a coastal town.

Of all the islands of the area, those that offered the best looting were Kos, Kalymnos, and Samos. The rest were small and poor, not worth the attention of the hungry eyes of the sea jackals. And from those three, the most appealing was Samos, rich and full of people who would yield a great deal of profit, and that is why he was sailing around it. However, the pirates were nowhere to be seen.

In the end, very stressed and annoyed, Theodosius ordered his captains to head south, taking the responsibility for that risky decision not to continue the search further north.

"Master droungarios," a sailor said, pulling him from his thoughts, "that light over there looks like a beacon fire."

"Where is it?" Theodosius jumped to his feet, as if having woken suddenly, and scanned the darkness that surrounded them. He saw the flames of the beacon fire on his right and his eyes opened wide.

His face shone with a smile of bloodthirsty pleasure and immediately gave orders. He knew that if he couldn't stop the raid in time, he would meet that filthy bunch at sea—and then not even all Hell's demons would save them.

Theodosius' ship listed as the quartermaster turned it southwest, while behind them, under his command, sailed the other three ships that had also been notified through fire signals. The second squadron was away, probably half a day northwest, and there was not a chance that it could help them in the pursuit. But their absence didn't trouble him in the least. He only prayed to God that the islanders would have enough courage to hold out until he arrived. With his two galleys and the two fire-bearing ships he could beat twice as many pirate ships.

He wasn't exaggerating, nor did he underestimate the pirates. He had previously confronted them five times, twice ashore and three times at sea. They weren't very competent seamen, unless they were Cretans who had converted to Islam. But ashore they were real demons, capable and fearless warriors who were very difficult to defeat. They might be barbaric and brutal men, but he couldn't help acknowledging their bravery and dexterity in battle.

"Oil the engines!" he shouted to the artillery men who stood next to the catapults and the springalds.

"Justin! Have the men get the ballistas from the hold. Place most of them on the starboard side. Eustace, put ten archers at the stern and ten at the prow. Romanus, signal Ignatius and Skuteris to have the fire-bearing siphons ready.

"We'll burn the Hajjis tonight—we're going to drown them! Men, in the name of Jesus and Mary, I really want to decorate the deck with the infidels' heads, otherwise I'll have yours!"

The sailors roared with laughter, shouted in approval, and got ready to execute the orders. At the same time, from the nearby ships similar joyful cries were heard as a reply to the encouraging speeches made by their captains.

The imperial fleet rushed to prevent the tragedy. However, this tragedy wasn't simply about ruthless pirates, but about something completely new and disastrous. . . .

By the time he saw the flashes of the Mnizurin being activated, Theodorus had only been worried about the Patmians, because he thought that they would lose their lives over nothing, during an unsuccessful ritual, for the sake of a false faith. He swore angrily to himself that should he survive the fury of the ruthless sorcerers, he would dedicate his life to the pursuit of all those heretics and the groups that performed human sacrifices. His eyes shone with rage, but when the flashes shot out of the basin and the earthquake happened at the same time, he froze completely and his breath was cut short.

Within moments, dozens of thoughts crossed his mind. He wondered how that group knew about the activation mixture and how they had come upon the Mnizurin; he instinctively placed his hand over the case of his tunic and felt his own. It seemed incredible to him that some people were opening the gate to time and space before his very eyes.

Perplexed, he looked at Rebecca and Leon. They were as surprised as he was, and he saw the fear in their eyes. The next moment, one single idea dominated his thoughts: he had to act, prevent the completion of the ritual and not let Dagon come through the gate.

He leaned forward and pulled out Abdul's book from the sack that Rebecca had in her arms. Not the translated, thick leather copy, but the original, cylindrical one. He opened it nervously and started reading quickly.

He shivered from the strain. He tried to find the point where there was the record of the death sound for the Iynges and the one that could foil Dagon. He could kill His subordinates, but not the elemental power itself; that creature was practically a god, so there was only a spell for sending Him away.

As he skimmed the verses, he racked his brain to recall where it was written. Remembering it by heart was almost impossible due to the scores of other sounds referring to creatures of other worlds, since for every Iynx from a different planet every sound for death is unique. Even Abdul only wrote about the ones that have appeared on Earth and have worshippers who wish to restore them.

The gloom and the mist kept him from seeing clearly. At a glance, he realised that the pirate behind him was astounded by everything he was seeing, heedless of the hostages. He immediately crawled to the front line, where the flashes cast more light. As he pushed aside the almost panicked Patmians, he remembered that during his translation he had written down the sounds for averting the so-called Old Ones on a separate piece of paper. He made an effort to focus on this fact, hoping that he had memorised the particular sound, but the hysterical screams by the people around him wouldn't let him.

From within the rift in the air, that black darkness, dozens of shadowmorphs sprang out and rushed to the bodies of the slaughtered residents. In rapid moves, they started sucking the blood and the flesh of their victims, while the Dagonists, stealing glances at the creatures that were taking on form, kept chanting the ill-sounding hymn that would summon their god.

The order members were glowing with joy watching the Iynges taking form in front of them. Their look was filled with emotion and displayed their admiration for their Lord's "angels." They knew that in a few minutes Dagon would appear and, even though they wanted to witness what was taking place, they looked at the rift with devout impatience.

The first creature that materialised raised its scaly torso in front of the fire, stretched out its two upper limbs and clapping them together, exposing the semi-transparent membrane that connected them to his body. Its winged limbs ended in four excrescences, similar to fingers. It didn't look like Yog-Sothoth's Iynges; this one was stouter, with a rounded torso, and it stood on two thick tentacle-like feet. But its most noticeable feature was its disproportionately large and slightly square head. In the middle of its forehead there

NECRONOMICON: THE MANUSCRIPT OF THE DEAD

were three rows of two blinking eyes and, underneath these, the creature's long and spiny muzzle started, looking like a proboscis.

An enraptured Dagonist stopped the invocation and removed himself from the circle. He fell on the ground, raised his hands, and kneeled toward the Iynx, uttering blessings and expressions of gratitude.

The monstrous creature let out a shrieking scream and swiftly jerked its proboscis at the worshipper's face. The man felt an unbearable stinging below his right eye and then, terrified over his imminent death, sensed the poison that ran through his veins, first swelling his arteries and then completely destroying them.

The next moment, the surprised Dagonists saw more of their god's "angels" attacking them. Five men and women fell to the poisonous blows, while just as many shadowmorphs began absorbing their vital fluids and taking shape.

At least half of the unholy believers broke the line and took to their heels. They had originally thought that the Iynges were their allies and would acknowledge their loyalty, but once they realised that this wasn't the case, they ran away. The "angels" were nothing more than anthropophagus demons.

Vuketes saw the commotion that was occurring, heard the wailings and the name-calling, but paid no heed. He raised his voice even more and adjured those who were near him to control themselves and go on with the ritual until Dagon appeared.

"They're not true believers!" he cried, justifying the Iynges' attack against the Dagonists. However, the victims' screams transformed instinctively into questions and frightening thoughts, undermining what his firm beliefs.

Some of the shadowmorphs that spread among the hostages found the bodies of the people that the pirates had made an example of by killing them, while others rushed to whoever had open wounds.

John Lambrinus was the first hostage to suffer an attack. His stomach wound was bleeding, and a shadowmorph seized him with a ravenous appetite. All those who sat around him fled screaming and left him on his own as he writhed in utter agony and felt his flesh being sucked away from the bones. The pain didn't last long, though, since the shadowmorph drained his blood, and most of his organs shut down.

Before taking his last breath, the abbot who had wished to reach holiness and aspired to an eternal Christian glory was shrouded in palpitating darkness. Dizzy and short of breath, he fixed his gaze upon the torchlight, which seemed to drift away inside a long and narrow tunnel, leaving him with the impression that there, on the other end, were the Pearly Gates. . . .

When the Dagonists had gone to the pirate Mukhtar al-Girah and asked his help for the raid on Patmos, he had refused at first and threatened them, saying that he would betray them to the master arch-pirate of Crete. The cunning man, however, was glad at the thought of the resulting profit. He had simply uttered that empty threat as a way of finding out more, to see what was behind their beautiful words and the shine of the gold he had been offered. So he forced them to confide in him their intentions and explain everything they were planning on doing. From their disjointed mutterings he knew that they belonged to a group that worshipped a strange god, which didn't surprise him, and he considered them fools. He and his men didn't believe in Allah, even though they posed as faithful Muslims. Once you have killed hundreds of men, women, and children, you no longer believe in God but only in the strength of your arms and wit. What god is this, anyway, that lets all those crimes go by unpunished, even if they are done against infidels?

Mukhtar al-Girah was sin itself. There was absolutely no crime he had thought of and not committed. He had grown up in a pirate ship ever since he was a boy, and the first man he ever killed was another Muslim, an Egyptian who treated him badly. He paid for that crime according to the pirates' code and survived. When he realised that his physical punishment wasn't followed by "divine vengeance," he started living by the law of Nature, killing and subjugating the weak.

At the meeting called by the pirates on the east coast of Crete to decide whether they would offer their help to the necromancers, he declared to his men that their financiers wanted to summon their god and, thus, they would perform human sacrifices, which they themselves did at every chance given for the sake of their own god, Wealth. That is why they shouldn't be afraid of any magic rituals like children, but should think of the abundance of gold they had been promised.

Indeed, the Dagonists were not the least thrifty in the money they had offered. They believed in the advent of a new era for people; and they, as the ones responsible for stabilising it, were no longer in need of material goods, since they would benefit from ruling over the world.

Some superstitions and childish fears the rest of the pirates had were immediately quashed at the sight of the glowing gold, even though almost half of them didn't accept the decision happily. They might not believe in the unintelligible theories of theologians, but during all those years at sea they had witnessed many strange and odd things, which could only be explained by the existence of an invisible higher power. However, since these sorcerers said that no harm would come to them, they eventually accepted, thinking of course that if something went wrong they would let their swords and bats talk.

But all those things that started happening before their very eyes—the mist, the earthquake, and those shadowmorphs that transformed into scary demons—didn't leave any room for second thoughts. All the pirates, shameless and amoral, as soon as they saw the Iynges attacking the hostages, dropped everything heavy they were carrying, apart from their weapons, and ran to their ships.

The first to waste no time watching the events was Mukhtar himself. Besides, in order to become the leader of a gang of pirates, one has to attack fast, steal faster, and run the fastest. That's the rule for surviving in the harsh pirate world, and Mukhtar, up until that day, was following it to the letter.

But no matter how fast he ran, clenching his teeth and mentally cursing his disloyalty, he didn't manage to get far enough. He suddenly felt an intense pressure on his stomach and saw his feet being swept from the ground. One of the monsters had grabbed him with its tentacle and lifted him in the air.

Astounded, his blood drumming the sound of death in his temples, he tried to free himself from that suffocating embrace. He attempted to cut off the tentacle with his sword, but the creature squeezed him harder, and Mukhtar felt so much pain that his weapon slipped from his hand. Before he could try anything else to escape, he found himself falling hard on a sharp rock.

The demon dropped him from a great height and crushed his head on the rocky ground. The last image Mukhtar saw before his brain was shattered to pieces was the face of Sindra, the only woman he had ever loved in his life. . . .

There were more pirates who were late in escaping and fell victims to the shadowmorphs, after the winged Iynges hurt them; some others, in their panic, instead of heading toward the ships, ran to the village along with the panicked residents.

Patmians, monks, pilgrims, and several pirates huddled like sheep; they didn't scatter, but moved in a herd, just as the mind dictated in the moment of panic. Such is human behaviour when fear takes over: people never act reasonably, but like a mob, as if they want to sense one another's presence. They do whatever the person in front of them does. Even if they see a person falling off a cliff, they won't stop, realising the danger; they will fall off too, considering this deed the only right or imperative solution.

So those who had run to the village didn't manage to get away and save themselves: the winged Iynges were suddenly before them and, mercilessly using the sting of their tentacles, the poison in their proboscis, and the sharp claws in their upper limbs, killed every man and woman of every age. People were completely lost in a frenzied violent slaughter, and that provided the rest of the shadowmorphs with enough blood and flesh to materialise.

Only those who had somehow kept their calm managed to survive, because they had hidden behind some bushes and rocks. They also knew that they had simply escaped death only for a short time, since the ritual was continuing and the Iynges that kept multiplying would try to find them sooner or later.

When the watchman from the front mast exclaimed that he could see the pirate ships, the admiral of the imperial fleet was surprised and didn't believe him. But then, the six biremes sailing close to the shore became visible to everyone and at the same time the pirates came running and yelling to be let on board. Theodosius Moschinus' smile was transformed into a sardonic wince.

Judging from the torches burning on the ships, he knew that the pirates had been trapped. The few sailors who were near the pirate ships couldn't move them and, possibly, only two or three guards were only inside each one.

At once, as if the sun had emerged through dark clouds, the heavy, suspenseful atmosphere on the deck changed. Seeing the anchored ships and the pirates who were screaming like madmen over their misfortune, every negative thought vanished from the seamen's minds; even the eyes of the apprentices, nervous about the

naval battle, shone with unexpected happiness, but also with devilish thirst for victory.

The admiral didn't let the chance go to waste. In a steady voice,
which always inspired his men with respect and fear, he gave explicit orders and, without slowing down the speed of the ship, he went
so near that his artillery men would not miss any shot.

The six pirate ships were moored one next to the other at the
shallow end of the sea, their waterlines almost touching the sand at
the bottom. They had anchored them so close to the coast because
they didn't use boats. So whoever wanted to get on board had to
tread water or swim to the sides, where the ladders were.

The second galley of the imperial fleet overtook the admiral's
ship with great ease. It was sailing so close that the sailors could even
exchange greetings and wishes for the upcoming victory. Further out,
the slower fire-bearing ships continued their circular route and
stopped only when they were right in front of the pirate ships' prows.

The lights that shone on the masts of the imperial vessels revealed light blue, red, and golden hues, Roman crucifixes on the
sails, eagles, dragons, and griffins on the figureheads, bearded iron-
clad men on decks and loud skippers with tireless hearts on the sterns
giving commands and instructions. The fire-bearing ships differed
from the galleys in that they had a huge metal double-mouthed si-
phon at their prows, and along their wide decks there were great
bronze cauldrons inside of which the flammable liquid was boiling.

The empty pirate ships were an easy target, so the galleys
weren't necessary for their destruction, yet the admiral wanted to
give all his men the satisfaction of victory. From where they were,
the clearing wasn't visible, nor was the way to the village, where the
Iynges were killing the Patmians. So, with the confidence of a victor
and the severity of a punisher, he gave explicit orders:

"Catapults and springalds, aim at the ships! Ballistas and archers, aim at the pirates on shore!"

The moment they heard the first command, the artillery men pulled the belts and the levers on their guns according to the distance required. Then, the clattering and squeaking of ramrods and breechblocks was heard and, lastly, that chilling whistling sound that the missiles made, jetting from the machines, tearing the air and landing heavily on the enemy vessels.

After the crash of the first firing, the happy cheers of the sailors overshadowed the terrified screams of the pirates. The strain of the hours spent at sea had exhausted the sailors; and at the moment of impact, after the successful shot, they felt a deep relief. They fervently watched the long and narrow missile crushing the waterline of the first ship and then, just as intensely, they watched a catapult hurl its stone shell, tracing a curved orbit and falling onto the hull of the same bireme. Once the missile pierced through the wooden frame, there was a jet of white water, as if the pumps from a fountain were on, and their joy was tripled and the fear had crawled back to the corners of their minds.

The next two shots both made the sailors cheer wildly. One springald shell struck the mast of a pirate ship, literally crushing it, dragging along two men as it fell into the sea, while the shell of a catapult smashed the waterline on the prow of a bireme. The stroke was such that it created a twisted chasm, like a toothless grin, through which the water flushed into its hull and by its weight lifted it vertically, with the stern sticking up in the air.

In a very short while, all six ships suffered huge damage. One of them had already sunk, while two more were heeling in the sea. The pirates, however, ignoring the damage, kept climbing up the ships, making the observant admiral Moschinus wonder about their behaviour.

Along with the catapults' shots, the ballistas that fired eight arrows at once hurled their deadly content onto the pirates who crowded in front of their ships. The arrows tore the air with that characteristic hissing sound, the melody of death, pierced bodies, heads, and extremities; they tattered the sails and were jabbed into the wooden ship frames, and their consecutive blows increased the panic.

The pirates shouted and screamed maniacally, trying hard to keep their courage, but the nature of the successive blows was such that any encouraging yelping soon turned to heart-breaking wailing. But their torment was not over yet.

After the last of the pirate ships was perforated by the ballistic machines, the fire-bearing ships spewed their lethal cargo on them, roaring. The Greek fire, the most ruthless and destructive weapon in the imperial navy's possession, the scourge of every enemy of the kingdom, jettisoned like a fiery spring through the siphons. The four fire pillars traced a curved route and landed on the decks of the nearby vessels. Instantly, the flames spread to every direction, burning everything down.

The composition of the Greek fire—a secret that, if revealed, was punishable by death—was such that even when the blazing material hit the sea, it kept burning unhindered, scorching all the ships' sides, even the ones that were underwater. Only when there was no more combustible substance did the fire go out. Inside the Empire they called it the "undying fire."

Men and ships became prey to the flames and, despite the horrid sight, the sailors cheered wildly. They saw people being burnt alive and they clapped, obsessed with an unquenchable desire for death; they were elated by the feeling of the irrational bliss that derives from images of destruction. They could hear the harrowing voices of men; the flames were burning their skin, melting their eyes, and scorching their bodies. The sailors felt satisfaction, as if all this macabre lamentation was a kind of an orgiastic musical performance.

The only person who didn't share the sailors' joy was Moschinus. The sea-beaten admiral, frowning and silent, was watching the pirates' absurd behaviour and wondered what had made them want to climb up the ships, even though disaster was evident. Throughout his turbulent life, he had seen numerous panicked people and was well aware of the reaction they have in the face of death; even so, he instinctively knew that the reason for their panic wasn't the imperial fleet, but something else that was happening on the island.

His guess was proven correct when he saw several pirates dropping their weapons on the coast, diving in the water, and swimming toward his ship in anguish. Among the clamour of the machines, the sounds of the fire that ate up the pirate ships, the sailors' loud cries, and the injured people's wailings, he tried to distinguish the voices of the men approaching. He stood near the side railing of the deck and listened, but the archers let their arrows spread death to anyone who came near the admiralship.

"Stop it!" he shouted and ordered his petty officer next to him: "Cease fire!"

At once, they all stopped shouting and shooting. Perplexed at the unexpected command, they turned around and looked at him in confusion. They never thought that their admiral would show mercy to rapists, kidnappers, and heinous murderers.

Now that fewer sounds were disturbing him, Moschinus could hear the distressed calls for help. Among the words, he was able to discern those that confirmed his feeling that something else was happening. The desperate pirates were spitting sea water while others, in Greek or Arabic, yelled about the attack of the beasts as they pointed at the island.

"They're saying something about demons and sorcerers, dear droungarios," the first mate, a bearded grey-haired man with a hawk's nose, said and raised a questioning eyebrow.

Moschinus didn't reply and, squinting, simply looked toward Patmos. He had also heard the pirates' voices clearly. From where he was standing, he could only see the flames of the fire, a few repeated flashes that fluctuated in size, and a deep darkness in the sky, without the bright marks of the stars.

"Christopher . . ." he addressed the helmsman, intending to command him to turn the prow, but saw a glimpse of something out of the corner of his eye and, astounded, looked at the island again.

Somewhere high above the low dune on the beach, there was a strange creature flying. Its features weren't very clear, but what could be seen was its significant size and its extremities, one on the head and two on its lower body.

The admiral, who bragged that when he was young he had travelled to the ocean off the Mediterranean and had reached the countries of the Franks, saying that he had seen everything there was to be seen, stood there gaping at the soaring monster. No, the *monsters!* While he had his eyes fixed on the island, he saw two more, flying behind the first one. But what shook him into action and lose the surprise from his face was that two of the creatures were carrying humans in their rear extremities.

"There!" "What are those?" "Take a look at the island!" One by one, the sailors stopped staring at the ships burning and the pirates swimming in the sea and turned to where the others were pointing their fingers. They stood, with bated breath, and watched the odd, winged figures and then, with the same agonising questions on their lips, they all turned to their admiral in unison.

Moschinus didn't have time to analyse the facts. Before he could think and give any command, a hysterical wave of screams was raised from the beach before the burning ships, where most of the pirates were.

At least twenty beasts attacked the terrified men and began killing them either by hitting them with their long muzzles or by jabbing them with the stings they had on their tentacle-like back limbs. Some of them lifted their victims and thrust them hard on the stone-covered ground, breaking their bones and filling the beach with blood the colour of darkness.

The sailors of the imperial fleet could see everything clearly, since the bluish-yellow flames from the burning ships lit the area and every little detail was visible. The monstrous winged creatures didn't look like the horned demons of the holy icons, but their destructive actions were similar to the stories mentioning the children of the Devil.

"Everyone keep your posts! Ballistas, aim! Archers, keep shooting!" Moschinus shouted in fragile calmness and unsheathed his sword. "Eustace, have everyone arm themselves. Don't let any of those monsters come near—"

The next moment, the air was torn by dozens of arrows that, whistling creepily and being thirsty for death, headed to the creatures above the pirates' heads. On the admiral's ship there was dead quiet, no one spoke, and the sailors who were arming themselves with bows and spears looked on breathlessly to see the result of the nervous volley of arrows. Only when they saw three of the monsters dropping on the ground and in the sea heavily wounded did everyone—including Moschinus—let out a sigh of relief.

"Don't stop, men! Whatever these things are, demons or beasts, you've seen that they can be killed. Aim well and shoot at them!" shouted the admiral at the top of his lungs.

Simultaneously, scores of missiles were launched from the rest of the ships and onto the shore, while the fire-bearing vessels, increasing their range, flung jets of Greek fire in the air, burning both the Iynges and the pirates. As a result, a few minutes later the whole beach was on fire.

It was now clear that nothing could resist the well-orchestrated attack of the fleet. The monsters could be both killed and burnt, just like any other living creature, and Moschinus couldn't wait to vanquish them all, so that he could later tell people that he was even able to defeat the Devil's army. His spirits, though, didn't remain high for long. He hadn't realised that a few dozen of them had dived in the water and headed toward the galley closest to the coast. Only when he heard the sailors' screams and saw several arrows falling close to him did he turn around and notice the massacre that was taking place.

The monsters emerged from the sea and attacked the unsuspicious sailors at great speed and in a vengeful mood. Flapping their wings, they jutted out their muzzles and their tentacles, poisoning or tearing apart every man in front of them with their stings.

Many sailors, astounded by the attack, jumped into the sea. Most of them, however, along with their captain were killed on the deck, unable to face that coordinated attack from every side and every level.

The skipper of the nearest fire-bearing ship, seeing the galley's men perishing, knew that he was next and, not hesitating in the least, turned his prow with great determination. In two bursts, his fellow seaman's ship was enveloped in flames. The men and the Iynges that hadn't managed to fly away were charred, letting out poignant screams and sounds of their tormenting calamity.

The events shook Leon terribly. His first reaction was to hug Rebecca protectively and follow Theodorus. He saw the terrified pirates and the panicked Patmians running for their lives; the distraught Dagonists following them screaming hysterically. Realising the danger, he tried to keep his composure.

He crouched behind Theodorus and watched him nervously. He wanted to know what he intended to do, because he himself could think of nothing but escape.

"That sound . . . Do you remember what the words are for the death of Dagon's Iynges?" Theodorus shouted anxiously when he sensed them near him. Further away, the shadowmorphs continued to materialise, as the human dead bodies kept increasing in number.

Leon shook his head, staring hard at his friend, who he thought had gone mad. He didn't remember or at least couldn't recall anything in that commotion of the massacre, the blood, and the unstoppable wailings.

"Let's go," he suggested and reached his hand to grab him. "Theodorus, get up!"

"Go where? We can't escape or hide. It's not the Emperor's guards who are after us, nor the Damascenes or the Kyrenians. We can't save ourselves now as before, by fleeing to another country. These creatures intend to destroy the whole world. Wherever we go, we'll always find them there. We've got to kill them and, above all, we must prevent Him from coming out."

Leon felt like collapsing. Indeed, when they had been persecuted before, they had the chance to leave and find refuge in another kingdom or duchy, because then they were chased by humans. But now things were different. The Iynges hadn't come with the intention of conquering a kingdom or settling in a specific area, but to dominate the entire world. He knew that his friend was absolutely right.

He scanned the clearing with his blurry vision and got lost within the savage and macabre activity. Everywhere around him, the shadowmorphs were draining their victims' vital fluids and took on form. Further away, the pirates and the Patmians ran for their lives; on his right, about ten Dagonists kept their ground and reiterated their god's name.

A flash caught his attention. He noticed a pirate's sword lying on the ground a few feet away. Without a second thought, he let go of Rebecca's hand and jumped to grab it.

The greenish mist was now thinner due to the gusts of the sea wind. The flashes that came off the Mnizurin were stronger as it was fully activated, and a terrible tremor shook the island for a second time.

"Leon!" Rebecca shouted in utter terror.

Theodorus turned around and looked at the rift. The dark opening had doubled in diameter, and at the sight of it his heart fluttered. He didn't care about himself; he only worried about what would happen once Dagon arrived. His heightened senses had revealed to him some of the events to come. He had seen the armies of the mutated creatures that would swarm the planet. The unholy union between humans and Dagon's Iynges would give birth to a new generation of monsters with hideous and repulsive features, but also with incredible martial skills. That was not all. He had also seen mighty Cthulhu waking up and rising from the depths of the sea, the rebuilding of R'lyeh, and the onset of the clash among worlds within the endless sky.

Once every planet had been subdued and every world had been destroyed, the mutation and preservation of creatures of a specific form would shatter the existing laws and the souls would forever disappear. The whole world would collapse and break in smaller uneven and incoherent parts, resulting in chaos.

"Leon!" Rebecca's voice brought him back to reality; he was at the clearing, holding *al-Azif*. Disoriented, he looked where his friend was and saw one of the Iynges attacking him.

The muzzle that was jutted out was aiming at his chest, but Leon reacted instinctively and thrust himself to the side. He fell to the ground, rolled on the rocks, and, holding his sword firmly, rose next to the beast. He thrust his sword into the creature and broke its top right limb. Simultaneously, he ducked to avoid the muzzle again and jammed his sword in the ribs of his unsightly opponent.

The monster let out a pained squeal, but didn't fall. In a swift movement, it leaned its body to one side and with its back tentacle hit Leon on the head.

The metal-hard sting tore Leon's forehead and his face was covered in hot blood. Unconsciously, urged more by survival instinct rather than knowledge and technique, he stabbed the Iynx' fat neck three times.

The creature slanted unstably and then slumped onto the ground, shaking with continuous spasms. It was writhing at death's embrace, just like any other living thing. Even its eyes were blurry with the realisation that it was about to die.

Leon stood for a moment over the body of his would-be killer and raised his hand to his forehead. His palm was shaking with tension and he knew that he had just been lucky, because he had pulled slightly back and the sting hadn't cut his upper skull completely.

He was about to return to where Rebecca and Theodorus were, but seeing their widened, horrified eyes, he knew that he hadn't been saved after all. Behind him two Iynges were drawing nearer, flapping their membranous wings.

"Run!" shouted Theodorus and, grabbing Rebecca by the hand, pulled her toward the fire in front of the Dagonists, where the Mnizurin was sparkling inside the basin.

At the second stride, he paused abruptly. A thought crossed his mind and it was immediately transformed into an image. He turned to Rebecca and locked eyes with her. His look had the brightness of determination and grief at the same time.

"Rebecca, run. Hide!" He let go of her hand and put the *al-Azif* inside his shirt.

Rebecca saw in her mind what Theodorus was planning to do and stepped back in fear. She could read his mind and he could read hers.

"Everything happens for a reason," he smirked and turned to the fire.

Ever since he took hold of the Mnizurin in John Lambrinus' cloister, Neophytus Vuketes had been extremely happy and felt omnipotent. He knew that the days of waiting, the banishing, the chasing, and all the secrecy had come to an end. Every failure and vexation of the past had gone now, and the only thing that flashed in his mind was the coming and the prevalence of his god. From the following day onward, he would no longer be a miserable alchemist who hid his faith and performed his sacred, bloody rituals in secret, but Dagon's grand preacher and the prophet of the Old Ones' arrival, a man whom all the people would respect and fear. The other members themselves chose him unanimously to be master of ceremony and gave him the black tiara of the prelate.

It was the happiest night of his life. He had never doubted his faith and had always dreamt of the moment when he would be in front of a Mnizurin, uttering the summoning words. Ever since he was a little boy, he had harboured the hope that he would someday see his ancestors' god, and he was convinced that his mission in life was to summon Father Dagon. He grew into a man with that impression and his desire never diminished, in spite of all the misfortunes he had encountered.

That is the reason why, during the ritual, he was excited, almost detached from reality. Totally devoted to the realisation of his dream, in total ecstasy, he performed everything in absolute perfection, as if someone were guiding him, preventing him from committing any mistake.

His joy grew even greater when he saw the rift in the sky, and he was enveloped by a sweet queasiness once the Iynges arrived. The presence of the "angels" proved that everything he had believed in was true and that his god would soon reward him personally for all his sacrifices.

The events that followed puzzled him. He kept his calm, despite seeing his companions being massacred, but inside him fear and doubt started growing. He wondered if he had made a mistake, but couldn't come up with anything. He saw that something had gone wrong, but he didn't know if it was his fault, the Dagonists' fault, or if the "angels" couldn't tell a friend from an enemy.

He kept summoning his master, getting angry at his other companions, who, instead of focusing on the ritual, had run to save their miserable lives; he only depended on his own faith to carry out his work. He knew that he could make it, and the Iynges wouldn't touch him.

Even so, his attention was distracted every time an acquaintance or relative of his lost his or her life. He saw his two brothers being torn apart; the actual prelate running away, but eventually dropping dead by a deadly stroke on the back; his uncles, who had initiated him to Dagon's worship, being crushed by shadowmorphs. He wondered whether the only truly loyal man was himself.

The situation was inconceivable. He thought that his ancient ancestors had probably forgotten to cast a protective spell, hence the "angels" were now attacking their worshippers. That was the only explanation he could find.

Out of the corner of his eye, he noticed a man and a woman approaching the fire and felt threatened. He didn't pause his summoning. Almost transfixed, he kept saying his god's name. That moment, nothing and no one could stop him from completing the ritual. He was sure he would achieve it.

And he did! Two enormously wide and long tentacles appeared at the end of the rift, and then four more. At once the rift tripled in size, while the tentacles touched the sea and then fumbled their way out of it.

A sickening stench of rottenness and decomposition filled the air, making his stomach churn. Liquid, ill-smelling mucus dripped from the rift, falling on the sparkling waters. The very next moment, dozens of dead fish came to the surface.

The admiration in his eyes didn't diminish in the least, despite the suffocating reek. He kept watching the arrival of his Lord in astonishment, kneeling on the ground and raising his hands.

"Welcome, Father Dagon!" he cried in the astral creatures' language. "Dagon, grand and beloved, this world is yours," he added rhythmically, and then he was astounded by the massive size of his god.

The diameter of the gate, which was wider than the island mountain, was filled with the greenish scales that covered Dagon's head. Vuketes immediately recognised his god from the icons and statues that the artistic Dagonists had created.

Yes! Dagon, God himself, was passing through the gate and the era of His predominance was beginning with his personal contribution and assistance. From now on, he would become an apostle, and blood-stained humanity would kneel before the one and only real world ruler.

Demetrius Meligrates' first instinctive reaction when he heard the harrowing screams of the people below was to run to their assistance. But he stopped at the fourth stride. His cassock became tangled up on a thorn bush, and as he tried to release it he looked at the clearing where the fire was burning. A gust of wind had cleared the thick mist hovering on the place, offering him a chance to see what was happening.

He froze at the sight of the shadowmorphs maniacally slithering among the people and was speechless at the Iynges' unsightly appearance. All the descriptions he had read or heard until that day about Satan's demons were like a children's story compared to reality.

He instinctively made the sign of the cross and, unable to form a sound thought, kept watching the events fervently. His heart was pounding, and the fear that gripped him was such that his whole body shuddered. His eyes misted and he felt his knees give way.

The gruesome massacre made him lose his courage. He saw people being torn to pieces, falling hard on the ground, writhing in distress, shadowmorphs taking on form and Iynges murdering without exception, unscrupulously and ruthlessly. He heard crying, pleas, and death rattles, and was unable to think of anything whatsoever. He didn't know what to do for those poor people, but also for himself, besides pray to God for help.

Even though he shut his eyes and focused on his prayer, he opened them every now and then; and through the blur of his tears he saw the dead bodies of the Patmians, the pilgrims, and his fellow hermits lying scattered in the path that led from the clearing to the village. His despair grew greater once he saw the winged demons multiplying and flying dominatingly.

For a moment he doubted his faith, which began to shatter in the face of the tragedy before him, and he moaned in fear. He had devoted his whole life to the service of God; he knew that he shouldn't be afraid of death, since Heaven awaited him. Even so, he couldn't handle the pressure and lost consciousness momentarily.

When he came to, he mustered every crumb of calmness he still had left and decided to accept his fate—that is, die by one of the demons' strokes. But the flapping of the sails and the imperial fleet sailors' commands lifted his dying hopes, and his face shone with joy.

At the sight of the masts and the flags, he decisively clenched his fists, believing that God had heard his pleas and worked His miracle. Thrilled by the hope of salvation, he ran to the edge of the mountaintop and watched the naval battle that followed, all the while praising Jesus, Virgin Mary, and all the saints.

But when he saw the Iynges attacking the galley, he lost his courage. They were unbeatable, and the damage they caused far outweighed what they suffered. They could, of course, be killed with weapons, but with difficulty and after multiple crucial strokes.

His face was again lit with joy at the sight of them being burnt by the Greek fire. Just like any enemy of the Empire, the demons had no means of escaping the undying blaze. They caught fire on the spot, their membranous wings melted; they fell into the sea like wounded birds and turned to ashes, disturbing the waves with their uncontrollable dying movements.

He was very sorry for the men who had been burnt along with the demons. His heart ached as he heard their pained shouting, as the flames ate up their flesh; but he was aware that their souls had been saved, since they had become martyrs of faith and sacrificed themselves in order to save the world.

From the movement of the ships, he understood that the admiral had commanded that they should approach the island. He had once met with the brave droungarios of the seamen and knew that he wouldn't retreat until he saw the last of the demons gone. His education and Christian morals didn't permit him to leave without saving at least one innocent life. However, what followed shook him hard, and his joy quickly turned to unbearable grief.

As soon as the two fire-bearing ships were near the island, causing death with their fiery tongues, the admiral's ship was under attack. The astonished sailors defended themselves bravely. Swords, spears, and shields resisted, cut away, and gave death, but these weapons would not offer victory to humans. One after the other were all killed.

As a result of the great distance, Meligrates couldn't see the admiral, but knowing that his place was at the stern and seeing the fierceness of the conflict between sailors and demons at that part of the ship, he had no doubts about what his end would be. As in a vision or with the eyes of his soul he saw the events that took place at the back of the ship, where the remaining living beings gathered holding their shields, as if at a citadel, ready to fight the ultimate battle. Among them, with clenched jaws and sword in hand, was Moschinus, who fought courageously against the hordes of the monsters that swarmed the deck, until one of them cut off his head in a fatal blow.

The rest of the sailors, without their brave commander's instructions, even after having inflicted substantial damage to their winged opponents, succumbed to the very last man. Then the rudderless ship was carried away by the waves and collided with the coast rocks, while the fiendish swarm, just like a flock of birds, flew toward the island in triangular formation.

That was when Meligrates stopped to watch what was happening at the clearing. His eyes turned to the rift that had been formed in the air above the sea, and he was scared to death when he saw the six gigantic tentacles emerging from within. His eyes opened in shock and his jaw dropped involuntarily as he watched Dagon's coming.

"And I stood upon the sand of the sea, and saw a beast rise up out of the sea." He whispered the verse from the Book of Revelation and fell on all fours, almost insane at the realisation that he was actually present at the events of doomsday. He lived on the island where the Christian book of disaster had been written; he knew every verse, all the terror that lies within them, but no matter how many times he had imagined its depiction in his nightmares, reality was far worse.

All of a sudden the demons stopped everything they had been doing. The flying ones landed on the ground and bowed submissively, turning to their master, who was emerging from the rift. They didn't move, only curtseyed in a docile manner; even those that were showered with Greek fire from the ships kept still.

"And they worshipped the dragon which gave power unto the beast: and they worshipped the beast, saying, Who is like unto the beast? who is able to make war with him?"

Leon didn't let this unexpected chance go to waste. Without delay, and as the Iynges were curtseying before Dagon, he ran and grabbed Rebecca's hand. They left that spot together until Leon noticed a hollow on the ground. Without a second thought, he pushed

Rebecca inside and then dropped on top of her and hugged her breathlessly.

Rebecca reacted promptly and tried to push him up, but he wouldn't go. He believed that any minute now the Iynges would stand up and continue the massacre.

"Leon, to the sea . . . We have to head to the sea," Rebecca struggled.

"We have no time. Don't be afraid." He pressed her on the ground and kissed her on the cheek.

Theodorus caught a glimpse of Leon and Rebecca leaving, and he placed his hand over the holster of his tunic. With sweaty fingertips, he fumbled for the Mnizurin.

The intensity he felt made his stomach turn, and his breath came out of his lungs in short, quick gasps. He saw Dagon emerging from the rift and knew that he couldn't waste any more time.

What he thought of doing wasn't inside the *Necronomicon,* but he believed that it was their only chance; his heightened senses revealed it to him. So he went near the fire, clenching the star-stone in his palm; but before he could complete his move, a sudden gale swirled him and thrust him to the ground.

Lying on his back, he saw two of Dagon's tentacles making the air vibrate above him. The god from the stars had grabbed the fire-bearing ships and had lifted them up in the air like twigs.

He didn't wait to see more; the sailors' screams betrayed the outcome. He crawled to the basin that lay in front of the fire and threw the Mnizurin he was holding inside.

The bang that was heard was so loud that his ears bled instantly. At the same time, the tremor that shook the island was such that it made him feel as if the ground had been lifted, while the flashes coming out of the Mnizurin blinded him.

The opening of the second rift caused a vortex that started pulling Dagon and everything around him inside. He couldn't see or hear, but he felt that unbearable pressure against his body. An infernal force was pulling him so fiercely that he thought his flesh would be torn away from the bones.

Vuketes ran toward the old man who was near the basin with the Mnizurin. He was surprised that the man wasn't afraid despite what was going on. This aroused suspicion in the alchemist, who rushed to prevent any action that would stop Dagon from arriving. Nonetheless, he too was knocked down by the force of the tentacles and, astounded, he saw the fire-bearing ships being snatched.

But the very next moment, he almost went deaf from the loud sound, and the flashes that shot out completely blackened out his field of vision. He cried with pain and later felt his body being lifted by the whirlwind and colliding with one of the scales that Dagon had on his body.

He didn't know what was happening, nor could he think straight because of the excruciating pain. Before perishing in the dark bottoms of the rift forever, he twirled at a great speed, uncontrollably crashed against burnt wood, stones, and the Iynges' rough bodies, and was eventually frozen by the unbelievable cold, still stuck on his god's membranous wings.

The same pressure that sucked Vuketes into the bottomless vortex also sucked Dagon. The immortal creature that travelled through the rifts in time and space without changing form was pulled into the second rift, unable to resist.

At once, his tentacles withdrew and were gone within the pitch darkness, along with human corpses, dead Iynges, burning pieces of wood, and anything that had been swept up by the unstoppable vortex. Then the two Mnizurin were rendered useless, causing an explosion that closed up the two rifts in the sky, and all the things that had risen in the air fell back to the burning ground.

The fiery blaze on the entire island was caused when Dagon lifted the fire-bearing ships with his tentacles off the sea. As the vortex sucked him in, he threw the ships away, one to the mountain above the village, where the monks' cloisters were, and the other to the south, at the parched stretch of land with the short bushes.

The ships' wooden frame cracked from the pressure, and as they flipped over, rolling in the sky, the Greek fire inside their holds spilled over almost the entire island. At the same time, the fire that came out of the broken siphons ignited the spilt flammable material and, almost in a heartbeat, the entire island of Patmos was wrapped in flames.

One of the cauldrons containing the Greek fire fell on the clearing near the hollow where Leon and Rebecca had hidden. The stern of a ship was jammed in the village, turning any of the Iynges that hadn't been sucked through the vortex to ashes. One of the siphons crushed the church on the mountain, where Meligrates was standing, and burned it to the ground.

The fire went out two days later. The entire island of Patmos had been consumed by flames, and a grey-black ash covered its ground, until the sea breeze and a strong sea storm scattered it away, leaving the task of cleaning it from the hundreds of human and Iynges' corpses to the scavenging birds.

10. The Palace of Whispers

A fragile silence spread over the boardroom as soon as the monk ceased his narration. The bishops and the patriarch kept looking at him, waiting for him to continue, until they realised that he had indeed finished recounting the events. Numb, somewhat disoriented, preoccupied, and pensive, they remained silent for a few moments, trying to sort out their feelings and thoughts.

Demetrius Meligrates observed them one by one, and in the end his look paused on the patriarch. Judging from their facial expressions, he could tell that some of them still had doubts, while others were shocked and at the same time perplexed. Yet they all seemed to want to pose some questions, because many of the things they had heard were unknown and inconceivable.

Relaxed now, breathing regularly, without the anxiety that had grasped him at the beginning, he rested his hands upon his knees, waiting for any questions or comments they would have. He wasn't sure if they had believed him, yet he felt relieved. He had managed to relate the events and alleviate his conscience from the heavy burden.

"I don't understand. Is Philetas still alive?" The bishop of Thessalonica was the first to ask a question. His stern look betrayed his temper. He looked as if he wished to attack and use force against Demetrius. His eyes gleamed with the intensity of his rage.

"The vortex sucked him in. He perished inside the rift. He's probably dead, but according to the story of Epimenides and the Seven Sleepers of Ephesus, he might be living in another world now. This sounds impossible: given where he ended up, I'm sure that he has been killed by the Iynges or by Dagon."

The bishops exchanged looks and grimaced enigmatically. It was obvious that something was troubling them, and Demetrius failed to understand what their problem was. Before he related the facts, they had all treated him with sympathy and an open mind. Now they seemed stern, forgetting about his tragedy and his traumatic experience.

"So the original *al-Azif* is also gone?"

The monk with the filthy bandages on his face nodded, without understanding the meaning of the question. He expected to be asked about the Iynges and the Old Ones, especially Cthulhu, the only one of them who is already on Earth, sleeping somewhere in the bottom of the sea.

"Since the original is nowhere to be found, we could assume that the work belongs to Theodorus himself and that he invented the Hagarene's story, so we won't accuse him of heresy, since the whole story leads to the formation of a cult," said Bishop Christopher from Nice and rubbed his beard with his right hand, while pensively pursing his lips. At the same time, he gave a meaningful look to the patriarch.

"What do you mean?" Demetrius broke out, astounded by their reasoning. He then restrained himself and in a calmer voice explained, "Theodorus, brothers, was neither a heretic nor a sorcerer. If he had written a book, he wouldn't hide behind a pseudonym, nor would he think up a whole story to deny his ideas. Besides, he was in agreement with everything mentioned in the *Necronomicon*—"

"Since you aren't making clear whether he died or not, there's the possibility of a plot," interrupted the bishop of Thessalonica, who expressed his irritation more than the others did. "You presented us with a marvellous story about demons, sorcerers, gods, and the effort of 'good' Theodorus to save the world by translating

a book. Who can guarantee that all this isn't a lie? We know that
Patmos was destroyed by an earthquake and was burnt in a fire he
caused. Moreover, according to the emperor's announcement, the
droungarios of the seamen, Theodosius Moschinus, and his fleet
squadron perished in a storm while pursuing pirates.

"Who's to say that you also didn't participate in a cunning plan
and that some time in the following months Theodorus doesn't appear to proclaim the new religion as a messiah?"

Demetrius gaped at what he was hearing, but said nothing. He
was astounded by the high priests' reasoning and was unable to
think of anything to refute it.

"What you recounted is extremely heretical and evil!" shouted
Patriarch Theophylactus. He had carefully listened to everything the
monk had narrated and had no doubt that his teacher had done all
that, but he was now given the chance to prove his faith before
God and the emperor. His brothers' deeds and his personal failures
had both tarnished his name, and this particular matter might clean
up his image in front of his fellow Christians. So, although he knew
he was being unfair and was breaking the moral code he had abided
by, he stated decisively: "Theodorus was separated by the Lord's
flock on the day he fled to the Hagarenes; we can't think of him as
our brother. On the contrary, his beliefs and actions prove to us
that he has been an ally of the Devil. I can't think of anything but
that he had an agreement with the Hagarenes and the Jewish in order to slander our faith—"

"The point, your Holiness, isn't what Theodorus believes, but
the fact that we're in danger," Demetrius interrupted him. His voice
cracked with despair, and his grievance was clear.

"Shut your mouth! Don't you think we already know that? Every day we fight to keep the demons away from the people, to protect and save the world. That's our mission; we don't need

suggestions from anyone, especially demon-stricken heretics like Theodorus Philetas!

"For the life of me, I cannot understand what this whole story's purpose was. What were you meaning to tell us? Abandon our faith and dedicate ourselves to the ravings of a Hagarene or the unproven notions of the Theurgists? The holy fathers of our church fought all those cults and anathematised the sorcerers. That's what I'm going to do as well: anathematise Theodorus Philetas because his thoughts and actions were derived from the Devil.

"And you, according to the vows you've taken, have dedicated your life to Jesus Christ, so you must confess your sins and repent for any doubts you may have."

Demetrius stared at the infuriated patriarch. He wasn't expecting such treatment and felt dizzy from all the thoughts that crushed him. The unjust attack against him upset and devastated him, because he saw that the high priests had their attention elsewhere and not to the importance of the facts.

"Calm down, my brother," the bishop of Adrianople told the patriarch. "Our young brother experienced and heard things that confused him; we are not to condemn him for that. I can understand his position, and I believe we should be lenient to him."

"My dear brothers," said Demetrius in a louder voice, regaining some of his composure, "you have obviously misunderstood my words! I didn't come here to preach a new cult or to speak of another religion. I have merely given evidence and stated the facts so that you can focus on the actual menace. Our world is threatened by astral creatures, not demonic spirits. I will not participate in a discussion about theological doctrines and religious notions. The circumstances dictate that we must see beyond dogmatism and intolerance."

He bent forward and opened his leather sack. In a swift movement, he took out the thick, leather-bound, arabesque book. He looked at it for a moment, indecisive, uncertain of his actions, and then raised it and showed it to the suspicious priests, who were gripped by conspiratorial obsessions.

"This is the *Necronomicon*. In here there are ways to vanquish the enemies of humanity. Theodorus translated it for that specific reason, and I am handing it to you because only you have the power to put things in order. You can use it for a good cause, but you can also bring on disaster, not just to humans, but to the whole of creation."

The bishops and the patriarch gaped at the grey-coloured book Meligrates was showing them. They had never seen a volume of such artistry and contemplated it in silence, with a glint of turmoil in their eyes—not because of its appearance, but because of all the punishable and damned doctrines it contained.

"It's infused with the ashes of men and Iynges. I found it next to the charred body of Leon Peleuses." Demetrius' voice broke as he uttered the doctor's name, and the flow of his speech was instantly gone. He remained there with his head bent low and then, once he had surmounted the obstacle of grief, he added: "You cannot destroy it. It can't be destroyed by fire or by the elements of Nature. It's protected by a special spell, so it can remain unaltered through time, until Death himself dies."

He stood up from the stool and took a step toward them. He saw that none of them had reached for the book and smirked. He left it on the stool and stood beside it.

"Rebecca was wrong to have been angry at Theodorus for translating it," he mumbled. "She didn't know then of course, but if she had, she might have done the same thing. We must rely on the kindness of people, otherwise our society has no meaning; we can't be suspicious and negative to anything strange and of a different faith. As a matter of fact, we don't need Iynges and demons to demolish us; we can easily kill each other on our own.

"Theodorus loved people and had faith in them; that's why he wanted the book to be spread, so that they could be saved from the imminent catastrophe. Abdul Alhazred thought the same thing; that's why he took the time to write the book and suffered so many hardships. That's what I also believe myself, I who have read it, I who saw Dagon with my very eyes, as my body was burnt in Patmos.

"We don't need to be so intolerant. Especially toward a man like Theodorus Philetas, who sacrificed himself in order to save the world—"

"We won't be making him a saint now," mocked the bishop of Philadelphia.

"I think we should," retorted Demetrius and narrowed his eyes to hold back his tears. Then, aghast at their treatment, shocked by their monolithic mentality, he turned his back on them and slowly walked to the door, his shoulders slumped. He didn't even want to say goodbye, so he left the boardroom, leaving them staring at the book on the stool.

The carriage driver outside the patriarchate winced in displeasure, seeing the revolting monk exit through the gate. He immediately opened the cabin door and lowered his eyes in servility. He had got inside to protect himself from the cold wind lashing at Constantinople since morning. Thank God he had, because it was already dark now and he would definitely have frozen to death after waiting all this time.

In one movement, he was out in the paved road and smiled sourly, stiff from the long dawdling. The order of his master, Duke Voreates, had been clear: he was to be of any possible service to the monk, and he couldn't disobey. He had to provide food for five people, thus he was forced to act as a kind and obedient servant. Otherwise, he would lose his job.

"To my master's mansion?" he whispered as the monk went past him.

"No, to the harbour," Meligrates ordered and got into the carriage cabin.

The driver was a bit surprised, but didn't pay much attention. He only wished he didn't have to carry anything heavy or to be asked to drive him all over the city. Thinking about all this, he hopped on his seat and grabbed the reins.

The streets were empty; no one was out in that cold weather, while the silent, locked houses created an atmosphere of death-like abandonment. The carriage rolled on the paved streets and went through the southern districts with no delay, until it stopped below the shelter at the guard post of the harbour. The wind was roaring, unimpeded by any buildings. The waves broke and crashed against the pier and the trees bent under the raging pressure.

No human or animal was in the street in front of the harbour. The huge brick storage rooms were closed, and the dockyard wasn't reverberating with the voices of the seamen and shipwrights, as it usually does in the morning. In the open market past the guard post there were just empty stalls, while the unlit oil lamps swayed and hit the lamp brackets repeatedly and annoyingly.

Five ships, anchored at sea, rocked from side to side according to the bidding of the gale. The boats that carried cargo and passengers were all docked and protected underneath a long and narrow wooden shelter, which rattled from the intensity, looking as if it were about to break and be slung into the Bosporus.

"We're here!" exclaimed the driver, clutching his overcoat tightly over his throat.

The monk opened the cabin door and stepped onto the paved street. The bandages on his face were lifted by the air and swung behind his head.

The driver was startled at first glance. He sat there gaping at him. At *her*, actually, for she was no man, as he had thought, but a woman. Her hair was short, but her face, her sensual lips, her thin nose, and her big black eyes left no doubt as to what her gender was.

Rebecca went near the driver's seat and stood by the lamp hanging from the left side of the carriage. She looked at the driver straight in the eye and, in a strict way that left no room for comments, she said: "Thank your master for me, for all the help he has offered me."

She was pensive for a moment. With her right hand she held the bandages batting her face and pursed her lips.

"Forgive me for making you wait so long," she said and held her hand out.

The wind lifted her cassock sleeve. In the half-light the driver saw the burns on her forearm and winced with a shudder, but then noticed the two golden coins in her gloved fingers.

"Ma'am . . . my lady, thank you," he mumbled, surprised and slightly embarrassed by the disgust he felt when seeing her arm, and gripped his handsome reward.

Rebecca waved her hand in farewell with a cold smile. She then hobbled to the shelter where the boats were. The strong wind made it hard for her to move; it pushed her body and brought tears to her eyes, which escaped to the corners and drifted away.

She wasn't crying. Those tears were merely caused by the wind. She had cried a lot during the last few weeks, though. She cried as she felt Leon burning on top of her; she kept crying at the sight of charred Patmos, when with every single step she trampled on the charred bodies and realised she was all alone on the island. She herself was saved because she was protected by the *Necronomicon*, by its imperishable spell, for she was holding it in her arms. The fire had only burnt her arms and legs, below the knee.

The village had turned to ashes. Only three or four families managed to survive, because they had time to hide in their basements. They didn't realise what had happened; they saw nothing, and whatever they heard wasn't clear.

Those few surviving Patmians offered to take her with them to Samos or Ionia, but she said no. She stayed there alone, knocking about like a damned soul among the ashes and debris, among the decomposed bodies of the pirates, the citizens, and the Iynges.

She carried Leon's body by herself, taking it to one of the abandoned, intact basements. She buried him in the earthen room and right there, above the ground covering him, she lay at night, when she was tired of reading. She crouched exhaustedly and felt as if she were sleeping in his arms.

When she realised that the leather sack with the *Necronomicon* was all she had left, she didn't think twice; she knew what she wanted, even though she was aware of the future. She accepted her fate with no complaint. She wished to see him again even for one last time.

He had desired the same thing when he saw her dead, slain by the Cypriot captain's sword. He wasn't afraid to face his fate; he loved her more than his own life. He was not daunted by the fear of dying. It did not deter her either.

Anyone who uses the sound for raising the dead dies or gets killed a few days later. *"You cannot chant the hymn of reanimation twice. A tragic death awaits you by Melanus' claws. Few are those fortunate ones who, within seven weeks, die from a different cause. He who offers life to a dead man loses his own,"* wrote Abdul in the *Necronomicon* and offered all the evidence.

Satenoth was slain by the Chaldean priests, who dragged his name through the mire, and whom legends transformed to lord of darkness. Orpheus was dismembered by Melanus the Darkness-walker, but the myth-makers wrote that he was mangled by the Maenads. Asclepius met a similar death, but the priests said that Zeus had burned him alive. Apollonius perished in the same way, while Jesus died on the cross before the shadow-morphed avenger and guardian could interfere, like Leon and Theodorus.

When Theodorus performed the reanimation of the dog, he hadn't read the whole book. As soon as he realised his mistake, he worried very much about Yog-Sothoth's Iynges, fearing that he might die before sending them away.

Rebecca estimated the distance to the shelter. She couldn't wait to travel to Patmos and knew that the ship would set sail at dawn. She would wait until the wind subsided so she could be taken there along with the rest of the cargo that was stacked and tied at the pier. She only hoped she would get there, that death wouldn't find her before she got back.

She wished to return to the grave of her beloved. If she was to die, she'd rather be at the same place he died at —for the second time.

She had taken this trip simply because she wanted to share Theodorus' story and give the *Necronomicon* to people who have the power to pass on the truth. Their narrow-mindedness had disappointed her, but she knew that there was still hope. That's what Theodorus had told her when he was sucked into the vortex. She heard him talking to her and sensed all his feelings during those dramatic moments of his swirling, before the rift closed up. He asked her not to hide the book, because when one day Cthulhu wakens, people will need the knowledge it contains. That was his last request before the rift closed: that the hope of rescuing the people from the star creatures remain alive.

She felt a burning sensation on her back, and the pain was diffused all over her body. It wasn't the same feeling that had melted the flesh on her arms and legs in Patmos. That was due to the fire; now she knew it was caused by a set of sharp teeth.

The tears that rolled down her cheeks, forming horizontal streams, were real this time. She felt as if she were immobilised, her limbs were gripped, and her body were being pulled to pieces.

She closed her eyelids without reacting. Melanus had come to do his duty. It was the creature that had paralysed her in Kyrenia, just like Bashar in Damascus. He moves about unseen, endlessly, in a constant quest for those who disturb the balance. He sometimes makes himself evident and shows his power to people like a warning, by stealing their breath and paralysing their body; but now he had come to take her life, just as he did to all those who had broken the laws of the dead.

She recalled Leon's image, not all burnt as he was when she brought him back, since she didn't manage to restore his body, but as she remembered him when she had come back, in the basement bedroom, reuniting after her death. She wouldn't—or couldn't—remember him as a reanimated body with decomposing flesh, melted eyeballs, and charred hands. No, for as long as she would live, she would remember him just as she had when she loved him, smiling and alive.

Her heart was beating fast and her mind filled with colours of spring. That heavy, black feeling of sorrow that crushed her due to her failure was now gone. All she could remember from the night of his reanimation was his heavy, whistling breath on her face. His words were incomprehensible, but she had read his thoughts and given in to his pleading for an end to his life. Besides, death would soon find her, too.

The carriage driver looked at the two golden coins in his hand, ecstatic, and imagined his wife's delight when he would give them to her. Because of his great joy, he had forgotten to ask the name of that generous woman. He wanted to light a candle for her sake in the temple of Hagia Sophia. He turned to her, his face alight with a huge grin, which froze as soon as he saw her.

From the left of the guard post, out of the corner of his eye, he caught the movement of a dark, spectral figure. It looked like a shadow, but it was wider, with numerous appendages, and blacker than anything he had ever seen in his life.

The next moment, in the blink of an eye, the creature enveloped the woman and made her disappear. All that could be seen was the throbbing spectral body behind her, which looked as though it was swallowing her.

He screamed in terror, felt his knees buckle with horror, and grabbed the reins. The last thing he saw before cracking the whip were the bandages waving uncontrollably in the wind and the shabby cassock drifting away to the wharf. The woman's body was nowhere to be seen, as though it had never existed, and so was that terrifying, shadowy being.

Evangelos Danasses entered the patriarch's spacious room and stood in front of the heavy oak desk. His forehead was marked by worry lines and his eyes looked tired. Hidden in the secret space behind the fireplace, he heard the story the monk had narrated to the bishops, and since then, many questions had been torturing his mind.

Theophylactus was sitting in a wooden armchair decorated with carved flowers and crosses. He glanced at the senior archimandrite and, with a linen handkerchief soaked in rose-water, wiped off the ink from his fingers.

"Here, I have the reasons for which I anathematise Theodorus Philetas," he said, raising the piece of parchment he had before him. "I am also adding threats toward anyone who follows his heretical dogma or reads any of his works. I didn't have time to add that his texts should be removed from the university, and that any man who owns any book of his must hand it to his parish priest or to a theologian, so that it can be destroyed. Here, you write this paragraph."

Danasses nodded. His weary look was fixed on the leather-bound volume next to the candlestick. Theophylactus followed it, smirked, and placed his palm on top of the *Necronomicon*. His last three fingers were adorned by golden rings, while around his wrist was a shabby prayer rope, with a burgundy bead.

"You have no idea what theories people can invent! Everyone has a theological opinion and they all believe they know what God wants. I don't think we'll ever get rid of cults, but I suppose I have eliminated the one Philetas tried to form before it was even born."

He tapped his fingers on the protective cover of the volume and smiled smugly. He yawned and rubbed his beard underneath his chin. He didn't feel guilty. Whether his teacher was dead or not, what he claimed was opposed to the Christian faith, so he didn't have second thoughts about blaming and punishing him. He did feel a slight tingle in his heart, though, because he took advantage of the situation so that he could preserve his position and his name.

"You knew Theodorus, didn't you?" he said wearily and blinked his sleepy eyes.

"We were classmates," admitted Danasses nonchalantly.

The patriarch bobbed his head meaningfully and stood up. He was tired and wished to sleep, because he had to attend the morning mass the next day.

"He was my teacher. I can still remember how much he tortured us with studying. 'Study! If you study, you'll wake up and learn, your brain will be full and you won't end up as pawns in the hands of the cunning.' And, of course, he talked about Plato whenever he got the chance. Plato this, Plato that. I knew he wanted to shift the political situation inside the Empire, but it didn't even cross my mind that he intended to form a new religion . . ."

Danasses made no comment. He just stood there, looking at the younger patriarch rubbing his eyes, so sleepy that he staggered.

"That," he pointed at the *Necronomicon*. "It must be locked away. Make sure it disappears. Tonight. I don't want anyone to be tempted to read it."

The senior archimandrite nodded and picked up the book from the seat. He placed the parchment with the anathema on top of it, said goodnight to his superior, and left the room.

In steady steps, he walked along the corridor that led to the boardroom and headed to the yard. He got into the chapel across from the marble fountain and pressed the lever behind the altar.

A hatch opened on his right, and under the light of the oil lamp he was holding, he could see the stairs leading down to the catacombs. He went down and, when he reached the landing of the tunnel that spread before him, lit one of the torches that were in the holders on the wall. He walked the distance until the crossing, where three different tunnels began, and crept into the middle one, which led to the palace.

Everybody knew about the tunnels underneath the city, but even so no ordinary man would navigate them. The first was opened when Constantinople became the capital of the Empire. Since then, every emperor added a new one, in accordance with the buildings he constructed or where he preferred to reside during his reign. An underground network of corridors weaved below the foundations of palaces, churches, public or private buildings, which in the stories the idlers used to tell was like an anteroom of hell; for in there a great many sinful orgies took place, enemies were tortured, and the ghosts of the murdered wandered about . . .

The reason they originally started building the tunnels was to have a safe means of escape, but then they continued, out of fear of conspiracies and the wrath of the people. Very few emperors were unafraid to walk freely along the streets of Constantinople during the day. Most of them, as a result of their religious beliefs, their regrettable financial administration, or their political adversaries, were fearful of exiting the palace; thus they built the tunnels so they could move freely everywhere, without fear of an attack against them.

Also, there were those who built entire halls and bedrooms, either for themselves or for their mistresses, or to hide their unacceptable and sinful habits. However, this specific room where Danasses was heading had been built during the reign of Theodosius II, almost five hundred years before. The only people who knew about it were a few ministers, who formed a secret alchemist group whose mission was to protect it.

In those first years, the room didn't have a specific name; they simply called it "the underground room" or "the library," until someone named it "the palace of whispers." Danasses wasn't aware of the reason for this name, but he had assumed that it was due to the whispers that came from the surface or to the different conspiracies being plotted amidst the cabinets and books. One of his fellow alchemists, though, had once told him that it had that name because in there, unlike the books that circulate freely, the stored books don't talk; they whisper.

"They whisper in the shadows, secretly, almost unseen, to their listeners who are so few that they could be counted on the fingers of one hand. They whisper because their readers don't have the right to carry what they have read outside the walls of the library, bring it up to the surface, and spread it." Those were his words more or less, and he might have been right, since in that exact room were all the books that the Church believed shouldn't be read by people; banned and cursed books of the ancient, the heretics, the infidels, the sorcerers, and so on.

Danasses pressed the small lever that was behind a stone in the wall, and the hatch that led to the room opened up. He went down sixteen steps and stood in front of the door. He unlocked it and got inside hurriedly, closing the hatch behind him.

The oil lamp didn't shed light across the whole huge, high-ceilinged room. He sat at a small table next to the door and sighed in displeasure. In swift movements, he wrote the title of the book, its author, and the year they obtained it on a piece of metal plate.

He looked at the date and thought that in fifty years it would be a millennium since the birth of Christ. That is when the scholars and prophets said that the world would be destroyed and the Second Coming would take place. He frowned. He knew Theodorus very well and didn't agree with the bishops' view that he was planning on forming a cult or religion. Also, it didn't seem irrational to him that he had indeed saved the world from Doomsday; after all, time is relevant according to theologians as well.

He sewed the metal plate to a corner of the book with a thick thread and lifted it in his hands. He almost opened it, but he stopped himself. It was late and, due to the fatigue, his head was not clear enough for him to read it. He would come on the next day, before noon, when he would have plenty of free time.

The hall was three times the size of the patriarchate boardroom, and apart from the cases on the walls, there were six rows of wooden structures along it. He moved quickly; the lamp flickered on cabinets that were filled with cylindrical books. He stopped at a certain spot and placed the *Necronomicon* in the cabinet. In the rest of them, there were five or six books together, but in that particular cabinet there was only one, and the name on its metal plate read *Chaldean Oracles*.

Acknowledgments

Every novel tells a story, but there is also another alongside it. It begins on the day an author starts writing and it ends on the day his novel has been published and put on the bookshop shelves. During this novel's course, I happened upon several individuals who helped me with advice, information and suggestions, and I'd like to thank them all.

I was inspired for this novel by the work of the author Howard Phillips Lovecraft, and especially by his *History of the Necronomicon*, which mentions Theodorus Philetas in 950 AD, the year when Abdul Alhazred's *al-Azif* is translated from Arabic into Greek and is named *Necronomicon*.

I would like to thank my friends, Christos Lazopoulos and Antonis Karantonis, who have read every one of my books and whose useful comments have helped me never to lose track of the story. My gratitude to my friend and researcher of the paranormal, Jonathan Bright, for offering me his insight, and whom I included in this novel, by the name John Lambrinus, since he wanted to have a Lovecraftian adventure of his own.

Moreover, I'd like to thank my good friend and graphic designer Photis Papadopoulos, who created an impressing cover for the novel.

Special thanks also go to my novel's translators, Maria Mountokalaki and Veta Georgiades, who managed to effectively render my Greek text into English.

I am indebted to my writer friend Angeliki Radou, through whom my manuscript reached the USA. My thanks to writer Wilum Hopfrog Pugmire who forwarded the manuscript to the writer and H. P. Lovecraft expert, S. T. Joshi, who evaluated it, cordially suggested it be published and later edited it. I sincerely thank him.

Last but not least, I'd like to thank Derrick Hussey, Hippocampus Press founder, for this lovely result, the book you now have in your hands.

—Antonis Antoniades

357

CPSIA information can be obtained at www.ICGtesting.com
Printed in the USA
BVOW05s0744281115

428727BV00026B/416/P